PRAISE FOR *THE PATH TO THE SEA*

'Atmospheric, emotional and full of mystery
– an absolute pleasure from page one'
Veronica Henry

'A wonderfully evocative story, packed
with secrets and emotion'
Judy Finnigan

'With a gifted storyteller's talent for crafting compelling
characters and putting them in alluring locations, Liz
Fenwick's books invite readers to open the covers
and explore a dramatic terrain of love, family, and
friendship. With wit and skill, Fenwick illuminates
the small, often overlooked moments that shape and
define a life. These are tales that draw you in and
keep you engaged until the last page is turned'
Deborah Harkness

'Evocative and compelling, a glorious tale of the
choices women make for love. I adored it'
Cathy Bramley

'Vivid and beautifully written, Liz
Fenwick is a gifted storyteller'
Sarah Morgan

Liz Fenwick was born in Massachusetts and after ten international moves she's back in the United Kingdom with her husband and two mad cats. She made her first trip to Cornwall in 1989 and bought her home there seven years later. She's a bit of a global nomad but her heart forever remains in Cornwall. For more information visit lizfenwick.com. Or find her procrastinating on Twitter @liz_fenwick.

Also by Liz Fenwick

The Path
to the Sea

Liz Fenwick

ONE PLACE. MANY STORIES

HQ
An imprint of HarperCollins*Publishers* Ltd
1 London Bridge Street
London SE1 9GF

This edition 2020

2
First published in Great Britain by
HQ, an imprint of HarperCollins*Publishers* Ltd 2019

Copyright © Liz Fenwick 2019

Extract of *The Road Not Taken* from *Poetry of Robert Frost* by Robert Frost. Published by Jonathan Cape. Reprinted by permission of The Random House Group Limited.

Liz Fenwick asserts the moral right to be identified as the author of this work.
A catalogue record for this book is available from the British Library.

ISBN: 9780008290535

MIX
Paper from
responsible sources
FSC™ C007454

This book is produced from independently certified FSC™ paper to ensure responsible forest management.

For more information visit: www.harpercollins.co.uk/green

This book is set in 10.5/15.5 pt. Sabon

Printed and bound in Great Britain by
CPI Group (UK) Ltd, Croydon, CR0 4YY

For the friend who has travelled the journey of my life, filling it with laughter, sharing the tears and the secrets, saving the memories and being an anchor when the waves of grief threatened to set me adrift.

Although we have chosen different paths, you remind me of the starting point and how far we have travelled. Great friendship doesn't require proximity, just great love.

Thank you Christine.

Two roads diverge in a wood, and I—
I took the one less traveled by,
And that has made all the difference.

Robert Frost, 'The Road Not Taken'

THE WAYMARKER

I

Lottie

3 August 2008, 11.30 p.m.

All was silent except for the sound of the waves reaching the beach. 'Happy anniversary,' he said.

Lottie frowned. 'Anniversary?' Turning, she tried to see his expression. 'Are you taking the piss?'

He traced her mouth with his finger. 'Would I do that?'

'Yes.'

She felt rather than heard his laugh as his body was stretched out next to hers, thigh to thigh, hip to hip.

'We've been together for a month and a half.'

'So, we're celebrating half months as well as months?'

He kissed her long and slow and she wasn't sure what they had been talking about as his hand ran across the skin of her back, just above her jeans.

'I celebrate every day, every minute, every second that you are mine.'

Her breath caught and held, and she looked up to the sky. The milky way stretched above, vast and mystical. She was captivated. The universe and all its glory filled her. Here on this beach, wrapped in his arms, was where she wanted to be always.

It could happen if they wanted it enough and she believed they did.

'Alex?'

'Yes?' His arm tightened around her.

'Will . . . ' Just then a shooting star sped across the sky and seemed to fall into the sea. She wished with all her heart that she could be in Alex's arms for the rest of her life. She rolled onto him. 'Did you see it too?'

'The shooting star?'

'Yes.' He kissed her.

'Did you make a wish?'

He nodded and pushed her hair back, tucking it behind her ears. 'I did.'

'I wonder if it was the same thing?'

'I hope so,' he whispered against her ear.

She brought her mouth to his, praying that he would be hers forever. 'Tell me.'

'No, because if I do it won't come true.' He pulled her even closer to him.

'You are all my dreams come true,' she said, wrapping her arms around him.

He hummed Gramps' favourite song, 'A Kiss to Build a Dream On', and she knew then they would make it happen . . . Alex and her and Cornwall forever.

SEA ROADS

2

Diana

3 August 2018, 12.00 p.m.

St Austell Bay gleamed in the distance as Diana Trewin turned left towards Porthpean and Boskenna. Once she had longed for Boskenna with everything that was in her. Every night she would clutch her pillow to her chest and pretend she could hear the sea, then she would dream. In those dreams she wandered sunlit rooms, seeing glamour and hearing the echoes of music and laughter. She would discover new rooms and new treasures then she would wake and the world around wasn't as bright or as beautiful. Those dreams still came to her, mostly at times of stress. She escaped to those visions of blue sea and sky, big lawns and a library filled with every book she could want. No real house could live up to what her mind had created.

Last night she'd had that dream again. She'd walked Boskenna's halls, seen the views and discovered new rooms. It was achingly familiar and yet entirely new. Something was forever just out of reach. She had always assumed that it was her father. If Diana found one more room, or the right book on the correct shelf then a secret door would open and her lost childhood with her father would appear. He would tell her that he'd just been playing hide and seek. She was his fierce huntress and she had found him. But no book, or panel or secret door would reveal her father, Allan Trewin. The morning light always showed the truth. Boskenna wasn't a palace of delights but a big draughty dwelling, housing two old people.

Now she was just moments away and the lane narrowed, funnelling her towards the beach. A sharp turn and she was through the gates. Yesterday the call that every adult child expects and dreads when their parents reach a certain age had come. 'Your mother's dying,' George Russell, her mother's second husband, had said. She wasn't sure how she felt about returning to Boskenna or about her mother. But that didn't matter. Some things have to be done.

She parked next to George's old Jag and grabbed her overnight bag. A shiver of recognition and homecoming covered her skin as she walked across the gravelled drive towards the house. She'd only been back to Boskenna a few times since she'd left it as an eight-year-old. Her heart had broken then – and a few more times since – and now it was whole, if patched. It performed its job a bit like the roof on the caretaker's cottage to her left where a bit of blue tarpaulin covered an eave.

Outside the front door she stopped and turned to the bay. The heat of the sun beat down on her and the happy cries rose up from the beach. The world went on, while somewhere inside her mother was dying. She paused, feeling that sharp contrast between life and death, between the holiday world on the beach below and the everyday life in Boskenna. Even back in 1962 when she had spent her last summer holiday here, Boskenna existed on a different plain. She had tripped lightly among the intelligent and interesting, the suntanned and the salt-encrusted. That was all she remembered because tears had erased the important bits.

A seagull landed on the lawn and peered at her. The tilt of his head asked her why she was here. Duty she guessed. She pushed a piece of gravel with her toe. Diana and her mother, Joan Trewin Russell, had nothing to say to each other. They hadn't for years. If Diana were honest this was a sadness she had sought to lose in her work. Travelling the world as a war correspondent had filled the void for years, but now she was slowing down and that left gaps. Unwanted thoughts and questions had begun to seep into the spaces.

Looking at the lawn, a memory of playing tag with her mother flashed in Diana's mind. She was laughing and so was her mother. Once they must have been close but since her father died over fifty years ago, that had evaporated. Her mother loved Diana in her way. Diana had wanted for nothing . . . except her. Everything changed and she knew it was because of that long weekend fifty-six years ago.

The front door was open, and she couldn't stand on the threshold forever, as tempting as the view was. George would be around somewhere. Striding in, she put the past aside to focus on what was happening now.

In the hallway the temperature dropped, and she shivered. The newspaper on the large round table in the centre of the hall flapped. Due to her early start she hadn't read the papers cover to cover as she normally would, but she'd listened to today's stories on the radio. They were eerily similar to those in her last summer here. She flattened the pages and placed an empty vase on top of it. In 1962 the world had been on the brink of nuclear war with the Soviet Union and currently the great bear was roaring again. The world moved forward and thought things would be better, but people never learned.

She peered into the drawing room then the snug, but George wasn't in sight and she was reluctant to call out. All was quiet aside from a lawnmower and the distant beach sounds. The small kitchen was empty too. There was nothing for it but to head up to her mother's room. She dropped her bag on an empty chair and took the stairs slowly, trying to prepare. She had seen the dead and the dying, but she knew this was different despite her ambivalent feelings.

On the landing she hesitated. A cough echoed down the hallway. Her mother was still alive. Diana was not too late to say goodbye. The floorboards complained as she walked the corridor. A closet popped open as she passed, and she glanced away. It would be full and what on earth would Diana do with it all? Maybe she would be lucky, and it would be empty. The house had been let for nearly thirty years. It wasn't until George retired in 1990 that Boskenna had become her mother's home again. Diana stopped. She'd seen her mother's will years ago. Boskenna would come to her but George had the right to live in it until his death. Her mother, of course, had expected to outlive George. That was the normal order of things but that hadn't worked for her grandmother either. Caroline Penquite, née Carew, had died of cirrhosis of the liver long before her husband Edward had passed away. Boskenna had bypassed him and gone straight to Diana's mother.

There were seven steps up to the landing in front of her mother's room. An odd detail to recall but she used to hop up and down them. Now the door was wide open, and the smell of illness hung in the air. Every few seconds as she stood there, she heard a raspy breath. Yet she remained motionless, staring not at her mother propped up in a chair but out of the windows. This room commanded an all-encompassing view, or it would have done if the trees hadn't been allowed to grow untended.

Boskenna had been added to over the years as the wealth of the family had increased. This room sat in the extension made in the 1840s. The ceilings were higher, and the sea-facing wall curved out towards the bay. Twenty years later the north end of the house was extended in the same way. As with all the windows at the front of the house, these framed a view. Gribben Head baked in the August sun while boats with white sails dotted the bay. It was postcard perfect, but what pithy lines would she pen on the back? Mother unwell but perfect holiday weather . . .

She could make out Carrickowel Point, the little headland to the left, which seemed to spring from the end of Boskenna's garden. Black Head to the right was just visible through the trees. Beauty could stop her in her tracks, but that wasn't what was holding her here on the threshold. Fear was. It was foolish because in the course of her work she had walked straight up to men holding guns pointed at her heart, but here she was rooted to the spot afraid of facing her dying mother. What could she say? She'd thought about this the whole drive and she'd rehearsed words and phrases. 'I love you,' being one of them. But then the questions that had gnawed at her for years popped up. They would not sink down into the recesses of her mind. Like children's toy ducks pushed to the bottom of the bath, they kept bobbing back up bringing unwanted emotions with them.

Clenching her hands, she took one step after the other, keeping her gaze focused out of the windows. A gull swooped down from the roof and she jumped. She was hardened and had seen death in its worst forms, but her head refused to turn to look at her mother.

George had been right to call her, but it would have been easier to come for the funeral. Being here now still gave her time, and time demanded action in some way. She exhaled. Standing here she couldn't avoid thinking of her father, missing what she could barely remember. She'd been eight when he died, and she only had one photo of the two of them. Years ago, when she'd asked for others her mother had shrugged and said she didn't know what had happened to them. Diana had found that hard to believe. Why wouldn't she know? But her mother had never changed her answer.

Around this one photo she had structured all her memories. The housekeeper at the time, Mrs Hoskine, had sent it to Diana at boarding school. Closing her eyes, she could envision the washed-out colours of the snapshot. Diana was on her father's shoulders and they were looking out to the bay. Both of them were smiling and pointing. On that day she had been a pirate about to sail the seven seas but always to return home to Boskenna. Now, home and Boskenna were two words she wouldn't put in the same sentence. Diana's last visit, ten years ago, had been because of her daughter, Lottie . . . artistic, flighty, and too trusting.

Her mother wheezed, and Diana turned to look at her. She had known what Lottie needed right from the start. Diana had been wrong. Not just then but in so much of her life. Yet she was sixty-four and still at the peak of her profession, about ready to slow down and allow others to move into her shoes. Her career, she was proud of but not much else and certainly not her mothering skills. Those she had learned from the woman in the chair. How she had longed for the closeness that Lottie had with her grandmother. Jealousy left a bitter taste and even now it lingered about the sides of her tongue.

Her mother's eyes were closed, and Diana watched the laboured rise and fall of her chest. Her brain told her to speak, to make her presence known. In the mirror on the wardrobe door she caught sight of her reflection but also glimpsed something else. She blinked. It was a dark-haired child, but there was no child in the room. She was imagining it. She was alone with her mother. The only figure in the mirror was Diana. Noticing the slight stoop, she straightened her shoulders.

Another step took her to the chair. Her mother's short, white hair was clean but not styled. Somehow it made her appear vulnerable. That was a word Diana didn't associate with her mother. No foundation covered the discolouration on her forehead and cheeks, yet she seemed younger. Only her dried cracked lips distorted the image.

'У меня не было выбора' Her mother moved her head back and forth.

'What?' Diana bent down to try and hear her better.

'Я не могла поступить иначе'

'Mum, what on earth are you saying?' She put her face close to her mother's but pulled back at the smell of her stale breath. Her mother's eyes opened wide, but Diana wasn't sure what she was seeing. Haunted and hollowed were the words that described her, and Diana began to process the scene as if with camera angles. Taking in the sweep of the room and the view before a close-up on a dying woman's face. Then it hit her, and she sank onto the edge of the bed. This wasn't a war zone and she didn't know what to do. There was no cameraman and she hadn't written a script.

3

Joan

Friday, 3 August 1962, 1.00 p.m.

The sun breaks through the low cloud and I squint at the brightness, slipping through the gate and onto the coastal path. In moments I reach the watchtower. The area is mostly quiet these days with only a few walkers venturing onto Carrickowel Point. Despite being built because of the war, this is a peaceful place. Clouds race across the sky and the sea below is splattered with their shadows. With sun one minute then rain the next, it is classic Cornish summer weather as the Bank Holiday approaches. Guests are due in the next few hours. Everything is in place. The larder is full of food, the menus are selected, and the seating plans are organised. Nothing is left to chance. All is as it should be, as it is expected to be.

Placing the flower trug on the ground, I climb the few steps up to the watchtower and kick aside the loose newspaper on the ground. A quick glance reveals it is from two days ago. Someone else must have stolen away here to read the news in peace. But that is the only thing peaceful about the news. It is filled with the Cold War. I've had enough four-minute warnings, nuclear tests and awkward diplomacy. Here in Cornwall, away from

Moscow, I want to escape that world. We need to relax. Too much tension surrounds us. I strike a match, light my cigarette, inhale and will the tension in me to leave. Slowly exhaling, I notice my pink lipstick marks on the cigarette.

The world is balanced on the edge, yet looking out at the bay below it all seems distant. A carefree laugh emerges from me unbidden and I take another drag on my cigarette. The smoke clouds my view of the beach, but through the haze I can see our sailing boat coming ashore. Allan and our daughter, Diana, have been out on the water for hours and the tide is just allowing them to return to the beach. They will be damp and weary which isn't ideal with guests arriving in a few hours. But it will be fine and I'm just jealous of their fun. The freedom of a day on the water is a gift, and I haven't had that pleasure this holiday. After this weekend I will go with them.

I roll my neck. From the moment when I woke until now I haven't stopped moving. Even cutting flowers hasn't provided the quiet reflection I'm seeking. At first I welcomed the activity, the focus on the beautiful, the surface of things, but now every muscle is tense, waiting. This weekend must be perfect. The sun will shine, and laughter and gaiety will abound. There will be a new guest, an important one, at the dinner table tomorrow night. Every reasonable bed in the house will be occupied. I glance down at the flower basket, knowing I should head back to the house and finish the arrangements, but the solitude here at the watchtower is a tonic. Closing my eyes, I try to still my mind so that I can hear the birdsong and the sound of the sea below, but instead names and faces scroll through my mind as if I am memorizing a sheet of paper. We will have eighteen at dinner tomorrow night and ten this evening.

In some ways, things will be simpler when we head back to Moscow. But only in some ways as my clenched stomach reminds me. If only life consisted of ballet classes at the American Embassy and helping Diana with her school work. I hold my hand out and roll my wrist gracefully. The ballet mistress would approve. I laugh. She has no idea that I understand every word she speaks, especially those muttered under her breath. She watches us so closely, pretending that she comprehends little of our chattering before and after the class. But she is no different than any Russian we meet on a regular basis. Nothing is ever as it appears.

My fingers flex, touching the concrete of the tower. I loved my war years here at Porthpean. My parents remained in India but felt I would be safer here. That proved to be wrong, with the endless bombing of Plymouth and near-misses along this coastline. But it was a magic time. The house had been filled with refugees and evacuees, including me. My governess taught us all, but I learned the most from the refugees . . . a French chef, a Czech scholar, a Polish linguist and Elena, a Russian countess who was a distant relative of my mother.

Elena had turned up on the doorstep after the Blitz. I clutch the enamelled locket at my neck. It is my good luck charm. It had been hers. She hadn't been wearing it when she'd been hit by a bus crossing the street in London in 1952. We had become close during our time together at Boskenna and I'd been touched when she'd left her jewellery to me. I release the locket, loving its touch against my skin. Because of the imperial connection I don't wear it in Moscow. All her jewellery remains hidden here at Boskenna for my return trips. On arrival I pull out my jewellery case and find the locket and wear it. Boskenna is a haven, and with or without the locket, luck abounds here.

Down on the sand they are about to play beach cricket, Allan carries the bat and Diana races across the sand before she comes to a halt. Turning, I can see her grin from here. I grab my trug and race down the path to join them.

Casting off my shoes, I drop my basket of flowers. The sand is cool and damp from the earlier rain. Diana bowls and I sprint to catch the ball. Allan runs back and forth until I tag him out, laughing. Squeals of joy fill the air and Diana picks up the bat ready for her chance. Allan bowls slowly and Diana makes the most of it. I fumble the catch giving her more time. She races, plaits flying. Finally I tag her out and Allan scoops her high in the air. We twirl together.

'Mummy, it's your go,' she says, grinning.

'I'm hopeless at batting.'

Allan raises and eyebrow. 'Can't say much for your fielding skills either.' He chuckles. 'Salome would be better.'

'Of course, she would Daddy. Dogs are brilliant at playing catch.' Diana smiles and I think of her and our dog playing ball in the parks of Moscow. The dog would love it here as we all do.

'Have a go, Mummy, please.'

I drop a kiss on her nose and take the bat. I remember playing here in summer holidays before the war. Allan makes a big effort of bowling. I can hear Diana moving behind me then I see Allan dropping the ball and running towards me. Frowning, I turn. A sailing boat is in trouble, caught over the rocks just hidden beneath the returning tide. Diana waves wildly trying to get their attention. Things don't look good. So much for quiet family time. No doubt they are tourists here for the Bank Holiday weekend, but today's wind and weather conditions are not ideal for the novice sailor. The sweep of golden sand is rapidly being covered by the sea and the easterly breeze is pushing the unlucky sailors onto the rocks.

I shake my head. In another hour their boat would be afloat but, no doubt, with some hull damage. However, Allan was already in the water. Damn fool husband and damn fool strangers. But I smile. Allan is quick to help and that is one of the many reasons I love him.

Diana and I watch as Allan, knee-high in water, is holding the strangers' boat from the side, bracing it as the wind pushes it further in to shore. Although I can't hear them, I know he is instructing them to get the sail down. By the looks of it, it is their first time doing it. Their incompetence would be funny to watch if guests weren't arriving shortly.

Diana frowns. 'Oh, it's the Venns.'

'Are these the people your father mentioned?'

She nods and right at that moment the best I can hope is that Allan won't invite them up to the house for a drink. He's been threatening to do it all week. I can't pinpoint when these people arrived in our conversations, but last night he'd mentioned them again. They look harmless enough and certainly hopeless with regards to sailing.

Finally with him holding the side of their boat, there is enough water to manoeuvre off the rocks. He takes their painter and walks the boat towards Diana and me. He points up at Boskenna and my heart sinks. I don't have time or energy for waifs and strays this weekend. Allan should know that, sense that, but he hasn't been himself since we have come here on leave. He can't be still but this isn't unusual when we are away from the fishbowl of Moscow life. But his restlessness is different this week and my concern is that I can't pinpoint why. Automatically my hand caresses my stomach. He has taken the last miscarriage harder than I have. For a man who had never wanted children he has become the ideal father, which surprised both of us.

The man from the boat leaps out. His swimming shorts display rather too much of his thighs. On top he wears a flimsy flower-covered shirt. He is almost pretty but along with having no sense about sailing he clearly doesn't know how to dress for a Cornish summer's day either. The east wind is touched with a cold underside. The forecast promises bright sunshine and warmth for tomorrow, but I will believe it when it happens. Right now, the sun is ducking behind the clouds and I wouldn't be surprised if we have rain.

Diana grabs my hand and I look down at her in her navy guernsey. She is sensibly dressed for a day on the water. Her cotton trousers are rolled up to her knees. She is the image of a Cornish maid with her dark hair and brown eyes. Whereas the woman climbing off the boat with her high cheekbones and full mouth, is as underdressed as her husband. I pull my shoulders back and push my hair off my face. I am clothed like my daughter, but this woman is attired for the Côte d'Azur, in snug white shorts and a sleeveless shirt tied at her tanned midriff.

Together with Allan they pull the boat onto the sand. With my public smile in place, I try to make eye contact with my husband, but he is watching the strangers, his expression animated.

'Darling.' He turns to me. 'I'd like you to meet Ralf and Beth Venn. The people I mentioned from America.' He grins at them both, boyish and engaging, looking far younger than his thirty-six years. 'They have rented Penweathers.'

'Hello.' I hold out my hand and Beth Venn extends her toned arm. Her hand limply grabs mine while she towers over me. I am not short, but I have to look up to meet her glance which falls away immediately.

'Welcome to Cornwall,' I say, then turn to Ralf Venn and offer him my hand. His grip is firm, but he quickly releases my hand too.

'Thank you. It's wonderful but the sailing is a bit different here.' He grins and doesn't quite look me in the eye. I don't like him, despite his physical beauty, and I can't explain this reaction to myself because it feels like jealousy.

I raise an eyebrow. 'Really? No sails then?'

He laughs, still avoiding eye contact unlike most Americans in my acquaintance. 'Good one. We're from Chicago and have sailed lakes only.'

'I see.' But I don't. His accent doesn't sound Midwestern either, or was it the syntax?

'I was just inviting them up to the house for a drink tonight, but they have other plans this evening.' Allan's glance meets mine and I stare back intently. 'However they can make it for dinner tomorrow night.'

I swallow down my immediate reply. Tomorrow night is important, and I don't need unknowns in the equation. I glare at Allan but open my eyes wide as I turn to his new friends and say, 'How lovely.'

'They've taken Penweathers for a year, so I thought it would be good for them to meet some people.'

'How kind.' I press my lips together slowly lifting the corners of my mouth into something resembling a smile. Two more people will bring the total to twenty for dinner. 'Wonderful. We'll see you tomorrow evening at six thirty for drinks followed by dinner.' I push a loose tendril of hair off my face, feeling flustered for no reason. 'If you'll excuse me, I must dash back to the house as guests are due any minute.' I lie. Picking up my basket I listen to Allan making plans with the Venns for tomorrow during the day when he and many of our guests would be enjoying the promised good weather. A piece of cobalt sea glass sparkles in a ray of sun light and I grab it, sighing long and low as I climb the steps on the path to the garden. Something isn't right about the Venns, I'm not sure what it is, but nor do I have time to dwell on it.

4

Lottie

3 August 2018, 3.10 p.m.

The traffic in front of her on the A390 came to a halt. Lottie's knuckles went white. Would she make it in time? Why hadn't she charged her phone last night? When she finally woke on the last morning in her flat and plugged in her phone, there were three messages from Gramps asking her to call. The final one said, 'My darling girl, she's leaving us. I don't think it will be long.' His voice had cracked, and Lottie had swallowed a sob. Her car had already been packed. She'd thrown the last of her stuff into the boot and waited for the estate agent to take the final set of keys for her flat.

It was fewer than three miles to Boskenna from here. She just wanted to drive up and over all these people. Didn't they know she had to get home? She exhaled, and her glance darted to the fuel level. In normal circumstances she would have enough fuel, but with this traffic it would be touch and go.

She turned on the radio for distraction. There was nothing she could do and that was proving to be the story of her life. Her fingers stilled on the scan button as Ray Charles began singing 'I Can't Stop Loving You'. This was the lead song in the soundtrack to her life. Just a few notes and she had time-travelled back to the summer of 2008.

That summer had proved that life could alter in a moment and now it was about to change again. Gran. She shifted from neutral to first and back again. The changeover traffic on a Friday in August had never been good but this was brutal. Cornwall was full of people and now that included her, except this was not a holiday. She would give anything to have this just be a visit, but she had heard the fear in Gramps' voice.

Traffic stopped again, and the only movement was on the other side of the road. There must be an accident ahead. Today was purportedly the hottest day of the summer and she was now watching the fuel gauge on her old Fiesta bounce in and out of the red. It was like her bank account. That too was empty. The trip meter said she'd done 286 miles since she'd last filled it up. She'd lived twenty-eight years never having let her finances or her fuel tank run dry. On the passenger seat her handbag contained only five pounds, her phone and not much else. She ground her teeth trying to think of positive things, which at the moment was very difficult.

She glanced in the rear-view mirror as traffic began moving again. The car was stuffed with her worldly possessions. That was something she didn't want to think about. She just wanted to make it to see Gran. She had to. Her last visit had been anything but good, and recent phone calls had been stilted. Lottie couldn't have that be the last conversation. She just couldn't.

As the car crept along at ten miles an hour, she spotted the problem: a broken-down camper-van. She tensed, waiting for the ancient engine powering her car to cough and die but it didn't. Finally turning left, she travelled past the new housing estate, and before long she went left again to Porthpean. That first glimpse of St Austell Bay caught her unprepared even though she'd made this journey thousands of times. Stretched out below, it looked as if she could touch it, but she always forgot the sheer jaw-dropping beauty and today was no different. The bright blue sea gleamed, and Gribben Head jutted out into the bay under a clear sky. The road narrowed, descending towards the cove, and her heart lifted then it crashed. Gran.

Even before the sharp turn through the gates, she pictured Boskenna and the view. White, green and blue. House, lawn and sea. Perfect harmony. Peace. The car spluttered its way past the green wooden gate on fumes. The gate was in need of painting and she might be wrong, but it looked like it was off its hinges and wouldn't close even if she wanted it to. This wasn't normal, but the sun was beating down on Boskenna and the view of the bay beckoned. It never disappointed even on a grey day. Here was home in a way she never felt anywhere else ever. It was in her bones. Every school holiday until university, this was where she lived.

Lottie parked and climbed out, taking a deep breath. The breeze was fragrant with sea air and freshly cut grass. She could do this. She stood tall. Gramps needed her. Dashing towards the front door, she caught a glimpse of broad shoulders walking through the courtyard. She stared for a second. Her brain said Alex but it couldn't be. It was just wishful thinking brought about because of an old song. She hadn't spoken to him in ten years and her last words to him had been unjust. But that wasn't really important right now. Gran was. She ran, seeing a blur of large agapanthus heads against the white wall of the house. The colour popped with the intensity of their blue petals. They glowed like Tanzanite. Boskenna was different from every angle, but this view by the front door was her favourite. It had welcomed her every time as it did now.

The front door swung wide and Gramps hobbled out, leaning heavily on a cane. This was new. In February he hadn't needed one. She swallowed then threw her arms around him. 'Gramps, I'm so sorry I missed your calls.'

'My darling Lottie, not to worry. You are here. That's all that matters.' His smile couldn't have been wider, but he looked like he would break. He was eighty-eight, his birthday just last month, but how could he have become so fragile so quickly?

'Gran?' She studied his face for signs of hope. There were none.

'Sleeping.' He sighed.

'Mum?'

'Still upstairs, I believe.' He shook his head and the smile slipped from his face. 'I haven't seen her yet.' His weariness broke her heart and she wanted to wrap him in her arms again. When she was last here, she'd had Paul with her and maybe that was why she hadn't seen their frailty. She'd been too bloody focused on making sure Paul had a good time. But he hadn't. He'd hated Cornwall. It had rained like they needed an ark. Maybe Cornwall had hated him, or it had simply been giving her a sign which she'd ignored. God, she'd wished she'd listened. Since then Gramps had shrunk. He had never been a big man, but he'd been fit for his age. He stood in front of her now looking old, really old.

'You must be desperate for tea. It's such a beastly journey.' His voice was still strong and distinctive with that peculiar mix of English vocabulary and American twang. It reminded her a bit of JFK in old documentaries.

'Is it OK if I just go see Gran and then have some tea?'

He nodded.

'I promise I won't wake her.'

'Go.' He smiled at her.

She hesitated. Should she stay with him a bit longer? But she might not have much time with Gran. She raced up to Gran's room. She was through the door, breathless, then stopped abruptly. Gran was asleep in a big armchair. Her beautiful skin was thin and slightly yellow with her white hair flat against her head. Lottie reached out to it. She could fix that for her. Even combing it would make Gran look more like Gran. That and a touch of pink lipstick.

An oxygen tube rested against her grandmother's sunken cheeks. Just six months ago she was working in the garden. The camellias were about to kick into full glory and Gran had held up one, and said, 'The red camellia represents love, passion and desire.' She'd tucked a bloom behind Lottie's ear and said, 'You'll know when you've found it and it will happen when you least expect it.' Lottie had thought it had been a sign, but if it had she'd misread it, thinking that Paul had been what she'd been looking for. A white bloom had fallen at Gran's feet. Lottie had picked it up and given it to her. Gran had smiled but there was sadness in her eyes. 'The white camellia can mean good luck, perfection and loveliness but in Japan it means death and bad luck.'

Lottie glanced around the room now. There were no flowers and that was wrong. She was sure the garden would be full of them. Gran always had flowers in her room and in the house. Even in the depths of winter. There was one particularly fragrant tree that should be in bloom now if she remembered correctly. Flowers would help somehow, even if they provided mixed messages.

She leaned down and kissed Gran's cheek. 'I love you,' she whispered. Gran didn't move, and Lottie backed out of the room with a heavy heart, but then Gran opened her eyes and smiled.

'Lottie, my love.'

Lottie returned to her side.

'I'm so pleased you're here.' She looked towards the door. 'Did you bring your young man?'

Looking away Lottie reminded herself to simply answer the question asked. 'No.' She turned to Gran. 'He's gone.'

'Ah.' Gran stared at her before putting out her hand to hold Lottie's. 'I thought I heard your mother's voice.'

'She's here but I haven't seen her.'

Gran nodded, and her eyes closed.

'Can I get you anything?'

She looked up and smiled. 'Nothing darling. I'm just tired . . . forgive me.'

'Rest and I'll find some flowers.'

Without opening her eyes, she said, 'That will be lovely. Thank you.' Taking a last glance at her grandmother, Lottie held back tears. How had she not known Gran was ill? Because she'd been wrapped up in her own life and what a bloody mess that was.

Downstairs the smell of the sea, low tide in particular, rushed in through the office window. God, she loved it here. Even though everything else was wrong, being here was right. She nipped out to the car to get her phone.

Three messages all from Sally, her solicitor and best friend.

Jamie Sharp, a private investigator, will be in touch. I told him all. Sxx

Lottie swallowed thinking of the cost. She opened the next message.

Don't worry about the cost. He owes me a favour. Sxx

Looking out to the bay, she didn't think this Jamie Sharp would be able to help. The police didn't know where Paul was nor did his mother. She opened the last message.

He's just pinged me to say he's found something. Love this guy. He'll be in touch. Hugs and send your grandparents my love. Sxx

Typing quickly, she replied.

Arrived. Gran not good. Gramps holding up. Thanks for all the help. Don't know what I'd do without you. Lxx

Even if they tracked Paul down it would all be too late. She sighed and grabbed her handbag, leaving everything else for later. She'd store her stuff out of sight. The last thing she wanted was for her current situation to be known and for it to become a concern. She was twenty-eight and she would fix her own problems.

Stopping in the entrance vestibule, she took a deep breath. Boskenna was unchanged, but she was altered since she had last removed her boots here. The Chinese vase still stood in the corner with enough brollies and walking sticks to equip an army. Under the large mirror, the bowl filled with sea glass was covered in a fine layer of dust, as was the table it sat on. Lottie ran her fingers over a cloudy aquamarine cabochon of the sea. It was pitted and rolled to the perfect shape. Her fingers turned it over trying to feel her grandmother who would have found this on one of her morning strolls. Those treasures of the beach had inspired Lottie's career. As a child, she'd used old bits of garden wire to form jewellery. Maybe she should have stuck with beach debris and string. She wouldn't be broke, if she had.

Through the glass doors into the hall, delicate flower-covered china plates still adorned the upper reaches of the wall in the 1840s addition to the house. Here the ceiling was high, and the white wooden panels covered the walls to six foot. Off to her right the drawing room beckoned, with the grand piano and family portraits, but rather than turning in there towards the view she walked through the arch that had marked the beginning of the original building. The afternoon sunlight streamed through the south-facing window, warming the wide wooden floor boards. Instantly the house closed around her with its lower ceilings. It felt like a much-needed hug. Clearly she was not the only one who felt welcomed. A spider web extended across from the ceiling light to the tall clock. A feather duster would tackle that later. She made a mental list . . . paint the fence, dust the hall. Other signs of things slipping appeared with each glance. Was their daily help on holiday? If that was the case Lottie didn't think there could be a worse time.

In the small sitting room, otherwise known as the snug, the tea things were laid out and the sight of a Battenberg cake set her stomach rumbling. Gran was dying but life here at Boskenna went through the motions as it always had.

Gramps hobbled towards her clutching the teapot at a dangerous angle. She rescued it from him. How was he managing? Had he brought the tea things in one item at a time?

'Did you stop for lunch?' He studied her, and she looked away, shaking her head. He'd been her confidant for as long as she could remember, especially when she couldn't talk to Gran or Mum. Now she hadn't the heart to tell him she couldn't have afforded to stop for lunch. It would require an explanation and that was one thing she didn't want to give. He had taken against Paul on that visit. It had been mutual, and it was one of the reasons she hadn't seen her grandparents or her beloved Boskenna since that wet February weekend. She should have listened to Gramps. But hindsight was a wonderful thing.

He frowned as he manoeuvred into his favourite chair by the fireplace. 'Will you be mother?'

She poured the tea and put a small spoonful of sugar into his cup. 'Shall I cut you a slice of cake?'

He looked at her as if he was surprised to see her there. 'Yes, thank you, just a small one, please.'

The silver handle of the cake slice was tarnished. Another job she could sort out for them. She had no idea how long she would be here, but the up-side of her situation was that she could be of use. She cut herself a big slice. This cake represented her childhood. Her life then had been divided into squares, time with Mum, time at school, time at Boskenna and time at friends'. The only misrepresentation was the size of the squares. The school and Boskenna squares should be larger. Now of course her life in cake would be far from neat. It would have a soggy bottom certainly and only one flavour.

Her mouth watered as she used the dainty cake fork. At least these were pristine. The explosion of sugar took moments to hit as it reached her empty stomach and blended with the caffeine. Over Gramps' shoulder she could see dust collecting in the corners of the bookshelves. Mixed among the local history books behind him were some of her favourite children's books. The cake dried in her mouth as she thought of her grandmother in bed upstairs.

'Tell me about Gran.'

He picked up his cup. 'It's not good.'

There was nothing Lottie could say. Gramps looked into his cup. His hand shook.

'Doctor doesn't say much.' He turned to the view. 'She's eighty-five . . . ' Out of the window she could see Gribben Head basking in the sun. Lottie had never known a summer like it. The atmosphere in London had been so close, but here the air was fresh with the scent of the sea.

'But she seemed fine a few months ago.'

'True.' His voice was wistful, and Lottie leapt to her feet. She knelt at his side. 'I'm so sorry.'

'Me too. Me too.' He patted her hand.

Her mother walked past the door without looking in the snug. Lottie stood.

'I hope she's OK.' He gave her hand a squeeze. 'Go to her.' His voice was gentle, but Lottie understood. Gramps knew things weren't easy with her and her mother, or for that matter between her mother and Gran. He was very intuitive. He'd read people well, especially Lottie.

'Don't worry about me. I'm fine. I'm just going to check on your grandmother. The nurse won't be in for a bit,' he said, pushing himself out of the chair then giving her an encouraging hug to send her on her way.

5

Lottie

Walking out the front door, Lottie noted a sea mist creeping across the lawn. Gribben Head had disappeared, the wind had dropped, and the air was still. In the past, she'd always felt that the world stopped when this happened, but looking ahead her mother hadn't. She stole through the gates and down the lane. Lottie raced after her.

'Mum?'

She glanced over her shoulder at Lottie, nodded, but didn't speak. Even at a distance Lottie noted the shadows under her dark eyes. Where had her mother been recently? It always took her time to decompress after each assignment. Lottie knew enough not to speak. She was simply grateful her mother was here too. Her feet slowed, expecting her mother to turn towards the beach, but she continued up the lane towards St Levan's Church.

She went straight to the small graveyard at the side of the building. There weren't many graves. For years it had been a private chapel to the big estate. She stopped in front of a plain granite stone.

Allan Edward Charles Trewin
Born 4 August 1926
Died 5 August 1962
Loving husband and father.

Thirty-six, just. So young. Allan Trewin was her grandfather and she had been to the grave before, but this was the first time with her mother. That fact felt wrong, but she could count on one hand the number of times that her mother had been to Boskenna. She closed her eyes. Now was not the time to dwell on the past, but that was challenging in a graveyard filling with mist. It had covered Porthpean and was now depositing minuscule drops of water on everything around them. They softened each surface, including her mother who appeared out of focus.

She turned to Lottie. 'Who put these flowers here?'

Lottie shrugged. Fresh flowers were always here, from what she remembered. Today they were bright blue hydrangeas with spiky red crocosmia. The one thing she was certain of was that it couldn't have been Gran. It wouldn't be Gramps. Why would he put flowers on the grave of his wife's first husband? People were weird but not that weird.

'Lottie?'

She blinked. 'I don't know.'

Her mother turned back to the grave.

'Why are we here, Mum?'

Her mother sighed and said, 'It's almost the anniversary of his death.' She traced her father's name then the dates. It must have been awful to have lost her father when she was eight, but at least she'd had him. Lottie had never had a father. Well, there had to have been one in the picture in some form or another but not one that her mother had chosen to share with her. Foolish, but Lottie was jealous her mother had a gravestone to acknowledge that she'd had a father. In fact, although her mother didn't like Gramps, she had a stepfather too. Lottie loved Gramps, but her mother didn't care for him. Well, that was the polite way to describe her attitude. Lottie had never figured out why. From what she knew, Gran had been a widow for thirteen years before she remarried. Lottie's mother was twenty-one then and no longer a child. But, maybe, for some things everyone was forever a child.

She peered through the mist at her mother who was still focused on the gravestone. Nothing made sense, especially being here now. Gran was dying, and her mother was standing in a damp churchyard touching a moss-covered stone. Lottie cleared her throat.

Her mother looked up, her eyes guarded. Lottie had seen that expression before. It was when she would lock things away inside, like all the horror she saw in the course of her work. She reached out and touched her mother's hand.

'Some things never leave you.' Her mother's voice was strangled. 'Everything changed.'

Lottie clutched her mother's long elegant fingers, so unlike her own small ones. As her mother glanced at her, Lottie caught pain in her eyes before she hid it again.

'I've looked into the past and I see so little.'

'Oh, Mum.' She took a step closer to her. 'Have you asked Gran?'

She nodded. 'She won't talk about it.'

'It must be painful for her.' Lottie pictured the frail woman upstairs in Boskenna now, who looked nothing like the vibrant woman in the black and white photographs in the house, with hair swept up, revealing a classic face. The clothes were elegant, and the makeup was so Sixties and Seventies. There were no pictures of Allan Trewin that Lottie had ever seen. His death must have been awful for Gran and her mother. Gramps didn't seem the sort to fuss about pictures of his predecessor being around. He was just Gramps, so easy. She swallowed the smile that came to her at the thought of him.

'I can look at this,' her mother pointed at the carved slate. 'With clear-sighted adult eyes and know my father died in a tragic accident.' She took a deep breath. 'But something eats at me.'

'What are you saying, Mum?'

She shook her head and glanced at the grave. 'I have only one strong memory.'

'What's that?'

She smiled, and her face became younger, lighter, happier. 'You know. I've told the pirate story many times.' She turned away from the gravestone. 'I can't picture any more than that, and that bothers me.'

Lottie looked down at her hand holding her mother's. Lottie's skin a smooth olive and her mother's an embattled English rose. Lottie's appearance spoke of somewhere else, but she didn't know where. Her father had never appeared, no matter how much she wished he would.

6

Joan

3 August 1962, 4.35 p.m.

The flowers are arranged, and I'd reviewed bedrooms for the final time with our housekeeper, Mrs Hoskine, and still Allan and Diana aren't back. Sighing I walk to the end of the garden and stand by the gate to beach path. Below Diana is skimming stones with Allan laughing beside her. She picks up a pebble and holds it out to him. He examines it carefully before handing it back and watches her form as she throws. It bounces twice then drops out of sight. He turns to the American woman, Beth, and her husband speaks to Diana, touching her shoulder. I frown. Allan isn't paying attention and he should be. He's become engrossed in conversation with Beth and his smile gleams. Something twists inside me. Why did he bring these strays into our world? Is he just filling the void again?

'Joan, that's a fierce look.'

At the sound of a familiar voice, I look up through my eyelashes and my stomach tightens. 'Tom.' I grin. 'You're early.' I kiss his cheek and step back to study him.

'Problem?' He raises an eyebrow.

'Never.'

'Good.' He studies my face. 'Not sleeping?'

I touch my cheeks. The powder I applied this morning must require another application. 'Can't fool you?' I turn back to the view.

'I should hope not.' He laughs then asks, 'New friends?' He opens his cigarette case, the one I gave him for his thirtieth birthday. It's inscribed with one word, *Always*. That was years ago and the feeling hasn't changed. Never have we ever crossed that line, but I don't know if that is true of Tom and Allan.

He lights a cigarette and hands it to me. I take it while he lights one for himself then squints into the distance. 'They don't look local,' he says.

Exhaling, I watch the smoke swirl. 'American.' I turn to him, noting the tell-tale darkness under his eyes. It only serves to enhance the blue of his irises. They remind me of a Cornish sky on a perfect summer day.

'Interesting.'

'Indeed, they are joining us for dinner tomorrow, so you can discover for yourself.'

He frowns. 'George Russell arrives tomorrow around noon.'

'Everyone will hopefully be out enjoying the sun they are promising.' I look at the darkening clouds. 'Which should give us some time alone.'

'It will be like old times.' He rubs his chin and a boyish grin appears.

'Yes.' I take his arm and we walk together towards the house. However it could never be like old times and we both know that.

We reach the front door where he picks up his bag asking, 'Usual room?'

I nod with my mind on the Venns then what he'd said sinks

in. 'Sorry, Tom, not the usual room. Due to numbers I've had to move you into the little one by my parents' old room.'

He smiles. 'Downgraded, eh?'

'Sorry.' I raise my shoulders.

'How many guests?'

I shake my head. 'Too many.'

'Allan?' He holds out an arm directing me to enter first.

'Yes, ever the host.' I check my watch.

'Some things never change.'

'True.' I chuckle. 'Shall I show you up?'

'No need, you are tight on time. I'll see you,' he pauses, 'just before drinks?'

'Diana,' I say. 'She comes to tell me about her day's activities then.'

'Ah, yes.' He turns away. 'A bit later then.'

He walks through the dining room to the far staircase and I remember the past. Things could have been so different. The scent of the roses in my trug catches the breeze. I pick up a bright red bloom and bring it to my nose. Its fragrance is a heady damask touched with spices. Arabia. Rose water. Souks. Innocence. A thorn pierces my index finger and I squeal, dropping the flower. Pulling the thorn out, I watch the blood pool then drip into the basket before I put my finger into my mouth. The blood tastes metallic. Memories . . . sailing and catching my finger on a splinter, Tom coming to the rescue, removing the bit of wood and placing my finger in my mouth. As I did that, he stared at me with such intensity, I shiver even now. Those intelligent blue eyes have haunted me ever since. I shake my head and dismiss the past, I have work to do.

7

Lottie

Just as they went through the gates and onto the gravel parking area, her mother's phone rang. It sounded important. Lottie prayed it wasn't some world crisis that needed her mother's award-winning reporting. Her mother veered back towards the gates where the phone signal was stronger. Inside the house Lottie checked downstairs for Gramps, but there was no sign of him. He must be with Gran or maybe taking a walk in the garden but she doubted that, with the fog. She couldn't see past the end of the lawn.

In the snug she found an old wooden tray resting against Gramps' chair and loaded all the tea stuff onto it. The small kitchen revealed more evidence of the neglect she'd noticed earlier, and her heart sank. She had been so bloody self-involved she hadn't realized what was happening here. Rerunning the phone calls in her head, the conversations followed a normal course . . . the garden here, the weather, but mostly it had been about the collection she had been putting together for exhibition of young designers at the V&A. They were both so proud of her and had planned to come to London for the opening of the exhibition in the new year. She held her breath for a moment as a sharp pain pierced her temples. There was no sense in dwelling on what was lost. In all those calls they never mentioned Gran's health, but there were things she'd never said either. She checked her phone: nothing.

But looking around there were signs of distress. Dishes and pans were washed but not put away. It wasn't just breakfast things either but items from the night before. Opening the fridge, she saw ready meals. This wasn't how her grandparents lived. Her heart sank further; she should have been here, no excuses.

After washing and clearing, she glanced out of the kitchen window towards the small walled garden. She would cut some flowers for Gran and the rest of the house. It might give her an indication of the amount of time her grandmother had really been ill. She knew Gramps wouldn't tell her. He might be American, but through Gran or maybe just his own nature, he did the stiff upper lip thing rather well.

Both her grandparents adored the garden, be it the special camellias or the vegetables. They grew most of their own produce so if the vegetable patch wasn't in good shape then they had been keeping Gran's illness from her for a while.

Out in the courtyard, the mist swirled across the cobbles – blazing sun to impenetrable fog in the same day. She smiled, pushing open the gate and thinking of all the happy hours spent here with both of them. Vegetables, roses, and in the glass-houses, peaches and tomatoes. Her nose twitched anticipating the smell.

Hearing a noise, she looked to the nearest glass-house and gasped. She had been prepared for anything but what she saw. Alex Hoskine, her first love, stood with hose in hand watering the tomatoes. She hadn't conjured him out of her memories earlier.

It had been ten years almost to the day since she'd last seen him. And during those years he'd haunted her dreams and she woke wanting to say so many things. Now she was standing here with her mouth open and her vocal chords seemingly disabled. Memories raced around in her head, from their first kiss to the last angry words she said to him.

He looked up and squinted at her. Damn. This wasn't going to be easy. She needed to apologise, but she also wanted to know what the hell he was doing here at Boskenna working in the kitchen garden. Where to start?

'Lottie.' His voice had become deeper since she'd last seen him. Back then he'd been twenty, lean and fit as hell, but now the promise of youth had been fulfilled and then some. Her mouth dried. She couldn't still be attracted to him, not after all this time, but her body was telling her years made no difference. She was standing in front of her first love and her body remembered each and every caress, whether she wanted it to or not. This was not convenient. Her focus must be on Gran and Gramps not on her romantic history.

He turned the tap off and put the hose down. 'Your grandfather mentioned he'd called you.' He walked towards her but stopped just short. This was awkward. How did she greet him after all these years . . . a handshake?

'Yes, this morning.' She looked down.

'She's been ill for a while.' He turned from her, giving her his back.

That said it all. She'd been too self-absorbed. 'How long?'

'There's been a sharp decline these past few weeks, but it's been months.'

She should have known. Closing her eyes, she took a deep breath, trying to think clearly.

He picked up the watering can. 'Where have you been? They needed you.'

'I didn't know.' She clenched her fist.

He looked up with a dismissive glance. 'You haven't changed then?'

That wasn't fair. Alex gave her one last look then walked away. She found her voice. 'What are you doing here?'

He looked over his shoulder. 'I would have thought that was obvious.'

'Yes, that might be, but *why* isn't?'

'I moved back and one of the first things I did was visit them.' He pulled out a weed. 'It was clear they needed help, so I moved into the caretaker's cottage to be close at hand.'

Ouch. There was no reply to that, so she took a step back. She should have known this, but she hadn't. She held her breath for a moment then fled before he could say anymore. Yet again she was at fault, but then she was always misjudging things.

8

Diana

3 August 1962, 5.15 p.m.

The sun had disappeared, and her stomach growled loudly.
Diana hoped Daddy heard it. He'd said he'd help Mr and Mrs
Venn set off then he would come up to the house with her. But
they'd been here ages and Daddy was just holding the Venn's
boat and talking and talking. She was tired of the Venns and she
wanted time with Daddy on her own. She'd had to share him
with them every day for over a week and now they were taking
him all to themselves again. It wasn't fair.

She picked up a mussel shell and moved it so the colours inside
changed. Every so often she heard a word. Meeting. Deliver.
Urgent. They were almost whispering but the breeze brought
their secrets to her. She loved secrets. Mummy and Diana played
the secret game all the time. Mummy said living in Moscow
made secrets important. Things had to be kept tucked away, just
like the little Russian dolls hidden inside the biggest one. She'd
brought her dolls with her to Cornwall and had set them on
her windowsill so they could see the sea. They had never seen it
before, only the Moskva. Diana liked saying *Moskva*. It rolled off
her tongue like when she said her piano teacher's name, Madame

Roscova. She could roll her Rs but Daddy couldn't. Mummy was very good at hers. Diana had heard her reading aloud from a Russian book. It was called *War and Peace*.

'*Rrrrrrrrrrrr*.' She dropped the shell and picked up a piece of sea glass. It was strange to find one so high up the beach. Normally she found them in the wet sand. She looked out to the point and there was a cormorant drying its wings. '*Rrrrrrrr*.' She loved the way her tongue vibrated and tingled a bit when she did it.

'Diana, what on earth are you doing?' Daddy looked over his shoulder. Mr Venn put his hand on Daddy's as a wave rocked the boat. She frowned. The wind was turning, which was good. They wouldn't have to row out into the bay – they could sail. They weren't very good at sailing, but they were worse at rowing. She just wanted them to leave. She and Daddy couldn't be pirates when they were here. Daddy became all serious with them around.

'*Rrrrrrrrr*.' She spun around looking up at the grey clouds. The gull's wings seemed to become part of the sky at the tips. But mizzle was beginning to fall. She liked the word *mizzle* but didn't like the actual thing.

'Diana.' Daddy spoke crossly.

She didn't know what she'd done wrong, but she heard Mr Venn say, 'See you tomorrow,' and to 'get' something. She fell to the sand and watched the Venns' sail flap until it caught some wind. It did and they frowned. They did that a lot when they didn't think they were being watched but Diana watched everything. Even when he was frowning, Mr Venn looked like a movie star, but Mrs Venn didn't. Diana didn't like her. She kept sending Diana on silly errands to get things the adults didn't need.

Daddy took her hand and pulled her to her feet. 'Let's see if Mrs Hoskine has anything you can nibble, as that tummy of yours is noisy enough.'

She smiled up at him and moved closer as they climbed up to the house. He kept looking over his shoulder. She wasn't surprised that he kept checking on the Venns. They were terrible on the water, but they didn't know that. Diana had noticed Daddy retying all their knots yesterday when they had been on the big sailing boat. They said they were from the Midwest in America and Diana knew from her geography lessons that there wasn't a sea there so that must be why they were so bad. She liked geography and maps. Uncle Tom had given her an atlas for Christmas last year. He had spent hours with her telling her about places and the people he'd met in them. She loved Uncle Tom. Mummy and Daddy did too.

'Daddy, why do you like the Venns so much?'

He stopped walking and looked at her. 'Why do you ask?'

Diana wrinkled her nose. ''Cause we've spent so much time with them.'

A smile spread across his face and his eyes smiled too. 'Well, they are new to Cornwall and I want them to feel welcome.'

She frowned. 'Why hasn't Mummy come along to make them welcome? She's good at that.'

'She is, but she's been busy with Boskenna.'

Diana looked to the big house. This was the place she loved most in the world, with its round ends and secret floor. It wasn't secret really, but it was easy to miss because everyone looked at the ends and the big windows. The second floor wasn't often used but Mummy had Mrs Hoskine airing out a room above hers for some American arriving tomorrow. The window was still open so the room must be very short of breath.

'Does Boskenna need Mummy?' They walked along the gravel path framing the lawn. They had played croquet yesterday before the rain, but Mr Hoskine had put the croquet set away.

'Yes, because the old dame has damp and the roof needs attention.'

'Is dame another word for house? What sort of attention does the roof need and is Mummy wiping the damp up?'

'Something like that.' Daddy laughed, and she joined him. She liked it when Daddy laughed, and he hadn't been doing it enough lately. Even Mummy said that. Diana had overheard them talking when they'd arrived. She had hidden in her favourite spot under the small table just outside the dining room. Mummy was worried about him. Daddy had said he was just tired, but Mummy had given him one of her looks. Diana knew those looks too well.

9

Lottie

With secateurs in hand and her grandmother's flower trug on her arm, Lottie walked out through the French windows in the smoking room. The name amused her as no one in the house smoked any more. It harked back to a time when men would have port and a cigar after dinner. She had no trouble picturing Boskenna then. Evening gowns, dinner jackets and household help. It was so far from today's casual world. It was easier now but some of the world's beauty had been lost with it. She rarely designed a formal piece of jewellery. Those rare pieces she did create were normally by special order for the Middle East. Fun, but she couldn't imagine anyone apart from a royal or a celebrity wearing those designs. Up until two weeks ago when she had to cease trading because she had nothing left to sell, most of her work was being sold through a few outlets and her website. She specialised in making wearable pieces featuring semi-precious gems with gold, silver and other metal. She'd only used precious gems for special commissions and for the pieces that were supposed to go in the exhibition at the V&A in the new year.

Stopping at the flowerbed beside the house, she snipped the

stem of a white Japanese anemone with rather more force than was necessary. She couldn't undo the past, she knew that. But what brought the bile to her mouth was her own stupidity and gullibility. How had she missed the signs? Had she been so desperate for love that she'd been blind to Paul's faults? She'd worked with him for five years and he'd been her mentor. Cutting another anemone, this time she took more care. She had landed herself in a huge mess and it would take time to fix. Somehow, though, she would find a way out and more importantly, a way forward.

The mist had deposited tiny drops of water on the petals of a pale pink rose. Here and there they had merged into large drops that magnified parts of the petal. She saw the fine lines that ran through it turned ever so slightly darker. With the bloom close to her nose, the fragrance was at first delicate but then musky overtones developed.

Towards the end of her degree course she had worked with pearls this subtle shade of pink. The rose, the pearls and the finished piece spoke of innocence. She cut the stem, watching out for the thorns. She hadn't been innocent for a long time, ten years in fact. Dropping the stem into the basket, she scanned the flowers at the front of the house. The agapanthus were at their best, but she wouldn't cut those. If she did there wouldn't be anything in flower visible from the front windows. Of course, the view outshone even the agapanthus.

Light showed in Gran's bedroom window and the snug, welcoming her. She loved the way the north and south ends of the house bowed out towards the sea. There was a satisfying symmetry about it. Although she knew they weren't built at the same time, she was pleased they had balanced the building when money had allowed. Of course, it did mean ceiling heights varied greatly throughout the house. As a child she had loved discovering all its nooks and crannies, dancing up and down the many sets of steps on the first floor and up to the attic rooms. Boskenna was a place of endless delight, or had been then. She had brought an end to her carefree days here and she had to live with that.

Raiding a few other beds and some hydrangeas, she went to the kitchen to sort the flowers for her grandmother. Once happy with the arrangement, she climbed the front staircase, carrying her overnight bag along with the vase. August was a tough month for blooms in the garden. Things were well past their summer glory. But Gran had always made use of the most interesting shrubs at this time of year. They provided the architecture for the agapanthus and annuals in flower. Some of the roses should be on a second display by now but she had seen so few. The kitchen garden may have had more but because of Alex she hadn't paid attention to anything there but him. It had been that way from the first moment she'd seen him, years before he'd become her boyfriend. He'd put her off her agenda then and now he'd unsettled her again, bringing the past to the surface. She sighed, resting the vase on the table outside her room before she went in to deposit her bag.

It was the smallest bedroom in the house, but it was the best. The single bed just fitted and from it she could look out of the window to the view. A view that never bored her even in the rain, or at the moment, fog. Placing her bag on the old chair, she saw nothing had changed from the Russian doll on the windowsill to her old books on the shelves. The dust on the chest of drawers told the same story of neglect she'd seen downstairs. Lottie was surprised to find the bed unmade, too. She'd sort that in a minute once she'd taken the flowers to Gran.

Out on the lawn, she could see Alex collecting the cushions from the garden chairs. Why had he come back to Cornwall? In the immediate aftermath of ten years ago, she hadn't wanted to hear about him, or Cornwall, or what people were saying about her. It had been a terrible tragedy and she was part of it. Her life altered that day, everything had.

Weary after the journey – hell, just weary from life – she closed her eyes for a moment, letting the sound of the sea soothe her, along with the distant sound of Gramps snoring downstairs. But it could be no more than a moment for time was precious. Eyes now wide open so as not to miss a thing, she grabbed the vase and headed down the hall and up the steps to Gran's room, listening for sounds of Mum chatting to her, but it was quiet. Sticking her head through the bedroom doorway, she found Gran sleeping in the chair and no sign of her mother. Lottie placed the vase on a table then walked back to the chair. She stroked Gran's forehead and Gran mumbled a few words. They weren't in English. She leaned closer to try and decipher the language. It sounded like Russian.

Lottie stepped back. They had lived in Russia so it shouldn't be a surprise that Gran could speak it. Years ago, at the back of the garden shed behind an old terracotta plant pot, Lottie had found the matryoshka doll that sat on her windowsill. When she'd asked about it, a sad smile had crossed Gran's face. She had wiped the grime off the outer doll and wriggled it until she could open it. To Lottie's delight she released the next then the baby doll inside. Gran had explained it had belonged to her mother from their time in Moscow. She'd put it all back together for her and said she'd thought it had been long since lost. Lottie could still remember holding it and feeling connected to her mother, who was then in Kosovo. There were three dolls . . . one for each of them.

Whatever Gran was saying now, her voice was too weak for Lottie to hear properly. She seemed to be in a fitful sleep. Lottie kissed her forehead and she stilled. Her eyes opened. 'Lottie.' Her smile filled Lottie's heart. 'Your mother?' Her voice was thin, like her frail body.

'She's downstairs I think, maybe with Gramps.'

'Help her to be kind to him.'

Lottie nodded. That would be a challenge. Without Gran, Lottie wasn't sure that her mother would give him the time of day. 'I'll look after him.'

'I know, dear one. He has loved me when no one else could.' She took a deep breath and closed her eyes for a moment. 'He has understood when no one could.'

'Gramps is wonderful.' Just thinking about him, Lottie grinned. He'd been more than a grandfather. He'd been a father figure, teaching her to ride a bike and fly a kite. He'd been there to listen.

'Yes, he is. But your mother has never seen that.' She coughed at first softly. 'She needs to be kind to him and . . . to forgive him.'

Lottie frowned. Kind, yes. Why "forgive"?'

Gran coughed again and her whole body, what there was of it, rattled. The effort took everything out of her, then she closed her eyes and her breathing settled. Lottie adjusted the blanket around her. Why did her grandmother want her mother to forgive Gramps? For marrying Gran and taking her father's place? Did Gran know that Mum didn't remember much of Allan?

'Lottie.' Gran was watching her.

'I'm here. I was just wondering if you'd like to come downstairs and join us?'

Gran frowned. 'Is Alex around?'

'I'm not sure, why?' She tilted her head.

'He could carry me down.'

Lottie paused for a moment. 'I'm happy to go and find him.'

Gran looked out of the window. 'It might be nice.'

'I'll do my best.'

'Thank you, my darling.'

She looked brighter and it was the right thing to find Alex. She could do this for Gran, Lottie thought.

On the way downstairs, she stopped in her room to pick up a sweater as the dampness from the fog had given her a chill. Her mother stood at the window holding the matryoshka doll in one hand with her other on the clouded window pane. The weather had set in and the visibility didn't extend to the end of the garden let alone Black Head.

Her mother turned to her.

'Travelling down memory lane?' Lottie smiled.

Her mother shook her head. 'No. I don't really remember Moscow from my childhood or rather I can't separate it from my visits as a journalist.' She frowned.

'Was Gran awake when you went in?' Lottie picked up a hoodie from the back of the chair. 'She's been asking for you.'

'Yes.' Her mother twisted the outer doll open, revealing the brighter smaller one. With a shaky hand she placed the smaller one down and put the largest one back together.

'How was she? Did she speak?'

Her mother twisted the middle one until it popped open and

the baby fell out onto the floor. Looking up to Lottie before bending down she said, 'Yes.'

'Is that all you can say?'

She nodded and arranged the three painted figures in order on the windowsill before she turned back to Lottie. She pointed to the window. 'It's a bit like right now. I know the bay, Gribben and Black Head are there but I can't see them because of the fog. I know I must have memories of those eight years with my father but . . . ' Her voice trailed away, and she picked up the smallest doll.

'Shouldn't you be focusing on Gran?'

'You're right, I should be but . . . ' She sighed. 'I need a drink.' She walked to the door.

'I'm sure Gramps is already organising that. I'll join you in a moment.'

Her mother disappeared down the stairs and Lottie pulled on her hoodie. She went to the old dolls and nested them again. The Cornish sunlight had faded the vivid colours on the mother doll over the years. They too would fade if left exposed.

10

Diana

Diana hurried downstairs on unstable legs. She had forgotten those dolls. Her father had chosen them with her. They had been beside the Moskva and the sun had shone brightly while the air was filled with . . . fluff. It floated like snow, but it was spring and hot. The memory was so clear she could almost taste it. She stopped on the bottom step. How could she justify being drawn to discover more about her father when as Lottie had quite rightly said, Diana should be focused on her mother. Her hands shook as she tucked her short hair behind her ears.

George emerged from the kitchen with the ice bucket in one hand. He looked up, a smile hovering on his mouth. She pressed her lips together before forcing herself to respond in kind. She was no longer a child, she could be gracious. 'Can I help?'

'I've sliced some lemon for your gin, but I'm afraid I can't manage that as well with the stick.' He raised it off the floor. 'Can't carry too many things at once.'

'I'll grab the lemon.' She watched him head to the drawing room then went into the small kitchen. For twenty-eight years since his retirement George and her mother had rattled around in this huge house. She'd never understood why they hadn't sold it years ago. They lived in such a small part of it, especially in winter. Four rooms out of twenty-four, if she had remembered them all – plus the caretaker's cottage, the lodge, the stables and a few barns. It was all too much for them and had been for a very long time. But her mother would never discuss it, so Diana had let it drop.

The lemon slices were in a shallow crystal bowl. Living here they had managed to hold onto the gracious past. How George would cope in Boskenna on his own was a mystery. For once, she felt sorry for him and that was a real change.

He'd entered her mother's life and had taken it over. She'd been twenty-one when they had married. It bothered her, he irritated her even now, which was ridiculous. Her feelings hadn't dulled with time as they should have. How could her mother replace Diana's father with him? Back then she had seen nothing of value in George Russell, but looking again at the lemons he sliced for her, she could now admit he wasn't so bad. He was thoughtful and he'd shown this in the past, but she hadn't wanted to see it.

Lottie hadn't appeared yet and George was free-pouring the gin into a glass as she walked into the drawing room. The size of his measure hadn't changed either. It had been a hot June evening in the small flat in Chelsea when her mother had dropped the bomb that she was marrying him the following day. Speechless couldn't begin to describe how Diana felt. George, sensing her anger, had immediately poured drinks – large ones – so that at the register office wedding the next day, Diana had a terrible hangover that had soured an already frightful situation. She'd been a right cow to her mother. But her inner child had been striking out. Looking back, she saw that her mother's marriage meant that she would have even less of her than she'd had before, which hadn't been much.

George took the lemons now and added a slice to her drink.

'Thanks.' Her hand wasn't as stable as she would have liked. Being here was getting to her. It was a place that should feel welcoming, but everything annoyed her because it wasn't familiar in the way it should be, despite her repeated dreams. A room like this spoke of family gatherings, Christmas carols around the piano and shared history with the portraits on the walls. Maybe they had had that once, but she couldn't recall. All she had was a sensation like something she might have witnessed on television and not in person. Among her old diaries and journals, she still had a letter from Mrs Hoskine, the housekeeper, saying how much she missed her, and that she understood how hard it must be for Diana not to come home to Boskenna. That implied that she had loved this place once.

'So, George, how long has my mother been ill?'

He looked up from his whisky, startled. 'I would imagine the cancer has been there silently for years.'

'She's done nothing?' The first sip of the drink tasted mostly of gin. The alcohol hit the back of her throat and her eyes watered.

'No.'

Part of her rebelled at this news but another part respected it. 'Hospice care here at Boskenna?'

'Yes.' His shoulders fell.

George and her mother had been married for forty-two years. He would be, and probably was already, devastated. Grieving could start before the loss. This she knew too well.

'How often do the nurses come?'

'Mostly twice a day now.' He looked out to the garden.

In the infrequent phone calls with her mother, George's devotion to the garden, and especially his passion for the camellias, always came up. Diana recalled he'd cultivated a few new ones.

'Have they said how long?' She glanced at him regretting she had phrased the question that way. He wasn't a warlord but a frail old man.

'I haven't asked.' His hand clenched the silver fox head on his cane. His knuckles went white.

'What will you do?'

Sad eyes looked at her and despite her dislike, her heart reached out to him.

'I don't know, I honestly don't know what I'll do without her.'

Diana swallowed and looked away. She didn't want to feel for him. She didn't want to care. She had done that once before. Not caring was the only way to cope.

11

Joan

Below on the edge of the lawn, Tom and Allan are side by side, their stance so similar. Allan's hair is darker with more wave than Tom's mid-brown straight fringe which falls onto his forehead if he hasn't tamed it with hair crème. Both still whippet-thin, not yet touched with the fullness of middle age, unlike many of their peers. Allan is the more handsome of the two, also the more charming. But Tom's eyes, their deep Cornish sky blue, are the more compelling. They take a step away from each other. Discord. In the past they had moved in unison and I was the third wheel, or so I felt. But now Tom plays that role happily, maybe even more comfortably.

He opens his cigarette case and Allan leans in to offer him a light. Allan's fingers brush Tom's. There is still a look in Allan's eyes when he watches Tom. I'm sure Tom was his first love, as he was mine. My passion for Tom was years ago and yet it lives under the surface of our friendship giving it an edge. But Allan was never one to be held in check, and Diana was the result. The memory of our first kiss still stirs me. I stand here loving two men, differently . . . one always from a distance.

As they turn to look at the view their faces are no longer visible, just their broad shoulders. A hunger creeps across my skin as Tom shifts his weight from one foot to the other and Allan mimics him. It has always been this way since the first time I saw them together. I'm not sure what I will do if Tom finds love and marries. I'm a strange creature, loving what I can't have. But my heart is filled with love for Allan and that is enough.

My husband's hands caress the air. What are they discussing? Both look solemn, with none of Allan's boyish charm on display. Diana runs up to them and Allan scoops her into his arms and Tom hands her a package. Even from here I can hear her delighted whoop of joy. She is a blessing and I never believed that would be the case. How wrong I was.

Turning from them, I walk to the dress hanging on the outside of the wardrobe. People will be arriving soon so I can't slip downstairs and join Tom and Allan. Hopefully there will be an opportune lull in the evening when I can talk with Tom. There is so much that I don't know, and my imagination is making things worse.

I pull the sleeveless shift dress over my head and the green silk reminds me of shallow waters on a bright summer's day. Like the ones when Tom, Allan and I sailed. I was nineteen and – against my mother's wishes – I had joined them sailing to the Scilly Isles. I was free as I never had been before. No school mistresses, no hovering mother or aunt. Simply me and two beautiful men in love. Innocent and free. Well, that will never happen again but at least I have those memories.

As I try to pull the zip up, I recall that it was then it was decided by the three of us that I should apply to a vacant secretarial post at the embassy in Aden. Tom thought I would be a shoo-in with my language skills, and of course the fact that Daddy was an ambassador wouldn't hurt either. I knew the ropes already, so to speak. I had completed finishing school the month before and Mummy wanted me to marry right away. The problem, aside from the fact that there were no candidates, was that getting married was last on my list of things to do. I wouldn't follow in her shoes. Somehow, I would find a way to a career and not simply become someone's accomplished wife.

Smiling, I look around the bedroom at all the accoutrements of just that. Mummy was accomplished, accomplished at keeping her drinking hidden. She was the life and soul of the party. I pause, looking at myself in the mirror with her pearls about my neck, in her house which is now mine. If she knew, she would approve. Allan is the political attaché in Moscow and I am the ultimate hostess. But looks can be very deceiving and a smile spreads across my mouth.

'What's so amusing?' Allan walks through the door and comes to stand beside me. He runs a hand down my bare arm. It is the only contact we've had in days. He hasn't been sleeping and I hear his footsteps in the darkness as he paces by the windows. After wearing the carpet out, he heads downstairs then outside where he lights up a cigarette. The smoke makes its way into the bedroom and I lie awake until he returns just before dawn.

'Nothing important.'

He pulls the zip on my dress up the final inch, running his finger along the base of my neck. 'You've gone a delicious brown.'

My skin glows, from the Cornish air if not the blazing sun. My dark hair is highlighted from a week here. I look like my younger self, more like the woman he knew as a teenager – long and leggy.

'It's all the gardening of late.' I look down at his hand as he links his fingers through mine. 'You've gone brown yourself.'

'Not sure how, with the dismal weather. Here's hoping for some sun this weekend.'

But I knew that being on the sea brought colour even if the sun wasn't bright. He's been sailing every day and spending time with the Americans. Diana has loved being on the water, so I haven't commented on the excessive amount of time he's spent with them. Allan is like that. Making fast new friends and cutting out the rest of the world until it drags him back. Mostly I haven't minded and many times it has helped. But I can't quite put my finger on what is troubling him.

He yawns and pulls his hand from mine.

'Tired?'

'Just the fresh air.' He laughs and turns away. 'I'll have a quick bath to freshen up.' He runs his fingers through his hair. Even though we've been here just a week a few freckles have appeared across his cheeks adding to his youthful look, but there is a slight greyness under that tan which is new. He strips off, desire fills me and he sends me a knowing smile, as he grabs his dressing gown then leaves the bedroom before I can act on my need or ask about the sleeplessness. He knows I know.

Eventually he will tell me. He always does.

12

Diana

3 August 1962, 5.50 p.m.

Diana watched Daddy go into the house. Uncle Tom was already dressed for dinner and he stood beside her. 'Shall we take a short walk?'

'Yes, please, and thank you for my book.'

'A pleasure. Have you had a diary before?' Uncle Tom put his hands in his pockets which pushed his jacket out of place.

They cut across the lawn and walked up the long path.

'No. What do I put in it?' She turned the red book over in her hands. It was beautiful.

'Your thoughts and what you did during the day.'

Diana frowned. 'Do I only write in it once a day?'

'That is entirely up to you.' He stopped to sniff a flowering tree. 'At your age you are already good with words, so you may want to write stories as well as what happened during the day.'

'Oh.' Diana stood straighter. She liked words a lot. 'Does being good with words mean that I'll be a writer when I grow up?'

'Possibly or maybe a journalist for a newspaper,' he paused and studied her.

'I like that idea. They write stories.'

He laughed. 'Technically they report events, but I do believe sometimes it is more storytelling.'

'Report events?' Diana decided to try to do that in her head. They passed the magnolia tree that was in bloom, it smelled lovely. She'd been told by the gardener that it was special, but she didn't remember why. 'I think I would like that.'

As the path rose the trees became taller and the camellia bushes bigger.

'It's an important job,' Tom continued. 'Think of all the people who read newspapers every day to discover what is happening in the world.'

She nodded. Mummy and Daddy did that, then they would discuss parts of what they'd read. 'So, I should read the paper to discover how to report?'

'You are a very clever soul, Diana.'

'Am I?' She stood straighter and took a bigger step forward.

'Yes, you are and I think you would be a very good journalist.'

'Thank you.' Diana looked up to the big Monterey pine tree and saw the birds gathering there. They must have a wonderful view of the bay. She was jealous of their lookout. To see further she frequently went up to the attic rooms of Boskenna. From the one above her bedroom she could see over the trees and onto Carrot Hole. No, Mummy would correct her: Carrickowel Point.

She turned and looked up at Tom. He was so handsome. Not as handsome as Daddy, though. 'What do you do, Uncle Tom?' She thought she must have asked once before but she couldn't remember. 'You are good with words, too.'

'I love words and history. But I look after people.'

Diana picked up a stone from the path. 'Are you a nurse or a teacher?'

He chuckled. 'A bit of both, to be honest.'

'Oh.' She wanted to ask more but wasn't sure what to ask because she couldn't think what job would be both nurse and teacher. Walking down the path towards them was Mr Carew. He limped ever so slightly, and Mummy had told her that he'd lost his leg in the war, but they had found him a new one when he came home to England. Diana had asked if they kept spare legs in England to replace lost ones. Once Mummy had stopped laughing, she explained it was made of wood and held in place with leather. Diana wanted to see it but hadn't yet worked up the courage to ask. Maybe this weekend she would.

'Hello, you two.' Mr Carew held out his hand to Uncle Tom then took hers and bowed over it slightly. 'I see as usual, Tom, you are escorting the most beautiful woman.'

Uncle Tom grinned. 'Always.'

In the distance Diana heard Mrs Hoskine calling her. She looked up and said, 'If you'll excuse me, please.'

'Of course.' Uncle Tom smiled then continued walking with Mr Carew.

Diana raced to the house hoping that Mrs Hoskine was going to ask her to help with the final touches for the silverbelle, Diana's favourite chocolate pudding, for tomorrow's special birthday dinner for Daddy. Diana loved chocolate and so did Daddy.

13

Lottie

3 August 2018, 6.00 p.m.

Stopping at the bottom of the stairs, Lottie was greeted by the voice of Bobby Darin. 'Somewhere Beyond the Sea'. Gramps had taught her to dance to this while Gran taught Alex. They had been invited to a big black-tie party at Eddie Carew's house for his eightieth. Neither Lottie nor Alex had known how to dance properly so the week before the party the drawing room rug had been rolled up and every night, just after cocktails, it had been like a session of *Strictly* for the hopeless. But by the time the party had arrived, both Lottie and Alex could dance. Even now she could remember how handsome he'd been in his borrowed dinner jacket and the feel of his arms around her. It had been a magical evening of dancing under the stars. A few days later it was over.

She couldn't fix the past, but she could make sure she didn't mess up any more of the future. Hopefully now she had learned to let no one in and to trust no one. That would be key to going forward.

In the courtyard she tapped on the cottage door. Alex opened it, dressed only in a towel. She looked at the top of his head for fear of staring.

'Sorry to disturb you but Gran would like to come downstairs and she said you'd help.'

'Of course.'

'Thanks.'

'I'll be there in a few minutes.'

'Do you need help?' She looked down at his bare feet.

'I can get dressed on my own.'

'Right.' She risked a quick glance up but wished she hadn't. He was amused but she felt an idiot. Exiting swiftly, she set a smile on her face and walked back to the house and into the drawing room with her head held high. No one here knew what a mess her life was at the moment and it would stay that way. It would cause Gramps so much pain and her mother would be disappointed yet again.

'Lottie, my dear. Gin?' Gramps asked, putting his hands on the arms of the chair.

'I'll get it, Gramps. You stay seated.' She walked to the end of the piano where the trolley sat and made herself a weak drink, tempting though it was to let the gin relax her. She couldn't afford to let her guard down. She turned back to the room and surveyed it. It felt too big and at the same time not large enough for the three of them.

Gramps was in his armchair because the sofa was now just too low for him to use without help. He didn't want assistance, as she'd discovered in February when Paul had taken the armchair. Gran had called him a stubborn old mule when he wouldn't be helped out of it and said to leave him to it. She hadn't been herself then, now Lottie thought about it. She had been quieter and greyer. She must have known but hadn't said anything. How could she have when Lottie had spent the weekend trying to get

Paul to see Cornwall, Boskenna and her grandparents for the wonders they were. She shouldn't have wasted her breath for he was a liar and a thief.

Her mother, gin in hand, paced in front of the French windows, looking out to the sea fret. She had been refreshing hers and Gramps' drinks with ice when Lottie had walked into the silence.

'Alex is going to bring Gran.' Lottie perched on the arm of the sofa halfway between the two of them.

'Alex?' Her mother turned. Lottie braced herself. A decade ago her mother had forbidden her from ever getting in touch with him again. Lottie hadn't blamed her. But Alex hadn't been the problem – she had. She was the one who had lied to her mother. True, it was because of Alex that she hadn't taken the internship her mother had arranged – but it was Lottie's decision, not his.

'Yes, Alex Hoskine has been a godsend to Joan and me.'

Lottie jumped to her feet. 'Is there anything I can get for her?'

'The nurse will be here shortly.' Her mother turned to look at her.

'Oh.' Gramps and her mother obviously had a chat. This was good, progress even. 'Should she stay upstairs?'

'No, if she feels up to joining us, that is wonderful.' He gave her a brave smile.

'How often does the nurse come?' Lottie asked, looking at Gramps' face. She saw him trying to hold it all together.

'Morning and evening.' He took a sip of whisky. 'Or more frequently if needed.'

Her heart sank. No wonder Alex had started helping.

'She should be in a hospice. Not here.' Her mother sighed and turned from the windows.

'She is where she wants to be.' He spoke with quiet determination.

'Mum,' Lottie stood.

'The place is a wreck, a relic even.' Her mother waved her hand. 'The upstairs windows are coated in salt and the woodwork is rotting from the constant assault of the weather while two people rattle about in a few rooms.'

Gramps put his drink down. 'Joan loves it.'

'Does she? Does she really?' Her mother shook her head. 'I can't see how.' She walked towards Gramps. 'I don't know how you can stand it, living in the house that they lived in together.'

'Mum.' Lottie moved towards her then stopped. Where was this anger coming from?

'We are all grown-ups here. No need to mince words.' She topped up her drink and Lottie raised an eyebrow. Her mother wasn't a big drinker.

'Why did she come back to Boskenna after so long?'

'What do you mean, "come back"?' Lottie frowned. This was Gran's home.

'Boskenna was let out until George retired.' Her mother sat on the sofa.

'It was.' Gramps relaxed.

'Why did you come here? Why not Cape Cod, where your family were?'

Lottie held her breath. Her mother had shifted into reporter mode – forgetting that, like him or not, Gramps was her stepfather and an old man. How could she snap her out of it?

Gramps put his fingertips together, making an arch with them like the childhood game he used to play with her. *Here is the church, here is the steeple, open it up, see all the people.* But this wasn't a game. Gran was dying and her mother, possibly as a way to distance herself, was interviewing Gramps.

'She wanted to. It's her home.'

Mum shook her head and pressed her lips together.

Just then, Alex arrived at the door – carrying Gran as if she was a child. With care, he placed her on the sofa and Lottie arranged some cushions behind her.

'Can I get you a drink?' Alex asked.

'I'd love the smallest taste of whisky, well-watered, please.'

'Of course,' he smiled, and Lottie caught his eye and mouthed thanks. 'George, does your drink need refreshing? Diana?' He glanced around.

She held her breath again. Her mother stared at him and everything in Lottie tensed.

'I'm fine, thank you.' Her mother turned and walked to the fireplace then turned back again as he handed Gran her drink.

Lottie watched her mother open her mouth, but Gran raised her glass. 'Thank you for coming.' She coughed.

The doorbell rang and Alex leapt to answer it. She couldn't blame him. Lottie's shoulders were around her ears. The atmosphere in the room was fraught.

The nurse came in and her mother glared at Alex before she left the room. That wasn't fair. Her mother had had every right to be angry with Lottie even now, because she'd believed Lottie had been in London all summer doing an internship when she'd been falling in love. It was never Alex's fault. It had been – and always would be – Lottie's fault.

14

Joan

3 August 1962, 6.10 p.m.

Diana sits cross-legged on the bed watching me while I clip on my earrings. Thus far today hasn't gone as planned and now I am faced with a handful of guests gathering in the drawing room for drinks. Tom would be among them of course, but there would be eight others. It is paramount that I find time alone with him before tomorrow afternoon.

'Mummy?'

I turn to her. She wears her serious look as she clutches the present that Tom has given her.

'Yes?'

She holds a leather-bound book aloft. 'Uncle Tom said this is a diary or a journal.'

I nod and perch beside her, taking the book from her hands. Flipping through the lined pages, it is apparent it was not made in England. At a guess the leatherwork indicated the Middle East, or possibly Spain at a stretch.

She looks up from under her long dark lashes so like Allan's. 'I can write things down . . . like what I do every day.'

'Indeed, your thoughts about all sorts of things, too.' I hand the book back to her. 'Or even sketches.'

'But there are lines on the page.' She runs her finger over one.

'True.' Trust her to worry about that. 'You could slip your drawings into the book.'

She frowns. 'No, this isn't a book for my drawings, I don't think.'

'OK, then you could write to it like it is your best friend.'

'But that's Maria.'

'Your next best friend then. But do remember that some things must never be written down.'

She looks at me as if she despairs of me.

'Of course, Mummy. I know all about secrets.' She wrinkles her nose and I hide my smile. She is so like Allan. Quick, mercurial and ever so clever. 'Uncle Tom said I was good with words.'

'Did he?' Turning, I look at her closely.

'Yes, he said I might become a writer or even a newspaper journalist when I'm older.'

'Very perceptive.'

'Perceptive?' she asks, tilting her head.

'He sees things well.' I stick another hairpin through the French twist in my hair. 'Did he say where it was from?'

'Beirut.'

Memories of 1955 in that glamorous city fill my mind. Dancing, laughing, loving.

'They speak Arabic there don't they?' She turns the book over.

'Yes.'

'Isn't that written back to front?' She peers at me and I love watching her thought process. My darling girl is so intelligent it scares me sometimes.

I stand and smooth my dress. 'You're a clever soul.'

'Thank you, Mummy.' She jumps up clutching the book. 'Maybe I'll begin writing my diary from the last page.'

I chuckle. 'That's a super idea. Make sure you tell Uncle Tom your plan.' I stroke her dark hair, loving its thickness. 'He'll be pleased.'

She stares at me. 'I think I'll become a journalist because I like to ask so many questions.'

'You'd be a very good one.'

'Would I, Mummy?' She takes my hand.

'Absolutely, you're curious and very good with words.'

'I like knowing the truth.' Her bright smile disappears and her eyes narrow.

'The truth is very important,' I say, but I know that much of the time it's best hidden. The truth can hurt.

We walk hand in hand into the hallway. Someone is warming up on the piano and begins playing the latest Bobby Darin song, 'Things'. Diana starts singing and dancing. Joining her until we reach the top of the stairs, I give her a twirl and her laughter lifts me. All will be fine. My concerns are unfounded. The scrutiny of living in the fishbowl of Moscow is intense and life here should be a balm. Sadly, this weekend has brought the world of work into my refuge. I laugh, remembering that it was years ago that the world of work invaded Boskenna, and maybe it had always been here. Daddy and his guests who visited here during our leave changed the carefree atmosphere.

'Mummy, what's funny?'

'Nothing important.'

'Funny is always important.' She gives me a piercing look. I make no sense to her, for I am intuitive and she is logical like Allan.

'I'm going to start my diary now.' She races to her room, which used to be mine. Twelve years ago I looked out of that same window and saw Allan for the first time. My heart missed a beat then and still does now as I begin down the stairs. The object of my thoughts is looking more handsome now than he had then. I had been eighteen and he twenty-four. My parents were celebrating their twentieth wedding anniversary. They never made it to their twenty-fifth.

'Darling.' Allan waits with a smile lighting up his face. The man is too handsome for his own good. He holds out a hand. Reaching the bottom step, I take it and he twines his fingers through mine. I shiver, loving his touch and yearning to take him upstairs, but instead we walk through to the drawing room, the picture of a golden couple.

Allan releases my hand, heading to the drinks table, and I move towards Lady Fox, Allan's aunt.

'Is everything in your room as it should be?'

'Of course, my dear.' She smiles. 'Thank you for giving us your parents' room looking out to Black Head. Mesmerizing. Despite the weather, I was so riveted by the view it's a wonder I managed to apply my lipstick properly.'

'True, it is a distraction.'

Outside, rain hits the windows obscuring everything but the sound of the sea, ever present. Tonight because of the weather, the windows are shut yet I can still hear the sea when the music pauses. The tide is high and the wind has picked up. Thinking of the beach brings the Americans to mind. They wouldn't have enjoyed this evening, despite the fact that many of the people they should meet locally are here. I can't see Lady Fox enjoying their company and with only ten tonight she couldn't have avoided them. Tomorrow it will be easier with more people, more distraction.

'Not sure how you can bear to leave Boskenna.'

My glance strays to Allan making a gin and tonic.

'Ah, yes, the things we do for love.' She picks up a devilled egg. Mrs Hoskine has done a marvellous job with the canapes and I take a deep breath. Life is about being flexible.

'I do admire you, dear, following Allan all over the world. How long have you been in Moscow now?'

I force a smile. 'Nearly two years.'

'Fascinating place to be living at the moment, I should imagine.'

'Yes.'

'Do you expect to be there much longer?'

I look down at the bracelet on my wrist. If I didn't know better, I would think I'm being pumped for information, but this is his aunt who I've known since childhood and this isn't Moscow. She, of all the people here this weekend, has nothing to do with the diplomatic world. She belongs to the gardening one, competing against Boskenna every year at the flower show. Each year Pengarrock, Boconnoc, Caerhays, or Boskenna would win. Of course, those gardens are far larger and Boskenna being so close to the sea with little protection from the east winds, faced different challenges.

'Here's your drink, darling.' Allan hands me the glass, looking up at his aunt. 'Have you seen the agapanthus this year?' he asks, leading her towards the windows. 'It's a wonder with all this rain this summer that anything blooms.'

I make my way across the room towards Tom. He is chatting to Eddie Carew and gives me a quick smile before replying to him. Again, I can see how drawn he has become but a few days here and he'll perk up. Despite being only thirty-six he is greying at the temples. Rather than making him unattractive, it adds to his appeal if one goes for the scholarly variety.

'Joan, how kind of you to invite me for the weekend.' Eddie beams while he taps his cigarette ash into the fireplace. Tonight a fire is roaring to keep the evening's dampness at bay.

'Always a pleasure.' I say, studying his face. He is such a dear man.

'I was just catching up with what Tom's been up to. It's hard to believe it was twelve years ago that I last saw him here.'

'At my parents' anniversary party.' It had been a momentous night in many ways. Aside from meeting Allan for the first time, my mother's drink problem became public which might have been caused by my father's mistress attending the evening as well. I'd fled to the watchtower to escape and Allan had followed me, concerned even though he'd only just met me. Years later he confessed that Tom had gone looking for me on the beach. But that had been the beginning. He'd asked me the following day to join him and Tom sailing. I'd escaped with two beautiful young men, leaving my mother to her bottle and my father to his mistress.

The Indonesian gong, a legacy from my father's years there, announces dinner. Tom takes my arm. 'May I escort you through?'

'Of course.' Glancing over my shoulder I see that Allan has the arm of the latest beauty in the neighbourhood. Nothing new in that. My dear husband does have an eye for it.

'Now, we need to have a chat.'

Nodding, I catch sight of Mrs Hoskine waving at me from the kitchen door. Tom sees her as well and releases my arm.

'Later.'

'Yes.' I sigh. One way or another I will find a moment alone with him before tomorrow afternoon.

15

Lottie

3 August 2018, 7.30 p.m

Lottie was digesting what little information the nurse had given her when Gramps reached her at the bottom of the stairs. She caught his expression as he went to the office. Devastated didn't begin to describe it. They had been together for over forty years. Their anniversary had been in June. She'd seen the pictures tucked away in a photo album years ago.

Her phone beeped, and she looked at the text.

Hello. It's Jamie Sharp here. Have made some progress. Have tracked down Paul's first wife. Will be in touch.

Lottie didn't see how talking to Paul's ex would help. She wouldn't know anything unless Paul had run off to be with her again. That wasn't likely. She sighed. Walking through the kitchen door to check her chilli, she stopped in the doorway. Alex, wearing a striped apron, was stirring the pot. Fresh vegetables were laid out on the table. She opened her mouth to say something, but nothing came out so she closed it and continued to stare.

He turned. 'I'm not much of a cook but the chilli was close to burning, which would be a waste as it smells good.'

She remained just inside the kitchen unable to move forward.

He was the last person she had expected to see cooking. Her mother possibly, but not Alex and definitely not Alex in an apron wielding a wooden spoon.

'Speechless at my beauty?' He raised an eyebrow.

'Something like that.' She swallowed. He had no right to look so good and she had no right to feel the way she did. 'More than mildly curious as to why you are here in the kitchen saving my chilli.'

He nodded. 'Perfectly understandable.' He paused. 'I'm making my dinner as the cottage doesn't have a functioning kitchen and I've been giving George a hand with cooking.'

'Ready-meals?'

'And fresh veg.'

She frowned. 'Mrs Blitho, the daily?'

'With her daughter . . . who is on bed rest expecting her second set of twins.'

'Not brilliant timing.' She frowned.

'No.' He left the stove and went to the sink and began to wash the veg.

She took a deep breath, she needed to speak now, not later. Lottie had longed to say these words for years and had rehearsed them in her dreams, hoping that somehow, she could make at least part of her past right.

'Alex.'

He turned with lettuce in hand. 'Yes.'

'It's been a long time . . . ' Her voice faded away and she took a step to the nearest chair, grabbing the back of it. He stared at her with a guarded expression on his face. She preferred the jokey one of a few moments ago.

'What's been a long time?'

'Sorry. Ten years ago.' She ran her hands over the battered oak of the chair, feeling the strength of the wood. She could be strong. This was the right thing to do. Taking a deep breath, she said, 'But I've told myself it's never too late to apologise.'

He raised an eyebrow. She took that as encouragement to continue. 'I'm sorry for so much and if I could, I would do many things differently.' She twisted her hands together. In her head the words had rolled out but now they were fading in her mouth, coming out at half strength. 'But I can't. But I can say . . . I'm sorry . . . to you.'

He leaned against the sink, remaining silent. She looked around the kitchen at the pine table and the painted wooden cabinet that lined the north wall. It was scarred with a few more marks and chips in the paintwork, showing the passage of time. 'I treated you appallingly in that whole mess. I should never have said what I did. It wasn't true.' She hung her head studying the red tiled floor and taking a deep breath, but then she glanced up, making sure she made eye contact. 'I'm sorry. I was so very wrong.'

Weighing a beef tomato in one hand, he passed it to the other. He didn't look away and she held his stare. She didn't deserve forgiveness, she'd been vile, saying things that were hurtful and untrue.

'Thank you.' He put the tomato down and turned back to the sink.

She stared at his back, managing to close her open mouth and swallow the reply she wasn't invited to give. The conversation was over. That was fine. At least she'd apologised and openly owned her wrongdoing. He had accepted it . . . not graciously, but he had. That was what mattered.

Now to move on and attend to dinner. This she could do. Her shoulders fell as she took the pot off of the heat and placed the lid on top. It would stay warm and be the perfect temperature for eating shortly. She gazed around, not sure what to do with Alex occupying the sink and in control of the veg. She was lost but maybe she had always been. Now she needed to find her way home.

16

Diana

3 August 1962, 7.45 p.m.

As her father popped his head through the door, Diana put down her book, *To Kill a Mockingbird* and slid it under the blanket.

'How are you, my darling one?' he asked, coming to sit on her bed. He was so handsome in his dinner jacket. She thought he looked handsome all the time, but tonight he had twinkling eyes. 'Did you have a good day?'

She smiled and nodded but decided not to say it would have been better if it had just been the two of them. He would make a face and might become cross. He'd been cross a lot lately.

'I'm pleased.' He brushed her hair off her face and put his hand on the book moving it into sight. He squinted at it. 'Are you enjoying the story?'

'Yes.' Looking at it, she frowned.

'It's rather serious, isn't it?'

Nodding, she said, 'But I am serious, Daddy, and many things in the world aren't right.'

He put a hand over hers and stroked it. 'And this worries you?'

She bit her lip, thinking. 'I can't do anything right now because

I am too little, but one day I want to make a difference.' Crossing her arms against her chest, she sat straighter.

He smiled. 'Then I know you will.'

'I think, like Uncle Tom said, I will try and make a difference with words.'

'Did he say that?'

'He said I was good with words.'

'Uncle Tom likes words.' He looked out the window and frowned.

She could hear the rain hitting the window. Was he cross about the rain?

'But enough about Uncle Tom. Are you ready for a day's sailing tomorrow?'

'Of course. How many people will be with us?'

He laughed. 'That is a good question and the success of tonight will tell me how many we will have tomorrow.'

'It will be a success. Mummy always has successes.'

'That she does, my little one. Your mother is the best hostess ever and very clever to boot.'

'Are hostesses not clever?' She wrinkled her nose. Most of the ladies she knew were hostesses. Were they not clever? She didn't like that idea.

'I'm not going to comment on that one, but your mother is a rare breed.'

'Breed? Like a dog or an exotic bird?'

He stood. 'You know, Diana, you *are* good with words.'

'Thank you. I learned a new one today.' She grinned. 'Perceptive.'

'Good word.' He picked up her new diary on the desk. 'Where did you hear it?

'Mummy.'

'Really?' He tilted his head and his eyes met hers. 'Who was perceptive?'

'Uncle Tom.'

He put the diary down. 'Of course. That's the perfect word for Uncle Tom.' He kissed the top of her head. 'Have you started the diary yet?'

'Yes, just a little while ago.'

'Are you keeping it secret?'

She nodded. 'Diaries are supposed to be secret. It's for me only.'

'Then make sure you keep it safe.' He tapped it then blew her a kiss as he left the room. Diana picked up her diary and looked at what she had written so far.

PRIVATE
This belongs to Diana Trewin of Boskenna

She turned the page.

3 August 1962

Dear Diary,
I'm still not sure what to write about in this diary that
Uncle Tom has given me. It is so beautiful. It's bright red.
It's mine!
Today was mostly boring. The sailing was good but
Daddy and I spent too much time with Mr and Mrs Venn.
No one but me will read this so I can say that I don't like
them and no one can tell me not to say it. I want Mummy

with us but although they haven't told me I know Mummy isn't sailing because she lost the baby a little while ago and she's tired. I never saw the baby and that makes me sad.

Right now I'm thinking about the raspberries and cream that I had. Not for my pudding. It was more second pudding, I think, like the Hobbit's second breakfast. Daddy finished reading The Hobbit to me two nights ago. My tummy is rumbling again. I wonder if they have even started dinner downstairs yet. They always eat so late. Maybe I'll sneak downstairs after I read another chapter.

Running her finger over the words, she knew she would have to work harder if it was to be interesting to read. It was boring. She needed to be more perceptive in what she wrote, she decided.

17

Lottie

It hadn't taken Lottie long to unload her things from the car into one of the stables. Someone, probably Alex, had been clearing and cleaning up the outbuildings. For years these buildings had stored lawnmowers, garden equipment that had last been used before WWI, old barbecues and spare furniture. Most of it was now either gone or neatly ordered. She was impressed. Whatever his reason for being in Boskenna, Alex Hoskine had certainly made a positive difference in the outbuildings.

Before shutting her stuff away, well out of sight, she pulled out the key paperwork file. It was her business, her problem, and on Monday she would make a renewed effort to sort it, including a proper chat with her best friend and solicitor, Sally. Right now, she wanted to focus on what she could do to help her grandparents. Pulling the gate back, she caught her shin on a small metal chest. It looked like an old tuck box from boarding school, but it wasn't hers. She picked it up to put it out of the way. From the weight of it she knew it had something in it.

Curiosity aroused, she opened it and two black glass eyes

stared up at her. She gently pulled the old bear from the box and a sheet of paper fell out. Lottie squinted at the faded writing...

> *Diana,*
> *Both Boskenna and I miss you. Look forward to seeing you soon. Here's Ben and your things to keep you company until then.*
> *With love,*
> *Mrs H*

Underneath it was a small navy Guernsey sweater covering a pile of books. Why was this in the stables?

Taking the box with her, she headed towards her mother's bedroom, but she wasn't there. Lottie turned around and went to her own. Would the contents reveal what her mother had been like back then? Gran had said Lottie reminded her of Diana as a little girl. But Lottie could never picture her mother as a child. There was something too reserved about her.

The teddy bear smelled of dust and was worn threadbare on the ears. They must have been soft once. Would her mother recall its name? Many of the books looked like they may have been Gran's once . . . except one, which had a beautiful red leather cover. Opening it, she saw in careful childish handwriting . . .

> <u>PRIVATE</u>
> *This belongs to Diana Trewin of Boskenna*

She went to the window, hoping to see her mother, but no luck. Returning to her bed, she flipped the diary open again. Empty. She frowned. Flicking through the whole book, she saw her mother had begun writing from the back of the diary. A quick scan of the words provided a glimpse into her mother's past. Eating, sailing, eating, eating and then Lottie's hand stopped. The last entry.

5 August 1962

Dear Diary,
Daddy is dead. It's my fault.

She blinked then she read it again. What did her mother mean?

'Lottie?' Her mother called from the hallway.

She shoved the diary under her pillow.

'There you are.' Her mother walked through the door, paused then took two big steps to the bed. She clutched the bear. 'Ben.'

'You remember him?'

She nodded and stroked the Guernsey sweater with her free hand. 'Where did you find this?' Her eyes narrowed. That momentary flash of a softer side to her mother vanished. Interrogation mode was back in place.

'In the . . .' Lottie hesitated. If she said the stables, her mother could possibly – and rightly – ask why she'd been in there. She mumbled as her mother began putting the books back into the box.

'It's good that you remembered Ben.' Lottie shuffled closer to her pillow where she could see the corner of the diary sticking out.

'Is it?' She stroked his ear. 'Or is it worse that I can recall a stuffed animal's name and not remember much about my father?' She placed the jumper and the bear on top of the books, picked up the box and left the room without a word.

When she was sure her mother was gone, Lottie pulled the diary out. Those words jumped off the page. Why on earth would her mother feel she was responsible for Allan's death? It was accidental. But thinking about it, all kids blame themselves for everything, be it divorce or in her own case, a missing father. Looking back, Lottie remembered believing that her father must have gone because of her. She looked out of the window, knowing she could still be right.

18

Diana

3 August 1962, 10.15 p.m.

The longcase clock in the hallway chimed and Diana crept downstairs. She could hear music coming from the smoking room. No one was in the hallway. The small kitchen was in darkness and totally cleared. She checked the refrigerator and found the bowl of whipped cream. But she couldn't dig into that without the evidence showing. That had happened before, and she'd been caught.

Back in the corridor, she raced upstairs then down the hall to the back stairway. She liked these stairs best. They had a lantern light above them, looking out to the sky. Right now, because of the lights on inside she couldn't see the sky, but on many nights she and Daddy had stared up at the stars and sometimes the moon. He would tell her stories while sitting halfway between up and down. It was their special place, a place of magic.

She stopped briefly, wanting all the guests to go so she could have Daddy on her own, but it was his birthday weekend and he wanted his friends around. She sighed then continued downstairs to hide against the doorframe at the bottom. The record player was on and Frank Sinatra was singing about night and day.

Mummy was dancing with Uncle Tom and she looked so beautiful. Her dress was all shimmery. When he spun her, her dress became like mermaid skin. Daddy put his drink down and cut in, taking Mummy in his arms. Uncle Tom laughed. He walked towards the door and she pressed herself against the wall.

Looking down at her, he whispered, 'Hello, Diana.' He put his finger to his lips and she smiled. He pointed to the big kitchen and she nodded, leading the way. He covered her dash down the hall. Once there, she peeked out. Uncle Tom was running his finger across the inside cover of his cigarette case. He looked up and winked at her. In the darkness, she found her way around the large table in the centre of the room to the larder. On the thick slate shelf were all the scones that Mrs Hoskine had made for tomorrow's adventures. No one would notice just one missing. But she would eat it here so that her escape upstairs would be easier.

She broke the scone open, longing to layer it in homemade jam and clotted cream, but they were both in the other kitchen and it might not be Uncle Tom who caught her next. It could be Lady Fox, who scared her. No matter what Diana did or said, she frowned at her and turned away.

The scone finished, she took a glass and filled it. The water was cool and sweet, unlike Moscow water. Diana had got very sick when she'd tried it when Mummy hadn't been looking. But apart from that, Diana liked Moscow. It was filled with palaces of gold. Mummy said they were churches but churches in England didn't have gold domes. The palace, in her favourite bedtime story about the princess who was loved, had many gold domes. Daddy changed the number every time because he couldn't remember, and it always made her laugh.

Diana slipped out past Tom with a smile, tiptoed back up the stairs and pulled her diary out from under her mattress. Daddy was right, she must keep it secret.

Looking out of my window now I can see stars. I hope that means it will be sunny tomorrow. That would be brilliant, in fact better than brilliant. We haven't seen much sun on this holiday. But it hasn't stopped Daddy and me from sailing every day. Both Daddy and me are very tanned. I have freckles across my nose and cheeks. Daddy loves them. But Mrs Venn says I should be careful with my skin. She wears a big hat which isn't very good for sailing. It gets in the way all the time. Daddy laughs a lot around them but I don't think they are funny.

I wanted more raspberries but I couldn't find any downstairs, just scones. Maybe Mrs Hoskine had made jam for tomorrow. I don't think the adults like the raspberries as much as I do. They come from the big garden across the road. It's all walled in and I love its fruit trees and the raspberry canes. The berries are so sweet and they give me red lips, and earlier I got red fingers. Mrs Hoskine caught me red handed, or red fingered, she said. I giggled.

I hate that Mummy has been so busy. She has had a lot to do to make people happy. She is very good at it. When I told her this she laughed. I love it when she does. She is so beautiful all the time but when she laughs, her eyes sparkle. I'm happy that I make her laugh.

In Moscow we spend so much time looking at art and attending concerts. And not talking about things. She has told me I must never tell anyone where we've been or who we have seen. I can tell Daddy, but never anyone else. And never when we are in our apartment. Only when we are outside and alone. I have asked why and she told me it was a secret and she knows I'm good at keeping secrets, like when we surprised Daddy with a party. So I don't tell anyone about the man I see her talking to when we take my dog, Salome, out for a walk. I haven't even told Daddy, I don't think. It's hard to remember all the things I'm not supposed to say.

I miss Salome and I wish we could bring her here on holidays but we can't. I hope she is having a nice time at the ambassador's residence. But she will have to behave so well. No barking in the beautiful rooms. I miss Moscow but I love being here at Boskenna. I wish we could be here always.

Goodnight, diary. I'm feeling sleepy and tomorrow we are going sailing even if the sun doesn't shine.

Diana

19

Lottie

3 August 2018, 10.20 p.m.

All Gran's stories of the bygone days filled the empty rooms as Lottie walked through the house shutting lights off. Thoughts of her mother's diary hidden upstairs vied with her current situation. It was still a struggle to accept that she could go from being a solvent, mortgaged, flat-owner with a promising career, to debt so quickly. Paul was the easy answer. She'd loaned him money for materials for an exciting new contract with a hotel chain. They had wanted him to make exclusive designs for them to sell. God, they had been excited about this. She'd even worked on the designs with him, neglecting her own work for a while.

She checked her phone. No new message from the private investigator. She shouldn't hope. Paul was gone along with all her materials and finished pieces, and she couldn't divorce him until they'd been married a year in April. Until then she was his wife thanks to UK divorce law. She shuddered then rubbed her neck to try to relieve the tension. Now was not a good time to let her thoughts tumble into a dreaded circular spiral. A walk would help.

The last light from the evening sky was hidden under the cover of the trees and the large camellias lining the path. But she knew this route so well, she could walk it blindfolded. It held so many memories. She strolled on, picking up the scent of the eucryphia. She stopped. A few trees were missing, and through the gap she could just make out the funny angle of the Judas tree. It was here by this tree that she had met Alex for the first time. It had been knocked over in a storm twelve years ago but it kept on growing, thanks to Alex and Gramps who had pushed it as upright as they could. Gramps said it was the tree of love, but she knew otherwise. Two years later she and Alex had said their parting words there. Or more correctly she had said the most awful things she could think of, wanting to hurt him.

Closing her eyes, she saw it all. Her friends from school were in the house. Alex had stormed out the back door. She'd chased him, grabbing his arm. 'Look at me.'

'Why should I? You've been all over John.'

She frowned. She had been leading him on a bit, but it was because Alex was being so . . . so bloody stupid. She loved him, but he'd gone all weird and monosyllabic with her friends. She hoped that by encouraging John a bit, Alex would sit up and take notice.

'It's clear you'd rather be with him.'

'If you act this way . . . then I might.' She crossed her arms.

'Well go right ahead.'

She opened her eyes wide. 'I thought you loved me.'

He raised an eyebrow.

'If you did, you'd fight for me.'

'Is that what you want? Local boy up against posh rugby boy.' He huffed.

'Don't be ridiculous. You're just not man enough to deal with this.'

He turned from her.

'The way you're acting, you're just not good enough.' She crossed her arms.

He looked at the house, shook his head then walked away.

She'd watched him disappear into the garden then she'd rejoined the others, still simmering with frustration. A few hours later when almost everyone had settled in the smoking room, she slipped back out into the garden for air. A few friends were playing croquet in the dark and John was one of them, which was a relief.

Turning left, she went up the long path. There was enough of a breeze to stir the tops of the trees but close to the ground all was still, except her head. It was swirling slightly. She didn't normally drink so much. However the fresh air was helping. But it didn't take away what she had done. How could she have been so mean to Alex? He was more than good enough, he was everything she ever wanted. She'd just been vain – leading on John, wanting the attention.

Tonight, so many years later, the feelings of the past seemed so close – like Lottie could reach out and touch her eighteen-year-old self. Yet right now the earth was dry though that night it hadn't been. The smell was different, too. She couldn't pinpoint it at the moment, but ten years ago the weather had been more variable and earlier that evening there had been a light shower, raining enough to dampen the topsoil. She hadn't known then that her evening would become much worse. She'd been an innocent up until then. Yes, she'd been wrong to treat Alex that way she had, but she could have apologised to him. What happened next . . . could not be fixed.

Looking back, it had the feel of a car crash: moving forward despite her foot pressed hard to the brake. Remembering, her skin went cold as she walked through the gate and turned to the watchtower. She paused on the path, unable to move forward or backward. It all felt too close. Closing her eyes, Lottie let herself recall what had happened.

Standing out at the furthest place on the point she dared, she had scanned the horizon looking for a falling star so she could make another wish. This time she longed to make a stronger one than the last so she couldn't mess it up. But the stars were dimmed because the moon was just rising and it was nearly full. It left a clear pathway on the sea. It looked like she could climb down the cliff and walk across the bay on the white road.

A twig snapped. She froze.

'There you are.' John's words slurred a bit. He had followed her. 'This place is perfect.'

She looked around. 'It's not bad.' He stepped closer and she moved back.

'I knew when I saw you leave that you wanted me to follow.'

She shook her head. That was the last thing she wanted. She wanted Alex right now. She needed to say sorry because she'd been a right idiot. John walked straight up to her and leaned in for a kiss. She dodged it.

'Sorry, John. I came out for fresh air and to be alone.' She put heavy emphasis on the last word.

'This will clear your head.' He kissed her, and she pushed him away.

'No.' She turned around and was about to leave but stopped. 'Sorry if I gave you the wrong idea.' This was her fault. Everything was. She had to find Alex.

'But you fancy me.' He held out his hands.

'No. You're a friend.'

His head dropped down.

'Are you coming back to the house?' she asked.

He shook his head.

'Sure?'

'Yeah.' He turned from her to stare out to the bay.

'Sorry,' she said as she walked away, pulling her phone out of her pocket. Had Alex gone home or gone out? She had begun to type a text when she heard John swear. She stopped and headed back. He was probably lost, and as much as she wanted to find Alex, she couldn't leave John on the point.

'John?' She called out. 'John?'

'Shit,' he said.

She heard fumbling.

'John, where are you?'

He screamed and her heart stopped. She raced forward to where she had left him. He wasn't there. Carefully she walked to the edge, her mouth dry, and peered over. The risen moon glowed off John's white t-shirt. Even from this distance she could see the awkward way his body lay.

'John!' she shouted, but she knew there was no point. Her hand shook as she dialled 999 and prayed. Sinking to the ground, she was sick and couldn't stop trembling. This was her fault. She never should have left him here alone. She rocked herself back and forth while she waited for the rescue services, but there was no comfort to be found.

Now Lottie shivered despite the warm evening. A decade had passed, and it was as fresh in her mind as when it happened.

That night had changed the course of her life. She hadn't gone to Ruskin School of Art. Instead she had lived in her mother's flat in London and gone to Central St Martins. All the while under the watchful eye of her mother's housekeeper. All trust between her and her mother had gone, and not without good reason. She was to blame. Had she taken the internship her mother had arranged, then she would never have been in Boskenna that night, and John would still be alive. Lottie lived with that knowledge every day. No wonder things had gone wrong with Paul. She didn't deserve love.

Instinct took her through the darkness and back to the gate. It was possible that the last time this gate had been used was in February when she'd taken Paul to the pub in Charlestown. His reaction to Cornwall and his behaviour towards her grandparents should have warned her something was wrong. But she always looked for the best in people and that was a mistake. Unlocking the gate, she kicked the post to unstick it. From now on she would be alone like her mother. The other way didn't work. She had tried, she had failed, and she had repeated the process, not learning. Now was the time for a new Lottie.

Peering into the dark, she realized that she hadn't taken a proper walk yet. And she still needed to clear her head. The evening was cool and she shivered as she retraced her steps. Part of her wanted to walk out to the point but doing it at night wasn't a good idea. She wasn't a fool, but many would not believe that if her latest problems came to light.

Changing her mind, she turned around and went towards Porthpean beach. The tightness in her chest eased and her mood improved listening to the sound of the waves. That was where she'd first kissed Alex. She closed her eyes, remembering. It had been as good as she had dreamed it would be. For two years before that, she had trailed after him while he worked for Gramps in the garden. Quite possibly, she had been the most embarrassing version of herself – finding ways to follow him, to see him, to do anything to catch his attention. Even now she cringed at her blatant lovestruck actions.

Gramps always used to sing the song, 'A Kiss to Build a Dream On', copying Louis Armstrong's style. The summer of 2007, when she was seventeen, she'd had the song on repeat in her head every time she saw Alex. He never even acknowledged her existence. She was too young and therefore beneath his notice.

Everything changed the following summer. She'd turned eighteen, A-levels were behind her and she was waiting for her results. The summer had begun with a two-week break with her grandparents, and that kiss on this beach had changed everything. She knew then that she wasn't going to take the internship her mother had planned, she was going to spend the summer in Cornwall with Alex. A summer to pull pints and have a boyfriend who was sexy as hell. He was the only one she had ever wanted, and she'd thrown him away.

Pulling her shoulders back, she set off slowly until she reached the steps down to the beach. Even now the longing she'd felt as a teenager, as she'd watched him as he mowed the lawn and trimmed the hedges, still stirred her. It shouldn't. She'd moved on long ago.

During those sun-drenched days, she would help Gran in the house then lie on the lawn in her bikini, pretending to read while watching him. He knew, of course he did. Then finally one night after a few pints, he'd walked her home and they had continued on past the gate and onto the beach. The moon had been full, and she'd been brave. After they had both skimmed stones for a bit, they stopped to watch a tanker in the distance. He was so close to her, she could smell the freshness of his aftershave. She'd leaned a bit closer and he turned his head towards her. Before she could stop herself, she tiptoed up and kissed him. In the light of the moon, she could see the smile hovering on his lips.

'That took you long enough,' he said, before he kissed her back.

Lottie laughed as she paused on the last step before she reached the beach now. Young and foolish. At least now she could remember the fun parts. For a while she had thought the only thing she would remember was the summer's end.

'Lottie?'

She stopped. 'Alex?'

'Yes.' He held a fishing rod and a bucket.

'Any luck?'

He nodded. 'What on earth are you doing?'

'Good question.'

'Travelling down memory lane?'

She cleared her throat. 'Might have been . . . '

Treading with care, she continued down onto the sand.

'You know the tide is on its way in?' He placed the fishing gear down and walked towards her as she strolled further north on the beach.

She didn't. 'Doesn't matter.'

The sound of the waves became louder and she stopped. Sensing, rather than seeing, if she went much farther, she would have wet feet.

She turned, and he was right behind her.

'I appreciated the apology.'

She breathed in the scent of the sea and the cool evening air. 'Long time coming.'

'Yes.'

Looking up at the sky, she tried to let go and be here now and not to think back to the past. She was on a beach in Cornwall with a man she'd once loved. This was all good. It was different. Nothing ever stayed the same, not even the rocks they were standing on. She would enjoy the moment for what it was. Peaceful.

They stood in silence. Lottie was reluctant to break it despite all the questions racing in her mind. Above she picked out the plough and Mars. Ten years ago they had been lying on this beach, looking at the stars and kissing. What would it be like if she kissed him now? Nothing could ever feel like first love's kisses. Everything was heightened, new and bursting with excitement. She shouldn't be standing here thinking about that. It would never happen again. 'Alex?'

'Yes.' His voice sounded almost sleepy.

She cleared her throat. 'I'm not complaining, but why exactly are you at Boskenna?'

'I wondered when you were going to ask.' She heard amusement in his voice.

She turned to him, but he was just shadow now and impossible to read. 'Well?'

'Do you want the long or short version?'

'Full, please.'

'In which case we had better head up the path, as the tide won't be high for another hour and already we will need to make a leap.'

'Oh.' She had been too lost in her thoughts and the stars to notice. He leaped and landed, and pebbles skidded.

'Here take my hand.'

She reached for it before jumping and crashing up against him. His arms steadied her, and his breath tickled the skin along her neck. She couldn't breathe, as though she'd been winded by the contact. Every cell in her came alive, reminding her of the past.

'Thanks,' she managed to say as she took a careful step away, conscious of the rising water behind her.

'No problem.' He let go of her. They would have to climb onto the wall as the way to the steps was covered in water. 'I remember this as being easier.' He levered himself up.

'Just thinking the same thing.' She took his hand again and scrambled to the top. Once she was stable, he released her hand.

'You were going to tell me . . . '

He fell into step beside her. 'Well, back in December I lost a close friend.'

'I'm sorry.' She let the back of her fingers touch his.

His fingers stilled, keeping the contact. 'Thank you.' He exhaled. 'And it made me see how short life can be.'

'Oh.'

'And the more I thought about that . . . the more I realized that although I enjoyed London, I wanted to be in Cornwall.' He moved his hand and cool air took its place.

'Your job?' She had no idea what he did. He'd been studying computer science.

'I was in IT and I had an idea that I'd build my own company based here.'

She paused. 'So, you're building it in Boskenna's stable block?'

'Your grandparents offered it to me along with the use of the cottage.' He looked at her. 'I'm grateful.'

'I should think your arrival was ideal timing to help them.'

'Possibly.'

They reached the gate behind the café. This all felt so familiar, yet odd. In the past, every thought revolved around spending as much time with each other as possible. It hadn't mattered whether they were walking the coast, swimming, or sailing. As long as they were with each other. Now they stood stiff like strangers.

She stifled a yawn.

'Get some sleep. You've had a tough day.'

'Yes.' She closed the gate behind them and looked up to her grandparents' room. The light was off, and she hoped they were both sleeping peacefully. She doubted she would.

20

Joan

3 August 1962, 11.30 p.m.

The bouillabaisse was a success, the summer pudding was delicious with just the right amount of bite, and now that the rain has stopped my guests are slipping outside into the fresh night air. I climb the front stairs to check on Diana. Unlike during most dinner parties, I haven't seen her slip into the kitchen. Maybe the day's sailing has tired her out, but that would be most unusual. She loves food and seems to be hungry all the time.

The door to her room is ajar and to my surprise she is asleep, with a pencil in hand. The diary has slipped to the floor. I pull the pencil out of her hand then tuck the blanket around her. Her dark eyelashes rest on her cheeks and my heart turns over with love. It never ceases to shock me how much I love her. Maybe I have lost the other babies because I can only love one child.

Picking up the diary, I resist the urge to take more than a quick glance at it. I would not spy on my own daughter. True to her word, she has begun writing in the back. She has underlined *private* and put it in bold capitals. I close the journal and place it on the bedside table. Private it will be, but I love that she has begun her first entry, *Dear Diary*.

I lean down and kiss her forehead. The scent of raspberry lingers on her skin. Her rosebud mouth is stained from the berries she ate earlier and there is a tell-tale crumb of scone in the collar of her nightgown. She must have slipped down unnoticed, after all. She is such a dear thing and I never thought I would feel such love. Life is funny that way. I never wanted her and now I can't imagine my life without her . . . or Allan. Below the open window I hear him chatting and smile. All will be fine. After each miscarriage he has mourned differently than I have. That's normal. Grief is different for everyone. But we do need to have a discussion about trying for any more. It takes so much out of us each time and of course, Diana. She feels it. I sometimes think she feels guilty. That she feels she is not enough, which isn't true. She is everything and more. How do I explain this to a child? Looking at her once more I slip out of her room, hoping that tonight won't be too late. I stifle a yawn.

Down in the dining room, I pour myself a small amount of cognac to settle my stomach and run my fingers over the spines of the books that line the wall until I reach the doors to the garden. No opportunity has yet presented itself for me to grab a moment with Tom. Outside, the sound of the waves competes with the conversation. During my life I have heard it through the good and bad, the calm and the stormy. A house this close to the sea is constantly aware of its position, proud above the beach, gleaming white. Even on this night of a waning crescent moon, the house glows. If I were on a boat in the bay, I would be able to see it without the lights. It makes its presence felt. At one point during the war the front of the house was coated in cow dung to dim the white and that seemed to work. But tonight the paint is bright and it shines.

On the path across the lawn, Tom is talking with Eddie. He glances my way and then sets off down towards the beach alone. There is no way I can follow him at this point. My duty is to my guests. I won't be free until the last one has departed or gone to bed.

Mrs Hoskine stands in the French windows of the smoking room. I nod at her and she heads off without a word. I don't know what I'd do without her. Boskenna wouldn't work, that is certain. Between her and her husband they kept it warm, dry and welcoming. When we arrived a week ago, I could have wept I was so exhausted. But thanks to the Hoskines, here everything is easy, not like the challenge of life in Moscow where nothing is as it seems. There I am on constant alert, and this weekend it feels like Moscow has crept into Boskenna while I wasn't watching. But, of course, that isn't true, I invited it in.

At the time it seemed the only way, but right at this moment I simply want to be a family on holiday, entertaining friends. I want to hold my husband and watch him sleep, peacefully, and I want to build sandcastles and make jam with my daughter. I don't want to be anything other than a mother and a wife. I laugh. Who would have thought that I could feel this way? Certainly not me.

'Darling Joan, thank you for such a lovely evening. The food and the company were divine.' William Parsons grins.

'A pleasure.' I smile.

'So like the evenings your mother used to run here.' He paused. 'I didn't think anyone could live up to her standard but of course her daughter can.'

'High praise.'

He clasps my hand briefly. 'We're off now. Hope to see you

in London when you are next back or maybe if you spend Christmas here this year.'

'That would be lovely. So kind of you to join us tonight.'

I watch them stop by Allan. I can't hear the words, but Allan glances up at me and smiles. My stomach flutters. Maybe we can get through this, after all.

21

Lottie

3 August 2018, 11.35 p.m.

The house was in darkness as Lottie climbed the stairs to her room feeling a bit drunk. The brandy she'd thought would make her sleepy hadn't done so. Her mind felt fuzzy, not tired. It had been a bad idea. But she was good at those. Spending any more time with Alex Hoskine would fall into that category. He'd lost none of his appeal. She shook her head and walked to the bathroom to fill her water glass. But she stopped before she reached it. Sitting cross legged on the hallway floor was her mother. The closet door beside her was open and she had an old shoebox on her lap. By the light of her phone torch she was going through photographs.

'Mum?' Lottie knelt down beside her.

'I don't remember any of this.' She held up a picture of her in Red Square with a man Lottie guessed was her grandmother's first husband. Her mother's hand shook. 'I only have the one picture of my father.'

'The memory you told me about.' Thinking of the diary, Lottie was grateful it seemed her mother didn't recall everything.

She nodded, and Lottie took the photo from her. There was

not enough light to see things in great detail, but her grandfather, Allan Trewin, was a handsome man. His charisma radiated from the faded snapshot. 'You never showed me that picture.'

'No point. But now I'm faced with all these new photos.' She dug into the box and pulled out another one with her father sharing a camel with her.

'How did you find these?' Lottie peered into the darkness of the closet.

'I went to go to bed and found I had no sheets or pillowcases.'

Lottie frowned. 'They aren't kept here.'

'I didn't know.'

Of course she didn't. She hadn't even stayed overnight that terrible evening ten years ago. She had stood by the bedroom door while Lottie packed her things. Once they were in the car the silence had been the worst. If she had shouted it would have been better. That silence was so damning. Here was a woman who made her living with words and yet she had had none for Lottie.

Taking her phone out of her pocket now, Lottie pointed its torch into the darkness. The closet was filled with garment bags and boxes. She'd never known this closet to be unlocked. She unzipped one of the bags and glimpsed the shimmer of green silk.

'Looks like it's all Gran's old clothes.' She ran her fingers over the fabric.

'She's hidden all this from me . . . ' Her mother's voice faded.

'I wouldn't say "hidden".' Lottie opened a box to find a pair of black pumps with a grosgrain ribbon bow. They were in beautiful condition.

Her mother stroked a black and white photograph. 'All this time I thought there were no other photos.'

'Did you ever ask?'

'She said she didn't know where they were.' She sighed.

'Well, then don't make a judgement.' Lottie winced. She shouldn't have said that. That was the brandy talking.

Her mother stood, taking the box of photos with her. She glared at Lottie then headed not towards her bedroom but her mother's.

'Mum, where are you going?'

'To ask about these.' She looked mutinous.

'It's nearly midnight and I hope both of them are asleep.' Lottie paused and took a deep breath, thinking maybe the gins had taken away her mother's normal sense. 'Tomorrow morning will be soon enough to ask these questions.'

She stopped and turned. 'She may not be alive tomorrow.'

Lottie couldn't argue with that, but she had to stop her. 'Then maybe you shouldn't ask.'

'I need to know the truth.' She rested the box on her hip.

'The truth about what?'

'My father.'

Lottie let out a long sigh. 'Mum, you know the truth: he fell from the cliff.' She flinched. The tragedy that two people connected with Boskenna had fallen to their death was still too close after her walk this evening and the coming anniversary of John's death.

'Yes, I've read the newspapers and the coroner's report.'

'Then what are you looking for?' Lottie hoped she was right that her mother had no memory of what she'd written in her diary.

'I wish I knew.' She walked towards her and Lottie dared to hope she would leave talking to Gran until tomorrow. As her mother passed, Lottie grabbed her hand. 'I know this is hard.'

She shook her head and went to her room, but Lottie was

sure she'd seen tears pooling in her mother's eyes. Yet again she'd said the wrong thing to her. Walking down the hall to the linen cupboard, she pulled out towels then sheets for her mother's bed and for her own.

Passing the closet where the clothes and photos had been found, Lottie pushed it closed with her foot. As she expected, the door to her mother's room was shut. She tapped lightly and said, 'I'll leave the sheets for your bed here, and some towels.' There was no response from within, so she placed them on the floor and went back to collect the ones for her room. But her way was blocked by the now wide-open closet door. No doubt this was why it had been locked in the past. It wouldn't stay shut.

Lottie tried to close it again to no avail. Looking closely, one of the shoeboxes had moved forward. She pushed them back, but it didn't work. Groping in the darkness, she found the culprit. One of the lids wouldn't sit on its box. She pulled it to the front and found not shoes in it, but a bulging notebook filled with bits of old newspaper, from what little she could see. Closing the door, she kept the shoebox and the notebook and walked to her room.

Turning on the bedside light, she sat on the top of her bed and opened the notebook. A yellowed page from *The Daily Telegraph* with a recipe for 'Chicken à la King' stared at her. Her grandmother was an excellent cook and hostess. The best in the Duchy, according to Gramps. Not that they had done much entertaining recently. A wave of sadness arrived with the thought that there would be no more entertaining for Gran.

On the first page Gran had written *Damascus, Syria* and the date, *30 September 1955*, the menu and the guest list. On the flipside she had jotted down things like *need more salt in the sauce* and *Mrs Phelps didn't eat the fish*.

Lottie kept turning the pages. It was amazing in the detail. Her grandmother had noted down whose parties she'd been to and what they served. Her thought process began to emerge. There was even a list of guests with food dislikes and drink preferences.

Lottie's stomach rumbled. Tonight's dinner of chilli con carne didn't stand up to beef wellington and salmon *en croute*. She loved Gran's little comments about seating plans gone awry and who had bored her silly at 'away matches'. She even noted what dresses and jewellery she wore to each event. It must have been hard to have that much pressure to look fabulous and to keep the dinner parties fresh. It was clear she'd made sure that no one had been served the same meal twice. Well, that wasn't quite true. The French ambassador clearly enjoyed her lemon soufflé, so whenever he was invited, she served it and he was always seated beside her. Lottie concluded he was either a very difficult guest or an easy one.

Yawning, she placed the notebook back into its box on the floor. Her head was spinning just having read the entries for September to December 1954. Her mother had been born in late December; how did Gran do all of this while pregnant? Before she married Allan, Lottie knew she had been a secretary at the embassy. She must have transferred her organisational skills to being a good hostess. Maybe it had been a way to combat the boredom. No, that was making a judgement on what she thought life as a Fifties' housewife must have been like. It had to have been challenging to source everything and make it all appear easy so far from home. But of course she would have had help. It would be the last thing on earth Lottie would want. Even if things had worked out as planned with Paul, cosy domesticity would never have been on the menu. Her career as a designer was paramount – or had been. Life could change very quickly if you trusted the wrong person.

22

Diana

3 August 2018, 11.55 p.m.

She stood staring out of the windows in her grandmother's old room at the north end of the house. Due to the darkness Diana saw a reflection of herself on the glass. Tall and lean. There was nothing comforting about her appearance. The lights from the tanker in the bay added highlights to her greying hair. The image was framed by the old chintz curtains.

Behind her, the bed was covered in faded photos. It told a story. Turning around she could see it. It was clear. A happy family. Love shouted from each smile, no matter the angle. Her hands shook as she picked up a picture of her as a toddler. Her father's arms were open wide, and she had a proud smile on her face. She sighed. This wasn't a memory she could have had. She was too young. But those first steps had been well documented. Turning the pictures over, her mother had carefully written *London, 1957.*

Her chest tightened. She'd missed Lottie's first steps because she'd been called out to Bosnia, so her daughter had toddled into George's arms here on Boskenna's lawn. Somewhere there was a photo. She should be grateful and she was. Looking at these pictures, maybe leaving Lottie with her mother had been the right thing. At the time it had been the only thing. No, she was lying to herself. She had run from her daughter, who had been like a puppy – big eyes and unconditional love. She had never asked for that love. She had never asked for the child, but by the time she'd discovered the pregnancy, fate had decided she would have it. She was thirty-six and a public figure thanks to her job. Being held hostage in Afghanistan for six months in 1989 had just added to her fame.

She closed her eyes. Unlike her childhood, Diana could remember every detail of those six months, no matter how she pushed it away. Of course, that was part of the problem with Lottie. There in her exotic eyes were her father's. No matter how she had tried, she couldn't separate her daughter's eyes from his. Each glance broke her. And yet she hadn't given her up. She should have but they had eventually found a way. It hadn't been perfect, but Lottie had never wanted for anything . . . except her love. That was why she knew she never should have become a mother. She couldn't love a child enough but looking at these pictures, Diana was wrong about the reason. She had been loved and she had loved in return.

On her most recent assignment, she'd met a young woman who had been searching for who she was. She had lost everything except – as she had phrased it – her bones, her essence that she carried inside her. She'd said it called out to her in the night, but she couldn't translate what it was trying to say to her. She had no home. She was far from the land she was born in and she was alone. Diana's heart reached out. It understood. She too had been alone, fearing everything had been lost.

Her words had opened up Diana's own history inside her.

After decades of being silenced, it shouted to her. For years she'd believed that the past was just that and had no impact on the present she was living. Diana knew why she operated this way. She didn't want to look back. She'd run from the past. Most people would run from what she'd seen in the course of her career, but it had called to her. She had covered her history so deeply with new images and memories that were richer, brighter and sadder so that she had squashed to oblivion what was underneath. Now, in the autumn of her life, she finally wanted to spring-clean and find out what she'd hidden.

Why did she think things weren't right with her father's death? Something about it had always worried her. Only now was she willing to acknowledge she didn't feel comfortable with the possibility that he chose to leave them? To leave her? Was that a pain too great to bear? It must have been.

She knew his death had been recorded as accidental. But it didn't ring true. Not to the man who had come to life in the process of her recent research. Allan Trewin was accomplished and brave. He had served in the RAF in the Pacific and – reading between the lines – he was in intelligence, which made sense of his later career in the Foreign Office. Her father had been a spy. This was not a surprise. It had been the Cold War and he had worked in the Soviet Union. It was simply an occupational hazard. But there was something else. She could almost feel the answer but it remained beyond her reach. Her mother might know more but Diana had left it too late to ask the questions, which was unlike her.

MILESTONE

23

Joan

4 August 1962, 3.00 a.m.

All is quiet. Allan is finally asleep, and I creep through the house to Tom's room. His door is ajar and, as I expect, he's not in his bed. I have read his signal correctly. The tall clock in the hall chimes three. Silently in bare feet, I move down the stairs through the hall into the rear kitchen. The door is unlocked. My plimsoles sit waiting and I grab an old cardigan. The night has gone cold with the clear sky. The path through to the top garden is slippery with dew. Only the slight scent of pipe tobacco gives Tom away.

I scramble across the part of the garden Diana calls Primrose Hill to the top path where I know I will find Tom. The crescent sliver of a moon is low in the sky. He's dressed in dark colours blending into the hedge. I sit beside him, taking one last look around and listening to be sure we are alone. Only the cry of an owl fills the night air.

'Hello.' My voice is husky. It feels like a clandestine lovers' meeting. I push the thought away.

'I'd wondered if you'd make it.' He taps his pipe on the seat.

'Touch and go, but Allan finally fell asleep.'

'Do you know what's bothering him?'

'You noticed too?' I relax my shoulders. What was the saying . . . a problem shared is a problem halved? But that meant I thought he was a problem.

'Hard not to.'

I nod, forgetting that Tom can't see my features any more than I can see his. 'I keep thinking it's the miscarriage.'

Tom shuffles closer to me on the bench.

'I'm sorry.' His hand reaches out, touching first my thigh, then my arm, before finding my hand and clasping it.

I hold my breath for a moment. 'Thank you.'

We are both quiet and I long to know what he is thinking.

'Has he behaved this way before?'

'Yes.' I take a deep breath. 'And no.'

'I wonder,' he says before puffing his pipe. The smoke catches the thin moonlight. 'Do you think it's the stress?' He releases my hand.

'Possibly.' I answer. It could be the cause of both.

'I should never have brought you back in.'

'You had no choice. You needed someone you could trust who was invisible.'

Animals scurry under the bench, rustling leaves. 'That doesn't make it right.'

'You can't live there and not be involved in some way.' I sigh. 'You know that.' Even before I became the key contact for the double agent Victor, the strain of our life in Moscow had been trying for Allan and me. We couldn't talk in the apartment. We spoke in code. Some days I think we forgot how to communicate naturally. The only normality in our life was Diana. She let none of the strictures infringe on her enjoyment of it all.

'There's involved and then there's . . . putting you at risk.'

'I've been at risk before.' I put my hand on his arm.

'Yes, but that was before – before Diana.'

I pull out my cigarette case and open it. It's empty. I forgot to refill it earlier. 'But this is important.'

'I can't argue with that.' He sighs; locating his cigarette case, he lights one and offers it to me.

I feel rather than see him slump beside me and I think back to Aden. It had been almost carefree in those days. I was good at checking people's personal diaries, overhearing conversations, and getting invitations into homes. 'What's happened?' I ask, bracing myself. This would explain the arrival of the American, George Russell, tomorrow.

'I'm finished.' He taps his pipe on the seat again.

'What?' I try to keep my voice quiet, but the shock is hard to contain.

'I've been blown.' His voice trails away into the night air.

'Who?' Images flash in my mind like a slide show of faces and locations.

'Don't know.'

I shiver. 'But you have an idea . . . ?'

'You might be, too.'

'How?' My thoughts race through everything, everyone. Nothing appears. No one could know. I am a housewife, a mother. I do nothing.

'As from later today, I'm no longer your handler.'

'No.' I have feared this from the moment I began. Tom knows me and my strengths. He is my anchor. 'You're not leaving me in this alone.'

'No. The Americans are taking it over.'

I shake my head. I don't know them. How can I trust them? Tom makes all of this easy and he always has. 'Is Victor blown?'

'We don't think so, but as you know he was itchy on the last drop.'

I nod in the darkness, remembering the heat of the Moscow day and the lack of air, even in the park. Diana had been reluctant to play and even Salome, our dog, was uneasy. She hadn't wanted the treat that Victor had offered, making things awkward, then Diana had come back. 'Was the info still good?'

'I believe so.' He sighs again. 'I hate leaving you alone in this.'

'Yes.' I look down to the house, thinking of all those sleeping peacefully. 'Does Allan know?'

'No.'

My head shoots up. 'Why?'

'There is a leak.'

'But it would never be Allan.' I fight the urge to strike out. This isn't Tom. He would sell his soul for Allan.

'It's no longer in my hands.' His voice catches.

I will not let emotion into this. I have a role to play. 'So he doesn't know?'

'No.'

'This George Russell . . .'

'Allan believes the cover story of the aunt in Penzance.'

I cough. 'Surely he doesn't.'

He laughs. 'We all believe things, Joan.'

My gut turns. 'Yes.' So many of us have been fooled, haven't looked when we didn't want to see.

'Right, we both need to get some sleep.' Tom stands and walks up the path away from the house and I retrace my steps back. I dry off the bottom of my plimsoles and replace the cardigan on the hook before returning to my room. Allan is in light sleep and I carefully slide into bed and lay staring at my husband. Is anything as it seems?

24

Lottie

'Damn.' Lottie rubbed her eyes and grabbed her phone. Six a.m. Yawning, she knew she could have used more sleep. It was way too early to be awake, but she'd forgotten to close the curtains last night. The rising sun filled the room with a blinding light. There was no point in drawing the curtains now and trying to go back to sleep. She had a lot to do today.

She swung her feet out of bed and kicked her mother's diary and the shoebox with Gran's notebook. Her grandmother was dying. The reality hit, and her shoulders slumped. There was no time to waste. With any luck her mother would still be asleep, and Lottie could do something to stop her from confronting Gran, or Gramps for that matter. She understood her desire to know. Lottie had that same desire. Who was her father? Maybe her mother didn't know, or didn't want to remember. When she was a teenager, she saw several articles about her mother's abduction and Lottie began to make a few guesses based on her age and her mother's time in captivity.

She went to the mirror. The dark haired, grey-eyed woman looking back at her was no English rose. Her mother and Gran both had dark hair and dark eyes, but they were fair skinned. Lottie's eyes, her best feature according to Paul, stood out against her tanned skin. Her irises were pale grey with a dark grey ring. They haunted her, and she thought they haunted her mother, too.

Looking away, her glance fell on the file. How could one pile of papers contain enough to explain how her life had collapsed? Yet they did, showing the refused insurance claim for the theft of the jewellery, the police report saying there had been no evidence of a break-in or damage to her safe, the legal paperwork for the sale of the flat, the outstanding invoices for the gems and the gold and platinum, and her Vegas marriage certificate. She sighed. Married in haste and repenting at leisure. He had taken her freedom, her money, her career and her self-esteem. She was an idiot. At least the money from the flat should have cleared by Monday or Tuesday, then she could close the chapter of her life entitled 'Lottie the up-and-coming London jewellery designer'. God, she had been blind.

She needed coffee before she did anything. Her old fluffy dressing gown from her boarding school days hung on the back of the door. Covered in teddy bears, it was the height of revolting taste, but it still did the job of covering the essentials. There was some comfort in wearing something that dated from before she had ruined everything.

The flowers she'd put on the hallway table yesterday felt right. Later she would gather more from the kitchen garden, but first she wanted to check on her grandparents. Boskenna's idiosyncrasies soothed her as they had always done. She loved the way the house was odd in its layout, the eccentricities of the additions over the years. It had begun life much more fortified, by all accounts. This was apparent if you looked closely. Some of the original stonework from the Tudor building was visible around the courtyard. Those stones formed the foundations of the house that stood here today. Gran had pointed them out to her years ago, along with all the other joins in the house. There were so many. She paused, overwhelmed. Boskenna without Gran. She was the very mortar that held it all together.

Taking a steadying breath, she climbed the steps up to her grandparents' bedroom. Those steps were another of the many visible joins. She stopped at the door, ready to knock. Gramps sat by the windows – not looking at the view but at her grandmother propped up in bed. She was speaking but her eyes were closed.

'Gramps?' Lottie came in and went to the bed. 'She isn't speaking English. It sounds like Russian.'

'Take no notice.' He shook his head. 'She's delirious.' He put his cup and saucer down on the dressing table in front of the middle window. There were two cups and saucers, one unused. She looked away. What would he do when she was gone?

Lottie sat next to Gran and stroked her forehead until she settled, and her breathing was no longer as distressed. 'I'll sit with her a while.' She gave him an encouraging smile. 'Why don't you take a bath or maybe a walk?'

She looked past Gramps to the view. The rising sun had washed the colour out of the sea and the sky, but there was not a cloud to be seen.

'Are you sure you'll be fine?' He pushed himself out of the chair. It took so much effort.

'Absolutely.' She smiled.

'A bit of cool morning air might do me some good.'

She nodded and turned back to Gran, listening to the thump of Gramps' cane on each stair then along the corridor.

'It's a glorious day, Gran.' Lottie walked over to the teapot and poured a cup. 'I might even be tempted to take a swim.' She smiled. 'Do you remember how I used to join you every morning for one?' So many days, rain or shine, she would follow Gran down the path to the beach. Frequently it was very early, before the families with buckets and spades arrived. Normally it would just be old Jacob with his fishing rod sitting on the far rocks. He'd wave to them as they dropped their towels and Lottie would race into the water trying to match Gran's stride. Oh how she'd wanted to be like Gran with her bathing cap and sleek black swimsuit. Instead she'd sported a spotted bikini with her hair in a plait.

'Do you remember Jacob? He was there every morning just like us.' She laughed. 'He was a man of very few words but many fish.'

Gran turned her head towards her.

'I wonder if he's still alive. I always thought he was ancient, but I saw him in the village a few years ago and he hadn't changed. I guess the sea had hardened his face early on and he hadn't aged.'

She looked down. Gran's eyes were open.

'Morning.' Lottie beamed.

'Yes.' Gran's voice was more of a croak.

Her heart lifted. 'I love you.'

Gran's hand came out from under the covers and she grabbed Lottie's. 'Forgive me.'

She pulled a face. 'There's nothing to forgive.'

Gran shook her head and lowered her eyes, so Lottie couldn't read her expression.

'Forgive me. I had no choice.'

'You've done nothing to forgive.' Lottie frowned. 'You've been everything for me.'

She shook her head and she fought for breath.

'Gran, I forgive you whatever you think you've done. I love you and nothing will change that, ever.'

She sighed. 'Thank you.' Her eyes closed and in moments she was asleep again. Lottie kissed her forehead and walked to the window. Below, Gramps hobbled around the path circling the lawn. He stopped every few feet and gazed out at the sea. She couldn't blame him. In the distance a gaff-rigged bark bobbed on the swell. The scene was timeless. Only the tower on Gribben Head dated it. She remembered Gramps telling her its history – that had been built in 1832 to help boats distinguish Gribben Head from Dodman Point. Lottie had felt it looked like a stick of rock stuck into the hill. This had made Gramps laugh because he'd thought it looked like a broken candy cane.

Hearing footsteps, she turned and put the cup on the table. Lottie knew it was her mother. She hoped she was wrong, and that a confrontation wasn't about to happen. But reading her mother's face, it wore not a daughter's concern, but the expression of the award-winning investigative reporter who left no stone unturned until she knew the truth. She'd seen it too many times. Lying was not an option with her mother. Lottie knew because she'd tried. She couldn't get away with it, not even by omission.

She held her finger to her lips and her mother stopped in her tracks, holding the box in front of her. For a moment Lottie saw her confusion but that didn't last long. She put the box on the bed and walked to Lottie.

'How is she?' her mother asked in hushed tones.

'She's just nodded off.'

'I'll wait.' She sank into the armchair by the window. It was where Gran would normally sit and read in the morning. Gramps would bring up a tray of tea and toast as he had today, and he would read the paper in his chair. Lottie looked for him below again, but he was not in front of the house anymore.

'Make some coffee, please.' Her mother picked up the book on the table, *To Kill a Mockingbird*. 'This was mine, or more correctly, I made it mine.' She turned it over in her hands and opened it. There in childish print it read

This book belongs to Diana Trewin of Boskenna
July 1962

'I knew I had a copy.' She ran her fingers over the cover then at Gran. 'I wonder what she thought when she saw the inscription?'

Lottie tilted her head to the side. 'Why?'

'I was very young to be reading this.' She flipped it over in her hands.

'True.' Lottie frowned, thinking of the diary. 'I'll go and make coffee but promise me you will be gentle with Gran.'

Her mother pursed her mouth.

'Mum, promise.'

'Fine.'

Lottie didn't like the word fine – it had too many connotations – but on this occasion, it would have to do because she wasn't getting anything further from her mother. Her nose was in the book. Lottie sighed.

25

Diana

Diana hummed as she walked down the stairs. It was the song about night and day that Mummy was dancing to last night. Diana took a spin around at the bottom of the stairs. The sun was out and no one else was up. But that was not true. She must pay more attention to things if she wanted to become a journalist. The front door was open. Someone else was awake. Looking around, she saw the newspapers were on the hall table. She must read articles to learn how to report.

She skipped to the table where three papers were laid out. The front pages didn't look very interesting. She kept flipping pages until she saw the words that she had heard mentioned in quiet voices . . . nuclear threat, Khrushchev, President Kennedy, Cold War. Goosebumps rose on her arms. Her glance stopped at the headline, *Keeping a Goat in the House*. That sounded fun, but she frowned. It was described as a parable. Jesus told parables in the Bible. Mr Khrushchev told them in the paper. Her nose wrinkled when she read about getting used to the smell. Mr Khrushchev called the goat *imperialism*. That was strange. She would need to ask what imperialism was. It didn't sound like a name. He also mentioned war and at that, Diana stepped away from the table. She didn't like reading that there had been more nuclear tests. She had asked Daddy what that meant, and she hadn't liked the answer. Mummy had made a serious face at Daddy and muttered that he shouldn't be telling her things like that because it would scare her.

Mummy would make more faces when she found out Diana was reading the papers. She studied the article again. It was confusing. But somehow the goat made the nuclear thermal weapons necessary. She sighed and decided she wouldn't ask Mummy about it, but would ask Daddy or Uncle Tom.

There was a picture of President Kennedy in the other paper. Mummy liked him. Diana thought he was handsome. Mrs Kennedy was almost as pretty as Mummy, but not quite.

'There you are little one. Hungry?' Mrs Hoskine walked through the front door carrying a broom.

'Yes.'

'Permanently, it seems to me.' She raised an eyebrow. 'It appears we have mice because there was a scone missing this morning.'

'Really?' Diana opened her eyes wide.

'You know it's best to tell the truth.'

Diana looked down. 'Sorry, Mrs Hoskine. I ate a scone last night because I was very hungry.'

Mrs Hoskine ruffled her hair. 'That's better my little one. Now let's see to some breakfast for you.'

Diana trailed behind her into the kitchen where she first smelt, then saw, fresh bread. 'Bread and butter, please, with jam.'

'Of course.' She sliced a piece and Diana layered it with butter and jam. The bread was warm enough that the butter melted right in and dripped down her chin. Mrs Hoskine wiped her face with a clean tea-towel. 'Is that enough for now or do you need more?'

'Enough for now, thank you.' Diana dashed out of the kitchen and went straight to the piano. She put the music away that was out from last night and pulled hers out of the seat. She was about to begin warming her fingers up, as Madame Roscova had taught her, when she thought of her diary. She needed to write in it.

She raced back upstairs and pulled it out from under her mattress. She had been puzzled to find it on her bedside table this morning. But then she'd looked in it and there was a pencil line dragged down one page. She must have fallen asleep writing. Mummy would have put it on the table. She knew it was Mummy and not Daddy because of the pencil placement. It was tucked just inside the cover. She did that with her own notebook. Mummy wrote in hers all the time. It was like a diary of sorts, except hers was all about food and clothes and people.

Peering out of the bedroom window, the sun was making steam come off the lawn. It was going to be a wonderful day for sailing. She put her diary under her arm. Today she would bring it with her and record everything that she saw. Maybe she would have another piece of bread, butter and jam before she practised the piano. Madame Roscova had told Diana she must practise every day and that she wanted to know all about her holiday in England. Recording everything in the diary would make it easier to remember. There was nothing that happened here that she couldn't tell Madame Roscova. She had to think hard in Moscow during her lessons, focusing on her finger placement and what she could and couldn't talk about. It was tricky but she did her best.

26

Diana

4 August, 1962 7.10 a.m.

'Good morning, my gorgeous girl.' Daddy sat down on the piano bench with Diana after kissing her head.

'Morning, Daddy.' Diana began playing 'Happy Birthday'. She sang as loud as she could while trying to get her fingers in the right position and hit the keys with enough force. Daddy placed his hand over hers lightly.

'Thank you, my darling one.' He kissed her hand. 'Maybe leave this, and even your practice, until later.'

She frowned and looked at him. His hair was all a mess, his breath smelled of cigarettes and there were dark shadows under his eyes. 'Why?'

'Because I think some of our guests might be a bit tired this morning and need a little more sleep before we head out sailing.' He smiled and reached into his dressing gown pocket for his cigarettes. She watched him light one.

'Can I play quietly?'

'Of course.' He put his cigarette down in the ashtray on the top of the piano. 'We could play together, if we're extra careful.'

'Oh, yes please, Daddy. 'Chopsticks'?'

'Of course.' He shuffled closer to her on the bench and they began by hitting the keys very quietly, but she began to giggle, and Daddy started to play with force until they both collapsed into a heap, laughing.

'That didn't work, did it?' He tickled her and she giggled and squirmed. 'Shall we go for a walk in the garden and see how the wind is doing?'

She nodded and grabbed his hand as they opened the French windows and stepped into the sunshine. Even without the flag up, she could tell there was no wind. But the sun was hot.

'It will improve later when the tide changes.' He scanned the horizon. 'No matter what, we have to be out of the house today so that Mummy can get everything ready for tonight.'

'But it's a secret.' She tugged on his arm.

He winked. 'You won't tell her I know.'

'Of course not.' She shook her head. Did he know about the cake? She hoped not. That was special. For the past few days Mrs Hoskine and Diana had been making copies of her matryoshka dolls in marzipan and Diana had created the gold domed churches too. On the sides of the cake they would apply eggs, like the small jewelled one Mummy had from her cousin. The little egg was made by someone important, but Diana couldn't remember the name. However, she loved the way it opened up to reveal a small boat. One day it would be hers, Mummy had said. Diana couldn't wait.

'Daddy, why is a goat called *imperialism*, and what does "imperialism" mean?'

He stopped walking. 'What a funny old question.'

'Why is it funny?'

'Because it's coming from you.' He dropped his cigarette on

the ground and crushed it with his slipper. She was barefoot and could feel the damp ground beneath her feet and the blades of grass that covered her toes. She took his hand as they walked to the front door where she stopped to scrape her feet on the mat so Mrs Hoskine wouldn't be cross.

'Good morning, Mr Trewin and happy birthday.' Mrs Hoskine was walking out of the drawing room carrying Diana's diary. Diana raced forward. She had forgotten she'd left it sitting on the piano. She would have to be more careful.

'There's fresh tea and coffee in the dining room,' she paused, and held out the diary, 'and this, young lady, is yours – although it took me a while to discover that, as you wrote your name in the back and not the front.' Diana thought about this. Maybe she needed to write it in the front, too.

Diana took it and said, 'Thank you, Mrs Hoskine.'

'Should I bring coffee upstairs to Mrs Trewin?'

Daddy smiled. 'I think she'll be down shortly.' He picked up the papers and walked into the dining room. He hadn't answered Diana's question. She would ask again later.

She went into the office, put her diary on the big leather covered desk and pulled out the chair.

Morning Diary,
The house was so quiet when I came downstairs. Just the old long clock ticking in the hall. I'm in the office now. The sun is filling the room and I have to squint as I write, it's so bright. In the distance I can see Mr Hoskine raising the flag on the front lawn. The flag doesn't flutter. I hope Daddy is right about the wind.

I will need to practise the piano more later. Madame Roscova will be cross with me if I haven't practised. It was fun playing with Daddy. He can be so silly and I love him so much.

Uncle Tom is walking in the garden with his hair all pushed up like he has been running his hand through it. Daddy has joined him outside. They looked serious. It must be because of the lack of wind.

I smell bacon cooking and I'm hungry again. I'll write more later, Diary.

27

Lottie

4 August 2018, 7.15 a.m.

While she waited for the coffee to brew, Lottie tackled the cobwebs in the hallway with a feather duster. At least the entrance no longer looked like a set for a Halloween film. With the warm dry weather and the missing daily help, the spiders were having a great time. After she delivered the coffee to her mother, she would tackle some hoovering. With a minimum of effort, Boskenna would be back to how her grandmother liked it. She could do that. It wasn't much but it was something.

She checked to see if Gramps was in the snug, but there was no sign of him. He must be in the garden somewhere. Although it was ten degrees cooler than in London, the air blowing through the open front door was already warm. She pulled off her fuzzy dressing gown and put it on the bottom of the stairs to take up to her room later.

All her summer memories were tinged with the feel of the sun and scent of the sea, yet when she looked through photographs many were of her in an old cagoule or Guernsey, braving the wind and the rain. Who was she fooling? Her memories centred on her summer with Alex. The heat of the sun, the warmth of their bodies and the soundtrack of Gramps' old vinyl records and the endless repeat of Sam Sparro's 'Black and Gold' on the radio as they drove to the north coast for the surf.

The aroma of coffee greeted her as she walked into the small kitchen and found Alex there.

'Morning.' His voice was deep and husky, like he hadn't long been out of bed. In fact, with his hair askew that was what it looked like. Desire filled her as he plunged the coffee then pushed the door open on the cabinet that covered the north wall. 'Your mother up?'

'Yes, sitting with Gran.'

He raised an eyebrow then pulled out three mugs. 'And how's that going?'

She laughed. 'Gran's sleeping.'

During that summer, cocooned in an old blanket on the beach, they had talked about her mother and her grandmother. Heck, they had talked about everything, even her father – or lack of one. He understood the hole in her life because he'd lost his dad when he was fifteen. That was when he came to live in Porthpean to be near his grandmother. He handed her a mug.

'Thanks.' Her gaze narrowed. He looked too bloody good. Better at thirty than at twenty. Why couldn't he have lost his charm in the last ten years? She pushed her hair back. His shirt had only one button done leaving an expanse of chest on display. Her fingers twitched, and she clenched her fists. They remembered the feel of him, even if she didn't want to. Hawaiian Tropic. She smelt it now. Was she imagining it? She must be. Having Alex here was wrong because she was still so damn attracted to him. Too much time had passed, and it didn't feel right. Plus she was still technically married even if she didn't want anyone to know and she had no clue where her husband was.

'How long are you here for?' He popped some bread into the toaster.

She opened her eyes wide. That was a question she didn't want to answer. She had no place else to go. But saying that would invite further questions. 'Don't know.'

He lifted his head and smiled. There were lines on his face that hadn't been there before, but instead of making him less appealing they did the opposite. There was knowledge behind the smile and laughter behind the lines. Who had helped him to gain the knowledge and who had made him laugh? Lottie looked into her coffee. She had no right to be jealous, but she was. Standing here so close, so casually dressed in a strappy top and silky shorts, everything between them felt incomplete. But it was over years ago. They were kids and now they were adults. She knew nothing of Alex Hoskine now and he knew nothing of her. For this she was grateful, and she needed it to stay that way.

'Depending on how things are with your grandmother, maybe we could go for a drink tonight?' He gave her a lopsided look.

Lottie cradled her mug, telling herself there was no harm in having a drink with him. She wanted to. Even just to remember the good times . . . but accepting would be wrong. There was an invitation in his eyes. It spoke of unfinished business and of longing. She felt it all, but she had to keep her distance.

Gramps appeared at the kitchen door. 'Sorry to interrupt.' He took the two steps down into the kitchen with care.

'Perfect timing. Would you like a coffee?' Alex asked.

'Oh, no, far too early.' He looked between them. 'Joan?'

'Sleeping – and Mum is sitting with her.'

He gave her a sideways glance.

'I've told her to behave and I'm bringing coffee up now.' She picked up the mug Alex had poured for her mother.

'Fine.'

There was that word again. Nothing about this whole situation was fine. It was far from it.

28

Diana

4 August 2018, 7.20 a.m.

The sun beat down on her back as Diana traced her childish handwriting inside the front cover of *To Kill a Mockingbird*. She had been cheeky to do it. It hadn't been hers and if Lottie had done it to one of her books she would have been livid.

Diana Trewin of Boskenna

Not of anywhere else, not of Moscow, not London where they had a flat, but Boskenna. At first, she hadn't run from the house, but had been taken from it. How had she felt then? The words in front of her spoke of belonging but she didn't belong anywhere. Her flat in London was only personalised by books and they could be packed into a few boxes. She hadn't created a welcoming environment for Lottie . . . not like Boskenna. The house dripped in history and warmth, with silver picture frames speaking of happier times. But there were no displayed pictures of Diana's childhood. Those had been locked away. Why? She shivered despite the warm breeze.

Reviewing the past sixty-four years she could see that she had done everything in later life to not be here and yet she returned in her dreams, pulled back by her sub-conscious when she wasn't in control. What was she afraid of? She had faced terrorists with no fear of death. She'd watched the man she loved die for her. Die for the child he knew she was expecting, even though she hadn't yet known. He had been so much more attuned to life than she ever would or could be. He died to set her free. Diana had felt more at home in the hovel that was her prison than she did here. She took a deep breath.

Here was alien, yet she knew it intimately. However, in her dreams the rooms had altered and this one she never entered. Looking around from the big wardrobe to the dressing table to the bed – nothing was familiar. Had she not found her father because her dreams never took her here? The only person who could tell her more was her mother.

She sat motionless except for a periodic rasp. Diana knew the facts of her mother's life, but she didn't like her or what she stood for. Joan Trewin Russell was a woman of the past, subservient. Yes, she'd had a career of sorts but once she had remarried, she'd thrown it in and become a housewife again. It was a wonder she had waited so long between husbands. Even now, she was beautiful. She would have been a 'prize' for any man, but she had chosen George Russell, a neat American. Diana had never seen the appeal. Her mother's remarriage had pushed them even further apart, and Diana hadn't thought that possible.

They must have been close once, though. The pictures showed it, but she felt nothing but distance. Diana stood and cleared her throat. 'Look, Mum, I know you can hear me. I'm not good at this talking lark unless it's scripted, and I haven't had time to write this one – although I have a lifetime of questions in my head.' She walked closer to the bed. Her mother's eyes moved under the thin lids so she pressed on, 'Now that there is so little time, words and questions desert me.' She paced the room glancing back at her. 'God, Mum, what happened to us?'

She picked up the box of photos and moved towards the bed. Her mother opened her eyes and Diana held up a photo of the three of them in front of St Basil's. 'We were happy but I don't remember it.'

She pulled out the picture of her taking her first steps and held it up. 'Why don't I remember him?' Diana knew all the facts. Allan Trewin had been drunk and had fallen from the cliff. She'd been through the police reports years ago. Her father's alcohol levels were high. Her mother had mentioned her last sight of Allan had been of him clutching a cognac bottle and heading into the garden. She had kissed him, she said. It had been noted in the report that he'd remnants of lipstick on his lips and cheek consistent with being kissed, being loved.

Diana moved closer to her. 'Please tell me what happened. Tell me he loved me. You loved me.' Her mother clenched her hand. The blanket crinkled under her fingers. Diana stepped closer to the bed.

'Mum, each year, each day you and I have pulled further and further away from each other.' She sat at the end of the bed. 'Why?'

There was no answer, but her mother's hand remained clenched.

'Through all the therapy sessions, I've asked why my memories begin at boarding school.' She lifted the box of photos and plucked out a few. Holding up a black and white picture of her father, her mother, a dog and her, she said, 'This picture speaks of happiness and love. On the back it is dated, '1961, Patriarchy Ponds.' They were all smiling, including the dog. 'I was seven. I should remember this, but no. All I recall is crying my eyes out in matron's office a year later.'

Diana watched her mother's eyes focus on her, then the pupils shrunk in the bright morning light.

'All these years I have been haunted. Did my father kill himself?' A lump loaded in her throat.

Her mother looked down and that simple glance told Diana that she thought the same.

'Mum.' She picked up her hand and placed the photo of the three of them and the dog in it. The thin fingers barely had the strength to hold the photo this morning.

'Did he love me?'

'Yes.' The word was strangled, and her hand shook so much the picture fell from her grasp onto the bed. 'He . . . loved . . . you.'

'Then why did he commit suicide?' Diana twisted her hands together. She had to ask otherwise she would never know the truth. 'Why did he leave me?'

'He didn't.' She looked out to the bay and not at Diana.

She was lying, Diana was convinced. Turning towards her, her mother opened her mouth, but nothing came out.

'Are you sure?'

'Yes.' Her eyelids closed, shutting down any chance Diana had of reading what she couldn't or wouldn't say. Her hand fell limp on the blanket and Diana pulled the photo out from under it. She didn't stir. Placing the snapshot back in the box, she fought the urge to upend the box and bury her in the photographs. She left the box on the bed, but then swung back and tossed a few more of them at her. It was petty. Diana knew that, but something inside her raged. She was being lied to.

Her mother dozed on, undisturbed by the patchwork of faded photos covering her. When she next opened her eyes maybe she would take some pleasure from the memories or maybe she wouldn't. Diana paused. Had her mother felt as betrayed by his death as she had? Was the pain still as raw? Those photographs spoke of love. She had loved him and he betrayed her too by killing himself. All these years her father's death had stood between them. She should have asked sooner.

29

Lottie

4 August 2018, 7.30 a.m.

Her mother wasn't in the room when Lottie brought her coffee. But her grandmother was awake and looking at photos strewn across her chest. Lottie's heart contracted. Gran didn't look at her but stared at the photo in her hand. Her other hand flailed around on the side table knocking a book off. Her reading glasses were just out of her reach. Lottie handed them to her. She glanced at Lottie then with her glasses on said, 'I'm so sorry.'

'Gran, you don't have anything to apologise to me for.'

Her grandmother had been the best . . . kind, loving, and understanding.

'Lottie.'

'Yes.' She sat and tried to see the picture, but it was turned away.

'My wedding, my first wedding.' Her voice stuck on the words.

'May I see?' Lottie held out her hand.

'We fooled no one.' Her grandmother laughed.

'Why were you trying to fool anyone?' she asked, as her grandmother finally let the picture turn towards her. Seeing the photo, she was instantly transported far away from Boskenna.

The ground in front of the church in the picture almost shimmered in the heat and the dust. Her grandmother held a bouquet of roses in front of her and then Lottie realized what she was saying. She had been pregnant. Despite the flowers, the angle of the photograph caught the swelling of her stomach. Allan Trewin stood straight and smiled directly at the photographer.

'You look beautiful.' Lottie turned to Gran. Those high cheek bones were still in evidence.

'Thank you.' Gran touched her hair.

'Who took the photograph?'

She beamed. 'Tom.'

Lottie frowned. 'Do I know him?'

'No. I don't think so.' She sighed. 'He was the best of us.'

'Did you work with him?' Gran's eyes flew open and her glance darted about the room before resting on Lottie again. She picked up another faded snap. In it her head was thrown back in laughter and on either side of her were young men. One Lottie recognised as Allan, looking rakish in a Breton top. The other man was dressed similarly but his look was more intense. He wore a bandana around his neck reminiscent of an old movie star. Was it David Niven or Cary Grant that she had seen in similar attire? She couldn't recall.

'Tom Martin.' Gran pointed.

'You look so young.'

'I was *nineteen*.'

'Who did you meet first – Tom or Allan?'

'Tom.' She looked out to the sea and groaned.

'Is something wrong?'

'No.' She closed her eyes and in seconds she was asleep. Lottie gathered up the photos, taking time to look at each one.

She paused, holding one of her mother in a tutu with a beaming smile on her face. It was so clearly her and yet so different. But aside from age, Lottie was hard-pressed to decide just what was different. Maybe it was the all-encompassing grin.

The sound of her mother's footsteps alerted Lottie to her imminent arrival.

'Your coffee's there.' Lottie pointed to the table. 'What happened?' she whispered.

Her mother glanced at Lottie and Gran. 'She fell asleep.'

Lottie raised an eyebrow. Still keeping her voice low, she said, 'So your latest interview technique is to throw things?'

'I didn't exactly throw things.' Her mother walked to the window, collecting her coffee on the way.

Lottie went to her. 'You once told me that sugar works better than vinegar.'

'Did I?'

Lottie nodded.

'I don't remember.'

She gave her a disbelieving look.

'Well, in some places it does.'

'And with your dying mother it might too.' She turned and looked back at Gran. From here she could see Gran still had a photo clutched in her left hand.

'I don't want to be here.' Her mother's shoulders dropped.

Lottie rolled her eyes. 'I wouldn't have known.'

'It hurts and . . . ' Her mother glanced at Carrickowel.

'And what?' She reached out and put a hand on her mother's shoulder.

She looked back at Gran then to Lottie. 'And nothing.'

'Mum.'

Her mother walked to the bed and pulled the Polaroid photograph from Gran's fingers. 'Christ.'

'What?' Lottie dashed to her side. The picture was a black and white shot of her mother clutching a book. She froze. The diary. She stole a glance at her mother.

'My diary.' She shook her head. 'I'd forgotten it.'

'Well, that's good you recognise it.' Lottie tried smiling.

'Hardly worth remembering. Not important. Just "Dear Diary" stuff.'

Lottie released the breath she was holding. She clearly didn't recall what she'd written.

'Ah, yes, you still have all your diaries from school until now.' Lottie pictured the white cabinets under the bookcases in her mother's study. Once Lottie had dared look in them and was told to respect her privacy. God knows what she would think if she knew that Lottie had her childhood diary, hadn't given it to her immediately, and had read it.

'Yes, but not this one. It was my first.'

'How old were you?'

'Eight.' She paced, looking at the picture. 'Tom Martin had given it to me the weekend my father died. The last time I was here.' She looked at Lottie. 'No, that's not true. The last time was in 2008.'

It always circled back to 2008. Sometimes Lottie was deluded enough to think she could move beyond that summer. Beyond the lies she had told. But looking at her mother now, it was as if 2008 formed a wall Lottie couldn't climb, no matter how hard she tried, despite having been the perfect university student and having worked hard at her career. No, she would perpetually be the eighteen-year-old who lied to her mother and dire consequences resulted ultimately from the lie.

Lottie couldn't forgive herself for what had happened to John. But she had hoped that her mother might have tried. Of course because of who her mother was, her name had been dragged into the whole terrible situation. Lottie could never let go of her guilt. It was just a damn good thing her mother didn't know about the latest jewel in her fool's crown. Paul was the bloody *Koh-i-Noor*.

30

Joan

4 August 1962, 8.15 a.m.

As I walk down to the beach, my thoughts linger on waking up to the sound of 'Happy Birthday' playing in my dreams until I'd realized that it had been Diana on the piano. I'd groaned, Allan had laughed, and now I smile just thinking about it. I'd wished him happy birthday and he'd asked, 'Did you drink too much last night?'

As the gulls cry, happily trailing a fishing boat, I stop to think again about Allan this morning. I'd watched him run his hands through his hair while the early rays of the sun caught the tanned skin of his abdomen. Desire rolled through me then and I'd held out a hand. A slow smile had crossed his face as he took it and gave me his cigarette. Chords crashed on the piano below. I winced.

He'd pulled away and grabbed his dressing gown, saying, 'I think I had better see to Diana before the rest of the house is awoken by her attempts at Mozart.'

'Shame.' I pushed myself up, not trying to hide my disappointment.

'Yes.' He leaned down and brushed the thin strap of my

nightdress aside, so it slipped down revealing my breast. He kissed my collarbone and then worked his way down to my nipple. I gasped, and Diana switched to Beethoven's Fifth, not her best.

He'd stood with a half-smile lingering on his lips. 'Tonight.'

'Yes.' I'd whispered as he left me wanting, aching and hoping that tonight we could put the past behind us and begin again.

Now I shake off the desire and let the sound of the waves soothe me. Squinting into the distance, I can't see a cloud in the sky. Today will be fine. Allan needn't be told that George Russell is my new handler and not Tom. The fewer people who know, the better. Victor is too important to risk and even if I know Allan isn't a threat, I won't jeopardise the operation. My small role is nothing in one sense, but essential in another.

The tide is out, and I search for sea-life as I head to the water. Yesterday morning a seal had watched me from the rocks. But this morning I am alone, and I need the solitude. My eyes burn and my thoughts are fuzzy. That is what lack of sleep will do to you, as I know only too well. However a swim will refresh me. It's one of the things I love most about being at Boskenna. The beach is forever available for swimming or walking or simply staring.

Ever since I can remember, this stretch of sand has loomed large in my thoughts. When we were in India and Indonesia I looked forward to the cool easterly breeze and the cold water of the Cornish sea. Much to my mother's despair, I would swim on all days of the year unless the sea was unsafe. It mattered not if the heavens were pouring down or the air had more than a nip in it. The practice had become ingrained during the war years when I was here and they were in India. I'd been sent home to be safe, but I'd been free, free from the formal life. Boskenna gave me freedom and my mother was never able to take it away again. She had been jealous until her dying day, but by then all types of jealousy and, of course, all types of gin cocktails had taken their toll. I was not like her in any way. I'd made sure of that.

The water circles around my ankles. I run in until I am up to my waist and I dive, holding my breath, trying not to gasp as the cold water wraps around me. I open my eyes as my chest tightens further. Holding still, I let my body numb before surfacing with my lungs begging for air, then I float. Every atom of flesh is alive and tingling. A bit like this morning when Allan touched me. We are coming out of the darkness of grief. Things are beginning to feel good, to feel right again.

The sky is blue, Cornish blue. Not the murky colour of a Moscow sky that seems permanently washed out to me. Slowly, I rotate my arms over my head and backstroke across the bay. My ears beneath the water hear the deep rumble of a distant engine. Maybe a fishing boat heading out. It doesn't matter. All that is important is today going to plan. I can do everything asked of me, even with the lack of sleep. The social side is automatic. I have learned that almost from birth. Deception is surprisingly easy, too. I have taken to it like I had to water. One moment simply a secretary then the next, a minor operative. I know my advantages. People think I'm too beautiful to have a brain. That I've been to finishing school rather than university tells the world my worth.

My father believed that university would be wasted on me. I tense as the anger runs through me. I should be thankful now. He doesn't know what I do. I made that a condition of doing the work. He would stop it, even now when he has no right to say anything about my life, he would try. He lives to control. He would be horrified that the life he provided for me has made me into a suitable spy. Foreign languages surrounded me during my childhood and I learn them with ease. And, of course, the whole culture of being seen not heard. For him that included women as well as children.

Flipping over, I begin the crawl with renewed force. As I breathe, I catch a glimpse of Allan and Diana walking along the beach. Diana waves wildly and I signal that I see them. Even at this distance her grin is visible. She loves it here. This is where she calls home. We all do. I turn around and above them I catch sight of the house. It dominates the view, despite the cluster of old fisherman's cottages and newer homes that have sprung up where my mother sold off some of the land. Thanks to Allan, I haven't had to do that to keep Boskenna. His brother inherited their family estate, but he had received a large inheritance from his grandmother and that pays for Boskenna's upkeep.

Maybe after the Moscow assignment we should think about giving up the Foreign Office. I laugh and take in a mouth full of salt-water. Both Allan and I would be bored to tears. We thrive on the pressure in a place like Moscow, but I know that once Victor is finished they will move us on. From what Tom has said, that might be sooner rather than later.

Kicking harder, I am certain no one suspects me, the wife of the political attaché. Between ballet classes, piano lessons, art lessons and school runs, I roam the city freely. No one is aware I speak Russian. I'm not sure if Allan even knows how fluent I am. By reading novels in Russian I am able to keep building my vocabulary. No one seems to notice them in the apartment. There are only a few and I've said I bought them because of the covers.

Changing to the breaststroke, I watch Diana and Allan leave

the beach via the steps to the coastal path and not up to the garden. I frown. Where are they off to? Sometimes I despair that he doesn't think of our guests. But that's what I do so well so that he doesn't have to, and in Moscow he has so little time with Diana. I swim to the shore and up on the path I see Allan is talking to the Venns. They glance down and wave. I respond but do not smile as I see the woman put her hand on Allan's arm. Towel clutched in my hand, I walk up to the house. There are things that need to be done.

31

Lottie

Lottie waved to the man bringing supplies to the little beach café. Later in the day she would go for an ice cream. Gramps had always lured her off the beach that way as a child. She would have stayed in the sea until nightfall if she'd had her choice. A few eager families were already setting up on the beach, despite the light mist that still hung in the air. Below it was murky but above at Boskenna it was vividly sharp.

She dropped her towel on the sand revealing her bikini and picked her way out to the sea, making sure to drag her feet to alert any lurking weever fish. Before long, her toes were numb and she was up to her knees. She saw old Jacob on the rocks, fishing. She could recall very few mornings when Jacob or another person wasn't fishing on the beach. Once the village had many fishermen but now it was just Jacob, and the old cottages were gone. Things move on and Lottie was at one of those stages of change.

Taking a shallow dive, Lottie floated underwater letting her body acclimatise to the shock of the cold. Gran had taught her that years ago, when her instinct had been to fight and kick. Now her body rose to the surface and she existed between the sea and the mist. It felt as if her problems were far away, but she knew they were waiting, and she couldn't push them aside forever.

She began to swim, enjoying a slow breaststroke across the bay. Swimming had become her sanity. In the water she left her awkward self behind. But that and all her problems returned as she left the sea. Looking up, Boskenna was just breaking through the mist. It looked like a palace set in a bank of clouds.

A searing pain sprang from the side of her foot. She swore and limped further up the beach. Weever fish. This was the last thing that she needed. She examined the side of her heel. There was a small dot, but she could see no sign of a spine. That was good news. Gritting her teeth, she made her way to the café. They took one look at her and put the kettle on. She needed to get this in hot water fast.

While she was waiting at a table outside, she squeezed her heel as best she could to push any poison out. She couldn't look at the blood.

'Here you go.' The man brought out an old washing-up tub and she could see the steam rising. 'See if you can tolerate that temperature.'

She braced herself and submerged her foot. It was hot, but she could take it. Having done this before when she'd stepped directly on top of a weever, she knew she was lucky. Although with the pain radiating up her leg, it could be debated. Just when she was needed to help out, she would be hobbling. All because she'd wanted a swim to clear her mind. Selfish, her mother would be sure to point out.

A steaming cup was placed down beside her. 'I thought you might need this.' The woman smiled and said, 'You're Lottie, aren't you?'

She narrowed her glance trying to figure out who this was. 'Yes, and you're . . . '

'Tegan. Alex's cousin.' She pushed her hair back and Lottie admired her bracelet, remembering. Tegan was just ten the last time she had seen her, and Lottie had made that bracelet for her birthday. She could hardly believe she still had it.

'I've given Alex a ring as I think you'll need a hand getting up to the house.'

Lottie looked down at the steam rising from the bowl. 'That's great.'

'No problem, and I'm sorry to hear your gran is so poorly.'

Lottie smiled at her and looked up. Alex was making his way towards her. She didn't need rescuing, but it would be churlish not to be grateful.

'The wicked weever strikes again.' He smiled and kissed his cousin's cheek. 'Thanks Tegan.' He squatted down by the tub. 'May I?'

'Yes . . . ' She flinched, waiting. His fingers gently lifted her foot out of the water. Pleasure and pain mixed as he rolled the foot over in his hand until he saw the puncture.

'Not too bad. I don't see a spine.' He looked up. 'Brace yourself.'

She tightened all her muscles as she waited. He was going to squeeze her heel more. Digging her nails into her palm, she felt the pain but also his fingers on her skin. She was breathless when he rested her foot back on the side of the bowl, blood trickling down.

He went into the café and came back with clean water and soap. With great care he cleaned the puncture mark. Then he rinsed it again. Her foot throbbed and her leg tingled with his touch.

Taking the two paracetamol tablets he handed her, she washed them down with the tea. He placed her foot on her towel while he cleared the bowl and the soap. She began to shake and held the sweet tea with two hands.

'Right, let's see if you can move.'

She put the cup down and took his hand to help her upright. She swayed, and his other hand wrapped around her back. 'Lean on me.'

She wanted to cry out but held it in as she hopped along, relying on Alex's strength until they reached the gate leading into the garden.

'The steps are a bit slippery. I think it would be easier if I carried you.'

Before she could say no, he had thrown her over his shoulder in a fireman's lift. Winded – and more than a bit indignant – Lottie prayed that no one would see this. When they reached the top of the steps, she waited to be put down, but he continued striding across the lawn.

'You know you can put me down now?' She focused on the passing grass so that she didn't study his legs.

'Easier this way.'

'It might be, but I'd prefer to be upright.'

He stopped. 'Fine.' He bent slightly and let her slide down his body. She put a hand out and steadied herself on his arm.

'Thank you.'

'No problem, but best to buy yourself some surf shoes if you are sticking around.' He raised an eyebrow. It was a question really. She was about to reply but stopped. Rather than speak, she nodded. Any answer would provoke more questions.

'Cat got your tongue?' He looked up from her foot and a

slow smile appeared on his mouth. Her breath caught. Stop, she lectured her racing heart. He was history. For all she knew, Alex had someone in his life. But his smile had had that effect on her from the moment she first saw him, when he and his mother had moved back to Porthpean. He was such an angry soul then, but Gramps had taken him in hand.

'Can you walk without help?'

She took a few steps and wobbled. 'No.'

He put his arm around her and she moved forward. More than aware that her bikini offered her no protection from the feel of his arm against her skin. She shouldn't react this way, but her body wanted him right now just as much as it had years ago.

In the hallway they stopped. Her mother was touching the hydrangeas Lottie had put there last night. They reminded her of Allan Trewin's grave and the flowers there. Her mother must have been thinking the same thing.

'What the hell has happened to you?'

'Weever fish.' With Alex's help she reached the stairs.

'You should know better.' Her mother looked hard at her and then at Alex. Lottie thought she might not be referring to the weever fish. And if that was true, Lottie knew enough not to play with fire the second time.

32

Diana

For her second – or was it third? – breakfast, Diana was eating porridge with raspberries. Everyone around the table was quiet and many were drinking tomato juice. She wrinkled her nose. It tasted awful. She loved orange juice almost as much as she loved chocolate. But orange juice wasn't often available, and she certainly didn't like them both together.

Daddy was beside her reading the paper. He turned to the page with the goat. He looked at her and smiled. 'Now I know what you were asking about, little one.'

'What does "imperialism" mean and what does a goat in your house have to do with it?' she asked.

Uncle Tom looked up and smiled at her. 'I see you have begun your education in journalism.'

'Yes.'

'Do you want to explain this one, Tom?'

'No, you are far better placed to do so.' Uncle Tom turned the page on the paper he was reading before taking a sip of coffee and winking at her.

Mrs Hoskine came into the room with a fresh pot of coffee. 'There you are, Diana. Do you want to help with the picnic?'

'Yes, please.' She ate the last mouthful of porridge. 'Will you excuse me, Daddy?'

'Of course.' He smiled.

As she dashed out of the room, she heard Uncle Tom say to Daddy that he had dodged a bullet there, which didn't make any sense. There was no gun in the dining room. She cast a look back at Uncle Tom and Daddy but both of them were reading the papers.

Diana walked into the big kitchen. The table was covered with all sorts of food, but her glance went straight to the cake.

'What do you think?' Mrs Hoskine asked.

'It looks like snow.' The cake was all white and, sitting on a plate beside it, were the marzipan figures they had made.

'Just what you wanted.'

Nodding, she went to take a closer look. The surface was smooth and not like the Moscow snow she had played in. That only looked smooth when it first fell but soon it was icy and dirty.

'Here's some icing so that you can place the figures on. Do you know where they should go?'

'Yes.' She pictured the whole scene in her head. From her bedroom window in Moscow she could see a dome of gold. Diana and her dolls would sit for hours just watching the snow fall. It fell so quietly from the grey skies. She picked up the church with the blue and gold dome, placing it on the far side of the cake, securing it as Mrs Hoskine had taught her with a spoonful of icing. Then she put the dolls all together in a line as if they were holding hands, making a family. When she was finished, she took a step back. 'It's done, and I've left plenty of room for the candles.'

'Do you think we'll fit thirty-six candles on there?'

'Well, last year you fitted thirty-five and we had sailboats on top.'

'True, very true.' Mrs. Hoskine sliced a chicken and put the slices into a box. Diana looked for the scones. 'They are already in the basket, young lady. Have you packed your things for the day out?'

She shook her head and raced up the back stairs, stopping halfway to look through the lantern light. She could see only blue sky. Hopefully the wind was picking up.

In her room she threw her swimming costume, her Guernsey jumper and a pair of trousers in a cloth bag. She pulled her diary out from under the mattress and began to write.

Dear Diary,
I helped Mrs Hoskine pack the food for the sailing trip.
I think Mr Martin had been right about people with sore
heads. But Mummy looked happy as she came downstairs
clutching her notebook. Once everyone was out sailing, she
will sit down with Mrs Hoskine and review all the yummy
food for tonight's party. I love being here in Boskenna
because the food is so good.

She jumped up to look out of the window. The flag was beginning to move. Daddy was correct. He would want to know what it would be on the Beaufort scale. Earlier this week he'd had to remind her what that was because she had forgotten. Right now, it was one or two but hopefully by eleven o'clock it would be three or four.

This morning he lifted me onto his shoulders then we
walked down the path and through the gate to the beach.

He scanned the water looking for pirates, I think. But we only saw Mummy swimming.

Mummy waved but kept swimming. Daddy smiled as he squinted into the distance. Then we walked the coastal path and met the Venns. They had a funny conversation with Daddy and said they would meet us on the beach later. The man who looks after our boats is bringing the big sailing boat over from Fowey where Daddy keeps it. It will be on its way now.

We walked back to the house and he told me the sea state was good and we'd need to get our skates on to head out to the yacht before eleven. I laughed. He asked why and I said he was funny because you can't skate on water that's not frozen. He kissed my nose and told me I was too clever for my own good. I told him I thought being clever was good and he laughed more then he called me his little love. He declared we would have a marvellous day on the water.

Back inside we joined some of the other guests in the dining room having breakfast.

I'll write more later when we are sailing.

Diana

She packed her diary and her pencil into the bag and headed downstairs.

33

Joan

4 August 1962, 9.30 a.m.

Dressed and ready for the day, I stop at the table in the hallway. The post has arrived, but nothing is important. The crocosmia in the arrangement on the table need refreshing. Fallen blooms are scattered across the polished surface. The withered orange flowers look like a sign that our time here at Boskenna is coming to a close, which is an odd feeling. A week lies ahead of me before I will be back in Moscow, walking Salome through the parks and having coffee at the ambassador's residence after ballet. I adjust a stem of the agapanthus and watch the blue flowers drop. Maybe the whole thing needs re-doing but I won't have time. Unlike in Moscow, where time is the one thing I have. When we return in a week, many people will still be on leave. The parks will be full of children but not the ones I know. Diana will be lonely until her friends return. No, she won't be. Salome will be delighted to have us back and my darling girl will read and practise piano. She is content in her own company in a way I never am. I railed against my solitude growing up but Diana delights in it.

I take a deep breath, gathering the dead blooms in my hands. Things will be fine. This morning showed me that. Allan still wants me. I want him. My life has taught me repeatedly that love can grow. Back in Moscow for the second half of August, without others around for distraction Allan and I will be able focus on each other. We can walk in the park, we can talk about where we go in the future. I don't want to try for another baby but if he really does, then I will do that for him. But maybe he'll see how each child we have lost has pulled us apart. Parts of me are missing. But enough of the past. I must think of the future. I smile. Tonight I am looking forward to being in Allan's arms again. Being the sole focus of his attention, his passion. My face flushes at the thought.

'Mummy.' Diana runs out of the dining room and catapults into my arms. This is love. This and Allan's is enough. We walk hand in hand until she veers off to the kitchen, no doubt to consult on some aspect of Allan's birthday cake.

Jaded smiles greet me in the dining room. I hadn't sensed that people had drunk too much. I must be more observant. There is no room for mistakes at the moment. After filling my plate from the sideboard, I sit opposite Tom and glance at *The Times,* which makes for uncomfortable reading. Being in Boskenna, the Soviet Union and its threat feel far away. But I just have to catch Tom's glance across the table and the Russian bear is sitting in the room. The knowledge that the whole operation could be blown had chased around in my dreams creating a restless sleep. I pause and try and swallow. The toast in my mouth is dry despite the butter and Mrs Hoskine's marmalade. I read the report on the Archbishop of Canterbury's four-day visit to Moscow. That must have kept those on duty at the embassy on their toes. Talks of future exchanges. Hah.

Folding the paper, between nerves and outright fear, I can't face the food on my plate. I need to be busy but what to do? Nothing for the moment. Sit still, be charming. A sigh escapes me. Here in Cornwall I am useless. At least in Moscow I play my part.

'*Telegraph* reports much the same.' Tom takes a sip of his tea. No one else at the table would take any notice of the conversation. 'But it does look like we will have good weather for today and tomorrow.' He raises an eyebrow and those blue eyes twinkle ever so slightly.

'Yes, we must be grateful to the weather gods for something. They are forecasting rain for the bank holiday itself.' I place my napkin on the table noting the splodge of marmalade I must have dropped on it.

'Always the way, a bit of good followed by bad.'

'What on earth are you two talking about?' Allan walks in holding Diana's hand. 'The weather?' He glances between us both, trying to read us. I have seen this before. They know each other so well from their shared history: school, the RAF, university. They even joined the Foreign Office at the same time. But I too have known Tom for years, in fact, all my life. His father was at Cambridge with mine.

Looking across the table, I see the boy I had my first crush on and I value the enduring nature of our friendship. His calm wisdom has helped me through personal pain and through professional trials. He must have suggested the handover here to make it easier for me.

Allan helps Diana to a piece of bacon from the sideboard. She is growing so quickly. In her free hand she holds *To Kill a Mockingbird*. I frown. I read the book last summer and she must have found my copy. She is too precocious. The book wasn't written for eight-year-olds, but I don't want to stop her reading. I can only hope she will not understand all of what she reads.

Tom catches my eye and he's trying to wordlessly tell me to leave her be. I sigh. He knows me too well. I must return to hiding my thoughts and my expressions better. It is vital and I will need it tonight especially. Standing, my fingers twitch. I'll go and sort the flower arrangement. It will clear my mind.

34

Lottie

The morning nurse had been and gone. Gran had been restless before Alex had helped Lottie settle her in the garden. Her breathing was distressed again, and Lottie guessed her thoughts were as well. Although her eyes were closed, she kept repeating 'I had no choice. I had to do it.' This made absolutely no sense, but Gramps had said she was delirious. Lottie didn't think so. Yesterday Gran sounded troubled.

Her mother wasn't around, and Lottie wasn't sure where she'd gone. Alex stopped mowing the lawn to pull his shirt off. If she didn't know better, she would think he was doing it deliberately. She looked at Gran whose words sounded like Arabic now, but Lottie couldn't be sure. But whatever she was saying, she was becoming more agitated.

'Gran, it's Lottie and I'm here.' She stroked Gran's hand. Her breathing eased but she was still restless.

Gramps appeared. 'Thought you might need a break.' His smile was wobbly, and she stood to hug him.

'How is she?' he asked, looking down on her. His hand clutched his cane so tightly his knuckles were white.

'Not very peaceful. I think she's speaking Arabic.'

He nodded but didn't comment as he lowered himself onto the chair beside her. 'Go take a walk if you can.' He glanced at her foot. 'At least enjoy the sun while we have it.'

'If you're sure.'

He nodded then rested his hand on Gran's forehead and spoke quietly to her. Lottie hobbled inside. Restless energy filled her now that some of the pain in her foot had eased.

Gran had married Allan in Damascus, so she must have picked up the Arabic then, and of course she was working in Cairo when she'd met Gramps. Years ago, Gran's fluency in French had made revising with her a joy. Back then she'd said she couldn't speak any other languages fluently just a smattering of phrases . . . the sort of thing needed to order in a restaurant, buy food in a market place. But that didn't ring true now because whatever she was saying, it was fluent. It could be, 'I'll have three tomatoes please,' but Lottie didn't think so. She went to her room to grab her phone and google what she thought Gran had said. But she came to a standstill when Lottie saw her mother sitting on the bed.

'Mum.'

'This.' She lifted Gran's dinner party notebook. 'Where did you find it and when?'

Lottie stomach clenched, and she glanced to her file. Under it sat the diary but it looked as if nothing had been moved. 'Last night, when I tried to close the closet door.'

'This is important.' She pointed to the book.

'Why?' Lottie tilted her head trying to read the page. 'You need a recipe?'

'She lied to me.'

'What?' Lottie flinched. Her mother had big issues with lying, as Lottie knew too well.

'She lied to me about something so important I can barely speak.' She shook.

Lottie sat down on the bed beside her. Her mother jabbed her finger at a page. A quick glance confirmed that it was Saturday 4 August, 1962. Carefully listed were the guests and some of them had the names of bedrooms in Boskenna next to them. The house had been full, but Lottie couldn't see what was upsetting her. 'What did she lie about?'

Her mother held her finger still next to a name. George Russell. Lottie frowned. 'They knew each other then?'

'He was here.'

'I thought they met in Cairo.' It had sounded so romantic. Love at first sight – but it must have been love at second sight. Lottie flipped through the next pages, but that weekend was the last entry in the book.

'That's what she said.' Her mother tucked her short hair behind her ear.

'You don't remember him from then.'

She glared at her.

Lottie shifted away. 'Stupid question.'

She shook her head. 'I thought that with the photos, maybe something would come back to me but nothing worthwhile has.'

Lottie touched her arm. 'What brought you in here?' She cast a quick glance at the file again, hoping her mother hadn't noticed it. If she saw the diary and the marriage certificate, she would explode.

She laughed. 'I suddenly recalled having a hiding place.'

'You remembered that?' Lottie swallowed.

'Well, I didn't know if it was a memory or a dream.'

'Did you find it?' This had been Lottie's room her whole life. She'd never found a secret hiding space.

'I didn't look in the end because I saw this on the floor.'

'Oh.' Lottie stood. 'Shall we have a look?'

'I just want to go to her and yell.' She shuddered.

'I get that but . . . '

'I know.' She put the box down. 'If I haven't dreamt it, there is a loose floorboard under the bed.'

Lottie stretched out flat. The floorboards showed no signs of anything. One by one she tapped and pressed them, but nothing moved. Dusting herself down, Lottie said, 'Unless it's been repaired, I think you must have dreamt it.'

'I don't know what's real and what isn't at the moment.' Her mother's shoulders sank.

'You never spoke about this before.'

She shrugged. 'What's there to say? You move on but being here . . . ' She picked up the book and headed to the door.

'Where are you going?'

'To talk to my mother again and find out why she lied to me.'

'Mum, she's delirious half the time.' Lottie heard the plea in her voice.

'It's the other half of that time I need.'

'Be gentle.'

'I haven't got time to be gentle.' She left, and Lottie debated whether to follow. Gramps was there so he could defend Gran. But it didn't make sense that Gran would lie about meeting Gramps. What purpose would that serve?

Pacing the room, she had to do something, anything, to make things better – even if it was just providing tea. She felt so useless. As she reached the bottom of the stairs, the tall-case clock chimed. It was ten thirty. It was a bit early for coffee, but it was close enough to Gramps' routine.

Lottie carried the tray outside half expecting to hear shouting, but silence greeted her as she walked up to them. Her mother looked mutinous and Gramps resigned. Gran's torturous breathing was the only sound other than the roar of the sea below.

The gentle thud of the tray making contact with the table broke the standoff.

'Coffee?' Lottie forced a smile and looked from her mother to Gramps.

'My darling girl, how lovely, yes.'

She poured his and whether her mother wanted a cup or not, she was going to have one. Maybe she should lace it with sugar to sweeten her. Lottie understood that she wanted to know her past, her father. And Lottie wanted to help, which was a strange irony. Her mother had never given her anything, anything at all, to go on about her own father. But Lottie could be bigger than that.

'George, why did you and my mother lie to me?'

She handed her mother a cup and tried not to flinch at her tone.

'I don't know what you are talking about.' He sipped his coffee.

'It's right here in my mother's handwriting. Guests staying at Boskenna: George Russell.' She pointed to the notebook she'd put down on the garden table.

'I wasn't here then.'

Her mother pressed her lips together, stood and quietly said, 'I know you're lying.'

He shook his head. 'I met your mother in Cairo.'

She walked to the chair her mother dozed in and leaned down towards her. 'I will find out the truth. I will,' she whispered as she left.

Gramps sank back into his chair.

'I'm sorry.'

'Lottie, dear, there is nothing to apologise for. Your mother is upset about my Joan dying. She is hurt, she is striking out.'

'Maybe.'

He reached across the table and picked up the notebook. 'Where did she find this?'

'I did, after she found the old photographs in the closet.'

'Photos?'

'Yes, a shoebox filled with them.'

'Oh.' He put the notebook down. 'Sometimes it's best not to look backwards, but it can be hard when you are at the end.'

Lottie jumped up and hugged him. 'I love you.'

'I love you, and remember that your grandmother does too.'

She released him and looked to Gran, whose eyes were open now. Gramps pushed himself out of the chair and went to her.

'My darling.'

'Yes.'

Lottie walked over and kissed Gran. 'I'll leave you two love-birds alone.'

Gramps smiled, and she heard him half whisper. 'It's all coming to a close.'

Her heart constricted. Her mother needed to let go of the past and make peace with Gran and Gramps. And she needed to make peace with the world. It hadn't been kind to her in many ways, but she had done good and that was what she needed to focus on.

35

Diana

The musty scent of unused places clogged her nose and Diana sneezed. This end of the house, with the large kitchen and larder, echoed as she walked around seeking a trigger to memories. The smallest of things could elicit one: the scent of spice, the angle of sunlight, the sound of a note played on an Afghan rubab. But memories not recalled for decades had often faded to beige, like a washed-out photograph with the detail lost and open to reinvention. Boskenna was the house of her dreams yet she hadn't slept in it for fifty-six years until last night, when she dreamed again.

Fate had twisted things with the days and the dates aligning. Her mother was dying, and her father had died here the same weekend in 1962. The story-hunter's instinct in her twitched – maybe it was a cruel form of symmetry. She must have walked these floors so many years ago not knowing that by Sunday morning her father would be dead, and her world as she knew it gone too, almost as if it had never existed. Yet the artefacts of her life were in front of her.

The large table was scrubbed but a fine layer of dust covered her fingers when she touched it. Looking up, she followed the cobwebs from the ceiling light to the row of bells high on the wall. Smoking room, dining room, drawing room . . . She stepped closer, looking at a relic from a long-forgotten world. The odd thing was she could picture Edwardian ladies with parasols on the lawn but not see her own time here despite the photos she'd found.

She'd tucked the memories to the back of her mind to examine later. Now it felt right to delve into those dark spaces because for all those years it had haunted her. No, not haunted, troubled her. The time had come for the adult Diana to look back, back through those elusive memories. She was not sure how to do this. Her slow walk through the house had showed her nothing of his. Allan Trewin had been erased from Boskenna. All that was left was his gravestone, which someone remembered. Images of the deep blues and sharp reds of the flowers at the grave swirled in her head as she touched the solid walls of the kitchen. The answers were here, she was sure of it. It was just a matter of asking the right question.

Diana had been born in Boskenna with a midwife in attendance. Whether she wanted it or not, she was connected to this house. Her father had not been here, she'd been told by Mrs Hoskine. He'd been in transit. Sometime when she was in her teens, she recalled an awkward conversation with her mother, asking about her father and her early life. She had paused only for a moment before reeling off the facts. Born here, moved to Istanbul then onto Moscow. Returning to Boskenna every summer and most Christmases until 1962. There had been no emotion, no joy or sorrow in the telling, as if she too had walled off those years. Her mother had lost as much as Diana had, but even now Diana felt she was part of her mother's grief. Diana had lost her years ago. Her death would simply underline what had already happened.

Looking out of the window over the kitchen sink, she saw the wood pile. Someone, probably Alex Hoskine, had been keeping it in order because it wasn't George. He looked dreadful but that wasn't a surprise. His wife was dying. She wanted to feel, but maybe all these years in ever more God-forsaken locations on the planet had worn the edges of her nerves away. They didn't respond any more unless it was tragic. It had to be more graphic, more everything. A simple death due to age and cancer wasn't shocking. Her mother was dying but she'd seen so many deaths, so many that weren't at the end of a long life but cut off lives in their prime, or before they had had a chance to know anything other than fear.

Something metallic fell and she flinched, not sure where the sound came from. Rolling her neck to release tension, she looked around but everything seemed to be in place until she glanced at the sink. There a baking tray sat at an awkward angle. That must have been what had fallen. She shrugged. She was still wound up after the refugee camp in Jordan and now the discovery that George and her mother were lying for some reason. Turning to the right, she flexed her shoulders and looked to the larder, taking a few steps towards the door before stopping. It smelled of chocolate. Her stomach turned, and she stepped away, her mouth dry. She couldn't remember the last time she'd willingly eaten the stuff.

Her phone pinged, and she glanced at it. Nothing important but it reminded her of the date. Today her father would have been ninety-two if he'd lived. With the logical side of her brain she could accept accidental death, but her instinct said that was simply a polite way to give the family peace. Family, a social structure. Sometimes useful, frequently not. She had seen more broken families than she had seen whole ones. Although the world held up the family as the ultimate goal, it wasn't essential. She would agree that children needed a structure around them to grow safely. But it didn't have to be a family and it didn't have to be loving to see a child to adulthood. Food, shelter, and education were all that was required. Love was not. A child would become an adult with or without love. Love only shaped parts of a child, making them more vulnerable. Yet it was everyone's holy grail. Living was simpler without love. Love created loss and the world was full of it.

Diana had loved her father. She'd now seen the proof. Maybe that was what she'd been searching for in her dreams. Yet here she was, standing in the unused big kitchen because her instinct had brought her to this place. Something had happened here. She was sure of it. She walked to the larder door. The handle turned easily. Somehow, she had expected it wouldn't. A blast of cool musty air greeted her. It was bare, with only an empty biscuit tin on the shelf.

A spider's web stretched from the top shelf to the small north facing window. That's all that was there yet she could still smell chocolate, and in the pit of her stomach was fear. It was a feeling she'd faced so many times. But she'd always won. What would cause fear here? What would make a child afraid?

Above her head a black iron hook dangled. Ominous but not frightening. The room must have been originally used for game. The cool air ran up her bare legs and goosebumps covered her flesh. She would not run, despite the urge. This room was key, she knew it. Now she needed to dig deep to find out what happened here.

Her mother had said her father's death had not been suicide. An hour ago she might have believed her but now she had seen proof that she'd lied about other things. George was lying too. He was good at it, far too good, but then he'd been a diplomat. No doubt if she delved, she might discover her stepfather was an old spook and lying was his profession.

Closing her eyes, she pushed out the anger and the frustration. There was no place for them if she was going to discover the truth. Although she was cold and fear covered her skin, she didn't feel vulnerable. That panic she knew too well. She was a woman and that fact alone had made her a target and a victim. No, the fear that ate at her stomach now was different.

She swung round and left the larder. It wouldn't provide the answers she wanted. There had to be something she was missing. As she walked out of the kitchen, she saw a pile of local newspapers. The top headline read 'Police break local drug ring'. That was the starting point, the police. She hurried to her room – she had some research to do.

36

Diana

4 August 1962, 11.00 a.m.

> *Dear Diary,*
> *I am sitting on the beach wall waiting. The tender, full of*
> *guests, is on its way out to the boat. But I am cross. The*
> *Venns aren't here. Why had they come earlier? And now*
> *when we wanted to go, why were they late?*

'Diana, what are you writing?' Mummy walked towards her. She was wearing her big dark sunglasses and Diana couldn't tell if she was cross.

'Just that I am stuck waiting on the beach.'

Mummy smiled. 'Well, if the Venns are not here by the time the tender returns, they will miss out.' She looked up and the wind caught the ends of her scarf wrapped around her head. Its red and oranges tangled through her dark hair. Diana's hair was in plaits again. She pushed one off her shoulder, smiling. It would be a better day's sailing if they didn't come.

'What are they like?'

Diana glanced up. She didn't like them, but it wasn't polite to say that. 'Pleasant.' Diana enunciated the word carefully.

'I see.' Her mother laughed. 'You don't like them.'

Diana pursed her mouth. 'I thought that was the correct thing to say but you knew.'

'Oh, darling I only know because I know you and I know your word choice.'

'So someone else wouldn't have known.'

'Absolutely not. The Venns are pleasant.' She shielded her eyes even though she was wearing sunglasses. The last of the guests was now on board and the tender, with Daddy at the helm, was making its way back to the beach.

'I wish you were coming too, Mummy.'

'Me too but we do want a special party tonight.'

'Yes.' Diana nodded, watching Daddy cut the engine out and lift it up.

'Hello.' Mr Venn walked down onto the wall.

Diana closed her diary. Mr Venn held up a camera and snapped a picture of her. She frowned as Mrs Venn joined him. He counted to ten then pulled something out of the side of the it and waved it about. 'Thought you might enjoy this Polaroid camera, Diana.'

'Why?' she asked, frowning.

'Because it gives you the picture right away.' He pulled the top sheet back and there she was holding her diary, looking a bit sad.

Mummy peered over her shoulder to take a look. 'How lovely but I don't think it will fare well on the boat.'

Mr Venn looked at her and said, 'Of course, Joan, you are right. How foolish of me.'

'I'll bring it up to the house now and she may have it went she returns.' She looked at Diana.

'Thank you so much for the present,' she said, placing her diary into her bag.

'Come on you lazy ones. Time and tide wait for no man,' Daddy called, holding the tender. Diana cast a quick look at Mummy then raced down the beach into Daddy's arms.

37

Joan

4 August 1962, 11.10 a.m.

The sun is out, the wind is fresh, and the sea flat. There might never be another day quite so perfect for a sail. I wave off my guests, my husband and my daughter. I want to be with them but because of their expedition I have time to prepare with Tom for meeting George Russell. Tom bowed out of the sailing party, blaming it on too much cognac last night. Allan didn't call him out on it. He could have but he had given me a look. It said it all. There was promise there. He would forgive me for keeping his best friend here with me. Tom and I work so closely together, but because of their friendship, no one suspects my role. Turning away, I consider the lie I will need to tell Allan if he asks what Tom and I discussed. The glow of happiness I'd felt disappears. Allan is no traitor, but the first rule is trust no one. Never before had that come so close to home.

I can wrestle with my qualms later, but first I must supervise the table for tonight . . . place settings, china, flowers, candles. It must be just right. It's Allan's thirty-sixth birthday. Every year we host a dinner in his honour while we are here. This year it provides the cover I need to meet George Russell.

On the sideboard in the dining room, Mrs Hoskine and the daily help have already put out the silver and the glasses ready to lay. What's missing are the table extensions and the placemats. It's still the size we needed for breakfast: eight. Twenty requires a full extension. I tap my fingers on the table. Why did Allan have to invite these new friends? A sigh escapes me. It is his birthday, so it is within his right, but it is annoying. I pause and lecture myself. I need to be bright.

'Mrs Trewin.' Mr Hoskine stands in the French windows.

I look up and smile.

'Shall I extend the table now?' he asks.

'Yes, that would be good then I can review where I've placed people.'

'Don't forget the vicar's deaf ear.' He chuckles.

'I won't.' I leave him to his task and walk straight into Tom coming out of the snug.

'Excellent.' He takes my arm. 'Do you have some flowers to cut?'

I nod. I don't, but in the garden we won't be overheard. My mind shifts to Moscow mode. I think I may have walked every park in that city. We remain silent until we are under the cover of the trees and among the camellia bushes. I turn to Tom. 'Do you know this George Russell?'

'I've met him.' Tom shrugs.

'And?' I snip at some eucalyptus branches.

He clears his throat. 'Seems sound.'

'That doesn't fill me with confidence.' I turn to him.

'Not much fills me with confidence at the moment.'

I put my hand on his arm. 'Tom, this isn't like you.'

'True.'

'There's more than you're telling me.' I stop walking.

He laughs. 'Always.' Lighting a cigarette, he offers it to me and I take it, waiting while he lights one for himself. 'Victor said in his dispatch that he felt someone was following him.'

I frown. 'I wasn't followed.'

'Are you sure?' He casts me a sideways glance and I search my memories seeing the park, the museums and the Arbat. I'd been followed on my first drop in Aden in 1955 and that taught me what it felt like. But the unease I felt in Moscow was different.

'I'm sure.' I take the secateurs out of the basket on my arm as I see Mr Hoskine in the distance. Here, under the trees, dew lingers on the leaves and I cut a white hydrangea head. The air smells of pine and petrichor and all I can see in my mind is the park bench in Moscow where I was sitting with Salome. Diana stood by the pond looking at another child trying to make a small wooden boat float. Victor entered the park and watched the children for a while. I'd let Salome's lead slip and she ran towards Diana. I began walking towards the pond. Victor caught the lead and brought Salome back to me with a smile. The scene is so clear. Were the women with the children watching us? Victor handed the lead back to me then bent down to scratch Salome's head and clipped the film inside the dog's collar. It was a seamless handover. He left the park and Diana and I stayed for another hour. No one had followed us home. Other than to say thank you to Victor we hadn't spoken.

'I'm sure,' I say again as we move to the top of the garden now.

'Victor is vitally important and if the information he's feeding us is true then Khrushchev is bluffing.'

I open my eyes wide. This is the first time that I have heard anything of what is contained in the films I transport. The less I know the better. 'Tom?'

'Sorry.' He drops his cigarette on the ground and crushes it on the path.

My heart breaks looking at his slumped shoulders. 'What will you do now?'

'I'm not sure. Whatever it is it will be office-based.'

'Sorry.' He loves the field and the travel.

'Perils of the job.' He plays with the catch on his cigarette case. Open, close . . .

'Yes.' The reality of what I have been doing hits home. Diana and her movements have been an easy cover. Neither I nor Allan have ever felt she was at risk. But what if we have been followed and we are known?

He touches my arm. 'You have to go back.'

I look up at him. 'Are my thoughts that visible?'

'To me, yes.' He pauses. 'Victor is too important.'

I know he speaks the truth. Pain sears between my eyes. I swallow down the gasp of agony. Diana is at risk and it's my fault.

'Diana could go to boarding school.'

'Yes.' I draw lines in the damp soil with my toe. 'She won't be happy.'

'I know, but . . . '

He doesn't have to finish the sentence. It is clear she is at risk even now. Closing my eyes, I think of her happy face as she scampered off holding Allan's hand. I'd do anything for her.

'I believe the next drop may well be the last.' He begins pacing and I cut another flower head. 'But I'm not in charge anymore and after this afternoon I will know very little of what happens going forward.'

'Oh, Tom.' He has been the safe pair of hands and now I

am being handed over to an unknown person who hasn't been involved. I sigh. That is the point, of course. They need someone who hasn't been connected with Tom. But this George Russell will be another person in the loop and the more who know, the greater the possibility of a leak.

Tom stops pacing and shakes his head. 'You mustn't tell Allan. He can't know. You understand this.'

'Is he really under suspicion?' I don't want to think about this and I try not to connect the pieces.

Tom nods.

'He's not the mole, Tom.'

He opens out his cigarette case again, removes a cigarette then taps it three times on the case before lighting it. 'He's one of a few people that it could be.'

'No.' I stare directly back at him not allowing my glance to waver.

'Have you noticed anything different about him lately?' He watches me, and I cut a branch from the Judas tree. I don't like this Tom, this logical doing his job Tom, but I understand this Tom. I shake my head, telling him no, but at the same time my stomach rolls over. Allan's restless behaviour is down to the miscarriage. It has to be. He wouldn't turn. He isn't a communist and he's never had a leaning that way. Tom knows this. He doesn't need to ask. He knows Allan like he does me.

'Be careful when you head back to Moscow next week.'

I take a deep breath. This isn't a game. 'You be careful too.'

He turns to me and says, 'Always.' Our glances meet then we look away, walking towards the walled garden where I can see Mrs Hoskine giving instructions, then I hear the sound of wheels on the drive.

'Your guest has arrived.'

'Yes.' I pick up my pace and head into the courtyard between the house and the cottage. Through the gate in the wall I watch my new minder step out of the taxi. Lean but short. I hadn't expected short. He is not much taller than I am. His hair is thick and as he turns to look at the house, I see intelligence in his eyes. His glance takes in the view, the garden before spotting me watching him.

'Joan?' His accent is east coast, Boston at a guess.

'Yes.' I walk forward with Tom a few steps behind me. 'Welcome to Boskenna.' I extend my hand.

'Beautiful.' He says, staring at me.

'Yes, we are very lucky with the location.'

'Tom.' George nods.

'Good journey from Penzance?' Tom drops his cigarette and stubs it out with his foot.

'The train was comfortable.'

'Do come in.' I lead him through the front door and drop my flower trug on the table. 'Would you like a drink, or should I show you to your room first?'

His glance takes in everything. 'Room please.' He raises the bag in his hand.

'Of course, follow me.' I lead him to the front staircase and stop on the bottom step. 'I'm afraid I've had to put you in one of the attic rooms as we are at full capacity.' I smile. 'But the advantage is that you have a bird's eye view from there.' As a child I had loved the room I was putting him in. Although the ceilings are low the view is spectacular, and I could survey my domain.

George remains silent as I take him up the short staircase to the top floor. This is in the oldest part of the house, built in the 1740s. In many ways, the house is misshapen with different levels and small sets of stairs where you least expected them. It is part of what I love about Boskenna, not all is revealed at first meeting.

The door is open and through the window the view is all blue sea and sky. In the distance I make out the sail of a yacht making way towards Gribben Head and then onto Fowey. Allan. I turn to George. Tom is downstairs, and this is his chance or mine to say something unheard by him.

He places his bag on the bed and looks at me and not the view. 'From this point forward, you will no longer relay any information to Tom or to your husband.' His voice is quiet and even. It is a command.

I remain silent.

'MI6 has become a leaky sieve and Victor is too key to lose with Khrushchev flexing his muscles in Cuba.'

I nod.

'You have to put Victor before yourself, your family, and your friends.' He glances to the door. 'We can't swap you out before the next drop.'

I swallow.

'I need you to be alert to everything and everyone.'

I cross my arms. 'How do I know I can trust you?'

A slow smile spreads across his face. 'You don't.'

I am alone. A cool breeze drifts in through the open window and goosebumps cover my arms.

38

Diana

4 August 2018, 11.30 a.m.

With a notebook in her hand and the information Diana had a colleague pull off the internet, she went to her mother's room. Her fingers worried the wire of the binder. According to the material, she had seen her father's body on the beach. That was in the transcript of the coroner's court. Local police had handed over to CID swiftly.

On the threshold of the bedroom she heard her mother. 'I had no choice.' This time she spoke in English. George sat beside her, stroking her arm and murmuring to her, trying to soothe her but Diana saw how troubled she was.

She cleared her throat and George looked up. 'May I have a few minutes alone with my mother?'

He turned to Diana, his look almost pleading, but he stood – ever the old-school gentleman. 'Of course, Diana. She's not very . . . she's . . . '

'Dying.'

His head dropped down to his chest. Her hand clenched as she watched him shuffle out the door. Once he was out of sight she went to her mother's bedside and sat down and picked up her cold hand. Her circulation was slowing but Diana knew she could still hear her.

'Mum, I need to know what happened fifty-six years ago.' There was no response, but she couldn't give up now. 'You know I don't really remember my father or Moscow or even Boskenna.'

Her mother's eyelids fluttered. 'I had no choice.'

Diana frowned. 'You had no choice to send me away?' Her voice caught on the last word. She too had sent her daughter away. It was the right choice and in her heart she knew that was true.

Her mother opened her eyes. 'Diana, I'm sorry.'

She began to speak then stopped.

She had waited years to hear those words. Now they took the fight from her.

Her mother's voice was so faint. 'I was wrong to do what I did but . . . '

'But what?'

Her mother's eyes closed again but Diana was sure she was still awake. 'Mum, talk to me.'

Her head moved from side to side. 'Forgive me, please.'

'How can I forgive you when you lied to me?' She pulled her hand away, thinking of the neat writing listing what room George was in and where he sat at dinner.

Her eyes opened wide before she said, 'All parents lie to their children.'

Diana gave a dry laugh. 'I'm not talking Father Christmas here.' She took a breath. 'George Russell was here when my father died.'

'No.'

'Yes, Lottie found your notebook. Don't lie.'

Her mother tried to take a deep breath, but it turned into a cough. Once she had stopped, Diana watched her lay motionless, all energy wasted. The only sign of life was the occasional rasp until she whispered, 'It wasn't important.'

'What? The man who became your second husband wasn't important?' She shook her head, but her mother didn't her see. She was looking out of the window. Her thoughts clearly faraway. 'You lied.'

Rising from the bed, she walked to the window. A few clouds had appeared softening the heat. How could she forgive her?

'I had to do it . . . you must understand.'

'No, I don't.' She wasn't sure if there was anything that angered her more than being lied to.

'I thought it best.'

'Ah, like sending me away?'

'It was for the best.' Her mother turned to her with eyes full of remorse. 'I did it for you.'

Diana swung around. 'Why didn't you love me enough to keep me with you?' Once the words were out, she wanted to take them back. If she had thought her mother pale before, she'd been wrong. A ghost lay on the bed in front of her.

'If you thought I didn't love you, I'm sorry.' Each word took more from her. 'I love you and have loved you since the moment you came into my life.'

Diana took a few steps back towards the bed, wanting to believe these words but she stopped. Her notebook still lay there, reminding her of her goal of more information about her father. 'Why did you push me away?'

'I didn't mean to but . . . ' She closed her eyes. 'I did.'

Diana swallowed. The truth, finally.

'You would have done the same.'

'No.' Diana moved forward but then stopped. She was right, Diana had.

She looked at the body on the bed. She didn't look like her mother but a corpse.

'I love you and I'm so sorry.' She sucked in air. 'If I could change what I have done . . . ' Her eyes closed.

'What? What have you done?'

'Forgive me.'

Diana went to her and took her hand. What was she forgiving? Her mother's fingers tried to hold hers and Lottie's voice rose up from the garden. Like her own mother, Diana had failed in so many ways. She paused then said, 'Thank you for loving Lottie.'

Her mother's eyes gleamed. 'Yes. Forgive me.'

Diana nodded and her mother's fingers clung for a second then fell away, hitting the notebook.

Diana still had no answers, but something had moved within her.

39

Lottie

4 August 2018, 12.00 p.m.

Next year's blooms were already forming on the camellia bushes. Some would be out before Christmas. Gran had always used the red and white ones in her Christmas decorating. Lottie associated the flowers with Alex. When he'd handed her a bloom that June, Gramps had whispered in her ear that a pink one represented heartfelt longing. Looking at one of the largest buds, she could see red appearing. Gramps had also told her that every year he cut the first red ones to appear and presented them to Gran, for they told her of his love, passion and desire. Lottie had imagined coming back to Boskenna for Christmas after her first term at Ruskin to find that Alex would do as Gramps had. Such lovely silly dreams. Flowers didn't hold messages except for the bugs and the birds. However, she loved that unlike roses which dropped petals, the camellia falls as a whole flower. Keeping its heart in one piece even until the end.

Her phone pinged with a text. It was from the private investigator.

Meeting with Paul's ex later. Will update you after.
Jamie

She rolled her eyes. It wouldn't help. Nothing would make the divorce happen sooner, return her money or her designs. On Monday she needed to chase the woman at the V&A to withdraw from the exhibition. Everything she had worked so hard for was lost because she had believed he loved her. How needy had she been. Turning back down the garden, she winced every so often. Damn weever fish and damn her own stupidity.

The walk cleared her head and from the tree cover of the path she saw her mother standing in Gran's room. Her arms were crossed, and Lottie could only hope that Gran had remained sleeping. Her mother hadn't looked pleased, but then that was not uncommon. What did her mother remember of her father's death? Why on earth would she think she was at fault?

'Hey.' Two hands grabbed her and steadied her. 'Head in the clouds?' Alex asked.

She gave him a lopsided smile. 'I wish.'

'What's up?' He fell into step beside her.

'Mum.' She sighed.

'Oh. Nothing new then.'

'I know she wants some answers that only Gran can give and well . . . ' She stopped walking and turned to him.

'And?' He raised an eyebrow.

'She feels Gran is lying . . . '

'Ah.' The corner of his mouth turned up. 'I understand.'

It could be the same conversation they'd had years ago. He hadn't understood why she hadn't told her mother the truth back then. She'd argued that she hadn't lied, and he'd kept whispering for days that there was such a thing as lying by omission.

The distant memory of him popping up behind her and calling

her a liar then kissing her came to the forefront of her thoughts. Probably because she was staring at his mouth. He had the most kissable mouth even now. She pushed the thought aside.

When she was investigating a story, her mother couldn't and wouldn't be led astray and Lottie feared she was treating Gran the same way. She took a deep breath. Her phone pinged, and she pulled it out of her pocket.

'Your boyfriend?'

She coughed and glanced away.

'George mentioned he met him a while ago.'

'I don't have a boyfriend.' This was true, she had a husband which was far worse. 'But this is just something I need to deal with.' It was Sally wondering if she'd heard anything from Jamie.

'Important?'

'It's nothing.'

'It's not nothing. I can see it on your face.'

'I have never been good at hiding things.' She smiled. 'Could never have been a spy.'

'Most definitely not. You're no good at lying.' He chuckled. 'You could only manage it by . . . '

She cut him off. 'Omission.'

He laughed but then the corners of his mouth dropped down. 'What's bothering your mum, other than her mother is dying and she doesn't want to be here?'

'She's just discovered that Gran lied to her.'

'What about – the tooth fairy?'

'Don't be cheeky.'

He grinned. 'All parents lie to kids, all the time, for many reasons.'

'Well, Mum as you know has a big thing about lying and this wasn't over something trivial.' She began walking again.

'What was it? Her father wasn't her father?'

'No, it has to do with Gramps.'

'With George?' He frowned.

She shook her head. 'It's weird, unless Gran has a really crap memory, which she hasn't.'

'You'd better tell me now as this is all too cryptic.' He caught up with her.

'Well, Gran had said she didn't meet Gramps until 1975 in Cairo, but looking through an old notebook listing all her entertaining, George Russell stayed here the weekend my grandfather died in 1962.'

He ran his hand through his hair then looked out to the bay. 'Odd, but have you considered that it might be a different George Russell?' He tilted his head. 'George Russell is not exactly like Archibald Guswinger, is it?'

'Archibald Guswinger? Where on earth did you come up with that name?'

'God only knows.' He smiled. 'George Russell isn't John Smith, either, but there must be many people bearing that name, I would think.'

'True.' She looked at him and she wished he was wearing sunglasses because his hazel eyes were bewitching. The last thing she needed was to fall under his spell again, so she removed herself from the temptation and walked into the house.

In the kitchen, she washed the lettuce and other vegetables she'd found on the table. Alex must have brought them in. Ripping the lettuce apart she flung it into the salad bowl. If she could kick something or someone, she would but that wouldn't help anything or anyone. There was nothing she could do but make food and be here. She couldn't even go grocery shopping, thanks to Paul. Her hands were tied, and she hated it.

'What's for lunch?' Her mother stood in the doorway looking a bit washed out.

'Who is with Gran?' Lottie asked.

She picked up a piece of carrot. 'The nurse called back in and is having a chat with George.'

'Oh.'

'You haven't answered my question.' The full strength of her stare landed on Lottie. This was something she'd learned to avoid as much as possible. Being under her mother's radar was best practice and essential at the moment.

'Thought the salad bowl made it obvious.'

Her mother squinted into the bowl. 'Anything other than lettuce and carrot?'

'Not at the moment.'

Her mother pulled open the fridge. 'Why haven't you gone shopping?'

Truth or lie? Looking at her expression it was a hard choice. Maybe something halfway in between. 'Haven't had a chance yet.' Lottie sliced a tomato. 'Why don't you do it while I'm doing this?' Her mother hated cooking, so this might work.

'I don't know what to buy.'

Lottie dug into her jeans pocket and pulled out a slip of paper. 'Here's a list.'

She grimaced as she read it. Lottie widened her stance ready for a fight.

'OK, anything else?'

'More coffee, maybe.'

'Fine.' Her mother put the paper in her back pocket and left the kitchen. Disaster averted. However, if she wasn't careful someone would find out and these were the last people in the world she wanted to share her failure with, absolutely the last people. Her humiliation would be complete. Marrying Paul and lending him the money had seemed a good idea at the time. But these things do, like ditching the internship and spending the summer here. Big mistake. Would she ever learn?

From the kitchen window she watched Alex walk into the cottage.

'No,' she said aloud then looked about to make sure no one had heard her. She would not think about Alex Hoskine and the plans they had had. There were more important things to think about. Gran, for one, and her mother's peculiar behaviour. She could do little about either one. She closed her eyes and wished. Wished that for once that she could do something right and help things rather than mess them up.

She put some eggs on to boil and thought about her mother's life and her life within it, or outside of it of late. The one thing that constantly represented her mother for her was seeing a passport. She had several in case one was tied up in a visa process and always had one on her person. In her bedroom, one drawer was permanently filled with black knickers and bras, grey t-shirts and dark grey utility trousers. Not quite monotone but not far off, especially with her dark hair. These days her hair sported big streaks of steely grey. Once Lottie had asked why all the clothing was so boring and laughing, she'd said, 'It won't show the dirt.'

Ever-practical was her mother and never there. Lottie assumed she was loved. She'd had her after all, but she'd never made it to a school play or a hockey match or a speech day. However, she'd attended every parent-teacher meeting. That had been important to her even if it hadn't to Lottie.

Rolling her neck from side to side her heart contracted, remembering the taxis that waited at the end of term. While other girls ran into their parents' arms, she was piling her kit into the back of an anonymous car. The upside had been Boskenna. If her mother hadn't been home, which had been most of the time, then Lottie had come here.

'Oh, you're making lunch.' Gramps sounded startled to see her. He grabbed the back of a kitchen chair. 'The nurse has popped back in.'

'All OK?'

'My darling girl, I wish I could say it was. I called them.' He shook his head. 'She seemed so distressed.'

Lottie dried her hands before hugging him. His weight, not that there was much of it, settled against her and he cleared his throat.

'I don't think we have her for long.'

Swallowing hard, she said, 'I know Gramps, I know.' She pulled him closer for a moment then rescued the eggs from boiling over. 'Shall I bring lunch up to you or would you like it in the garden?'

He looked at her, but she knew he wasn't with her in the here and now. She only hoped his thoughts had taken him to a happier time and allowed him to escape for a moment.

'She won't take any real pain relief,' he said turning back to her.

'Why not?' She didn't know much about lung cancer or any cancer, for that matter, but Gran must be in terrible pain.

'She doesn't want to lose control over her mind, her thoughts, her emotions . . . ' His shoulders sagged. 'She wants to be conscious until the end.'

'Oh Gramps.' Lottie threw an arm around his shoulders and helped him up the three steps to the courtyard. 'Take some fresh air and grab me a few cucumbers if there are any ripe ones.'

'I will.' He squeezed her hand.

She kissed his cheek and watched him enter the walled garden. Once he was out of sight, she raced upstairs to try to catch the nurses. They might not tell her much, but she needed to know how she could help. There was no reason for Gran to suffer for the sake of suffering.

40

Joan

4 August 1962, 12.30 p.m.

Opening my notebook, I glance up at Mrs Hoskine then back to the menu and the seating plan, so carefully wrought but now in ruins. Everything had been as it should have been, but no longer. Tapping my pen on the page, I don't need this right now. I would rather be sailing with Allan and Diana. Instead I am sitting here chewing my lower lip and tasting the remnants of my lipstick, waxy and unpleasant.

I flip back to last year when the menu differed, but the guests – bar the Venns and Eddie Carew – had been the same. Now I am stuck trying to fit these newcomers into the seating plan. At least I know I have never served these dishes to them. Of all our guests tonight only Tom has had a repeat of any of the food. The pudding is the exception. Since Diana had been old enough to express an opinion, she has chosen silverbelle, a chocolate charlotte. Her thinking is beautiful. It is her favourite and therefore it must be her father's. Of course, she is right. Allan loves anything chocolate, just like his daughter.

Last year I wore a navy strapless gown with my cousin's aquamarine eternity brooch on a choker. This year I plan to wear a sea-coloured silk gown with an empire waist and a bow just under the bust like the one I'd seen on a photo of the U.S. president's wife. It is a favourite and I always have a wonderful evening when I wear it. It will give me confidence like a suit of armour. I'm on edge and feeling uncertain and it isn't just because of the ruined seating plan. Allan's restlessness, Tom's unease and George Russell arriving are all playing havoc with my calm.

Mrs Hoskine hums along with the wireless. Last night she did a superb job with the adapted bouillabaisse. I flip to my recipes. Between the two of us, over the years we have altered it to Cornish fish and English tastes. When she's not looking, I add my secret supply of dry chilli flakes given to me by the Italian ambassador's wife. Despite her collection of Robert Carrier's recipe cards from *The Times*, she looks on most spice with reluctance. She will not have foreign flavours ruining good Cornish fish. It tastes best simple, she says. I can't argue but I can't serve steamed fish to my guests for dinner either. We had planned to have a relaxed dinner last night, barbecuing, however the weather had other ideas.

Looking back down at the seating plan that had worked perfectly, I say, 'Allan has invited the Venns to join us for dinner tonight.' I pick up a pencil and pull a clean sheet from the back of the ring-binder.

'Two more to feed.' She puts all the tomatoes on the table. The aroma is earthy and my mouth waters. I long for fresh bread, salted butter and sliced tomato.

'Indeed.' The feeding is the least of my worries as I sketch the table again and mark it with twenty place settings. With eighteen it had worked. I'd made sure the vicar – who was hard of hearing in his right ear –was seated next to Allan's godmother, as she spoke as if she were controlling fractious children in the nursery. I suspect she regards us all as children in one way or another. On my left I'd placed the lovely Eddie Carew to make sure the conversation flowed at the end of the table. Now I am faced with placing these two strangers, not knowing a thing about them except that Allan has taken a shine to them and they are from the Midwest. I nibble the top of the pencil and Mrs Hoskine gives me one of her looks. Although younger than me, she is wiser and so like her mother. Her mother's death at the same time as mine hit me much harder than my own had. I put the pencil down and she resumes sorting the vegetables.

The Venns. I close my eyes thinking about them. Something isn't right. Their accent possibly? The wife of the political attaché at the US Embassy was from Chicago, born and bred, and there was no resemblance to the Venns' pronunciation of the most basic of words. Shutting down that train of thought, I return to focusing on balancing the needs of my guests that I do know. But it just wouldn't come. I glance up. 'Mrs Hoskine, have you heard anything about the people who rented Penweathers?'

She dries her hands on a tea-towel before she speaks. 'No, but I had heard that the place was rented, and it all happened very quickly.' She looks at the notebook, running a finger over their names. 'Venns, you say? English?'

'No, American.'

She raises her brows. 'Interesting. I did hear that they weren't looking for any help, which is odd.'

Sitting back in the chair, I tilt my head to the side.

'Don't seem right, not with a house of that size and with no one having lived in it since the war.'

I shudder. Wood lice, spiders, damp . . . a house so close to the sea needs more attention, not less. I know this. Ever since my mother died and Boskenna came to me, it has been a constant battle to stay ahead of repairs brought on by the position, the weather and the age of the house.

'What do they look like?'

I snort. 'Tall, handsome, athletic and entirely too clean.'

'Sounds about right, thinking of the GIs we had here abouts.'

'True, but this couple aren't like the troops, not at all.' I still can't quite pinpoint what it is that makes the Venns different but there is something. Normally reading people is easy for me. Sleep deprivation is clouding my thinking.

'Sit him next to Mr Trewin's godmother and her next to the vicar.'

I laugh. 'You're a genius, an absolute genius.'

'I wouldn't be so rash, but I'm not a bad cook and I'll need to talk to Jacob to get more fish. I think we have enough of everything else.'

I ran my finger down the menu. Chilled vichyssoise followed by sole meunière, dependant on today's catch, cheese, then silverbelle plus birthday cake. We would have drinks in the garden then dinner followed by dancing. The smoking room would be cleared and the carpet rolled up. It would all be fine, and I am seeing problems where there are none. There is nothing to be concerned about at all. Allan is always bringing home unexpected guests and this is something fun. I am tired, that is all.

Carrying the notebook into the office, I take a seat at the desk and review the details for this weekend. Making sure my writing is clear as it should be, I enter in the extra guests and finalize the seating plan. My pen rests a moment too long on the name of Ralf Venn, thinking of the camera he presented to Diana. The ink feeds out into the thick paper. I withdraw it before more damage is done. Most people looking at the book wouldn't notice the extra ink on the end of the N, but it jumps out at me. Ralf Venn is marked. All the other names, even George Russell, are uniform.

I shake my head and look out at the garden. An agapanthus head, big and blue, is in my line of sight then a big stretch of the lawn before the sea. Boskenna is so connected to the sea. What is that poem I loved as a child? 'Sea-Fever'.

Boskenna, the sea and my gypsy life moving from one country to another. The poem captures it all. I smile thinking of my merry fellow rovers, Diana and Allan. I can almost hear their laughter carrying in on the breeze, but it must be other happy souls playing on the beach. Boskenna grounds us and returning here reminds me that life can be normal.

I glance down at my notebook. Real life. This is it. Each event, whether attended or hosted, is here in detail. This weekend is no exception, but I wish it could be. Everything must be the same as before. All anyone reading this strange record of my life since I'd married Allan would see is a woman obsessed with perfection in entertaining. The irony isn't lost on me. My mother had kept a similar notebook, but not as detailed. It is one useful thing she had taught me. Not to mix my drinks is another.

I close the notebook. All will run like clockwork. Mrs Hoskine is a saint, and with fresh food the meals will succeed. I won't let two incomers ruin it and this George Russell will be fine. He knows the drill as a Harvard boy with the right credentials. I've met his type before and to my surprise have enjoyed their company. It won't be long before I know what I think about Mr Russell. Anything will be better than my feelings about the Venns.

On the blotting paper, I see the impression of Allan's writing.

Taking a sheet of paper and pencil from the bottom draw I shade in the white sheet until I can see what was written. He must have used a ballpoint pen for it to be this clear. It was not like him, but it was his writing.

4 August

Meet me tonight as agreed.

My heart stops and I look over my shoulder in case someone is around and then methodically I go through the desk. Who? Why? Finding nothing else, I dash upstairs to go through Allan's things. But aside from a missing cufflink, there is nothing out of place. Walking to the window I wrap my arms around myself. The sun shines relentlessly and I am slowly freezing from within as dread runs through me.

41

Diana

4 August 2018, 1.10 p.m.

Diana had whizzed through the shopping on Lottie's list and was in the library sitting at an empty computer in less than a half hour. It didn't take long to research her father's death. She'd gone over the main facts many times before. The local news had been full of it, but the key fact she needed now, the name of the local policeman first on the scene – Pat Treneer – took a bit more digging. A few more searches confirmed he was still alive and living here in St Austell.

Leaning back in the chair, she listened to the librarian chat to a woman about the wonderful weather and hadn't the rain a few days ago been a blessing. Diana couldn't remember the last time she'd spoken about the weather unless it was in regard to safety. It only interested her if it caused a famine or flood. By trying to raise awareness of people's plight, she had shut off her own needs. Sitting in St Austell public library was not the time to have an existential crisis. Her work had given her life meaning. Nothing else mattered in the end. And yet her mother, nearing her death, had asked for forgiveness.

Diana wrote down Pat Treneer's phone number and cleared

her searches from the computer. She was certain that with just a bit more information she would piece together this puzzle and finally resolve the question in her mind regarding her father's death. Logically, she knew that it was history and it didn't matter if he had fallen from the cliff or jumped. But part of her was still a child and that child wanted to know her father hadn't willingly left her. It shouldn't matter but it did.

Leaving the library, she dialled Pat's number.

'Hello.' A man answered.

'Is that Pat Treneer?' She unlocked her car.

'It is, who's asking?'

'I'm Diana Trewin.' The sun beat down on her. She found it hard that the weather was so beautiful while inside her thoughts darkened.

'Of Boskenna?'

She leaned against the car and laughed silently. Not Diana Trewin from the television. 'Yes.'

'How can I help you?'

'I was wondering if you could talk to me about my father's death.'

'Ah.'

'Mr Treneer?' she asked, opening the car door and placing her bag on the seat.

'Yes, I remember it well.'

She straightened. 'How well?'

'What do you want to know?'

Looking at the box of photos on the passenger seat, she had put them in chronological order. If nothing else, they would give her a visual map to help her to find her way forward. 'I can't remember much about it.' She slid into the car.

'You were young and very broken up about it.' He took a deep breath. 'Are you in St Austell?'

'Yes.'

'Come round now, if you like.'

She put the key in the ignition. 'I'll be there in ten minutes.'

'You know where I am?' he said.

She clicked on her seatbelt. 'Yes.'

'Bleddy internet, I bet.'

She laughed.

'Would have made my job a lot easier back in the day. See you soon. I'll put the kettle on.'

Diana hung up, smiling. Finally, she was getting somewhere – but she didn't know where it would lead.

42

Lottie

Gramps had his lunch on a tray upstairs with Gran. Lottie didn't feel hungry, but she knew that she needed to eat.

Alex stood by the door to the courtyard. 'Hi, any spare?'

She smiled. 'Yes, come join me.' Grabbing another bowl out of the cupboard, she handed it to him.

'Thanks.'

She sat down and passed the salad. 'Must be hard not to have a kitchen.'

He grinned. 'Not really, with two in this house.'

'True.' She laughed. Boskenna was big and so much of it not in use, like that old pantry next door. She had no idea when someone had last ventured in there. It could have been her and Alex looking for chutney. They'd never found it but had spent a long time kissing in the dark before Gran had come to look for herself. She grinned.

'Good memory.'

She lifted her eyes. 'Yes, it was.'

'Share?'

She tilted her head to one side and said, 'Relish.'

'Oh, that one.' He blushed, and she laughed again. He'd been much more embarrassed being caught kissing than Lottie had been.

'Yes, that one.' It had been one of many and looking at him now she wanted to do it all over again . . . but have it end differently.

'About that drink tonight?'

She took a deep breath. 'Gran.'

He nodded.

She stood and put the kettle on. She should just tell him she wasn't free. Gran wasn't good, but Paul was the real reason she couldn't and shouldn't have a drink with him. She'd hurt Alex once, she wouldn't do it again. She turned around and bumped into him.

'Lottie,' he said, standing so close she could have stood on tiptoe and kissed him, but she stepped back – just as her mother walked in with groceries in her hands. Alex's grandmother, Mrs Hoskine, followed close behind. When Lottie was little, she'd been still doing occasional work for her grandparents but she had retired years ago.

'Look at you, all grown up.' The depth of her smile caused her merry eyes to disappear almost completely.

'How lovely to see you, Mrs Hoskine. It's been years.'

'It has, my love, it has. I was heading this way because young Alex told me Mrs Russell is not well.' She looked to her grandson.

Lottie nodded, wishing 'not well' was all it was.

'Your mother found me walking down the lane.' Lottie sent her mother a questioning look. So Mrs Hoskine hadn't been the cause of her delay. Where the hell had she been? It didn't take two hours to shop, even on an August Saturday.

'Would you like to see her?'

'Yes, dear I would.' She stepped forward and Lottie let Mrs Hoskine set the pace. She was pleased to see that, although nearly the same age as her grandmother, she was still fit and able, climbing the stairs well.

'The house hasn't changed at all.' She looked around. And it hadn't, in essence. But Lottie had never seen the house look so tired, not even back in February.

'She's still in her room?'

'Yes.'

'Good. She loved the view.' Mrs Hoskine stopped on the threshold. Gramps wasn't there and Gran was restless. Lottie had spoken with the nurse. Morphine would ease her breathing and reduce her stress, but Gran wasn't having any of it and Gramps wouldn't overrule her.

'Oh dear.' Mrs Hoskine took small steps to the bed. She cast a glance over her shoulder at Lottie. Her happy expression slipped away. 'Oh, my dear.' She picked up Gran's hand. 'There's no rest for you, is there?'

Lottie frowned as she thought she'd misheard the softly spoken words.

'I had no choice. I had no choice.'

'We always have a choice my love, always.' She straightened the covers on the bed then rested her hand on Gran's shoulder. 'You were wonderful to me and I hate to see you suffering like this.' She turned to Lottie. 'Can we do anything?'

'Sadly no. She's refused all but the most basic relief.'

She shook her head. 'There's no need to suffer like this. It won't change things.'

Lottie frowned. What was she on about? Gran didn't need to suffer but she did seem determined to.

Mrs Hoskine walked to the window. 'So much sadness.'

'Do you mean when my grandfather died?'

She nodded. 'Everything changed.'

'How?'

'Well, once your grandfather was buried your grandmother let out the house.' She sighed. 'Under her instruction I put all personal items except the books away in the closets in the hallway and locked them up.'

'Ah, that explains it.'

Mrs Hoskine turned towards Lottie. 'What?'

'Mum found pictures of her childhood last night.'

'I asked about those, but your grandmother wanted it all locked away.' She turned and looked at Gran. 'I went against her wishes and sent my favourite picture of Mr Trewin and Diana together to the mite at school.'

Lottie swallowed, the diary.

'I know that your grandmother was trying to make everything less painful . . . ' she paused, 'but I'm sure it did the opposite. A soul needs to grieve properly.'

'I found some of Mum's old thing in the stables, too.'

Mrs Hoskine frowned then smiled. 'Is that where they ended up?'

Lottie nodded.

'I was going to post them to her, but we had the new tenants due and they arrived early.' She shook her head. 'I must have put them in there thinking I'd come back to them later and never did.'

'How quickly did Mum and Gran leave?' Lottie glanced at Gran, wondering if she was listening.

'Just days after.' Mrs Hoskine turned to her. 'She came back down briefly for the inquest, the funeral and to hand over the keys to the agent.'

'What did you do?'

'Ah, Pete and I stayed on in the cottage as caretakers. Pete kept on gardening and I made sure no real damage was done to the house by the various tenants who lived here.'

'Mrs Hoskine?' Lottie glanced again at Gran.

'Yes, my love?'

'Did my mother ask you any questions?'

She laughed silently. 'Pretty much the same ones you have.'

'Ah.' Her mother was still digging. She didn't know how to not be a journalist.

'Diana doesn't seem peaceful.' Mrs Hoskine made a clucking noise which sent Lottie straight back to her childhood. It was such a gentle reprimand and sign of disapproval.

'That's true.'

'Your mother says she doesn't remember her father or much of those years, which is a pity. She was so loved, adored by both Mr and Mrs.' She walked to the bed. 'They were a beautiful family and then it was gone. Mrs gone back to work overseas and Diana off to boarding school at only eight.'

She picked up Gran's hand. 'I think this is goodbye, Mrs Russell. May peaceful sleep find you. Rest.'

Gran's breathing stopped, and Lottie's did too, but then the raspy sound began again.

'It won't be long, Lottie.'

'How do you know?'

'It's all in the breath. I learned it being with too many people as they took their last one.'

'Oh, I'm sorry.'

'Nothing to be sorry about. It's a blessing and curse to be gifted with it. It's something you never forget.'

'Now, Mrs Russell be peaceful. If the good Lord is ready so must you be.' She put Gran's hand down and wiped Lottie's cheeks with her hankie. The good Lord may be ready, Gran might even be, but Lottie wasn't. Mrs Hoskine gave her a bear hug.

'I didn't mean to, I didn't mean to. I had to.' Gran's voice croaked.

Lottie went to her. 'Gran, it's me Lottie.'

'I had to. I had no choice.' Gran repeated.

'Shall I call your mother?' Mrs Hoskine bustled through the doorway.

Lottie nodded. 'Oh, Gran, please don't be so upset.'

'I didn't mean to. I had no choice.'

In the hallway, Lottie heard Alex chatting to his grandmother.

'Rest, Gran,' she said wanting to help somehow but not sure what to do.

Her grandmother opened her eyes.

'I love you.' Lottie took her hand in hers. It was icy. Lottie froze.

Gran turned her head and focused on Lottie. 'I had no choice, no choice.' Each word took so much effort, Lottie hurt watching her. She looked around and Alex came up to her and took her hand in his. There had to be something she could do. Something to stop Gran leaving her.

'Sssh, it's OK. You had no choice, I understand.'

'You do?' She looked directly at her.

'Yes, you had no choice, it's OK.' Lottie touched her cheek. She would do anything right now to erase the anguish in Gran's eyes.

'I had no choice because of Diana.'

Cold air ran down Lottie's back as she thought of her mother's diary. 'What?' She looked up and her glance met Alex's as Gran dragged air in, her whole body shaking with the effort.

'I couldn't, I couldn't let him.'

Lottie's mind ran to places that she didn't want it to go with that phrase. Was this why her mother didn't remember him? If he had interfered with her in some way, it began to make more sense. Her skin crawled at the thought. Her poor mother. No wonder she didn't trust anyone. 'Couldn't let him what, Gran?'

Alex put his finger to his mouth and she frowned at him. Lottie wasn't stopping – she needed to know. Her mother needed to know.

Gran looked her in the eyes. 'I had no choice, I killed him.'

Lottie froze.

'I had to.' Her head thrashed. 'Forgive me.'

Lottie had to do something. 'Gran?'

Her eyes closed. Air escaped from her mouth and Lottie wanted to scream. She stared, praying this wasn't the end. Gran's chest began to move. She hadn't left her yet, but it wouldn't be long.

'You OK?' Alex picked up her hand.

Lottie gave him a look to tell him he was insane then whispered, 'No, how could I be? My grandmother has just told me she killed my grandfather.'

'Don't jump to that conclusion.' He spoke to her as if she was a child who couldn't understand a concept. 'She didn't say that.'

'Alex don't play games with me.'

'I'm not but all she said is she had no choice and she killed him. It could be talking about the family dog, for all we know.'

Lottie wanted to hit him and hug him at the same time. But would Gran be that upset about a dog? She rose to her feet shaking. He pulled her into his arms and she closed her eyes and let herself feel protected for a moment. That sense returned that all was OK when she was in his arms, but it was an illusion. She opened her eyes and looked down on Gran, forcing her brain to accept what it didn't want to. Gran was leaving – and leaving Lottie holding her guilt.

Her mother burst through the door. Alex looked at Lottie and she nodded. She wouldn't say a word, not yet anyway. Not until she understood more. But if there was a way she could help her mother, she would.

CROSSROADS

43

Lottie

4 August 2018, 3.00 p.m.

Lottie walked in circles. In her mind, the blue of the sea merged with the green of the lawn and the white walls of the drawing room. All of this was dotted with blurred ancestral portraits. Each step she took didn't clear her thoughts, in fact, quite the opposite. Gran had killed someone. Someone who was a threat to her mother.

'Stop that infernal pacing.' Her mother slumped into the sofa. Gramps was sitting upstairs with Gran, and Lottie wasn't sure where Alex had gone. Hiding possibly, Lottie would if she could. She wanted to unhear what Gran had said. How was she going to avoid telling her mother? Her stomach clenched. Her mother's childish words on the page and her grandmother's words chased each other in her brain.

'Did she say anything else? Did she speak?'

Lottie swallowed, stopped pacing, and looked out of the French windows. What should she say? Best to not say anything.

'Did you hear me?' Her mother came up to her.

Lottie avoided her gaze. 'Sorry, Mum, I was lost in my own thoughts.'

'Did my mother say anything? Did she come back to consciousness?'

Lottie's glance darted about the room looking for escape. 'Nothing new.'

She crossed her arms. 'What does that mean?'

'I couldn't make out her words.' She looked down at the carpet. 'I think they were Persian, maybe.'

'Persian? She was never posted to Iran. Makes no sense.' She strode to the fireplace. Picking up the porcelain dog that sat there, she turned it in her hands, feeling the weight of it and the detail. Lottie held her breath, waiting for the smash that she was sure to follow.

'Well, that's what I thought. The other day she was speaking Russian and then some Arabic.' Why had she said Persian? Almost any other language would have been better.

'The last two make sense but not Persian.' She put the ornament down.

'Were you expecting her to say something?' Lottie took a step towards her then thought better of it.

'I'd hoped.' She adjusted the dog on the mantle.

'Did you have a dog?'

Her mother swung around. 'What does that have to do with anything?'

'I don't know.' Lottie glanced towards the fireplace and saw the ornament. 'You were looking at that thing so intently.' She took a deep breath.

'The pictures show me with a dog in Moscow but I don't remember.'

'What type was it?'

'It looked like a Cavalier King Charles.'

'Oh.' That was not the type of animal that would be a threat to a child.

'You're behaving really oddly.'

Lottie tilted her head and gave her mother a hard stare. 'My grandmother is dying.' She paused. 'I'm not really myself.'

'Fair enough.' Her mother turned and walked out of the room and Lottie wasn't sure if she was relieved or lost. She wanted to hold her mother and to be held, but if anything with Gran leaving, her mother felt further away. She wrapped her arms around herself trying to keep everything together. She rocked back and forth looking at the increasing cloud covering the bay. It felt right somehow.

Alex stood in the doorway. 'You OK?'

She shook her head as he walked up to her.

'Do you want to talk?' He brought his hand to her chin lifting it, so she had to look at him even though she didn't want to.

'About what?' His eyes were so intense and so honest.

He raised an eyebrow. 'The elephant in the room.'

She turned away. 'It wasn't a dog.' Walking to the fireplace she put the china dog in its correct position.

He frowned.

'They had a spaniel.'

'Right.' He came to her side. It was hard to focus but she needed to.

'My grandmother killed someone, and it is clearly distressing her.' It just didn't fit the grandmother she knew. Beautiful flower arrangements and superb meals fitted Gran, not killing someone . . . not someone . . . him.

'It's in the past.' He threaded his fingers through hers. It was so tempting to let it go but she wasn't going to. Gran felt it was important enough to use what might be her last words confessing it.

'It won't help anyone.'

She cocked her head to the side. 'Look, it's not really your business, Alex.'

'I heard her too.' He stepped back.

Taking a breath, she said, 'I know but she wasn't talking to you, but to me.'

'It could have been drug induced.'

'It wasn't. She's refused drugs.' Lottie shuddered.

He sighed. 'She was confused.'

'No, she wasn't.' Lottie huffed. 'This isn't your problem.' She left him there and walked through to the hallway. She should be grateful for his help and not cross with him, but she was. Her grandmother had just confessed to killing someone and he was trying to tell her what to do. Why on earth should she listen to him? She should call the police. She stopped, closing her eyes. No, she wouldn't do that. That wouldn't help anything or anyone right now. But she had to do something.

Opening her eyes, she bolted up the stairs and went straight to the closet where Mrs Hoskine had said she had put all the personal things. Lottie had no idea what she might find in there, but anything would be a start.

44

Joan

4 August 1962, 4.00 p.m.

Tom walks across the lawn and takes the path to the sea. The others will be dropped off any time now. I have watched the yacht make its way into the bay. Picking up my father's old binoculars, I make out Diana at the helm. It takes me a while to locate Allan. He's stripped to the waist and leaning over the American, Beth Venn, handing something to her husband, Ralf. They are all too close together. My breathing quickens, and I put the binoculars down, racing out the door towards the path. In moments I have caught up with Tom. Glancing back at the house, I see George standing at the window in his room, watching.

Slipping my arm through Tom's, I ache for the innocence of earlier days when all I wanted was to marry him and live in Cornwall, sailing, reading, and ignoring the world. A bitter laugh escapes me. Today of all days, innocence is a thing of the past and my heart aches.

'Are you OK?' He stares at me as he unbolts the gate.

'Yes.' I force a bright smile.

'Liar.'

'Never.'

He strokes my cheek, saying, 'I'm sorry.'

'For what?'

'Bringing you into this game.'

I take a deep breath. 'I went in with my eyes open.'

'Hmm.' He drops his hand. 'You did it because you were in love with me.'

I gasp.

'Of course I knew.' He turns to me.

'But . . .'

'Joan, if I could have loved anyone it would have been you.'

'But . . .'

'No buts. What is, is.' He strides down the last few steps onto the sand. The tide covers most of it and in the distance an over-full tender is making its way to the beach.

Clenching my fists, I catch up to him again. He is focused on the boat. 'What do you know about George?'

'Harvard. Likes his Scotch with three ice cubes and has a real taste for Cuban cigars. A straight-shooting American. No dark underside, or one that's so well hidden he's forgotten it.'

'That tells me nothing.' My nails dig into my palms.

'Which tells you a great deal.'

I uncurl my hands. No information. No one to trust. Just me. Maybe my mother's life wasn't as dull as I thought. All I know, as I look at Allan pressed up against the American in the dinghy, is that I want to keep my husband and above all, to keep my daughter safe. Nothing else matters. Not Tom, not George and not Victor.

I shake my head. I am a cog in the wheel and not important at all. I must remember that. Diana scrambles over the side of the tender and runs to me, covering me in kisses. 'Mummy I missed you.' I search her little face, all serious. The sail has not gone well from her point of view. Over her head I watch the American woman place a possessive hand on Allan's arm. He's only known them a week, but that is the familiar action of an old friend or a lover. Tom's glance meets mine.

'You missed a brilliant day.' Allan walks up to me and kisses me on the mouth. My eyes narrow as he scoops up Diana. 'Wasn't it wonderful, Diana?'

She nods but I know my daughter only too well.

'How's the head, old man?' Allan turns his attention to Tom. 'Or was it an excuse to lose yourself in a book?'

'After all the travel of late, I spent the day resting.'

Allan cast him a look. 'Good, then you'll be on form for a long night of celebration.'

'Of course.' Tom smiles and his eyes dance. I know a party is the last thing he wants. He's been made impotent by the mole and his clever brain will be assessing his options. The real question is, what are mine? I look back to the house, but George is no longer at the window.

45

Diana

4 August 2018, 4.15 p.m.

A young woman with her blonde hair pulled back in a ponytail was putting a large bouquet of flowers on her father's grave. Diana watched her. She was young, early twenties at a guess. Her clothes didn't give much away. She wore cropped jeans with white trainers and when she turned around Diana saw David Bowie on her t-shirt.

'Hi,' she said, smiling as she walked past me to the gate.

'Who are you and why are you putting flowers on my father's grave?'

The woman stopped. 'He belongs to you?'

Diana nodded.

'Oh.' She took a few steps towards Diana. Her face was open. 'I'm Hannah Hollis and I come here once a year – normally on the fifth – but I'm heading up to London to begin a job on Monday, so I hoped no one would mind if I did this a day early.'

'Should I know you?'

She grinned. She had an open face. 'No, I doubt it. I only met Old Tom in 2011 and I made my first visit here in 2012.'

'Old Tom?' Something stirred inside Diana.

'Sorry, Tom Martin.'

Tom Martin. She knew it. 'Are you related? His granddaughter, maybe?'

'No, just a friend.'

Diana's eye's narrowed.

'Sounds weird but he befriended me when I moved to Cornwall.' Her smiled widened. 'He saw something worthwhile in me when I sure as hell couldn't, and I'm not sure anyone else could.'

'Oh.' Diana looked at the roses and the lilies resting against the gravestone. 'The bouquet?'

'Old Tom brought flowers here all the time when he was alive and made provision in his will for someone to continue.' She peered at her. 'I gather they were long-time friends and had been to school together. I only come once a year. But I feel it was important to him if he wanted someone to be tending the grave even after he couldn't do it.'

'They were friends.' As Diana said those words, an image flashed in her head.

'I've never seen anyone here before – not that I've been here loads.'

'No, I shouldn't think my father has many visitors.' She sighed. She should have come but even now a kind of fury filled her.

Hannah looked at her closely. 'I don't visit my own father's grave.' She paused. 'It hurts too much and to be honest I'm still angry with him.' She shrugged. 'But every time I'm home in Cornwall I spend a lot of time at Old Tom's grave.'

Diana frowned.

'I know it's weird, but I find peace or maybe as he would have said, solace from it.'

'You loved him.'

She nodded. 'He loved me and taught me that love is worth having. And importantly you show your love by what you do.' She laughed. 'If anyone else had tried to teach me that I would have sworn at them then stormed off – in fact I did do just that many times.'

'Thank you for the flowers.'

'A pleasure.' She took a breath. 'I feel connected to Old Tom when I do this.' She held out her hand. 'It's been lovely to meet you.'

Diana took her hand and held it for a moment. 'Good luck with your new job.'

'Thanks,' she said as she set off then turned and walked back. Out of her bag she pulled out a silver cigarette case.

Diana's breath caught. She hadn't seen one since she was a child. Opening it, Hannah pulled out a card. Diana smiled and noted that the case was engraved on the inside with one word: *Always*. 'That's beautiful and it makes good use of something that has gone out of fashion.'

Hannah grinned. 'Yes, it was Old Tom's and I keep it with me.' She stroked it. 'Even though he smoked a pipe when I knew him, this was in his pocket.' She handed Diana the card. 'If you want to reach me about the flowers . . . for any reason.'

'Thanks.' Diana watched her go then went to the gravestone. Picking up the bouquet, she breathed in the scent of the lilies and the roses. Her tears pooled on the petals. Someone had loved her father.

46

Lottie

Shoebox by shoebox, Lottie began going through Gran's things. Black silk court shoes, flat ballet pumps with a ribbon bow, penny loafers, white sandals. All immaculate. But no more hidden photographs, lost letters or dinner party diaries. Aside from some truly beautiful shoes, there was nothing of interest. Lottie slipped on the silk court shoes. They fitted her perfectly. No doubt the gown they had been worn with was hanging protected in a garment bag. Had she waltzed in a Moscow ballroom under crystal chandeliers, whispering about diplomatic scandals?

She stood and began going through the garment bags. There would be nothing here that would tell her what Gran had done, or more importantly why she had killed someone – or who. However as she ran her hand over the fabrics, Lottie sensed her. Looking over her shoulder she expected to find Gran there with a quick smile on her face and questions at the ready. What would she be saying to Lottie right now as she held an evening gown of sea-coloured aqua silk? The tailoring was immaculate with darts on the bodice and fine stitching around the neckline. The colour would have set off her dark hair. Had she swept her hair up or left it down the last time she wore it? Turning, Lottie was about to ask her when it hit her that it was unlikely that her grandmother would utter another word. She looked up the hallway towards the bedroom and swallowed down the taste of loss.

Checking the clothing bags, she had some sense of her grandmother's life, elegant and glamorous from the Chanel suits to the silk gowns, but these were not the details she was looking for. The hatboxes yielded nothing more. They were pillbox style and so typical of how she pictured the early Sixties.

Strangely defeated by the process, Lottie went downstairs. Her foot still ached and she needed to take more paracetamol. She longed to see all the photographs that her mother had found. There had to be more information somewhere about Allan's death. The internet would be the best place to begin, after she had put together the ingredients for soup. The dinner party notebook wouldn't be any help for such a basic vegetable creation, but this soup was one she had learned at her grandmother's hip. The image of her cutting carrots from the garden didn't fit with the gowns upstairs nor her words in the bedroom.

Once the soup was cooking, Lottie went into the office. It took minutes for the ancient desktop PC to come to life. She typed 'Allan Trewin' into Google. A short Wikipedia entry on him was the first listing. It stated his education – Eton and Oxford – RAF flight lieutenant, and his diplomatic service, last post: political attaché in Moscow. Scrolling down the page there was one sentence regarding his accidental death on 5 August 1962.

In the citations at the bottom, she clicked on the link to the newspaper article reporting his death. It was sparse on detail as well. A fisherman discovered the body on the beach at the base of the cliffs. At the inquest the coroner had declared it a tragic accident. There was a picture of him looking very . . . debonair. Funny word that, but it described him perfectly. She touched the screen tracing the outline of his face. Her mother looked like him, but it was the angle of his head that most reminded Lottie of her.

All in all, it told her very little. Further searching brought up an obituary in *The Times* which included a very glamorous photo of Gran with him. They were the model golden couple. But despite more family history it shed no further light. She shut the computer down. She needed to check on Gramps and Gran.

He wasn't with Gran in the bedroom, but the nurse was there. Lottie found him asleep in the snug.

'Gramps?' She whispered. His eyelids fluttered. 'Thought you might like to eat a little something.'

His eyes opened, and he stared at her blankly then shook his head. He pushed himself up. 'I just needed a little nap. I'll head upstairs now.'

'The nurse is there.'

He nodded. 'I don't think she will wake again. It's just a matter of time.' He held out his hand. 'I must let her go.'

'Oh Gramps.'

'We've had a good life. I'm not complaining.'

Her heart broke as she watched him walk away. What would he say if he had heard what she'd said? Collapsing into a chair at the kitchen table, she knew these thoughts were wasted. It didn't matter. Maybe she should forget what Gran said. Following it up would only lead to pain. She knew that, even an idiot would. But then she was good at doing idiotic things.

But Gran hadn't said she'd told a lie or stolen some jewels. No, she'd confessed that she had killed someone. That she'd had no choice. Maybe she had been delusional, but Lottie couldn't convince herself of that. Her eyes had been clear and focused. Gran had known exactly what she had said. She hadn't wanted to say it. It had come unwillingly. It came with the desire for forgiveness. But Lottie might be reading more into it than she should. Maybe it all meant nothing? Gran was in pain.

Her mother's cheeks were red and blotchy as she entered the kitchen. She didn't do tears. Never. Her mother faced the most horrendous things and never cried.

She stopped by the table. 'George killed him.'

'What? Who?' Lottie jumped up as her mother blew her nose.

'It makes sense.' She focused on Lottie.

'You don't make any.' Lottie spoke with a calmness she didn't feel. She hated this sensation. Everything felt like her fault. She shook it off. Her mother was struggling with grief like Lottie was.

She looked at her, puzzled. 'George killed my father.'

'Mum . . .'

'I'm serious. He was here but denies it, yet there is proof in the notebook and the police reports.'

'It only proves that *a* George Russell was here.' Lottie took a step towards her wanting to help somehow. Gramps couldn't have and wouldn't have killed Allan Trewin.

'I don't believe in coincidences. It was him.' She pulled out her phone.

'Did you ask Gran?'

'No. I didn't have the chance, she fell asleep.' She rocked from one foot to another. 'She wanted forgiveness. She kept asking for it.' Her mother ground the words out.

'Did you give it?' Lottie walked closer, taking in the wild look in her mother's eyes. Where was the tight control of the past? Her mother nodded. That was a relief.

Lottie's phone rang. It was the private investigator. 'I need to take this.' She walked out into the courtyard.

'Hello,' she said.

'Lottie?'

'Yes?'

'It's Jamie Sharp. Sorry to disturb you with your grandmother being so ill, but I just wanted to touch base.'

'Thanks.' Lottie looked around. 'I don't suppose Paul's ex had any idea where he is?'

'Yes, she did. He's in Thailand.'

'What?'

'She postponed our meeting but confirmed that's where he was.'

'Great.' Lottie rolled her eyes.

'I'll be in touch when I have more news.'

'Thanks.' The phone clicked. She was trapped in a mess of her own making.

47

Diana

4 August 1962, 4.35 p.m.

Diana drank the milk down in one gulp. Sailing back had been fun but the rest of the day had been boring. Someone had been ill. Daddy became cross and Mrs Venn fussed over Diana's skin again. She also kept trying to read Diana's diary, and when Diana had gone to help fix a sail she'd come back to find Mrs Venn doing just that. It just wasn't right, and she'd told Mrs Venn it was private. The woman had laughed. Every time Mrs Venn had turned her back, Diana had stuck her tongue out. Daddy had seen her and they had had words. It wasn't right that the woman was trying to read her diary. It was private.

Mrs Hoskine handed Diana a scone with jam and clotted cream. 'Are you all right?'

She nodded. 'Thank you.' She tucked her diary under her on the chair. She would be very careful with it. At the end of the kitchen table was the camera that she'd been given. She didn't want it. She didn't want anything from the Venns.

Uncle Tom walked into the kitchen. He smiled and Diana felt better. 'New?' He held up the camera.

She nodded.

'From the United States?'

'I think so. Mr Venn gave it to me.'

'Did he?' He raised an eyebrow then he studied the camera. 'Did they give you film for it?'

She shook her head.

'Hmmm.' He put it back down the on the table. 'I suppose you could use it to take some photographs of the party for your father.'

She grinned. 'I could make a book for Daddy.'

'You could.' Uncle Tom pinched a scone that Mrs Hoskine had just unpacked. 'May I?' He said, and she smiled at him. Everyone liked Uncle Tom. He walked out into the courtyard with his scone.

She pulled out her diary and looked at what she had written.

Dear Diary,
I am sitting at the front of the boat as I write this. This is the best day we have had, and I'm bored. There is the smell of sick coming up from below and it makes me feel ill. Adults are strange. The sailing was fun, but Mrs Hesketh got seasick, and everyone thought it was funny and spoke about the wine. She looked too white, but no one took much notice of her and the smell was disgusting.

She pulled the pencil from her bag then took another bite of scone. The jam and the clotted cream stuck to her lips. Mrs Hoskine laughed when she looked at her. 'I don't know where you put all the food, but you have grown since you arrived.'

'Have I?' Diana sat straighter then began to write but stopped. Out of the window Uncle Tom talked to a man she didn't know. Uncle Tom looked unhappy. She hoped she was wrong, but she felt sad just looking at him.

48

Lottie

4 August 2018, 4.45 p.m.

The beach was huge with the tide almost fully out. Kids were crabbing in the pools between the rocks to her right. Lottie walked along the firm sand keeping her flip flops on. Her foot felt almost normal. Around her some families were beginning to call it a day, packing up their things. She looked down at a piece of seaweed. It was rippled and in the ripples were drops of water and her fingers twitched. She wanted a pencil and paper to sketch the design. She pictured silver and gold bent and twisted to look like the seaweed and gems acting as the water drops.

She sighed. It was good to know the desire was still there. After the debacle with the theft, she couldn't work. It wasn't just that her raw materials were gone but when Paul stole it all, he took the desire with it. She had collapsed. Everything that saw beauty in the world had left her.

Now was not the time to think about that, she had other concerns. She looked up to the watchtower. Gran. Allan Trewin. Mum. Her hand went to her mouth. No wonder Gran had been so quiet ten years ago when Lottie's world had broken wide open.

'It's history.' Alex said, and she jumped.

He held two ice creams and handed one to her. 'I thought you could use some bolstering.'

She laughed and took it. 'Thanks.' They walked to the wall together and sat. Lottie stared out to the point thinking about John.

'It's best to leave things in the past.'

'Easier said than done.' She licked the ice cream around the cone before biting the flake. 'If I hadn't been a needy idiot all those years ago, John would be alive.'

'No, you can't think that way.'

'But I led him on and he followed me.' Seagulls darted out from their nests along the cliff.

'Because I was a dick.' He stared at a dinghy coming in to the beach.

'No you weren't.' She bit the ice cream and regretted it. Her teeth ached.

'I was. I was so afraid of losing you.' He shook his head. 'So I pushed you away.'

'No, it was me. I was so insecure.' Her ice cream dripped, and she licked her hand attempting to clean up. 'I was trying . . . '

He placed a hand on hers. 'Lottie, I know you. You were, and I think still are, trying to do the right thing, to please everyone.' He looked at her. 'I was jealous as hell.'

She frowned.

'Yes, they had it all – especially John.' He finished his ice cream. 'I hate what happened, but by the time that dinner had ended I had heard enough of his success at rugby, the cars, the holidays and the way he was looking at you.' He picked up her hand. 'I was so envious . . . so jealous and I'm not proud of the role I played in what happened.'

'It wasn't your fault and for the record you had no reason to be jealous.' She took a deep breath. 'There was only ever you.' She dropped her eyes, rushing on, 'I'm responsible from start to finish. I said they could come and stay before the festival. I wanted to be liked by the in-crowd.'

'Everyone makes mistakes.'

'Yeah, they do, but not so big nor so deadly. If I hadn't flirted, John wouldn't have followed me and . . . '

'Stop. You didn't push him over the cliff. He was drunk, and he stumbled.'

A cormorant landed on a rock at the end of the point. He spread out his wings to dry them. 'I pushed him off me and left him. He didn't know the headland.'

Her hand shook, and her ice cream dripped on to her wrist. She tried to lick it off but ended up with ice cream on her nose.

'Lottie, look at me.'

She stared at the sea. It was all her fault. He placed a finger under her chin and turned her head. 'It wasn't your fault. You don't have to carry this.'

She blinked. He wiped the ice cream off the tip of her nose with his thumb. 'Sorry I don't have a napkin.'

She smiled, and a tear fell down her face.

He dropped his hand. 'It was a terrible tragedy but not your fault.'

'You really think that?'

He nodded. 'And I think that might be what your grandmother meant.'

'But . . . '

'You've blamed yourself for the past ten years. I can tell you, hand on heart, John's death wasn't your fault.'

'But . . .'

'Your grandfather fell from that cliff many years ago. Who knows, they may have had a fight and he stormed off with a bottle of brandy and got stinking drunk then missed his footing when he went to come home.'

She opened her eyes wide. 'You think that's what happened?'

'I do.'

'But she said she had no choice.'

'Who knows what he'd done? Maybe he'd kissed another woman in front of your mother. Any number of things – but she has held onto to it all this time and blamed herself like you have.'

'Oh.'

'Are you going to just let that melt?' He pointed to her ice cream.

'No.' Lottie smiled. 'Thanks.' He stood and offered her a hand. She took it and finished the rest of her ice cream as they walked back to the house.

49

Joan

4 August 1962, 5.10 p.m.

Afternoon light falls through the window, hitting the wooden floor and picking out the colours in the carpet. This one is from Turkmenistan. The intricate pattern tells a story in repeat. A bit like my life. The fear that tightens my chest at the moment is not the first time it has happened. It was Cairo. My nostrils flare as I force myself to breathe. This morning's actions are a cover. He doesn't want me – or if he does, it is in addition to, not as the main course.

I pace the hallway. I can do this. He loves me. He loves Diana. Breathe. My father loved my mother despite his mistresses. He said he had, and he had been devasted by her death. It will be fine. When I was pregnant with Diana, Allan roamed. We recovered. I forgave him for his weakness. I close my eyes and let my love fill me.

Guests are in their rooms preparing and here I am wasting time. The hall clock chimes the quarter hour. Everything is ready except for me. The ground floor is empty with only Mrs Hoskine in the kitchen. I climb the stairs slowly, listening to the sound of the radio in Diana's room. From the vibrations of the floorboards

I know she is dancing. A smile spreads across my face and I tap on her door before putting my head around it. She jumps, holding her hand out and I join her swaying to the sound of Bobby Darin singing 'Things'.

I am still humming the song when I walk into my bedroom. Allan stands in a towel and I catch my breath. A slow smile spreads across his face.

'Hello darling.' He drops his towel and walks toward me. 'There's no reason to wait until later.'

The lines from the song run through my mind . . . the things we used to do.

'This is superb timing.' He releases my belt while kissing my neck. Timing. We don't have time, but I don't care. It has been too long to wait another moment. This is exactly what I need.

50

Diana

4 August 2018, 5.15 p.m.

Diana sat on the bed rocking back and forth clutching Ben, the bear, and the Guernsey. The ancient motion of soothing she'd seen the world over as mothers who had nothing left to give rocked to try and provide solace. Not sure what to feel but feeling it anyway, her fingers worried Ben's ears and she recalled sitting on a bed reading to him with a call to prayer in the background. She must have been very young, but now the memory was sharp and it cut, leaving a gash and allowing tears to find their exit.

For years she'd tried so hard to remember and when nothing appeared, she'd convinced herself it was unimportant. She didn't need her past, her mother, or Boskenna – but at this moment she wanted her mother in a way that ripped through her.

Taking Ben, Diana walked down the hall seeing the peeling paint. She stopped, seeking a map that wasn't there. She touched the wall looking for evidence that the old map of Cornwall wasn't purely from her imagination. Opening another bedroom door along the hall to allow the early evening light to flood in, she ran her free hand over the wall. There was an empty nail hole. A vision flashed. She saw the map and she'd held her father's hand. Closing her eyes, she prayed this was true, not a creation of her imagination because she'd seen the old snapshots. But there had been no picture taken in this hallway. Last night she had gone through each and every photograph trying to create a past from them. But it hadn't worked for she didn't have the stories that went with them.

Walking to her mother's room, Diana longed for the stories but her mother lay on the bed, eyes closed, barely breathing. She stared. With the life force leaving her, the body only vaguely resembled the woman Diana had known. Her eyebrows were so like Lottie's but other than that, her daughter's appearance reflected her father's genes. This had made her striking, but every time Diana looked at her daughter, she saw the man who held her captive in so many ways. That wasn't Lottie's fault, but Diana blamed her anyway.

She sat beside her mother and picked up her waxy hand. The fingers were elegant. A platinum wedding band encircled her ring finger. Would George remove it? Would she be buried or cremated? A funny thing to think about but she was sitting here facing her mother's death and Diana didn't know what her wishes were, and she should. Today her mother had said she was sorry and that had to be enough. It must be, but it wasn't. It was unfinished and yet looking at her, Diana accepted the time for words had gone. She was surprised she was still alive. In fact, she would say she wasn't. It felt as if her soul had left. Was her mother dancing with her father now?

In front of Diana the ghost of an image hovered. It was of her young self sitting on the bed in this room watching her mother dress. She could almost touch it. The hint of her perfume, Chanel No. 5, and hairspray filled her nose. Her mother was putting on earrings. They were diamonds and pearls. She had jewels, many of them. Diana had played with them and they had laughed together. Looking at her now she wanted to tell her she had remembered something good, but the words died on her lips.

Where were her jewels? Diana hadn't seen them in years. Had she sold them? Lottie would have loved them. Her fingers twitched, and the bald fabric on Ben's ears scratched her skin. Diamonds and bright colours. She looked at her mother. She hadn't really known her at all and now she never would. She was an orphan before she'd enjoyed being a daughter.

51

Lottie

4 August 2018, 6.00 p.m.

Lottie's shoulders slumped. Her mother was tricky at the best of times, but right now she was a nightmare, thinking that Gramps had killed Allan. Lottie needed to know the truth. With the diary out again, she reread the last page. Why would her mother think it was her fault and why had Gran said she had killed him? She didn't believe either of them. There was one person who might be able to help – Mrs Hoskine.

It was a short walk to the cottage where she lived and as she passed the church, she glanced towards Allan Trewin's grave. New flowers had replaced the previous ones. Maybe it was her mother this time. A crow swept down from a tree with a deep mournful cry. Soon Gran would be joining him. She paused. She'd made that assumption, but she hadn't checked it with Gramps. He might want something different. Gran might have told him what she wanted. There were so many questions she was afraid to ask.

As she left, Alex had been sitting with Gramps watching Gran. Death watch. She should be there too, but restless energy filled her. Walking on, she listened to the rooks in the trees above.

What was it about this time of day? They lined up on rooftops, trees and telephone wires . . . watching and chatting. What had they seen? What could they tell her of the past?

Lottie looked back over her shoulder. The bay glistened and Gribben Head was golden in the evening sun. Her grandfather had fallen to his death on this weekend fifty-eight years ago. Her mother was just eight. Her grandmother was glamorous and by the evidence in her notebook an accomplished hostess . . . and by her admission a murderer. What Alex had said made sense but seeing her mother's words in the diary had put doubt in her mind. She clearly felt she was at fault, just as her grandmother did. What could an eight-year-old child have done to even think that? Lottie just couldn't imagine. Was that why her mother's memories were so sketchy?

She reached Mrs Hoskine's bungalow. The front door was open, and she could see her in the kitchen.

Lottie knocked on the door frame and called, 'Hello.'

'Who's there?' Mrs Hoskine turned, wiping her hand on her apron, bringing with her the scent of freshly baked scones as she walked down the short hallway.

'It's Lottie Trewin.' She smiled.

'Ah, Lottie,' she said, steering Lottie towards the kitchen. 'I thought you might come visiting.'

'You did?'

She nodded. 'Tea?'

'Yes, thanks.' Lottie followed her into the kitchen, remembering the warm and welcoming space with the old Cornish range. The sunlight streamed in through the back door which looked out on to a well-stocked garden. Nothing had changed. As Mrs Hoskine put the kettle on, Lottie noticed the photos tucked among the plates, cups and jugs on the old pine dresser. Lottie frowned as among the pictures of Alex growing up there was one of him in a naval uniform. How had she not heard he'd been in the Navy? There was also one of Alex and Lottie together, looking suntanned and relaxed and so young. It had been taken the weekend before everything had gone wrong.

'Sadly the scones are too hot to eat but I have a sponge.'

'I had an ice cream not long ago.'

'You always had room for cake.'

'Can't lie.' Lottie grinned. 'I do always have room, especially for yours. What can I do?'

'Grab the milk and some cups and take them out to the table by the rose arch.'

In the garden Lottie caught the scent of sweet peas and watched the bees loving the agapanthus. She put the things down and dashed to take the tray from Mrs Hoskine's hands.

'Thank you, dear.' She sat in the old iron chair. It had had a new coat of paint since Lottie had last visited the garden years ago. Back then it was blue and flaking. Now it was black and shiny. 'What do you want to ask my lovely?'

Lottie sighed. 'Tell me about my grandfather's death, please.'

'It was terrible.' She poured the tea. 'Jacob, the fisherman, found the body and your poor grandmother was with Tom Martin looking for him, as were my Pete and your mother. They came to the beach and they found him. My Pete told me he and Diana were laughing as they walked the path to the beach not expecting anything untoward and then the poor mite saw him.' She shook her head. 'She went all quiet.'

'No.' Lottie shook.

Mrs Hoskine nodded her head with a sad expression on her face.

No wonder her mother didn't remember, but why would she think it was her fault?

'The whole affair was all a bit odd, if you ask me.' Mrs Hoskine took a sip of tea. 'Your grandmother came downstairs that morning looking for him and he wasn't in the house. We all assumed he'd fallen asleep somewhere.'

'Really?'

'Well, it had been his birthday party and there was a great deal of alcohol consumed, judging by the empty bottles the following morning.'

'His birthday?' She had forgotten that.

'Yes, they made sure they were at Boskenna for his birthday every year.' She poured more tea. 'Your grandmother threw the most elaborate parties for him and the house was filled with friends.'

She took a sip of tea. Gramps. Lottie had to ask about him for her mother, but maybe she had asked already. 'Do you recall all the guests that were here then?'

'That weekend is still so clear to me, unlike yesterday.' She shook her head as she added a drop of milk to her tea.

'I found Gran's hostess notebook.'

'Ah, yes, her bible of entertaining.' She pulled the cake closer and picked up a knife. 'She was religious about it.'

'It has George Russell down as a guest.'

The knife stopped halfway through the cake as if it had hit stone. Mrs Hoskine's hand fell away. 'I . . . ' She blinked then rubbed her eyes. 'I . . . yes, I think he was.'

'Are you sure?'

She nodded. 'He was younger and fitter and didn't stay long.'

'How do you mean?'

'Once he was interviewed on the Sunday he left. Some of their friends stayed on until the Monday.' She resumed cutting the cake.

'You're sure it was him?'

'Thinking about it now, yes. He hadn't been before. He was in the attic bedroom.'

Lottie nodded and took the slice of sponge Mrs Hoskine held out to her.

'It's all coming back to me now. He arrived in the early afternoon on Saturday.' She cut herself a slice. 'From Penzance, I think. Something about a relative.' She took a forkful of cake. 'Yes, that explains why he always looked a bit familiar, but I could never place why.'

'Oh.' So, Gramps *had* lied. He wouldn't have forgotten being here when Allan died. He and Gran must have decided that it would have upset her mother. That made sense.

'It was all so awful.' Mrs Hoskine stared off into the distance. 'Everything changed.'

Lottie frowned. 'How exactly?'

'Well, renting out the house. Your mother going from the happiest little mite to the quietest and then your grandmother going back to work.'

'What did Gran do at the time?'

'She'd always had a knack for languages, so she went back to work for the Foreign Office.' She sipped her tea. 'I'd secretly hoped that she would find her way to Tom Martin.'

'Oh.' Lottie remembered the pictures Gran had showed her.

'Tom Martin was a great friend to both your grandmother

and to Mr Trewin. Lovely man. Never married.' She smoothed down her skirt. 'I always thought your grandmother and he would make a good match.'

'Oh.' Lottie put her fork down. 'Is Mr Martin still around?'

'Oh no, dear. He passed away a good few years ago. I went down to the funeral in St Martin church in the Meneage. Such a lovely man. Mr Trewin's death shook him up badly.'

'How did my grandmother react?"

'Bless her, she kept her head, kept cool. Kept everything moving, handling everything. I thought she would crack but it's not the way she was brought up. Poor thing hadn't seen much of her parents. Those two were colder than fish in winter. Never once showed any warmth to her. But she wasn't like that with Diana . . . ' she trailed off and picked up her cup.

'But Mum and Gran don't have a very good relationship.'

'I know. I saw that when you were born. Made no sense but I hadn't seen them in the years in between.'

'Hello.' Alex's voice carried across the parched lawn. He stood in the kitchen doorway. 'Shall I bring some more hot water?'

'Yes.' Mrs Hoskine beamed, watching him head back into the kitchen and Lottie wrenched her thoughts away from how the sunlight had caught the highlights in his hair.

'He's a good lad.'

'Why isn't he staying here with you?' Lottie took a bite of the cake.

'I can't be doing with anyone under my feet, even my own grandson.' She chuckled. 'I'm just surprised no one has scooped him up yet.' Her glance narrowed as she looked at her. 'He was mighty keen on you once.'

Lottie swallowed. 'It was mutual, but a long time ago.'

'Time means nothing to love.' She gave her a hard stare.

Alex strode up the garden with the kettle and cup. After topping up the teapot with hot water, Alex wedged himself beside her on the bench, making sure all Lottie could think about was his proximity.

52

Joan

4 August 1962, 6.10 p.m.

My skin smells of Allan's aftershave and I haven't time to take a bath. Adding my own scent would make me smell like a bordello. What the hell is happening? I yank my gown over my head. No sex for months then a delicious quickie. It is like we have started over. We need to. The stress of our life outside is eating into family life. Allan is always travelling and has so little time for Diana. She needs him. I know exactly what having a distant father does to a daughter.

I wriggle in order to get my zip up. Teasing the front of my hair to achieve a lift, I sweep my hair into a French twist, securing it with a few pins and a diamond clip that had been my mother's. I look like her, but act nothing like her. She had been typical of women of her day. Well-read but under educated. Like the clip that adorned my hair, she adorned my father's arm until her end. No, I am not like her at all. In fact, I am more my father, wily and evasive. He gave nothing away, not even love.

In the bottom of the wardrobe, I pull out my jewel case and run my fingers over the pearls, but my fingers settle on the diamond necklace that Allan had given me for the birth of

Diana. He'd never expected to become a father and his delight had surprised us both. It was never meant to happen, Allan and me. We were both letting our hair down. A tense operation finished. We were alive and before we knew it, we were making love. The following morning, we had laughed while smoking in bed listening to the *muezzin* recite the *adhan*. We would say no more about it. These things happen and all that.

A month later a decision had to be made. But due to work I could not travel. Rage ensued. This was not the plan. Allan and I married, sealing my fate and providing me with a different cover. Diana arrived not quite eight months later. She changed me in ways I'd never expected. Love was one of them.

The diamonds catch the light as I lift the necklace and place it around my neck. It is Cartier. Memories. When Allan had presented it to me, I recalled wearing it and nothing else. Looking at myself now, that carefree abandon feels very far away from here.

It is funny how the evenings are drawing in already or is that just my imagination? When we go back to Moscow next week, I will feel the winter even though autumn is weeks away. As I clip my earrings on, the glint of yellow gold reminds me of the churches with glistening domes. What had Diana called them? Castles of gold. That was two years ago. Diana had been six. Time is flying.

Glancing in the mirror, I adjust my bra strap before pulling on my gloves. The sound of our guests gathering on the lawn below my bedroom window mixes with the music coming from Diana's room. It was Elvis Presley now. Diana was singing at full volume and no doubt my guests are enjoying her rendition of 'Good Luck Charm'.

The quartet isn't due to begin playing until after dinner. Last year we were still dancing as dawn broke behind Gribben Head.

Instead of sensibly heading to bed, ten of us went swimming and Mrs Hoskine had provided breakfast and Bloody Marys on the beach.

It will be a wonderful party tonight and I will enjoy being in Allan's arms again later on. His laughter carries above the hum of conversation below. He is in his element. How he loves to be at the centre of everything.

A final check of my appearance in the mirror and I see I've forgotten my lipstick. Slipping off my glove, I take care applying the pale pink. It shows off my tanned skin as does the wonderful watery aqua silk of the dress. Outside, the Venns' voices rise above the rest of the guests. No, that isn't quite right. They aren't actually louder, but their accent stands out. I pull my bedroom door to, noting the sun catching the sailing boats in the bay. It is a glorious evening for a bank holiday weekend and I will enjoy all of it. I am determined, and I head down to greet my guests.

'There you are.' Tom smiles.

I turn at the bottom of the staircase to see him.

'Looking breathtaking as always.'

I kiss his cheek and put my arm through his. 'Has no one given you a drink?'

'Pacing myself.'

'Hmmm. You are off-duty now.' I whisper, arching an eyebrow as we walk through the drawing room out to the lawn.

'One never knows.' He gives my arm a squeeze and I wonder if I am ever able to let my hair down, to be Joan Trewin. I don't know quite who she is or how I feel about her at the moment.

Mr Hoskine mixes Negronis, and I long to be in the heat of Italy suddenly, away from here and now. But looking at the view I can hardly complain about it. I grab a vivid drink and do what

I am known for . . . be the most outstanding hostess. As I kiss the powdered cheek of Lady Fox, I see Tom wink at me. A smile spreads across my face. It is his fault of course. All his fault that I was a society hostess, a Foreign Office wife and a mother. He brought Allan here in the first place.

I don't quite gulp the drink but dispatch it with more haste than is sensible. Tonight, I'm at least partially off-duty. The handover is complete and until I return to Moscow, I'm free to enjoy my break. As the gin makes its way into my system, my shoulders relax. I will have a good time tonight. My husband has shown he still wants me, and I still have a role to play that is more important than tonight's dinner. This matters to me even though no one else knows.

I grin and Ralf Venn catches my eye. He matches my expression and I taste the bitter kick of the Campari. His white dinner jacket glows in the evening light and the cut of it is perfection. I have not met many Americans who have their suits made in Jermyn Street. But we are not in the Caribbean and although the sun shines today, his choice marks him out. His wife is well dressed, too. Her strapless gown shows off her long limbs and hourglass figure. It is all a bit obvious and so not what appeals to Allan. I'm not sure why I'm concerned. Allan has always been attracted to the elegant and understated.

'You have no worry there.' Tom whispers in my ear.

'Just what I was thinking.' I sip the last of my drink.

'I know.'

I look up at him from under my lashes.

He glances down at my empty glass. I wrinkle my nose at him. The man knows me too well, unlike George Russell. He, unlike these other Americans, had the sense not to dress for a cruise ship in Cornwall.

'Where's your drink?' I ask, noticing Tom's hands in his pockets. 'Still pacing yourself?'

'Gin is not my friend.'

I laugh, remembering. 'True but I see there is whisky on the table.'

'I'll save myself for the wine with dinner.'

I cast him a sideways glance. He grins and wanders away to talk to Eddie Carew. Tom is all out of sorts but looks as cool as anything if you didn't know him. But I did.

'Joan, what a glorious evening for a party.' Anthea, who I went to finishing school in Switzerland with, walks over looking glamorous as ever. 'To think we were stuck inside last year.'

'Yes, and the roof began leaking we had so much rain.'

She chuckled. 'Gosh, I can still remember the hangover.'

I nod. The rain had stopped by two, the sky had cleared, and I'd ignored the roof, dancing as if my life had depended on it.

'Well on the way to this year's hangover.' She raises her glass. 'These are lethal but so delicious.'

'That's the point.' I hold up my empty glass. 'I seem to be in the need of a refill.'

'Me too.' We walk towards the house. 'We never learn, do we.'

I shake my head, but wonder are we destined to repeat the same mistakes, or does that only apply to alcohol? My mother had used drink to numb her life. Was that because it had been in her control or was she just a victim? I didn't want her to be a victim, but the other option wasn't any better. I, however, am in control of my life and as I hear the gong sound, I am reminded I am in charge of this evening and nothing is going to ruin it, not even the thought of a hangover tomorrow morning.

53

Diana

4 August 1962, 6.30 p.m.

Everyone except Mrs Hoskine and Mary, the daily help, were out in the garden. Diana had checked before she entered the kitchen to take a picture of the cake. It would go on the cover of the book she was making for Daddy. She pressed the shutter, flicked the switch at the front, then one on the back and pulled the sheet out. Her glance kept darting to the clock, watching the second hand until she could open the back and see if the picture had come out well. Flapping it as she'd seen Mr Venn do, she then took a close look. It was a success.

Mrs Hoskine handed Mary a plate of food to take outside. It had prawns in it and Diana hated them. They felt funny in her mouth. When Mrs Hoskine checked the oven, Diana grabbed a piece of bread and her picture of the cake.

Once up in her room she placed the photo on top of the chest of drawers and searched for paper and glue she'd brought up from the office in preparation. She carefully folded the unlined sheet in half and centred the photo on it before applying glue. While that set, she peered out of her window. Gribben Head baked in the sun. Below, everyone looked beautiful – especially

Mummy. Diana picked up her camera and leaned out the window and took a picture then went through the steps until she could take out the photo. With a quick glance to be sure it had worked, she left it by the first one then dashed back down the stairs. She would have to take the pictures quickly so that she could give the book to Daddy today as a surprise.

Before heading outside, she took a picture of the dining room table from where she could see Daddy's name on the place card. His seat looked right down the table out to the garden. Mummy had made the table look beautiful with all the flowers. The smell of the roses and the honeysuckle was wonderful. Tucking the picture into her pocket, she stood at the French windows, watching. Mummy was chatting to Mr Carew. Uncle Tom was speaking again to the man who arrived this afternoon. Diana had heard he was American. They turned to look out at the bay and Uncle Tom pointed at Gribben Head. The light was changing. The headland was bright one minute but then dull when a cloud covered the sun.

Daddy stood next to Lady Fox and Mrs Venn. They were talking about the weather. Diana smiled. Everyone talked about the weather, even in Moscow – except there it was normally about the snow and here about the rain. Mr Venn stood with his back to Daddy, taking a drink from Mr Hoskine's tray. She crept out onto the lawn and stood by a planter. From this angle she saw the side of Daddy as he smiled. She took that picture. He was enjoying his party.

As carefully as she could she slipped around to take a picture of Mummy. It was just as Uncle Tom and the American man joined her and Mr Carew. Diana pointed the camera and captured Mummy laughing with Uncle Tom on one side and the American on the other. Mr Carew had turned so Diana only had the back of his head.

Someone was playing the piano in the drawing room. Inside she found the vicar looking at the painting of a boat. She didn't want to take his picture, so she slipped back outside. From this angle at the curve of the house, she tried to include everyone in the photo with the bay in the background but it didn't work. She would need to try that from the windows in Mummy's room.

Daddy saw her and winked. Mr Venn frowned at her. Diana wondered if he was cross she was using the camera. She didn't know why she thought that, but she did. Before going upstairs, she went into the study and took two quick photos. One of Mummy looking across at Daddy and the other one of Daddy looking all serious and handsome while he spoke to Uncle Tom. From this vantage point no one realized she was here.

She sat still on the top of the desk just watching the way people moved when they spoke to each other. Many were having fun because there was a lot of laughter, but some, like the American man and the Venns, wore different expressions. She couldn't think what they meant but they weren't party ones like everyone else's. Mummy would be disappointed if people weren't having a good time.

She returned to her room to put all the photos together in the book. It didn't take her long to assemble it. The only thing missing was a picture of her. That would require someone else. She frowned. It couldn't be Daddy as that would spoil the surprise. Mummy would be too busy, as would Mrs Hoskine's. Maybe Uncle Tom could. He had looked like he knew about the camera this afternoon. She searched but couldn't see him. There was still time. She would find him later. Right now, she would report everything in her diary. But first she went to see what was happening. Her doll sat watching too. She twisted it open so the other dolls could enjoy the party.

Dear Diary

I'm looking out of my window and I can see Mummy chatting to her friend from finishing school. Mummy says I will go to university if I want to. She had wanted to but her father wouldn't let her. This made Mummy sad. She didn't say so but I could tell. Right now she looks so beautiful, more beautiful than anyone else. Daddy is talking to the Venns, Mr Venn is standing awfully close to Daddy and Mrs Venn has her hand on Daddy's arm. He doesn't look happy. He should be happy. It's his birthday party. Most people are laughing so that is good.

Down below I saw Uncle Tom walk back onto the lawn and again he is talking with the American. This one is staying at Boskenna. Both he and Uncle Tom are watching Mummy. I'm not surprised. She glitters like the diamonds around her neck. I want to be just like her when I'm older and I want a husband as handsome as Daddy.

The dinner gong sounds and people start moving inside. Mrs Hoskine said she will come and find me when it is nearly time for the cake, but I might go downstairs in a bit and sit hidden under the small table by the door to the dining room. It's my favourite hiding spot. Mrs Hoskine found me there earlier this week. She said I was growing so fast that by Christmas I'd be too big to fit there anymore.

She put the pencil down, put the diary away, and tiptoed downstairs.

54

Lottie

It was easy to forget the intervening years as Alex fell into step beside Lottie leaving his grandmother's house. The key difference was that her hand wasn't in his. The longing for what they had in the past hung in the air currents created by their swinging hands, caressing their fingers. It would be so easy to take his hand in hers, but she wouldn't. There could be no going back. Ten years and so much more stood between them. Besides, he might not be thinking these same things at all. It was most probably in her mind alone. A cool breeze blew up from the bay and she shivered despite the warmth of the evening sun.

Only a few cars remained in the car park and a family walked past them up the lane carrying baskets and blankets. She turned towards the sea. Alex hesitated. His hand brushed hers. Her breath caught. But one long stride gave her the distance she needed to keep a clear head.

'Why the visit to my grandmother?'

She turned to him. Here she was thinking about their past and he rightly was firmly in the present. 'I had a few questions.'

'Oh.' He raised an eyebrow.

'Nothing important.'

'Sure.' He continued walking by her side. 'Is your mother OK?'

She laughed. 'Good question. I don't think she is.'

'Do you know why?'

'I can make some guesses – like being here is painful – but it's all speculation.' She stared at him, debating whether to say what was puzzling her. 'Why is my grandfather relying on you and not me?'

'We've always been close since I worked for him.'

She remained silent.

'Well, he's been like a father.'

Lottie winced. She knew how much the loss of his own father had meant to him and how his grandmother had been grateful for Gramps' kindness and quiet guidance. Her question had been spiteful. 'Sorry.'

'George mentioned that when you last visited, there was a boyfriend in your life and he may have said that he monopolised you.' He took a step away.

'Did he?'

Alex nodded. 'So where is the boyfriend?'

'As I mentioned, he isn't my boyfriend any more.' She looked out to sea, suddenly thinking of Thailand.

'That will please George.'

She laughed. If he only knew. She longed to tell someone what an idiot she had been, but silence was best. No need to confirm what people thought of her already. She walked onto the sand and picked up a shell.

'Did my grandmother help?'

She walked to the water's edge. 'Yes, she confirmed that Gramps had been here that weekend my grandfather died.'

'So?' He shrugged. 'You're trying to play detective . . .'

'No but Gran said she killed someone.'

'I seriously doubt that she meant it literally.' He didn't look at Lottie when he said that but picked up a piece of sea glass and handed it to her.

It was vivid green-yellow like a peridot, but with the pitted finish of the tumbling sea. She rolled it between her thumb and forefingers before holding it up to the sky. 'Why do you doubt it?'

He laughed. 'I told you what I thought earlier.'

Frowning, she said, 'Yes, you did but people do kill people . . . all the time.' She bent to pick up a mussel shell and placed the glass where the animal would have been, picturing a pendant.

'Can't argue with that.' He began walking along the water's edge. She followed, studying his footprints in the sand. The angle of the sun casting shadows in the indents.

'Look, the more I think about it, I know Gran, she wouldn't say it unless it was true.' But why would she say anything at all? Whatever happened, happened a long time ago. Lottie stopped walking. Forgiveness.

'Has she always told the truth?' He threw a rock into the water.

She took a deep breath. 'No, I'm sure she didn't and it's clear Gran has lied to Mum about George, and that raises questions.' She was certain that the words in the diary were written because her mother was in pain and kids always think they are somehow at fault, be it divorce, a death or lack of a father, as in Lottie's own case. 'Why would she lie when she was dying?'

'Can't answer that.'

She glanced at her watch and turned towards the house. This wasn't important now. She wanted to be with Gran. 'See you later.' She marched to the steps and she didn't turn around when she heard Alex behind her. Out of breath when she reached the hallway, she stopped. Her mother was facing Gramps. Silence hung in the air. Lottie looked between the two of them.

'You killed my father.' Her mother glared at Gramps. The round table stood between them.

'Mum!'

'He was here that weekend,' she huffed. 'The police records show his statement.'

'How the hell did you get access to that on a weekend?' Alex asked, coming to stand beside Lottie.

She sent him one of her looks. Lottie knew her mother hadn't reached this point in her journalistic career without making contacts or by taking no for an answer. But she couldn't work miracles.

'Just because Gramps was here didn't mean he killed your father.'

'They lied.' Mum placed her clenched hand onto the table. 'My mother and George both lied.'

Lottie looked at Gramps, who wobbled while his cane remained steady.

'People lie all the time.' Alex stepped forward.

The telephone rang.

'Do something useful and answer it.' Her mother looked at Alex before taking another step towards Gramps. Lottie darted between them and placed a hand on her mother's arm.

'Let's go and sit like civilised people and speak calmly.' Lottie led them into the big drawing room where she could engineer more space between everyone. Did Lottie see sweat on her mother's brow?

Once she'd settled Gramps, who looked at her with worried eyes, she studied her mother again. She wouldn't sit and instead paced in front of the fireplace.

Alex walked in with the tea tray. 'I thought this might help.'

It was after six and gin would have been wonderful, but Alex was right. 'Thanks.'

'Was it one of those nuisance calls?' Gramps' voice was weak.

'Something like that.' Alex handed him a drink. 'It was Pat Treneer.'

George frowned, and her mother hopped to her feet.

'He'll call back later.' He placed the tray down on a side table.

'I would have spoken to him now.' Her mother blew air out through her pursed mouth. 'Someone came in to visit Pat just after I arrived at his house earlier.' She gave Alex a searching look before walking towards Lottie. 'Something isn't right about my father's death.'

Lottie looked away. Taking a deep breath, she schooled her features. She could do this – she looked at her mother.

'Has your grandmother said anything more to you?' Her mother took a step closer.

Lottie looked down thinking about Gran's words, then said, 'I think Gran has said everything she is going to say.'

'Yes,' her mother sighed, and her shoulders slumped.

'Now is the time to just be with Gran.' Lottie gave her a sympathetic look and Mum grabbed her hand and held it.

'Yes, you're right. I'll head up to her now.' She let go of Lottie's hand and Lottie watched her go before closing her eyes. She hadn't lied, she simply hadn't told her everything. Opening her eyes, she saw Alex helping Gramps to his feet. He gave her an encouraging smile. At least she had pleased someone.

55

Lottie

4 August 2018, 7.30 p.m.

'I've just had a chat with the nurse and she's just leaving. We're to call her if we need her.' Lottie stopped next to the record player. 'What was Gran's favourite?'

Gramps turned to her. 'Any song by Nat King Cole.'

'The nurse mentioned Gran can still hear so . . . ' Lottie swallowed a lump. 'I thought . . . '

'I'll bring it up.' Alex took the player and Lottie pulled out an old LP.

'You two go on ahead.'

'Can I help you, Gramps?'

He wiped his eyes. 'I just need a moment.'

Lottie looked back over her shoulder and her feet slowed on the stairs. She knew the time to say a final goodbye was near. Alex set the record player up on the dressing table and she gave him the LP. She went to the bed taking Gran's hand in hers, it was so cold. Lottie swallowed. 'Hello, Gran. We thought we'd bring some music up to you.'

The rich tones of Nat King Cole's voice filled the room with him singing 'Unforgettable'. Gramps arrived and Lottie stood. 'Shall I give you both some time alone?'

Gramps nodded, and Alex waited for her by the door. He took her hand as they walked downstairs and straight out into the garden. The music floated down through the open window and Alex pulled her into his arms and they danced. Being this close it was easy to stop thinking about Gran, her mother and what she knew. Resting her head on his shoulder, she could forget everything and just remember how good they had been together.

The song changed and the tempo was more upbeat. Alex picked up his pace but didn't let go of her. As they spun around, he whispered in her ear, 'You handled your mother well.'

'By avoiding her question.'

He nodded. 'It wouldn't help her.'

'I think you're right.' She tilted her head to the side and looked at him closely, loving the way the green in his eyes blended with the grey.

He pulled her closer as they turned. 'You don't sound certain.'

'The truth is important for her and not knowing it will eat at her.'

'Only if she finds out there's anything else to know.'

'She's good at finding things out.'

He chuckled. 'This is true but sadly I don't think your grandmother will be around for much longer so there is very little chance for her to discover anything.'

Lottie sighed. Her mother would go ballistic is she knew what Gran claimed to have done. As it was, Lottie wanted to know why Gran had killed . . . 'him'.

'You've gone all serious.'

'Just thinking.'

'This worries me.'

She shook her head. 'Don't be – after all, it's my family that's messed up.'

'True, but I do care.' He stopped dancing.

'Thank you.' She looked up at him and his glance met hers. Once he wouldn't have hesitated. He would have kissed her and that was exactly what she wanted this moment as his head lowered closer to hers. But she and Alex, as a couple, were history – so she stepped away. 'I'll just go and check on them.' She couldn't go back, and her future was solo like her mother. It was safer.

56

Joan

4 August 1962, 9.00 p.m.

Despite the gleaming silverware, the flickering candles, the laughter and the flowing wine, Allan isn't as relaxed as he should be at this point. The last of the dinner plates have been cleared. I glance at the door. No sign yet of Mrs Hoskine, Diana and the cake. I long to see Allan smile but there is a tightness around his mouth. He is swift to laugh but the sparkle isn't reaching his eyes. Tom, however, is arguing with Anthea to his left. He's enjoying the wine and my earlier worries proved wrong. He had spoken the truth about waiting for the wine. Is my ability to read people off? Maybe it is just the lack of sleep fogging my brain. At least the vicar is happy staring down Beth Venn's cleavage. My mouth twitches, fighting a smile.

'Happy birthday to you.' Diana's voice is high and slightly wobbly as she enters and holds the cake aloft, with Mrs Hoskine behind her. Everyone stands and joins in and the atmosphere lifts.

'Blow out the candles, Daddy, but don't forget to make a wish.'

Allan places his hands around Diana's to steady the cake and blows. All but one candle go out and Diana swiftly takes care of it. Allan kisses her then places the cake on the table for all to admire. Mrs Hoskine hands him the knife.

'Don't forget to make another wish, Daddy, and remember not to tell anyone.' Diana is intent, despite her smile. She is so serious, even about something so frivolous. Allan holds the knife poised above the cake. The matryoshka dolls look out on the guests from their world of snow-white royal icing. Allan pushes the knife through looking at me, eyes sparkling. I shiver.

Diana rushes into the kitchen but returns just as quickly with her hands tucked behind her back. I watch as she theatrically pulls out what appears to be a handmade book.

'I made this for you, Daddy. Happy birthday.' She goes on her tiptoes and he bends down so she can kiss him.

He grins. 'You made this?' He holds it up. 'How clever.'

Diana turns to looks at Ralf then Beth Venn. 'Thank you for the camera. I had so much fun with it.'

'You're welcome, darling.' Beth smiles and I don't like her at all.

Diana hides a frown under her hand, but I see it. Allan turns each page admiring the pictures, but his fingers still on one page in particular. No one else notices it while Mrs Hoskine and Mary serve the cake. He flips two more pages and I make a note to have a closer look later.

Over the table, Tom's glance meets mine and I walk up to Diana. 'What a talented chick you are.'

'She is wonderful.' Allan closes the book.

'Maybe Diana should take it up to her room so there's no chance of food getting on it.' I stroke Diana's shoulder.

'Good idea.' Allan looks up at me briefly then gives the book to Diana. She holds it under her arm and Mrs Hoskine hands her a plate of cake before bustling her back into the kitchen. Champagne corks pop and I jump, spilling a bit of the red wine in my glass. George makes eye contact from the other side of the table. He misses nothing. Allan laughs loudly at something Beth Venn says then knocks back a glass of champagne. I mop up the spilled wine with my napkin but there remains a tell-tale drop of red on my glove.

57

Lottie

4 August 2018, 9.05 p.m.

Dinner was ready and Lottie had no idea where her mother had gone. At the top of the garden, the gate to the path was ajar. The only sounds were the waves. Lottie reluctantly turned left and walked towards the watchtower. Her stomach tightened uncomfortably. This time ten years ago she was sitting at the dining room table and was already pretty drunk. This evening the footpath was deserted, but she could hear happy sounds coming up from the beach.

Lottie stood in the middle of the path knowing her mother was at the watchtower. She had to go there. Alex had said John wasn't her fault but at this moment, guilt weighed her feet down. A bat swooped low in front of her and she fell against the fence. Her heart raced as she looked through the brambles to the beach below.

In all her visits to Boskenna since 2008 she had never again stepped off the footpath and onto the headland. She crossed the invisible barrier now and in a few strides, she was beside the old concrete structure. The air was cool and she rubbed her bare arms. Her mother was perched on the steps leading up to the lookout platform.

'Hi.' Lottie whispered but her mother jumped any way.

Her mother turned away from the view. Her eyes were filled with tears. 'I remember.'

'You do?' Lottie took a step back, thinking of the diary tucked under her pillow.

'Not much. But I remember the body, my father on a rock.' She shook her head. 'From the path,' she pointed. 'It looked like he was sun bathing in his evening suit.' She took a gulp of air. 'I don't know if I want to remember more.'

'Oh, Mum.'

'But what bothers me is that he was on his back.' She took a breath. 'I have spent the past hour moving every which way trying to work it out but . . . but I think he would have fallen forward.'

'Oh.' Lottie walked near to the vegetation-covered fence. There had been a few landslips over the years, and when she had looked at the cliff from below, the grassy edge hung over the gentle concave indent of the cliff. Birds nested under the overhang. She'd noticed them that afternoon when she'd been on the beach with Alex. She peered down then took a step back.

'What if he staggered backwards?'

'I've been thinking about that, wishing I'd paid more attention in physics.'

Lottie laughed. 'You were no help with maths either.'

'True.' She stood and walked down the few steps. 'I'm sorry.'

Lottie tilted her head. 'What for?'

She stood a foot from Lottie. 'For being a shit mother.'

Lottie moved backwards. That was the last thing she expected. 'You weren't.'

She shook her head. 'I was.'

'You loved me.' Lottie looked away, trying to keep her voice steady.

'From a distance, I think I may have.' Her mother glanced over the edge of the cliff and shuddered. 'I let my mother raise you . . . which was wrong, as she didn't raise me very well – or at all, in truth.'

'I'm sorry you and Gran weren't close.' Lottie took her hand and she looked down at their fingers. Her mother's were long and elegant and Lottie's were short and workman like.

'Me too. Forgiveness came too late.'

'Oh, Mum.'

She locked her fingers with Lottie's. 'Forgive me.'

'Nothing to forgive.' Lottie echoed the words she'd said to her grandmother.

'There is. Both of us know it.'

Lottie looked down at their hands. 'Mum.'

'I'm sorry.'

She glanced up at her mother. 'I love you and forgive you.'

'Thank you.'

She kept hold of Lottie's hand. All Lottie could think about were the years she had longed for this moment. She was grateful that Gran had been around to hold her hand and listen.

'What are you thinking?'

She cast a quick glance at her mother, trying to read her mood. Should she dodge the question to keep the moment, or tell the truth and hope any anger would dissolve in the pink evening light?

'Grateful for you and for Gran.' Lottie held her breath, watching the emotions cross her mother's face.

'I'm glad I thanked her for loving you.'

That broke Lottie and the tears that she wouldn't let come before began. Her mother pulled Lottie into her arms and she cried more, trying to speak.

58

Lottie

Her mother had gone upstairs to see Gran and she didn't want to eat. Lottie walked through to the kitchen. Alex turned from the stove. 'Hello, did you find her?'

'Yes, but she's not hungry.'

'So you told her I was cooking?' His eyes gleamed, although he managed to keep a straight face otherwise.

He took the pot off the heat and walked over to her. 'I think George might need something.'

'Yes.' She closed her eyes for a moment.

'I'm just warming the soup.'

She noted that he'd laid the table for the four of them. 'After that shall we take a walk?' He placed a hand on her arm.

She stared at it as if she'd never seen it before. She swallowed. 'Not sure.' There was so much he didn't know. 'Shall I get Gramps?'

He nodded, and she walked away.

In the snug Gramps sat with a glass of whisky in his hand.

'Some soup?'

He shook his head. 'Haven't the appetite.'

She nodded. 'I'll let you off this time.' She held his hand and it was cold despite the warmth of the evening. She pulled the throw off the sofa and covered his legs.

'I'll be back shortly.'

'No rush,' he took a sip of his drink, 'I'm not going anywhere.'

She kissed him and went back to the kitchen, catching the scent of the roses in the vase on the hallway table.

Alex was about to pour the soup.

'Just the two of us.'

'Oh.'

The toast popped up and she grabbed it. It smelled good. It was something normal when nothing else felt the way it should. She put it in the toast rack and sat opposite Alex. Steam rose from the bowl and blurred his features.

'There was a picture of you in uniform at your grandmother's.'

He raised an eyebrow. 'I think that was the last thing I expected you to say.'

She smiled. 'Pleased I can still surprise you.'

He grinned. 'After uni, I joined the Navy and now I'm an IT geek.'

'But you'd never mentioned the Navy when we were together.' She raised an eyebrow.

'Ah, no it had never crossed my mind.'

She frowned.

'But I realized that you were right when you said I wasn't man enough or educated enough. I was going nowhere, and the Navy solved that.' He laughed. 'From a boy who'd only been to London twice, I suddenly saw the world.'

She pushed her hair back, regretting her words yet again. 'Did you enjoy it?'

'Yes, but Cornwall kept a hold of my heart.' He looked up at her and gave her one of those sexy half smiles of his.

'Living in Cornwall was always part of your plan.' She blew on her soup. She shouldn't have said that because she too had been part of his plan, their plan. She dared to look up and her breath caught when she saw the emotion in his eyes. He still cared for her. She swallowed. This wasn't good. She would just hurt him again and that was the last thing she wanted to do.

'So that's me, what about you? George mentioned a big show coming up.'

She buttered a piece of toast planning what to say without saying anything. 'I love what I do.'

'I always knew you would.'

She looked up. 'Really?'

'Yes. It was the way you were forever taking bits from the beach and put them together.' He smiled. 'You made that sea glass bracelet for my cousin Tegan for her birthday.'

'I'd forgotten about that until I saw her still wearing it this morning.'

'Everyone asks where she bought it.' Alex dunked a piece of his toast into the soup.

She pictured the mussel shell and the sea glass she'd seen this afternoon. That thought led to what she'd lost. She'd been so stupid. Pushing those thoughts aside, she cleared her throat. 'My grandfather, Allan Trewin . . . ' She looked down and then back up again.

'Why don't I think I'm going to like this line of conversation?' Alex smiled, and her heart melted a bit.

'He was a political attaché in Moscow.'

He passed her the butter dish. 'He was a spy.'

She looked up, eyes wide.

'It was at the height of the Cold War.' He handed her another piece of toast. 'But I'm sure that had nothing to do with his death. He was here in Cornwall not in Red Square.'

He had a point, she had to admit. 'Do you think my grandmother knew?'

'I would think so.'

'Oh.' She blew on the surface of her soup. It was still too hot to eat.

'But not much.' He stood and brought a jug of water to the table. 'If I were you, I'd forget what she said.'

'Why?'

'Because whatever she meant, it's in the past.'

This was true. She heard Gramps footsteps in the hallway. He had been in diplomatic service then too. Had he been a spy for the Americans? No, she couldn't see that at all. But thinking of Allan with his dashing looks, he fitted the movie star picture of a secret agent, which meant he had probably been too obvious.

59

Diana

4 August 1962, 9.50 p.m.

Back again, Diary.

*They are all eating cheese downstairs, yuck. I like seeing
the room all glowy with the tall candlesticks burning bright
and people laughing a lot. Mrs Hoskine says that the wine
might have something to do with the laughter. She saw me
scoot under the table again when she brought the silverbelle back into the kitchen, but no one else had. I loved
watching and trying to figure out who was bored because
Mummy said it happens a lot at dinner parties. Daddy was
chatting to Lady Fox but he was looking down the table.
He hadn't really liked his birthday cake. He frowned when
he first saw it. Maybe he didn't like the dolls on it, but then
he laughed. He did like his book though and he called me
a clever girl. Maybe we shouldn't have made the cake like
Moscow. Maybe we should have made seashells to put on
it, or sailboats like last year. Last year Daddy had been
happier but Mummy had sailed with us then.*

*They think I don't know Mummy lost a baby. I don't
know how she did, but she cried a lot about it and they*

fought. Daddy slammed doors and she cried more. But things have been better since we have come home.

Diana closed the diary and put it under her pillow. She pulled out her book. The band had begun downstairs so it was too noisy to sleep.

60

Lottie

The phone rang and Lottie dashed to the office.

'Hello, Boskenna.'

'Is that Diana Trewin?'

'No, I'm her daughter, Lottie.'

'This is Pat Treneer.'

'Mum was talking with you earlier.' She leaned on the desk.

'Yes, she was asking me what I remembered about Allan Trewin's death.'

'She mentioned it.' Outside in the garden she saw Alex chatting to Gramps but her mother was heading down the path to the beach.

'Is she there? It's just that I remembered something else.'

Lottie leaned forward to see if she could call out to her, but she had disappeared from sight. 'She's just gone for a walk in the garden. Can I take a message?'

'Well, I hadn't thought about the case in many years, you see.'

'I can imagine.'

Alex sat on the bench next to Gramps now. They appeared to be in a serious conversation.

'And I was angry at the time I handed over to CID and they didn't listen.'

'Oh.'

She stood straighter. 'But it was an accident.'

'Yes,' he said. 'But my gut told me all wasn't right.'

'Are you sure?' She turned from the view. She didn't want to hear this.

'I've seen enough poor souls that have accidently fallen off cliffs, but he didn't look like any of them.'

'It's a pretty steep cliff.' She thought about what was there now. Was it a straight drop or more of a slope then?

'It was dead straight, and I felt he should have been face down.' Her mother had been thinking the same thing earlier.

'But surely if he took a step backwards. . . ?' She closed her eyes wishing she hadn't heard what her grandmother had said.

'Then I don't think he would have landed where he did.'

'Oh, but that doesn't mean he was murdered, does it?' Her grandmother's words echoed in her mind as she turned around. Alex was pacing in front of Gramps outside now.

'There were other footprints there.' He coughed.

'I'm sure it was a popular place.' She looked at the framed pictures of her as a child on the desk.

'Yes and no . . . '

She took a deep breath.

'But that wasn't what I remembered.'

She frowned, looking at the shelves lining the north wall. So many books on camellias and gardening in general. 'What was it?'

'Jacob, the fisherman, said Mr Trewin was clutching a silk bow in his hands when he found him.'

'A tie?'

'No, like it came off a woman's dress.'

She went cold. 'What colour?'

'Like the blue of the sea on a perfect summer's day.'

'That's rather poetic,' She said, thinking of the beautiful aqua silk dress she'd seen in the closet.

'Well, that's how Jacob described it.'

'What happened to it?'

'It had disappeared by the time the body was taken from the beach.'

Lottie let that sink in and didn't like where her thoughts were heading. 'Was it ever found?'

'No and they had to dismiss it because Jacob couldn't be certain.' He coughed again. 'Now tell your mother what I remembered.'

'I will, but just one more question if you don't mind?'

'Of course.'

'Was my mother interviewed?' She ran her fingers over the battered leather on the desk top.

'Yes, yes she was. She was very distressed, poor thing.'

'Understandable. Thank you, Mr Treneer.'

She put the phone down then headed outside to Gramps and Alex. As she approached, they stopped talking. She slowed her steps waiting for them to resume but they didn't. 'Where's Mum gone?'

'She wanted a walk.'

'Really?' The sky was dark, and a few stars shone above.

'We were thinking of a cognac,' Alex stood.

'Gran loved it.' Lottie sat next to her grandfather.

'Yes.' Gramps half smiled.

'It doesn't feel real that we're losing her.' She took his hand in hers.

'I wish it wasn't happening.' His voice wavered. 'I always thought I would go first.'

'I'll grab some glasses and the bottle.' Alex said as he went towards the house.

'Gramps?'

'Yes?'

'Gran said something . . . odd today.'

He took a deep breath and his chest wheezed. 'My darling girl, she isn't very well, I don't think we can rely on her words any more.'

'I know but it was troubling her.'

He looked out to the sea. The half-moon hung low in the sky and nearby an owl called.

'Gramps, she said she . . . '

Alex returned. He placed the glasses and the bottle down on the teak side-table.

Gramps reached out and squeezed her hand. He whispered, 'Whatever she said, it doesn't matter.'

Alex handed her a glass and she inhaled the sweet yet burning scent as he sat down beside her. Gramps' hand shook has he held his glass aloft and looked to the bedroom window. The silhouette of the nurse moved about the room.

Lottie sighed, and Alex placed an arm around her shoulder. She leaned into him for a moment.

'Thank you both for your help.' Gramps took a sip.

Alex nodded and raised his glass. 'Thank you for believing in me.'

Lottie welled up and snuffled. This was all too much, and she searched the darkness looking for her mother. It would have been good to have her here with them.

61

Joan

4 August 1962, 10.15 p.m.

After cheese and port, I am surprised that any of us can move but the musicians are playing in the smoking room. A glance down at my stomach confirms my fears are unfounded. It isn't bulging. There is no sign of over-indulgence on show. I noticed the vicar's wife discretely burping into her napkin as she places it on the table. Allan walks past me, running his fingers along my upper arm. I shiver, watching him head out of the opened French windows into the garden, picking up a box of cigars. Several of the men of the party follow immediately, but I head to my bedroom to replace my gloves. I have another pair and if I rinse these now the stain will come out, but if I leave it until the morning, its shadow mark will be there always, ruining them. Then they would only be fit for Diana's dressing up box.

The light in the bathroom colours my skin sallow. Where has the healthy glow from the sun and the sea gone? Dark circles are highlighted, and I look older than my thirty years. Sighing, I turn the cold tap on, wet my glove and rub a bit of soap on the spot. Despite my diligent work, the stain doesn't want to lift. I shut the tap off and wring the gloves out. It will require bleach.

Locating the second pair, I bring the soiled ones downstairs via the far stairway. If I leave them by the sink in the kitchen, I will remember to deal with them tomorrow. Muffled footsteps sound on the path outside by the woodshed. I glance up to see someone in a pair of black trousers walking away. Dropping the gloves, I head to the back door and slip off my shoes. A squeak comes from the larder behind me. Diana is standing rigid, pressed against the counter. I put my finger to my lips, she nods, and I point up. She races off. Only then do I head out the back door. Something isn't right.

The faint scent of cigar smoke fills the air. The grass is already damp with dew as I walk on the edge of the path. I'm not sure what I'm looking for. But it didn't seem right that someone, or probably more than one person, had walked out of this door of the house. Most of my guests are standing on the lawn at the front or dancing in the smoking room.

It is said that curiosity killed the cat and I have no intention of getting killed but I am questioning and unsettled. I know why Diana was in the larder. She had chocolate all over her face but why was her face ashen under the mess? I should have asked what she'd seen, but sound carries and that would have alerted whoever it was to our presence. And I knew in my gut that I didn't want anyone to know that Diana had seen anything. As always, the fewer people who knew, the better.

My eyes adjust to the darkness and the small amount of light from the young moon helps me to pick my way through the garden. The sound of the footsteps continues along the top path and I catch sight of two shadows close together. I hide behind a tree, grateful I'm not wearing white unlike the dinner jacket on the American. He is one of the men, for I am certain now it is two men.

They turn and head to the gate that leads out onto the coastal path. I wait, listening but other than the scrape of the bolt on the gate, I hear nothing for they aren't talking. My heartbeat sounds loud in my ears, vying with the waves reaching the beach below. Once the gate is closed, I dash and try to see which direction they went. This is not normal behaviour. If this American wants to talk business, there is no need to slope off out the back door. My mouth dries. Trust your instincts, I tell myself because as of today, there is no one else I can trust.

On the footpath, I assume they would have turned to the beach. The sound of the sea would cover any voices. Yet as I pick my way down, I don't see the white jacket, so I retrace my steps and make my way to the old watchtower, keeping myself hidden. From the sounds I can tell what is happening and my stomach turns. The outline of Beth Venn's pale pink dress shimmers ten feet from me. She is watching, she must have been waiting here for them. A honey trap, but not as I'd expected it. I remain glued to the spot behind the trunk of a fir tree. Hoping that I am wrong, praying. But then I hear my husband's voice as he climaxes. I sink to the ground covering my mouth. My stomach threatens to revolt while my mind puts everything together. His role is hardly a secret but mine is. It has to stay that way.

First Ralf Venn leaves and walks towards the beach. Then Allan goes through the gate to the garden. Beth is last. The moonlight catches the metal object in her hand. My heart falls further. I hear another set of footsteps behind me. I run before I am seen.

62

Diana

4 August 1962, 10.20 p.m.

Diana shook as she crept upstairs. The music was loud so no one would hear her, but she might be seen. Her right hand was covered in chocolate up to her wrist. When she had seen Daddy, she had leaned back and her hand went to the bottom of the glass dish. Even now her stomach turned as she reached the bathroom in the hallway. At the sink she ran the tap, trying to get the chocolate off her fingers.

'I'll be down in a minute,' a woman's voice said. Diana turned the tap off and grabbed the hand towel, wiping her fingers and her face. Chocolate covered the white surface. It looked awful. She held it tight as she raced back to her room before she could be found out.

Closing her bedroom door, she leaned against it. Her heart beat so hard she could hardly breathe. Her head felt wrong, all swimmy. Tucking the hand towel into her dirty clothes pile, she tried to hide it. But the stained white kept peering out at her.

She turned out her bedside light and walked to the window. Below, light from the rooms fell onto the garden. The noise was loud but the sound of her heart beat was louder still. What had she seen? Where was Mummy? What would she do? She rested her head on the glass and turned her dolls around. She didn't want them to see what was outside.

Daddy had kissed Mr Venn. Or maybe it happened the other way. Where had they gone? What would Mummy do? She didn't know what to think but her tummy didn't feel good. She crawled into bed and her head hit her diary.

Pulling it out, she decided to report what had happened. Opening the pages, her fingers left marks. They showed her guilt. She shouldn't have gone downstairs for more silverbelle. She'd been greedy. Gluttony was one of the seven deadly sins. Her stomach rolled like she was going to be sick. If she hadn't been greedy then she wouldn't have seen anything. Her head began to hurt. She was confused.

Dear Diary,

I'm sorry my fingers are leaving chocolate prints on the pages as I write. I was in the larder when I heard Daddy's voice in the kitchen. He was talking to someone. Talking about being quiet. I leaned against the shelves because I knew I shouldn't be up. The party was noisy and I couldn't sleep and my tummy growled. Daddy and Mr Venn stood by the back door. Daddy looked around and even in the larder. I held my breath waiting to be scolded or maybe just told to go to bed.

But he hadn't seen me. He opened the door then he took the man's hand. The man leaned forward and kissed Daddy. Daddy didn't pull away but looked around again. It didn't make sense. Daddy only kisses Mummy and me. He might kiss his godmother's cheek but that is all.

Diary, I pushed back further, sticking my hand in the silverbelle, trying to become invisible. I don't know what was happening but I'm afraid. I feel sick in the tummy. Why was Daddy holding the American's hand and letting him kiss him? What will Mummy do when she finds them? Diary, I'm scared.

63

Joan

4 August 1962 10.40 p.m.

I slip into Diana's room and as I suspect she is reading under her blanket. I pray she hasn't witnessed anything. She loves Allan. She is too young to understand. How can I explain?

'Hello darling, are you all right?'

I push her hair off her face and she looks so sad. I know then what she may have seen.

'Tell me what's wrong.'

She crunches up her nose. 'Nothing, Mummy.'

I sit down on the side of her bed and she looks at the book in her hands, *To Kill a Mockingbird*.

'How was the second or was it the third serving of the silverbelle?'

She smiles but her eyes don't. 'It was yummy.' She rubs her stomach.

'Was it?' I watch her swallow and her thinking is almost visible.

'Well . . . my tummy hurts right now.'

'I see.'

'Mummy?' She looks at me and her confusion is apparent.

'Yes.'

'Why would Daddy hold Mr Venn's hand?' She frowns. 'He's not blind. He can walk without help.'

I swallow. 'Maybe he stumbled, darling.'

My poor child has been here trying to make sense of it. But there is no sense in it. The most important thing is that she hasn't told anyone. Maybe I can contain this.

'But he didn't, Mummy.'

I took a deep breath. If Allan were here now, I would strangle him. But if he saw his beloved Diana right at this moment with her face ashen, her brow creased, and her rosebud mouth chewed I wouldn't have to. He would kill himself. 'I don't know then, darling. Just don't think about it. Put it from your mind and never tell anyone what you saw.'

Her eyes are wide open. 'You mean lie?'

I take a deep breath. 'You know how I ask you not to repeat things you might hear or see to anyone when we are in Moscow?'

She nods.

'This is the same.'

'But Mummy what was Daddy doing?' She gulps. 'When they stepped outside, Mr Venn kissed Daddy.'

'Darling, I'm sure they were whispering.'

Her little face is serious, and I can see her replaying what she saw in her mind. She must forget it, or I must convince her she saw something else entirely. But first I need to know everything. 'Did they see you?'

'No.' She shakes her head.

That is something I can be grateful for at least. 'Just forget all about it and I'll talk to Daddy. There's nothing for you to worry about. Try and get to sleep.'

She nods. 'Can I read a few more pages?'

I kiss her cheek. 'Yes, just five though.'

She snuggles down into the bed and pulls the blanket up over her head. I stand, walk to the window and pull the curtains closed. Below, my guests are drinking, dancing and smoking. My husband stands clutching a cognac in his hands seemingly unaware of the damage he has done. I have only one thought and that is to talk to Tom. But today has taught me one thing. I am truly alone.

64

Joan

4 August 1962, 11.30 p.m.

Eddie Carew is playing the piano and George Russell sits on the fire fender, his foot tapping to the Cole Porter tune. I study his shoes. But as with anyone who has been in the garden, they are damp on the bottom and have bits of grass stuck to them. I don't know why I feel he could have been out there too, but I do. His glance meets mine and I turn away.

Tom is dancing with the vicar's wife and I watch Allan pour another brandy. The Venns are nowhere in sight in the drawing room, the smoking room or on the lawn. However, the house is big and the garden bigger. I run through all I know about them and it's not much. They are not a couple from the Midwest of America who like to swing, but something far more sinister.

I leave the drawing room and stick my head into the small kitchen. It is spotless with things ready for breakfast tomorrow. The lights in the keeper's cottage are off. Hopefully the Hoskines are sound asleep and haven't witnessed any unusual activity. The dining room is deserted so I head again to the smoking room. Lord and Lady Fox are dancing and the Vicar is availing himself of the drinks tray. Stepping out through the French windows, I begin a head-count. Most of the guests are staying over but the Venns aren't.

'As always a fabulous celebration.' Anthea yawns. 'I'm going to call it a night.' She kisses my cheek. 'If you see my husband, tell him where to find me.'

I chuckle. 'Not expecting him to wander into someone else's room, are you?'

'Not after the quantity of wine and the other delights he's consumed.' She waves. 'No one would want him. Believe me.' She walks through the dining room and I lose sight of her. I know that Anthea's husband, Rupert, has wandered in the past, and Anthea has as well. It doesn't matter to them, and in my heart, I could dismiss Allan's wandering if we were normal – but we aren't normal.

By the time I reach the drawing room via the garden I have a head-count of seventeen. No sign of the Venns. Allan is by the piano, singing. I take a deep breath, grab a glass and pour myself a single malt.

'That sort of night?' Tom asks as he walks up to me.

'Yes.'

He stares at me. 'You look a bit peaky,'

I smile. 'The whisky will help.'

'If you think so.' He raises an eyebrow.

I glance down at his shoes. Could he have been out there? Old habits die hard.

'A good night's sleep might be better.' He looks pointedly at the generous measure I have poured.

'Indeed, my friend, but you know I will not disappear until all my guests have.'

'Not much hope of that for a while.' He smiles.

'Thus far I seem to be down three.'

He scans the room. 'Doing your sheepdog impression?'

'Of course.' I turn to him and kiss his cheek. 'You haven't seen the Venns, by any chance?'

'As it happens, I noticed them setting off in their tender about twenty minutes ago.'

'Hmm.' I raise my glass to my lips. Their deed done, no need for the politeness of saying goodnight to your hostess.

'Not a wise thing to do without running lights and knowledge of the waters.'

'Somehow, I think they'll make it.' But in my heart, I wish them dead.

'You don't sound pleased.'

I smile and move on. It would be so easy to confide in Tom but I mustn't. Allan slips away from the piano and I walk across the room to see where he is heading. From the bottom of the stairs I watch him enter Diana's room. I hope she'll be asleep by now. But no matter what he may be or may have done he has always been brilliant at convincing her to close her eyes and dream.

65

Diana

Diana's stomach hurt worse than earlier. She shouldn't have eaten the chocolate. She shouldn't have gone downstairs. If she hadn't gone, she wouldn't have seen Daddy.

She walked to the bathroom to get a glass of water. But when she arrived her stomach turned over and she threw up. Shaking and scared, she sat down on the floor waiting to see if it was going to happen again. She wanted Mummy, but she knew Mummy was with her guests.

Blowing her nose, she rinsed her mouth and tried to stop shivering. It wouldn't stop so she went back to bed and rocked herself. She was still rocking when Daddy came into her room. He stopped at the chest of drawers and looked at his birthday book. Diana tried to speak but her tummy was rolling again. He stayed there a long time staring at one page.

'Daddy.'

He turned, and a smile spread across his face. 'My Diana, what on earth are you doing awake. What's wrong?' He walked to the bed and she slid over to make room for him. He pushed her hair off her face. 'Are you OK?'

Diana nodded. 'I was sick.'

'Too much chocolate?' He touched her chin.

She nodded and looked away. Had he seen her there?

'Did you ever finish your piano practice today?'

Diana frowned. 'No.'

'What's Madame Roscova like?'

She smiled. 'She's lovely but . . . '

'But what?'

'Tough.'

'How so?' he asked.

'She knows when I haven't practised enough.'

'Does she talk to you much?'

'Yes, but I don't say much, like Mummy told me.' She shook her head.

'I'm sure you don't.' He picked up her hand. 'Do you like her?'

'Oh, yes. She's lovely and she always smells nice, like flowers.'

He laughed. 'Is there anything particular she's interested in?'

She closed her eyes for a moment. 'About Salome and where we take her for walks and she sometimes asks when you've been away.' She wrinkled her nose. 'She's not like the art teacher who asks me all sorts of questions.' She flexed her fingers. 'But she always talks to me when I'm trying to put my fingers in the right position.'

He went quiet and he said so softly she could barely hear him, 'They knew but they turned me anyway . . . I'm as good as dead already.'

'What Daddy? Who is dead?'

'No one, my angel.' He tickled her then took his hankie and cleaned her face. 'You don't keep secrets from me, do you?'

She shook her head. 'Never.'

'I love you.'

'I love you, Daddy.' She gripped the blanket tightly. 'You love Mummy, too?'

He frowned. 'I love Mummy, too.'

'That's good.' She released the blanket.

'You're not to worry about anything, little one.'

'I won't.'

'You'd tell me if you were?'

She pushed her hair back. 'I'm sorry I went into the larder. I shouldn't have.' She nodded and looked away. Mummy had said to tell no one what she saw but that wouldn't mean Daddy.

'Ah.' He glanced at the chest of drawers. 'You haven't told anyone have you?'

She shook her head and closed her eyes, thinking of Mummy. 'No.'

'Good.' He kissed her cheek. 'Nothing to concern yourself with. Just forget it.'

She nodded vigorously. That was a word she liked. Daddy had taught it to her. 'I will.'

'Good.'

'Will you tell me a story?'

He smiled. 'Which one?'

'The little princess.'

'I will if you close your eyes and relax.'

She snuggled down in the bed and looked up at him. His eyes were shining, and she reached out and touched his hand. He looked sad.

'Eyes closed,' he said.

'Yes, Daddy.'

'Once upon a time in a castle far away lived a little princess

299

who was so loved by her parents that she glowed with happiness. She and her little dog Salome ran through the kingdom bringing joy wherever she went . . . '

Diana listened, not hearing the words any more just Daddy's voice telling her he loved her. Everything would be fine.

THE CAUSEWAY

66

Lottie

Alex helped Gramps up to bed. Lottie had suggested earlier on he might want to use a different room, but he refused. He wanted to be with Gran while he could. She could understand that.

She looked for her mother, but she hadn't returned from her walk and she'd been gone for ages. As Alex came downstairs, Lottie was pulling out the big old torch.

'Problem?'

'No, Mum's not back so I'm off to have a look.'

'Want company?'

She paused. It would be good, but her mother might not feel that way. 'Thanks, but no.'

He smiled. 'You know where to find me if you need me.' He stopped at the kitchen door. 'George was almost asleep before he lay down.'

She walked towards him. 'Although he knows – well, we all know – what is coming, it knocks you off your feet. Thanks for all the help.' She stood on tiptoes, balanced herself with a hand on his chest. His heart beat beneath her fingers. She kissed his cheek.

He put his fingers on hers for a moment. 'No problem.' He dropped his hand and stepped away, closing the door behind him. She walked out of the open French windows in the drawing room. The sound of the sea and the cry of an owl filled the air. It was mournful, but Gran had loved listening to them and Lottie wondered if that was her way of saying she was on her way.

No, that was too fanciful for Gran. Lottie laughed and cut across the dew-covered grass and onto the gravel path. Her mother must be in one of two places. Lottie heard the voices of some teenagers coming from the beach, so she would try the watchtower first.

The darkness grew the further up the long path she went, and she switched on the torch. The beam of light picked out the way and she recalled taking this path so often with Gran. On one particular evening stroll Lottie had asked her about Allan. Lottie must have seen his grave that day. Gran had spoken about him with such love. 'He made me laugh and he could win anyone over to his point of view. Your mother adored him and so did I.'

'Is that why you didn't remarry for so long? You loved him too much?'

She'd taken Lottie's hand in hers. 'Yes. Love that big is hard to match.'

'But you love Gramps?'

'I do.' She smiled.

'He loves you.' Lottie giggled. 'He tells you with flowers all the time.'

'That he does.'

'It's like a secret code.' She skipped a few steps ahead and turned to Gran

'Indeed.' She laughed.

'Do you think I'll ever find someone who loves me like Gramps loves you?' Lottie asked.

Gran bent down so she could look her in the eyes. 'I know you will because you have a huge heart.'

'But why doesn't Mum have someone loving her, aside from me and you?'

'Ah, I think . . . I think she might be afraid of love, or maybe she is complete without another.'

'Oh.'

Lottie had looked at her elegant grandmother and wondered what being complete meant. Now as Lottie reached the gate that led out onto the path, the smell of the pine needles beneath her feet scented the air. The ground was so dry. She couldn't remember a summer so hot. Never had she so looked forward to rain and never had she felt less like going to the watchtower. Earlier it had been bad enough. Somehow it was different in daylight but in the darkness her skin prickled, and her feet slowed.

She wasn't alone. Whispered voices and the sound of feet filled the air. She suppressed the desire to scream. She fled to the watchtower, switched off her torch and stood still, waiting for whoever it was to pass. But the footsteps came closer. A beam of light showed their progress. Lottie pressed herself against the concrete support holding the platform above her.

'Are you sure this is the way, Robert?' the woman's voice was soft and well spoken.

'It looks different at night but yes.' He cleared his throat. 'Take my arm.'

'I know I thought it was a good idea to come here at the hour of his death. To . . . to let go finally, but . . . ' Her voiced trailed away and Lottie's heart sank. John's parents.

'What time do you make it?' he asked, and they walked right by Lottie.

'About quarter past, I should think.'

She watched the beam of their torch move further out onto the headland and she followed. They were making a pilgrimage and she shouldn't be a part of it. But she had to face her role in it. He had been their only child.

She stopped on the path, listening to the sounds of the night. Something moved in the undergrowth as John's parents made their way out to the point. The backbeat of the music from the beach shook the still air. Lottie peered into the darkness below, looking to see lit cigarettes or phone screens but all was dark.

'Hey you.'

Lottie spun around, heart thumping, but she realized it was from the beach, forgetting how sound carries around here. She knew this small headland like the back of her hand having used it as her personal playground for years. John hadn't.

Now his parents had reached the bench and the light from their torch caught the bouquet of garden flowers his mother held.

'Robert, I can't do this. I can't let go.'

'We can. It's what he'd want.'

'But . . . '

Lottie stood by a tree. She shouldn't be witnessing this. It was wrong. That night ten years ago, the music was all Groove Armada, who were headlining at the festival in a few days' time. She didn't recognize the music coming up from the beach now.

'Be careful up there,' a voice from below shouted.

'Yeah, we don't need our night ruined.' Laughter followed the reply and she could smell their weed.

'OK, I can do this.'

Lottie saw them hold hands and walk a bit further towards the edge. Her heart in her mouth, she prayed they weren't about to do something reckless.

'That's done.' Their torch shone in her direction.

The woman wasn't carrying the flowers anymore. 'We won't stop missing him,' she said.

He cleared his throat. 'No, but we don't need to come back here again.'

A branch snapped as Lottie stepped on it. She flinched.

'Who is there?' he asked.

Lottie watched John's mother move closer to his father.

'Sorry.' She stepped into the path of their torch and they walked right up to her.

'You're Lottie Trewin,' his mother said.

'Yes.' Lottie rubbed her arms feeling the wind rising.

'You came too.' His mother held out her hand and Lottie took it. 'These years had to be hard on you, too.'

Lottie swallowed. 'Yes, but not as hard as for you.'

'Thank you.' She squeezed Lottie's fingers gently. 'It's time we all kept John in our hearts and moved forward.'

'Yes, he'd want that.' John's father's voice faded away.

'I know.' Lottie managed to say.

'He'd want all of us to live, to laugh and to love.' His mother paused. 'We must do that.'

'Are you heading back?' his father asked.

Lottie shook her head. 'Not just yet.'

'Take care of yourself and be careful.' John's mother took a deep breath. She leaned forward and kissed Lottie. 'Embrace life.' She snuffled. 'It's what I'm going to try to do again.'

'Yes.' Lottie managed to reply. Living was hard. She watched the light of their torch until it disappeared. She was alone. Her mother wasn't here, and Lottie doubted she was on the beach with the teens. She knew today had been tough on her. To finally find some peace with Gran and to know the end was so close. Lottie began to make her way off the headland when suddenly she remembered her mother's diary. Her mother had to try and understand so much as a small child, like her father's homosexuality, but it was the diary's final words that haunted Lottie.

Daddy is dead. It's my fault.

Was it like Lottie feeling responsible for John's death? Or had her mother played a role in her father's death and if she had, did it matter? Whatever happened, her mother had her ghosts and Lottie had hers and so had Gran.

67

Lottie

5 August 2018, 12.45 a.m.

Everything ached, including her head, when she reached the house. She went around locking doors and windows but left the back door by the larder unlocked in case her mother was still out, but it was now almost one in the morning and she hadn't seen her. She was probably sound asleep in bed, which was where Lottie should be. Stifling a yawn, she climbed the far staircase. She would check on her grandparents before she called it a night. Tomorrow, or more correctly today, could prove to be a long day. She needed to make a proper list of all the things that needed to be done on Monday.

When she reached the landing, she saw her mother in the hallway taking everything out of the closet once more.

'There you are.' Lottie walked up to her.

Her mother looked up with a haunted expression. 'They are all so beautiful.'

Lottie nodded. Her mother had taken each dress out of their garment bags and unboxed all the shoes. There were only a few things left hanging. Seeing all the clothes Lottie thought of her earlier conversation with Pat Treneer. She looked for the sea-blue dress he had described. Was it the one she had seen on Friday?

'It was such a different age.' Stroking a pillbox hat, her mother sat on the floor.

'Jackie O.'

'Yes, when she was the first lady and white gloves were *de rigueur*.' She picked up a pair of long calfskin gloves.

'Do you remember?' Lottie knelt beside her.

'Flashes of things and jewels.'

'Jewels?' Lottie raised her eyebrows. Gran wore pearls but nothing else that she recalled.

'Diamonds.'

'I've never seen any other than her rings.'

'Diamonds were only to be worn after five.' Her mother chuckled.

'Where did that come from?'

Her mother shrugged. 'Somewhere. I wish I knew,' she smiled. She stroked the silk of the dress in front of her. 'Maybe . . . Lady Fox?'

'Who?' Lottie froze. She'd read that name in the diary. Her mother was beginning to remember more.

Frowning, her mother said, 'My great aunt, possibly.' She shrugged. 'My mother had beautiful jewellery.' She closed her eyes. 'Even some Russian ones.' Her hand went to her neck. 'There was an enamelled locket and other pieces.' She opened her eyes and dropped her hand. 'I wonder what she did with them.'

'Maybe she sold them.' Lottie frowned.

'I guess money was tight.' She waved her hand. 'She rented out Boskenna and went back to work.'

'We could ask her about them.'

'Sadly, I think that possibility has passed.' Her mother yawned.

Lottie nodded with a heavy heart. 'Why don't we leave these

here and go through them tomorrow when we've had some sleep?' She stood as the longcase clock downstairs chimed the hour.

'Yes.' Her mother rose and rubbed her back. 'It's strange. Here I am trying to piece together my mother or maybe my childhood through things.' She picked up a silk scarf and let it slip through her fingers. 'I'm not sure how it will help, though.' She turned towards her room. 'Night.'

Lottie smiled. 'Night, Mum. I'm just going to check on them.'

'OK, get some sleep and . . . thanks.' She smiled then disappeared around the corner of the hall.

Before she reached her grandparent's room, Lottie could hear his snoring. At least Gramps would be rested in the morning. As tired as she was, her brain was running around like a puppy chasing its tail. She wished her body had that energy.

She leaned on the balustrade. Would hot chocolate help? Her mind kept thinking of Gran's words, her mother's diary and Pat Treneer's conviction that Allan hadn't just fallen. She walked back to where Gran's clothes were laid out. Turning on the nearby bathroom light, she went through the dresses and gowns on the floor. No sea-blue ones and none missing bows. Taking a deep breath, she checked the remaining garment bags. The first two were more silk and cotton shift dresses but the final one tucked in the far reaches of the closet was an evening gown she'd seen yesterday. Even in the dim light the silk shimmered like the sea.

Pulling it out, she carried the garment bag into the bathroom and closed the door. Laying it on the floor, she freed it from the bag. The zip was on the side and a thin band ran under the bust. She swallowed as she turned the dress around. There was no bow but maybe there had never been one. The light from the single bulb above was dim. She lifted the dress watching the colours of it shimmer. It was exactly as Jacob had described it to Pat. Gran must have been stunning in this.

She pulled the wooden chair from the corner of the room under the ceiling light. It groaned as she stood on it, clutching the dress. Beginning at the back she turned it over studying the band. If the bow had been on the back Allan could have grabbed it as he fell. But the were no threads or even needle marks. She slowed her breathing and moved her fingers around praying she wouldn't see what she knew she would. At first, she thought it was all fine. No threads were visible but when she held the fabric up to her face there was a tear that had been carefully mended. Her heart sank.

Once she had the dress back in the bag and hung in the exact place it had been, she went down into the small kitchen and put milk on to heat. If she hadn't spoken with Pat she probably could have let go of her grandmother's words, like Alex suggested. But she couldn't un-know, un-see, or un-hear. Her grandmother had killed her grandfather. Gran had said she had no choice, but Lottie knew there was always a choice. Murder was never right. She made cocoa and sat with her head in her hands. Gran had murdered her husband. Those words kept running through her brain. She told herself it didn't matter. Gran was dying. But she knew it did.

68

Joan

5 August 1962, 3.30 a.m.

The hall clock chimes and I watch Allan light a cigar in front of the French windows. He doesn't see me as he grabs the half-empty bottle of cognac and staggers up the garden. I switch a few lights off and make sure my guests are in bed. Once I'm sure the house is clear, I change into my plimsoles and set off to the watchtower. It is his favourite spot for an end-of-party smoke. And if he hasn't gone that way, I would know far quicker than if he has opted for the beach.

The bottom of my dress is soaked from the dew as I creep through the shrubs and trees, making sure I can't be seen from any of the windows. Once I am far enough from the house I return to the path. The moon is gone and the darkness complete. Instinct and the smell of the cigar smoke guide me.

I pause, taking in the peace of the early morning. The sound of the sea is gentle, almost whispering while my heart is hammering. I roll my shoulders to release the tension.

'Hello.' I say holding myself straight. Only the burning tip of his cigar was visible.

'Darling.' He slurs.

'Really?' I can't keep the irony from my voice

'Always.'

I freeze, wanting to see his expression, but it is too dark. Only the angry burning edges of the rolled tobacco glows as he puffs. I sniff. It is not his usual. Cuban I would guess. No doubt from the Venns. 'Why?'

'I've asked myself that question too many times.' He snorted. 'I suppose you have, too.'

I nod but know that he can't see me. 'Yes.'

'What gave me away?'

'Many things.' I clasp my shaking hands together in front of me. This ladylike pose is somehow comforting.

'I was careful.' He sits on a step.

'I'm sure, but they had you tightly.'

'Unfortunately, yes.' He tapped the ashes from the cigar. My glance follows its burning trail.

'How much have you leaked?'

'Nothing important.' He inhales deeply.

'I doubt that.'

His laugh is bitter. Self-hate emanates from the sound. I fight the urge to comfort him. It has gone beyond that now. 'Tell me.'

'Nothing can be done.'

'Something can be done.' I take a step closer, wanting to make this better.

'No.'

I shift my weight onto my left foot, thinking. 'You betrayed Tom.'

Silence.

'Allan.'

'Well, yes,' he pauses, 'you see they needed something big

or I was done, and it would affect you.' He drops his cigar and grinds it out. 'You see it was you, or Tom.' He laughs. 'It always has been.'

I stand still. Me or Tom. I'm not blown. Relief floods in but then I know the pressure will build. It would never be enough. Tom and the operation wouldn't be enough. He would have to give more. That's the way it worked.

'So you blew Tom and which operation?'

'Vauxhall.'

'Not me?' I step back.

'How could I? Think of Diana.'

'You only chose Tom because of Diana?' My mouth dries. The truth is never easy. I squint through the darkness. I would choose Diana over him, but I would also have chosen Tom over him.

'Darling, he was my first love but she, she is everything.' He fumbles in his jacket, finding his cigarette case.

I swallow.

'She saw you.'

'I know.' He lights a cigarette then grabs the bottle of cognac from the concrete steps of the watchtower and takes a slug. 'I asked her what was wrong. She wouldn't say at first but then it came spilling out.' He laughs madly. 'Poor mite didn't understand. I asked her if she'd told you. She lied.' He took a swig. 'Not that it matters now.'

'What do you mean?'

'Nothing.'

'Allan?' The clunk of the bottle against the concrete startles me. I jump. I need to control my emotions.

'It will all become apparent soon enough.'

I grit my teeth. 'That's not an answer.'

'No. But it will have to do.' He stands.

'No, it won't. I need to know.'

'In this world that rarely applies. You don't need to know.'

'What have you done?'

He sways. 'More than Tom?'

'Yes.'

'It's only Tom that matters and I've probably saved him.'

'When did they turn you?' I stand my ground as he moves closer. I have been the drop for a year and a half. How much did Allan known about what Victor has been giving us? How much has Tom shared?

'You remember the trip to Budapest?'

'Yes.' I nod, thinking that he was not himself when he returned but I'd just had a miscarriage before he'd left.

'Then.'

'Are you that weak?'

'Or are you just not enough?' He paused. 'I could never have what I wanted so everything was always a substitute, even you.' He took a drag of his cigarette. 'But you knew that, and you gave me the one thing I hadn't known I longed for.'

'Diana.'

'You love me, you need me.' The bright end of his cigarette made circles in the air. 'What does it matter if I'm a double agent?'

All I can focus on is him putting Diana at risk. He is the weak link and Tom has known this for years, as have I. Not that I want to admit it to myself, but between the two of us we have covered for him.

'Come on, Joan. Our little game doesn't matter in the big picture.'

But I know it does. Victor is worth protecting. I owe a duty to my country but more importantly, I love Diana.

'I know you think you are helping with Victor but he's not giving you anything they don't want you to know.'

I press my lips together as he takes another swig and staggers towards me. 'Tell me his real name, Joan, and we will be free.'

I back away. 'No.'

'Come on, Joanie. It's nothing.' His cognac breath covers me. But I know it is everything. They don't know Victor's name or aren't sure. This operation could be saved.

'It's all blown. All of it.' He moves closer. I step back again.

'Don't do this, Allan.'

He throws his head back and chuckles. 'It's too late, my lovely one. Too late. I'm done.' He tips the bottle up and downs the last dregs. 'You're done too, my clever one.'

'No.'

'Don't be all mightier than thou on me. I know you love Tom more than me, but in the way of irony he loves us both . . . as friends.' He shakes his head and I see his teeth. 'Neither of us could have our way with him, though God knows we both tried, until we fell into each other's arms as compensation.'

'Don't do this.'

'Don't do what? Puncture our love?' He drops the bottle. 'The sad thing is, I do love you.'

'I love you, too.' I sigh, knowing it is the truth.

'I know, silly woman, I know.' His words slur more and more. 'But that doesn't matter right now. What I need is the actual name of Victor.' He stepped closer. 'And you, my love, can get it for me.'

'How can you ask me that?'

'Because I need to.' Two steps bring him to me. I can't move back any further. Despite the darkness, I know we are on the edge of the cliff. The sea sounds below as it sucks the water away from the beach.

I need to think clearly. 'What are they threatening you with?'

'What is my one weakness?'

I gasp. 'Diana.'

'Yes. So, tell me and they will leave us alone.'

My chest is tight, and I can hardly breathe. 'I can't believe you would do this to us.'

'Our beautiful girl is the one who led them to us.'

'No.' I shake my head.

'The piano teacher.'

My stomach turns, accepting the truth of this. 'But you are the one who betrayed us.'

'You know me.'

I can't deny that. But now because Allan couldn't keep it in his trousers, he is risking Diana.

'Don't go all "God and country" on me, Joan.'

But he is right. I am left with only one choice. 'Don't ask me to do this.'

'You'd choose Queen and country over Diana.'

I step closer to him. The smell of cognac was intoxicating. I kiss him.

'See, women are ruled by their feelings.'

'True.' My lips hover over his.

'Love binds you.'

'It does.' I place my hands on his arms and he leans in

towards me. He is so drunk. As I kiss him again, I brace myself, moving one leg back then I whisper, 'I love you.' And push him over the edge. I feel a slight pull at my heart as his hands reach for me, but I step back. He doesn't make a sound, but his body does when it hits the rocks below. A deep and cracking thump.

69

Joan

5 August 1962, 4.00 a.m.

'If you hadn't done it, I would have.' George steps out from behind the watchtower.

I jump, and he grabs me and pulls me close. I shake until my teeth chatter. They will not stop.

'It's a shame he finished the cognac, you could use some.' His American twang pounds in my ears, but I know he is whispering.

'Diana.' I stutter.

'She'll be fine.'

'How . . . how can you be sure?'

'I promise.'

He holds me close and I try not to think but it doesn't work. 'How?'

'It's simple.'

I rock my head back and forth. Nothing will ever be simple again.

'It is.' He holds me away from him with a hand on each arm, gentle but firm keeping me standing. 'Listen. Everyone saw how drunk Allan was. It will look like he stumbled off the cliff.'

I glance over my shoulder. Somewhere below Allan is on the rocks.

'No one knows you are here except for me, right?'

I nod. 'No one. I made cer—certain.' My teeth chatter. My hand flies to my mouth forcing him to let go.

'What's wrong?'

'My lipstick.'

'Lipstick?'

'Yes, I kissed him. He'll have my lipstick on him.'

'Breathe.' He strokes my shoulder while holding me upright. 'Of course you kissed him. You're his wife.' He takes a breath. 'You tell the police you kissed him on your way to bed. He was still up.'

'No.' I shake my head.

'Yes. No one was up when you left the house.'

'You were.' I step back.

'Yes, but I was waiting.'

I think about his room. It overlooks the bay. He must have seen Allan leave.

'Why?'

'Because it's my job. And now we need to get you back into the house without anyone else seeing or hearing you.'

I nod then turn and look behind me.

'There's nothing more that can be done tonight, just know that you have done the right thing.'

I cry out. 'Murder is never right.'

'It wasn't murder. It was manslaughter at a push – if that. He was a traitor to your country, he was a traitor to you and he risked Diana's safety.'

'No, he didn't do that.'

'Yes, he did.'

'No, I did that, using her as a cover.' I push a strand of hair away from my neck. The diamonds catch my fingers. I want them off. If George hadn't been standing with me, I would have ripped the necklace off and thrown it down the cliff with Allan.

'This is bigger than you or Allan or me or even Diana.'

He leads me through the garden gate and then waits in the shadows until I am in the kitchen. I remove my plimsoles and wipe them clean then lift my dress. The bottom is sodden and heavy. Holding it high, I climb up the back stairs on tiptoes and continue along the passageway to the front of the house, hoping that no one is on their way to the loo.

Once in my room with the door closed, I lean against it and look at the empty bed. Sliding to the floor, all I can think is that I've killed my husband and it was so easy.

70

Lottie

5 August 2018, 5.00 a.m.

Lottie paced the kitchen. She'd had no sleep, just tossing and turning while her mind circled. Why did Gran have to say anything? Why did she do it? According to Mrs Hoskine, they were the perfect family. But what did that mean? Perfect meant different things. In the case of a gemstone it would mean near flawless. But to her, those stones were the ones of the least interest. She preferred ones that had inclusions showing the stones' history, what forces had shaped them.

She stopped pacing. Why would her mother think she was at fault? What had Gran said? She did it to save Diana. She raced upstairs to the diary.

> *The man leaned forward and kissed Daddy. Daddy didn't pull away but looked around again.*

Allan was gay or bi. This was 1962. Homosexuality was illegal then. Lottie read on.

> *Morning.*

I still don't feel very well. Last night when Daddy came to check on me, his breath smelled of brandy. He asked me what was wrong. I said I'd been sick. I can still taste it in my mouth. He asked if I'd eaten too much chocolate. Maybe he had seen me?

I love him so much but, Diary, I am worried. Both Mummy and Daddy are cross. I know because of their mouths. They went straight like when I've done something wrong. I know I've done something wrong, but I don't know what. Diary, I'm scared. I also saw someone standing outside my room while Daddy was in here. I saw their feet shadows under the door.

Lottie looked out into the growing light, trying to piece it all together. Flipping through the notebook, she wanted to see what else her very observant mother had noticed. Both this Tom Martin and a young, handsome Gramps watched Gran closely. But she was beautiful, so that was not surprising. What she was sure of was that Gramps knew more than he was saying. Lottie had a feeling Mrs Hoskine might as well.

The next entry in the diary was the last. Lottie read the whole thing again looking for something. Anything that would take away the knowledge or provide her with a reason why Gran pushed her husband off the cliff.

The sky had gone from leaden to a Ceylon sapphire blue and now was a blaze of pink and orange with Gribben Head like a dark finger stretching out into the grey water. The sun hadn't appeared above the headland yet. She threw on some jeans and an old sweater. The morning air was fresh, and an easterly wind blew through her open window. Lottie looked down, trying to picture what her mother would have seen fifty-six years ago. She imagined the dress hanging in the closet catching the light and her heart hurt.

Heading towards her grandparents' room she could hear Gramps snoring again. They were both sleeping – her grandmother was still with them. When she was a child, she used to think someone was moving a table back and forth in the attic room above her. Lottie smiled at the memories of how Gran had laughed when she'd told her this. These were the things Lottie wanted to remember. Laughter, joy and fun. Instead, as she reached kitchen, she was thinking of murder.

She was about to put the kettle on but turned and headed out of the back door to visit Mrs Hoskine. She was always up early and Lottie had a few more questions for her. Outside the air was cool and damp. The sky was cloudless and would be deep blue soon but right now it was washed white with soft pink edges. Lottie waved to a dog walker in the field. With each step she tried to formulate what she wanted to say. The question was how to broach it. Did she just come right out with it?

'Morning,' Alex whispered in her ear.

She jumped. Where the hell had he come from?

'Sorry. Didn't mean to startle you.'

'Startle? Scare the hell out of me, you mean.'

'Off to see my grandmother again?' he asked, walking alongside her. They passed the church and she glanced at Allan's grave.

'How did you guess?'

'Might be me hearing you whisper her name, or it could be the direction.'

'No, was I talking out loud?' She rubbed her temple.

He nodded.

'That's what lack of sleep does for you.' She yawned just to confirm it.

'Thought I saw a light on in the small hours.'

'Why were you awake?'

He shrugged. 'I didn't see you come back.'

She turned to him. 'Why were you watching?'

'I was worried about you. Joan is dying, and your mum is taking it and being here, hard.'

She was about to bite back that she was well aware of that but swallowed it. 'Thanks.'

'Now why are you off to see my grandmother?'

'Looking for more answers.'

'Let it go. Your grandmother was talking nonsense.'

She turned towards him. He was pushing this 'forget it' stuff too much. 'She wasn't, and I know she killed my grandfather.'

'Come on, that's ridiculous. Joan couldn't hurt a fly.'

That was what she had always thought but now she knew differently. She stopped, hands on her hips. 'She pushed him off the cliff.'

'No.'

'Yes.'

He tilted his head to one side and gave one of his half smiles. 'You're imagining things through lack of sleep.'

'I wish.' She marched off.

'No, I'm serious.'

'So am I. Last night Pat Treneer called looking to talk to Mum but she wasn't around.' Lottie took a breath as they reached his grandmother's gate. 'He remembered something, something that bothered him and something that told him it wasn't just a drunk man falling off the cliff . . .'

'And what?' He crossed arms.

'Allan was clutching a silk bow from a woman's dress.'

'That wasn't in the coroner's report.' He frowned.

Why had he read that, Lottie wondered. Morbid curiosity?

'It might not have been your grandmother's. He could have picked it up because he'd found it on the ground.' He ran a hand through his hair.

'I found the dress last night and the fabric was ripped.'

She waited for a comeback but there was none.

71

Joan

Sunlight burns directly in my eyes. I hadn't closed the curtains last night nor had I made it to the bed. I am on the floor where I had cried myself to sleep. Everything hurts but nothing more than the empty feeling inside. I killed my husband. Looking in the long mirror, water stains mark the silk at the bottom of my dress. Slowly I let my glance rise, expecting to see something different in my face. But what looks back at me are large bloodshot eyes and dishevelled hair, the diamond clip at a perilous angle. The only thing sitting perfectly as it should is the damn necklace. I have looked this way before, having enjoyed a party too much. It feels wrong to even think that.

Pulling the clip from my hair, it tumbles down, and I wiggle until I can loosen the zip on my dress. The silk pools at my feet while the diamonds at my neck gleam in the morning light, damning me. I pull at them then stop. With shaky fingers I release the clasp, then store it with my mother's clip and my earrings in the case. I place them in the space beneath the false bottom of the wardrobe.

Thinking about what I would normally do, I drape the dress

328

over the chair. My nightgown is laid out on the bottom of the bed. I remove my undergarments and put it on. The silk is cold against my skin and I shiver. For some reason I think of Allan touching me, but then coldness fills me. I need to keep focused and cannot let my thoughts wander. Pain, regrets, grief are for later. Now is for shock, horror and surprise.

In a moment I need to raise the alarm. Not a big alarm. I will wander downstairs in my dressing gown looking for Allan, expecting to find him asleep on a chair in the drawing room. It will be light and humorous. I slap my hand to my mouth smothering a scream. Diana. My poor girl is fatherless now.

I tear away the bed clothes, trying to make it look like I have slept here. Laying down for a moment, I begin to toss and turn. My thoughts aren't clear, but instincts kicks in, and I will make this look right. Today and the days that follow will be the performance of my life. No one must know the truth, most especially Diana.

The sound of scales being softly played rises from the room below. Damn Madame Roscova. My poor darling girl. I sit up and take a last look about the room, knowing the police will be all over it soon and Diana's world will be broken. I will be strong for her. Everything has been for her. I pull on my dressing gown and head downstairs.

Popping my head into the small kitchen, Mrs Hoskine is not there and the smell of coffee turns my stomach. The soft sound of Mozart fills the hallway. There is no sign of anyone else. But *The Times* is laying open on the hallway table. My glance falls to the article entitled 'Russia Begins New Nuclear Tests . . . Forty Megaton Blast Reported.'

I have done the right thing, but knowing that doesn't make

me feel any better. I close the paper. Who is up aside from Diana? George? Would he have left the paper open for me?

The music changes to 'Twinkle, Twinkle, Little Star'. I have to go to her, but once she knows I don't think I will be able to face her grief. The hall clock chimes the half hour. It is half past six. Just a few hours ago I pushed my husband over the cliff and now he will be lying on the rocks as the tide comes in. I need to act. If he is swept away it will draw more attention to the problem. God, it isn't a problem. It is . . . I don't know, but whatever it is, I am the cause.

Forcing my feet to move, I look in the snug in case anyone is watching. It is empty. I then make my way to the drawing room. Her back is straight. Her ballet mistress would be proud. She plays '*Frère Jacques*' with growing intensity. She is having a little joke with us after yesterday morning, no doubt. I swallow and sit on the bench next to her.

'Morning, Mummy.' She smiles. 'Thought this might bring Daddy downstairs. It's such a glorious morning, I'd like to go for a swim.'

I draw in a sharp breath. She mustn't go to the beach. 'What a lovely idea, but I'm not sure where Daddy is.' I glance about the room.

'Surely he's in your room.'

'No, I woke up and he wasn't there. I thought he might be asleep down here.'

She giggles. 'He does that sometimes, doesn't he?'

I nod, stand and look about the room. Mrs Hoskine has already been through and gathered all the glasses.

Diana jumps up. 'I'll help you find him.' She grabs my hand. 'You look very tired, Mummy.'

I run my free hand through my hair, still sticky with hair spray. 'I'm not surprised. It was quite a party last night.'

She nods. 'I heard someone singing rude songs at one point.'

I glance down at her. 'Sorry.'

'I was awake anyway.'

Searching my mind, I try to remember when Simon Heskith was singing rugby songs. It must have been about 1.30. I need to cement the whole evening in my mind. It won't be long before the police are here. We begin walking into the hallway then I stop. What if someone else finds the body? It is a holiday weekend. The sun is shining, and people will be heading to the beach. The one thing I know is that I don't want a child to find him. No one else needs to be haunted by what I've done.

Diana leads me into the little office. 'He's not here.'

Pulling me through to the dining room, she is quietly singing '*Frère Jacques*'. The table is laid for breakfast. It just seems wrong knowing what I know. Instead of laughter and heavy heads, this room will be filled with silence and disbelief shortly.

Diana pulls away and looks around the smoking room. 'He's not here.' She frowned. 'Maybe he's in the garden. It would be a funny place to fall asleep but that must be where he is.'

She comes back to me and pulls me down so she can whisper in my ear. 'Mummy, Daddy wouldn't be with Mr Venn, would he?'

My heart stops. She is too astute. I fix a smile on my face. 'Definitely not. The Venns left by boat quite early in the evening.'

'Good.' She kisses my cheek and my heart breaks. 'He loves you, you know.'

I close my eyes for a moment.

'He told me last night.' Her breath tickles my cheek.

'Thank you my darling. I kn—know he does.' I stand upright.

'Morning.' Tom pauses in the doorway.

'Have you seen Daddy?' Diana grins at him.

He shook his head. 'Have you lost him?'

'Yes.' I pause. I must get this right. 'I left him about three o'clock and he was heading out into the garden.'

'On his own?' He raises an eyebrow.

'Yes, everyone had gone to bed and I couldn't keep my eyes open.' I yawn.

'Looks like yet again you haven't had enough sleep.'

I give him a lopsided smile. 'Diana, why don't you find Mr Hoskine and see if the two of you can have a look around the garden.'

'OK.' She dances off to the back of the house like she is playing hide and seek. If only it could be so innocent. I think about George. When will he appear?

'Shall I go and have a look on the beach?' Tom walks towards me. I swallow hard. He shouldn't find the body alone.

'I'll throw some clothes on and come with you.' Forcing a bright smile, I say, 'The fresh air will blow the cobwebs away.' I dash away, digging my nails into my palms.

72

Lottie

'What a delightful surprise before seven a.m.' Mrs Hoskine smiled but Lottie could see the question in her eyes. Why was she at her house with her grandson at this early hour? 'Is it coffee we are wanting or a good cup of breakfast tea?'

'I think I need coffee.' Lottie smiled.

'You don't look like you've had a wink of sleep.'

She half laughed and fought the urge to cry. Why was she doing this? Gramps didn't need to have the memory of his beloved wife destroyed. Her mother didn't need to know. Lottie bit her lip. That might not be true. But her mother had finally found some peace. Yet Lottie was sitting at Mrs Hoskine's kitchen table, with her brain in a muddle from questions and lack of sleep, wanting to know more. Gran wasn't a murderer. She was a kind, loving woman who saved the bloody baby rabbits who ate her plants from the neighbour's cat. Lottie had to find out why she did it. Did she mean to do it? Gran's faint voice saying, 'I had no choice I had to,' kept mixing with all Lottie's memories of this elegant loving woman. She had never once raised her voice with Lottie, let alone lost her temper – even when John died and the police called her from the station looking for Lottie.

'Drink that down and I'll make you some breakfast.'

'No need.' Lottie smiled.

'Lovely, you haven't seen yourself.' She laughed. 'Alex, pick me a few tomatoes, please.'

He cast her a funny look but did as his grandmother asked. Lottie guessed the Navy had made sure he was good at following orders.

'Now what brought you to me this morning?'

Lottie sighed then said, 'My grandmother had a sea-blue silk dress.'

'Yes, I recall it. It was Mrs Russell's favourite.'

She cleared her throat. 'I found it this morning. It has . . . '

'It's missing a bow.'

'You remember?' Lottie opened her eyes wide. 'This all happened fifty-six years ago.'

'She was upset about it. I found her about to burn the dress.'

Lottie choked on the coffee in her mouth.

'She was so distressed and wasn't thinking straight in the hours after Allan's death.' She shook her head. 'On one hand she was cool-headed, holding it all together, but then I found her doing strange things.'

'Like what?'

'Throwing out her plimsoles and grinding the soles of another pair.'

Lottie cradled the mug in her hands. 'Did you ask her about it?'

'No, we do funny things when we grieve.' She gave Lottie a quick look and her glance darted away to the dresser.

'What about the dress?'

'I took it from her.' She turned back to the hob. 'I think she had a breakdown.'

'And the police, were they . . . ?' Lottie didn't know what to say.

'Are you talking about Pat?'

She nodded.

'He was young.' Mrs Hoskine grinned. 'And keen. It was his first big case. He was sure Mr Trewin had been murdered.' She drew her brows together. 'There *was* something funny.'

'What was that?' Lottie thought about the bow again.

'The American couple. The police interviewed them then they were never seen again. That always troubled me because they had rented Penweathers for the year.'

Alex returned with the tomatoes. 'Gran, I fixed the tap. Why didn't you tell me it was broken?'

'Was it? I forget these things. Anyway, the American couple were the Venns.' She washed the tomatoes, sliced them thinly and tossed them into the pan with the bacon.

'What Americans?' Alex asked.

'Ones Mrs Russell didn't care for, but they'd been sailing all that week with Diana and Mr Trewin.' Mrs Hoskine looked at Lottie over her shoulder.

'Now eat.' She put the plate down in front of her. 'You need energy.' Lottie didn't argue. 'While I think about it, your poor grandmother was quite tired out having had the miscarriage just before they came home.' She shook her head. 'Stressful life in Moscow is what she put it down to, but I knew it wasn't the first baby they had lost.'

As Lottie ate her breakfast, she added this to the information that Allan was having an affair with a man. 'Was it a good marriage?'

'Oh yes, even if it happened because of Diana.'

'Gran had mentioned it.'

She laughed. 'It was a bit of a surprise because I knew she had been keen on Tom Martin.'

'You mentioned that the other day.'

'Yes, well she followed him out to Yemen to be his secretary. I fully expected that we'd hear of an engagement in months. But we didn't and suddenly she had been transferred to Damascus and then swiftly married.' She topped up her coffee cup. 'When they came home for leave and she had Diana, Joan was so happy.'

'And Allan?'

'He was a doting father. Loved that baby to bits. We fully expected a second one when they were next back for leave.' Mrs Hoskine sat down. 'Poor Joan.'

'How so?'

'She was like my sister. Managed to keep the first one, but lost the rest.' She sighed. 'Each loss chipped more of her heart away.'

'And Gran?'

'Well, she devoted herself to Diana. Teaching her. That little girl was destined for Cambridge by the time she was three. So good with words she was. And look at her now. Everyone knows her, a household name.'

Lottie nodded. She knew all about that, remembering the tabloid headline, '*Public school boy dies in cliff fall. Diana Trewin's daughter being interviewed*'.

She cleared her throat, then said, 'This Tom . . . '

'He was devastated when Allan died. They'd been best friends all through school, served in the RAF together.'

Lottie made a mental note to google Tom Martin. While Mrs Hoskine chattered on, Alex was silent and her brain was racing with the help of coffee, but kept returning to Gramps. He had been here that weekend too. She would have a gentle chat. He'd always been a confidant. He was the missing key to unlock Gran's actions. She was sure of it.

'You mentioned that Gran seemed to be having a bit of a breakdown.' Her grandmother must have been destroying evidence.

Mrs Hoskine stood. 'I've held my thoughts close to myself these years but maybe this will help.' She walked to the dresser. 'It can't hurt now, when she's so close to leaving us.'

Lottie's mouth dried. Mrs Hoskine pulled out the drawer and turned it over on the table, emptying the contents. From the bottom of it she pulled out a few sheets of paper stapled together with a black and white snapshot of a birthday cake with three Russian dolls on the top of it. Lottie's hand shook as she opened the handmade book emblazoned with the words, Happy Birthday Daddy in her mother's childish hand. The cake, the table, the guest, the bay. Her grandmother flanked by George and another handsome man. 'Who is this?'

'That would be Mr Carew.'

The next photo showed Allan chatting to some woman, but as Lottie studied the picture she saw a man in a white dinner jacket with his hand on Allan's bottom. Lottie looked up and Mrs Hoskine's mouth was pressed into a straight line. It wasn't an accidental motion caught by the camera. It was deliberate. It was sexual. Lottie looked up and swallowed before saying, 'Did you know?'

Mrs Hoskine frowned. 'I had my suspicions but when I looked

through Diana's book, I knew.' She picked up a cloth and wiped the clean table. 'I went up to her room and took the book.'

'Why?' Lottie's eyes narrowed.

'I didn't want the police to find it and ask questions that your grandmother didn't need to face.'

Lottie turned to Alex and handed him the book. Had Gran killed Allan to protect Diana from the scandal of Allan's homosexuality? No, that wasn't Gran at all. Divorce, yes. Murder, no.

'May I keep it?'

Mrs Hoskine nodded. 'Will you show your mother?'

Lottie looked through the book again. 'I don't know.' She put the book on the table. Maybe it was best to leave it here for the moment.

73

Joan

5 August 1962, 7.00 a.m.

Tom is reading the paper when I come back down the stairs.

'This isn't good. Khrushchev's build-up in Cuba is nothing but provocation. I hope Kennedy will hold his nerve.' He folds it and puts it on the table.

'Me too.' We head to the front door and walk the gravel path at the edge of the lawn. The bay glistens blue below us. It is another beautiful day. This is wrong. I know what we will find on the beach. I want clouds, big and threatening.

'I don't know what I'm going to do now.' He pulls his jumper off and throws it on his shoulders.

I study him, looking for signs, but he doesn't know. I breathe. 'With your mind, maybe . . . analysis?' I scan the horizon. Gribben Head is softened by a distant haze that will burn off in the growing sunlight.

He shook his head and says, 'Doesn't appeal.'

'Boring after the excitement of the field.'

'Something like that.' He chuckles.

There is a light easterly breeze coming off the sea as we walk the path down to the beach and I shiver. As I release the bolt on the gate, I pray somehow that these next few minutes will be different. That last night hadn't happened.

We step onto the walkway and the most perfect summer's day sight meets us. The tide is almost in. The sea is bluer than the cloudless sky above, and a child and his mother are playing with a bucket and spade. I swallow.

Raising my hand, I shade my eyes and scan the sweep of beach.

Tom takes the last of the steps down onto the sand and says, 'If he's down here he'd be sleeping over on the rocks.' He points to the cliffs. 'God, I remember getting so pissed with him one night, and both of us passed out on the beach, waking only when the tide reached our feet.' He laughs.

I force a smile wishing I was so carefree, but I can't speak as my chest compresses. I follow him, not sure whether to rush ahead or hang behind. I've seen dead bodies before. I found my mother. She had died in bed and looked peaceful. But I knew what waited up ahead wouldn't be a peaceful face. Just the thought of his handsome features smashed stops me.

'You OK?' Tom calls over his shoulder.

'Yes, just a little bit hungover if I'm honest.'

He laughs. 'Well, you were hitting it a bit harder than normal last night.' He pauses. 'I did mention it.'

'I know. Very rude of you to say so.' I grin at him. 'I never learn.' I shrug. I'm not hungover. I had burned through all the alcohol in my system long before I confronted Allan. Then I had cried out anything else that had been left in me.

'Allan seemed to have a bee in his bonnet last night too.' Tom shakes his head. 'Haven't seen him hit the bottle like last night in a long time,' he says with a sideways glance at me. Does he know? My stomach drops, but there is no way he could be aware of what he is about to find. As his eyes study me, I see the black of Allan's dinner jacket a few feet in front of us at the base of the cliffs. He has landed closer to the base than I had imagined. But then I hadn't had to use much force. In fact, thinking about it, hardly any at all.

'Christ.' Tom grabs my arm. 'Sorry, don't look, Joan.' But it is too late. The sight of my husband broken on the rocks will stay with me forever.

He takes his jumper from around his shoulders, bends to his knees and gently covers his friend's head and shoulders pausing briefly. I didn't think I had any tears left, but the devastation on Tom's face as he rises and turns to me breaks me in two and I double-over in pain.

74

Diana

5 August 1962, 7.15 a.m.

'*F*rère Jacques, Frère Jacques, dormez-vous, dormez-vous?'
Diana sang, thinking she should change the words to make the
song especially for Daddy. She and Mr Hoskine had searched the
whole garden but there was no sign of her father. She tugged Mr
Hoskine's hand and asked, 'Should we help check the beach?'

'Can't hurt.' Mr Hoskine continued humming as they walked
to the gate onto the coastal path. She hoped that today the Venns
wouldn't be around and she would be able to spend time with
Daddy and Mummy and maybe Uncle Tom. The other guests
would begin to leave today although tomorrow was the bank
holiday. Mrs Hoskine said rain was forecast so today would be
a wonderful day for swimming and some beach cricket. Maybe
it would be good if a few of the guests did stay for that. It was
always more fun with lots of people playing.

A bird hopped onto the path just before they were about
to walk down the steps. Diana smiled. 'Morning, Mr Magpie.'
It tilted its head and gave her a good look before it flew away.
Below on the beach she could see Jacob, the fisherman, with a
policeman. 'What's happening, Mr Hoskine?'

He frowned as they reached the bottom step. Jacob and the policeman walked up to Mummy who was in Uncle Tom's arms. Diana squinted. The policeman bent down to something behind them. Mummy was shaking her head. Diana watched the policeman. Had someone had an accident? The policeman pulled Uncle Tom's jumper off what he was looking at. She froze for a moment then yelled, 'Daddy.'

Her legs took a moment to move and she evaded Mr Hoskine's hand. The sand was hard to run on, but Daddy needed her. He was hurt.

'Diana, stop!' Mummy ran to her and Diana kicked and squirmed as Mummy held her fast. Uncle Tom and Jacob all stood shoulder to shoulder and she couldn't see Daddy, she needed to see him to tell him she loved him. She hadn't meant to lie to him. She should have told him the truth that she had told Mummy she'd seen him kiss Mr Venn.

Still holding her tight, Mummy put her on the sand. 'Stop. Diana, look at me.' She turned her head and saw Mummy's red eyes. Diana fell to the sand. Mummy bent down to her and picked up her hands.

'My love, you can't go to Daddy.'

'I need to.'

Mummy swallowed.

'He needs to know I love him.'

Mummy wrapped her arms around her. 'He knows that my love. He loved you.'

'Why can't I talk to him?'

Mummy took a deep breath. She hugged Diana even tighter. 'Daddy is . . . '

'Daddy's right there lying down.' She pointed.

'No, Diana, he's . . . gone to heaven.'

'Heaven?' Diana frowned then she looked Mummy straight in the eyes. 'He's dead?'

Mummy nodded, and she pressed her lips together like she was cross. Daddy was dead, and it was Diana's fault.

'Mr Hoskine can you take Diana up to the house?'

'Come Diana, let's go.' He held out his hand and she took it. With each step she repeated in her head *daddy's dead, daddy's dead, daddy's dead*. She looked over her shoulder. Uncle Tom's jumper covered Daddy's face. It was all her fault – she'd lied.

75

Lottie

5 August 2018, 7.30 a.m.

The tide was still out, and Alex hadn't said a word since they had left his grandmother's. Yet Lottie knew he was bursting to speak, and she wasn't ready to listen. This playing sleuth was hard, but harder still was knowing only a half truth. Or thinking of the dolls on the birthday cake, it was as though Lottie had opened the largest one, but she wasn't able to loosen the grip the middle doll had on the smallest. Years ago when she'd found them, Gran had opened them. She sighed.

Leaving Alex by the wall, she walked to the rocks by the cliffs. From here the watchtower was nearly invisible. At the moment, on the furthest rock sat a fisherman. She made her way out to him. He turned as she approached. 'Lottie Trewin, I'm so sorry to hear your grandmother's not well. She's a fine woman.'

'Thanks, Jacob.' She perched on the edge of a rock and peered into his bucket. 'Much luck?'

'Not bad. Enough for dinner tonight anyway.' He grinned. 'I see you're spending time with young Alex again.'

'Not like in the past.' She blushed, thinking of Jacob once finding her and Alex in a state of some undress in one of the tenders pulled up onto the beach. She looked at him closely and said, 'You were the one who found my grandfather.'

He nodded. 'Your mother was asking me about it and now you are.' He reeled in his line and rebaited it. 'They are hungry this morning but cautious.' He cast the line. 'It was a long time ago. I never will forget. But I've learned somethings are best left in the past.'

'Is that what you told Mum?'

'Yes. Told her there was never any good in digging up dead bodies. Things always stink.' He chuckled. 'Don't think she paid any attention. She's spent her whole career uncovering the awful things in life.'

Lottie couldn't deny that.

'The bow?'

'Pat's been talking.'

She nodded.

'Mr Trewin had a bow in his hand when I found him.' He sighed. 'When I came back with Pat, it was gone.'

'What happened?'

'Don't know. But it don't matter now.'

Lottie frowned.

'Best to look for the good.' He smiled, and his sun-worn face lit up. 'Alex is coming for you.'

'Thanks, Jacob. Good luck with the fishing.'

He waved and she met Alex on the rocks. 'Not letting go?'

She shook her head.

'Are you better off for what you know?' He held out a hand when she slipped on a slime-covered rock.

'I wasn't given any choice. Gran wanted me to forgive her and Mum too. We did, but neither of us knew what she was asking.'

346

'If you had would it change what you said?'

'I honestly don't know.' She looked up to Boskenna glowing white in the morning sun. 'I don't know, but I see Gramps is awake.'

'Don't trouble him with this.'

She turned to him. 'I know you care for him. I love him, but he was here, and he went along with Gran's lies.' She squinted, trying to see what Gramps was doing but it was just too far for her to focus. Something wasn't right. She just didn't know what. 'That tells me he knows something, maybe not everything. But he's no fool.' She walked across the sand.

'Lottie!' Alex stood feet apart and hands at his side lightly clenched. 'Wait.'

She stopped and turned to him.

'When you find your answers, what will you do?' He walked towards her.

'What does that matter? As you've pointed out, Gran won't be with us for much longer.'

'Will you tell your mother?'

She looked at him and then the gentle waves caressing the sand. 'After the fiasco of ten years ago, I promised her I would always tell the truth . . . if asked.' She swallowed, thinking of what she hadn't told anyone here. But they hadn't asked. She hadn't lied.

'Is this an answer she really wants to hear?'

'Not my decision.'

'That's where you are wrong.'

She began walking again. She knew now that Gran had killed Allan, but she didn't have the reason. Would she have done it because of the affair? Jealousy was a strong motive.

Reaching the house, she found Gramps walking out of the kitchen.

'Morning, Lottie.'

She went to him and hugged him. 'Gran?'

'The nurse is here.'

She nodded and took his arm, leading him into the snug. Once he was settled, he gave her a piercing look. 'What's troubling you?'

Lottie sat and looked down at her hands and locked her fingers together. Alex had more than indicated that she shouldn't ask Gramps, but in her heart she knew he held all the answers.

'Out with it, Lottie.'

She looked up. She'd heard that phrase from him so many times, but never had it been so difficult. His expression was guarded. He knew.

'Why did Gran kill Allan?'

He gasped.

Lottie regretted her words. She picked up his hand. 'I'm sorry, Gramps. I didn't mean to be so blunt but . . . she asked for my forgiveness and then confessed.'

'She said she killed Allan?' He leaned back, releasing her hand.

'No.' Lottie thought through exactly what happened. 'She said she had no choice then confessed she'd killed "him".' She sighed. 'I pieced the rest together.'

'Oh.' He sank back into the chair looking as if someone had taken the stuffing out of him.

'You knew.'

He glanced at her then to Alex who had appeared at the door. 'Your mother has gone to talk to Pat. I've called him and warned him.' Alex shook his head. 'I should have thought of that before.'

'Why?' She looked from Gramps to Alex then back again. He didn't answer.

'I'm going to tell her.' Gramps picked up her hand again.

'Fine, I may head to Pat's too, then.' Alex sent her a funny look as he left.

'You knew all this time?' She asked, staring at Gramps. None of this made sense. In her head she'd pictured a moment of anger, jealousy.

Gramps nodded slowly. 'Yes, I saw it happen.'

'What?'

'Things are rarely what they appear.' His face fell.

'Gran murdered her husband and you witnessed it?' She shifted on the sofa. 'Were you Gran's lover?'

'No, I'd only met her a few hours before.'

She rubbed her hand across her face. None of this added up. 'I don't understand.'

'If I explain, will you tell your mother?'

She closed her eyes thinking of the conversation she had had with her yesterday. 'I don't know. Don't you think she has the right to know what happened to her father?'

He sighed. 'Joan told me that Diana had forgiven her, accepted her love and Joan found some peace in knowing that.' He wheezed. 'That moment was fifty-six years in the making. She loves Diana so much that what she did destroyed her.' He shook his head slowly. 'All she could see was what she'd done to Diana, and that drove a wedge further and further between them and to be honest, between Joan and everyone . . . except you.'

She frowned.

'She loves you, Lottie. She gave you the love she couldn't give Diana.'

Lottie stood and spun around. 'She loves you, too.'

'Yes, in the end she did – because I knew. She didn't have to hide the trauma within.'

'I don't understand.' She ran her fingers through her hair.

'Joan was a spy.'

Her legs wobbled. Of all the things he could have said, this was one she hadn't expected. 'What?'

'Yes. And brilliant at what she did.'

She sat back down and studied his face. 'Come on. Gran was a cultural attaché, a socialite.'

'Which meant she had access to people's homes.'

'What?'

'In Moscow she wasn't snooping on her own people, she was the main contact for a double agent, but before that she kept tabs on our side.'

'I still don't understand.'

'Her father was a career diplomat and her mother the ultimate hostess. Joan was "family".' He held up his hand to make the quotation marks.

'So . . . Gran spied on friends?' She ran a hand through her hair.

'When asked, yes.'

She studied him. 'I don't like the sound of that.'

'Sadly, it was necessary in our world. The Cold War was real.'

She squinted at him seeing him anew. 'Were you a spy?'

He sighed. 'Not as such. I was a handler.'

'Were you Gran's?'

'I was about to be. The double agent was a joint operation and the handover took place here hours before Joan acted.' He squinted into the distance.

'Was that why she killed him?'

He nodded. 'Allan had turned, honey-trapped.'

'Honey-trapped?' She frowned.

'Allan was a very handsome man and although he wanted other children, she told me he wouldn't touch her when she was pregnant. During one of the failed pregnancies, he had an affair and they held it over him to get to Joan to discover who the Soviet double agent was.'

She sank back against the cushions. 'She didn't have any choice.'

'No, she didn't. But it killed her.' His hands shook.

'But she had you.'

'That took years, but she never forgave herself for taking Allan from Diana.'

'Oh.' She tried to absorb it all, but her tired brain was swimming. 'And Alex, is he a spook too?'

Gramps pressed his lips together for a moment then said, 'He's a friend.'

She assumed that was code. Alex had served in the Navy – maybe it had been in intelligence. 'Speaking of friends . . . this Tom Martin?'

'He was Joan's handler, and Allan's, but Allan had betrayed him and that's why I was brought in.'

'How did Tom take it?'

'Not well. Although he was never told the truth, he was smart enough to work it out.' He patted her hand. 'He left the service, returned to academia, did a PhD, became a teacher then a headmaster. Joan and I saw him now and then once we moved back here.'

'Oh.'

He cleared his throat. 'Don't think less of her.'

'I don't, not at all.' She swallowed. 'If anything . . . I'm in awe. I couldn't have made that decision.'

'Oh, you'd be surprised. We're all stronger than we think.'

They sat silently, and tears rolled down Gramps cheeks. She kissed him. 'Thank you for loving her.'

He smiled. 'I had no choice. She stole my heart from the moment I saw her.'

76

Joan

5 August 1962, 7.45 a.m.

Once Diana is out of sight, I turn around and walk back to Tom.

'You're in shock.' Tom moves and blocks my view, so I must look at him and not Allan. 'You need to go to the house.'

I shake my head, but he is right. I didn't think I would be in shock. After all, I knew what we would find on the beach but nonetheless, I am. I close my eyes for a moment and I hear huffing and puffing.

'Oh, dear God.' Mrs Hoskine stood, staring. 'Pat?'

'Carol, best not to look. I'll be up to the house shortly.' Pat put a hand on her arm.

'It's a terrible business.' Mrs Hoskine shakes her head.

'Terrible.' Pat looks at me. 'Mrs Trewin, this is no place for you.' He turns back to Jacob.

I look from his serious face to the watchtower. It is a long way up. The sky is bright blue. No clouds. The morning sun is golden and softens the colours of the rocks. On any other day I would be overwhelmed by the beauty, but today the beauty is almost offensive. I glance down at Allan's legs, which are all I can see.

'You need to go up to the house,' says Tom. He turns to Mrs Hoskine. 'If you would be so kind as to take Mrs Trewin. She is in shock.'

'Of course.' She nods.

'I'll stay here.' Tom places a hand on my cheek and pushes a tear away with his thumb before she directs me through the crowd which has been gathering. I note a few of our guests on the beach as people part to let us through. George stands at the back of the crowd. He doesn't look at me, which makes me feel worse somehow. How did I not realize how awful this would be? If I had, would I have done anything different?

She leads me behind the low concrete buildings to our gate. The view of the house baking in the August sun is so peaceful, sleepy even. Judging by the pulled curtains several of our party are still sleeping, in blissful ignorance of the tragedy that lies below.

We reach the front door and Pete Hoskine says, 'Mary's in the kitchen with the mite.'

'Thank you, ' I say.

'I thought you might be needing me on the beach,' he says. Mrs Hoskine is whiter than her apron. I must look a fright, still in the remains of last night's makeup and my skin blotchy from my tears.

'Let me get you something to drink. Tea, I think.' She bustles off as I nod, unable to speak more. My mouth is dry, and I am shaking. There is no need to act. I look around. Nothing has changed. The newspapers are on the hall table. The tall case clock is still working. This is wrong, everything is wrong.

Diana bolts into the hall. I bend down and open my arms. 'Mummy, tell me it isn't true. Tell me it was a bad dream.' She presses her tear-covered face into my shoulder.

'I can't lie to you, my darling.'

'No, Mummy, no. Not Daddy.'

I pull her tight against me. There is nothing I can say.

77

Lottie

Lottie opened the door to her bedroom. Her mother was sitting on the bed with the diary in her hands. Lottie braced herself. Had she been so tired this morning that she'd left it out? How was she going to explain this?

'When were you going to tell me?' She held up the book. 'Why were you keeping this from me?'

Lottie sat beside her on the bed. 'I'm not sure you want to read it.'

'Too late.' Her mother's shoulders dropped.

'Are you OK?'

'No.'

Looking closely Lottie could see how pale she was. Her hand fell shaking onto the diary. It was open to the damning page. 'I killed my father. That's why I don't remember him. That's why my mother found it so hard to love me, ran away from me.'

Lottie swallowed. 'Mum, you can't believe that. You were an eight-year-old child.'

'It makes sense. It makes sense of all of it now.' Her head hung over the book. She ran her fingers over her words. 'Why

355

we didn't come back here. Why there were no photos.' Tears collected in her mother's eyes.

Lottie knew the truth. She opened her mouth and closed it again. Gran. 'Mum.' She put her hand on her mother's.

'What do I do?' She looked up with such a tormented expression.

'Mum, stop.'

'Lottie. I killed my father.' She rocked back and forth.

'Look at me, Mum.' She turned her mother's head gently towards her. 'You didn't kill your father. You were eight. You didn't kill him.'

She stabbed the page. 'I did.'

'No, you didn't.' She took a breath. 'What you've written is normal. It's what kids do . . . they think they caused everything.'

Her mother took a deep breath. 'I did something that caused his death. I can almost remember.'

'Mum, you need to listen to me.'

'No, I need to take responsibility for my actions. I need to accept what I've done. Accept my blame in the failure of the relationship between my mother and me. What I did to her, to us.'

'No.' Lottie jumped to her feet. This was terrible. 'Stop.'

'Lottie, don't try to smooth over this.'

'I'm not.' The truth would certainly destroy the peace that Gran and her mother had achieved.

'You are.' Her mother chewed her lip. 'I appreciate it.' She smiled at Lottie. 'Thank you for trying . . . it means a great deal.'

Lottie could barely breathe.

'I know it's nearly too late, but I will go and apologise to my mother and then I need to contact the police.'

'No, you can't do that.' Lottie looked at the dolls on the

windowsill. The outer doll was faded and worn. The two dolls inside were bright and shiny. Gran had protected them. She had borne the guilt. Lottie swallowed. She had to choose.

Her mother walked to the door. 'I'm going to talk to her.'

Lottie took a deep breath and said, 'Stop, I know what happened.'

Her mother shook her head. 'I remember. It's time that I faced up to it.'

Lottie's legs gave way and she leaned against the chest of drawers. 'It was fifty-six years ago. You haven't remembered for all that time, so how can you know what you recall at this moment is the truth? Memory is a tricky thing at best.'

She stared at her. 'What do you know?'

Lottie took a deep breath. Would knowing her mother killed her father help? What would her mother do with the information? Contact the police? Gran was dying but Gramps . . .

Her mother tilted her head and said, 'Thanks for trying to make this easier but I've read the diary and I've read in between the lines.'

'Your father was a spy.' Lottie winced as she said it.

She nodded. 'He was a political attaché and he was bisexual.'

'Yes.' Lottie moved to the window and picked up the dolls.

'But I was the one who leaked the information.'

Lottie turned. 'You were a child.'

'That doesn't matter.' She grabbed the diary. 'I was the source.'

Lottie twisted the doll in her hands and the middle one dropped to the floor. Her hand shook as she picked it up and put it back on the windowsill and whispered, 'Gran was a spy, too.' She glanced at the door, half expecting Alex or Gramps to appear.

'What?' Her mother stood.

'Yes.' Lottie put the doll down.

Her mother put her hand against the doorframe. 'No, I would have known that.'

'Why would you know? You were young.'

Lottie closed her eyes, she was about to betray Gran. 'She was a spy and she had no choice.'

'My mother was a spy?' She turned and walked to the window. The very end of Carrickowel was visible. Her mother picked up the middle Russian doll and opened it revealing the smaller one. She turned around. Her expression was thunderous. 'She had to do it . . . '

Lottie steadied herself as her mother took two steps towards her.

'My mother killed my father.'

Lottie nodded. 'And I think it killed part of her.'

'Surely he couldn't have been that important?'

Lottie twisted her hands. 'It was the Cold War. You were living in Moscow.'

'Christ.' Her mother sank down on the bed. 'She's asked me to forgive her.'

'Yes.'

'But I bet she can't forgive herself.' She put the smallest doll down and walked to the door.

'What are you going to do?' Lottie tried not to wince as she said this.

'I don't know.' She rubbed the back of her neck. 'I should call the police.'

'Mum.' The word stuck in Lottie's mouth and came out more like a stutter. Gran was going to die without forgiveness – with the secret she'd held until her deathbed exposed to the world – and it was her fault.

'What a bloody mess.' Her mother sucked in air in gulps. 'What a waste of lives.'

Lottie reached out to her, but her mother walked out of the door. As Lottie closed her eyes, she saw the three Russian dolls glowing in the afternoon sunlight.

78

Joan

5 August 1962, 9.00 a.m.

Eddie Carew, dapper in his panama hat and cravat, is lighting a cigarette for Anthea. She looks like she has the hangover from hell. Her husband has gone back to bed. A week ago, I had planned the events for today. Croquet, a walk to the pub in Charlestown, and a picnic on Silvermine Beach. The weather is ideal for these events, for once. But now my guests wander without a purpose until the detective inspector arrives. George went for a walk. No doubt to the phone box to report. He has said no more than the required words to me. I know this is right, but I am lost.

'Go and take a bath. You'll feel better for it.' Mrs Hoskine gives me a piercing look. 'You don't look at all right.'

I glance back at her. Did she know?

'I've washed your gloves for you.'

My eyes open wide. I'd forgotten them. 'Thank you. I'd foolishly spilled red wine on them.'

'I saw.' She turns away.

Taking a deep breath, my mouth tastes grainy from all the sugar in the tea I held. The large amount of milk in it has furred my taste buds, too. I'm not myself. I am a killer. That thought keeps repeating in my mind and I must stop thinking it or it will come out. It has to be buried so deep within that it can never escape.

'You're right. It will make me feel better.'

'Yes.' She peers at me briefly and then sets about making lunch for my guests.

'I'll check on Diana.'

'Good.' She smiles then returns to the kitchen.

After a quick phone call to my doctor earlier, he'd said it would be safe to give her a half of one of my sleeping pills. She hadn't wanted to take it, but she wouldn't be consoled, and I can't blame her. The light of her life has gone, and I am responsible.

Opening her bedroom door with care, I creep to her bedside. She is wrapped around her father's old bear, Ben. Her long dark hair covers most of her face, but the redness of her cheeks is still visible.

God, what have I done? Last night it seemed the only way to protect her, to protect Victor. For them, I pushed the man I loved – the father of my child – over the cliff. It had all been so clear. Despite the bright sunshine breaking through Diana's curtains, nothing is clear now. I cover my mouth as a sob threatens and I long to hold my beautiful girl, but it feels wrong. I am the cause of her sorrows so how can I soothe them? How can I comfort her? I can't and I flee from her room.

Tom is walking down the stairs. He stops and looks at me. His glance is filled with a message, but I can't decipher it. 'I've called Allan's brother for you.'

'Thank you.' I turn away. I'd forgotten him.

'And the rest of the family.'

I nod. This I understand.

'Can I do anything else for you?'

I step towards him but stop. 'No.' I shake my head.

'A walk?'

I open my mouth to say yes but pause. 'No, I need to clean myself up.'

He nods. 'Later, perhaps.'

'Yes.' But I know that walk will not take place. It can't. He continues down the stairs and I have lost Tom too.

79

Lottie

5 August 2018, 12.30 p.m.

Lottie couldn't find her mother in the house and she stood in the hallway unsure what to do. Had her mother already confronted Gran? If she had, would Gran have heard her? The nurse came downstairs and Lottie asked, 'How is she?'

The nurse shook her head. 'It won't be long now.' She touched Lottie's arm. 'I left Mr Russell with her. They're listening to music.'

'Thank you for all your help.' Lottie headed up the stairs and stood in the doorway for a moment. Alex came to stand beside her.

'My darling,' Gramps said, taking Gran's hand in his. He looked up and saw Lottie and Alex.

'Do you want to be alone?' she asked.

'No.' Gramps looked at Gran. Alex went to the window as she sat on the far side of the bed, picking up Gran's other hand. She looked to Alex. 'Can you see Mum?'

He shook his head and she let go of the breath she was holding.

She turned to Gramps and asked, 'Has she been to see Gran?'

'Not that I'm aware.' He caught her eye and she nodded. He sighed, shaking his head.

Lottie took a deep breath then said, 'Gran, I love you and thank you for everything.' Her grandmother opened her eyes. Her eyes said so much that Lottie found it hard to breathe. 'I know Gran, and I forgive you. You had no choice.'

A tear slipped from the corner of Gran's eye as she closed her eyes.

'I'm here, my darling one.' Gramps stroked her hand and she turned to him. 'It's OK to go.'

She opened her eyes again and Lottie held her breath.

'It's a beautiful day. It reminds me of our trip to Maine.' He ran a finger down her cheek. 'We argued over the lobster. You said Cornwall's were best, but I held my ground.' He laughed. 'You conceded, but I knew you were only letting me win.' He sighed. 'You were good at that.'

The song changed. Lottie's glance met Alex's for a moment.

'Do you hear the music, my love? "Night and Day".' He swallowed. 'Dancing. Cairo.' He closed his eyes. 'Can you smell the night scented jasmine? I proposed, and you accepted, making me the happiest man alive.'

Lottie turned to the window where Alex was looking at the bay. Gribben Head glowed in the midday sun.

'How we would dance, my love.' He looked heavenward. 'Dance on, my darling.'

Tears pooled in Lottie's eyes, but she wouldn't let them fall.

He picked up Gran's hand and held it to his lips. 'I love you, Joan.

Gran looked at him then her eyes closed. 'Always,' she said. Her breathing faltered then she didn't take another breath. Lottie waited, holding hers, willing her to take in more air.

She sank to her knees. 'Gran.'

Her grandmother's mouth fell open and stayed that way. Despite what seemed like another gasp, she was gone. In that moment, Lottie knew what Mrs Hoskine had meant. Lottie blinked then looked up. Gramps sat still holding Gran's hand. She couldn't watch. His pain, his loss, it hurt too much. He loved Gran so much and now he was alone.

'Gramps?'

He looked up. 'It's OK.' His cheeks were damp. 'It's OK.'

Lottie shook her head. It was anything but OK. She went to him and rested her cheek against his.

'It's fine. She went with love.'

Lottie frowned but didn't ask him what he meant. He cleared his throat. 'I'm just going to sit here for a while.'

'Do you want me to stay too?'

He shook his head and gave her hand a squeeze. 'No, my darling girl.'

She kissed him, and Alex appeared at her side. He took her hand and together they walked down the stairs. The sound of Nat King Cole's voice followed them as he led her into the drawing room and poured her a brandy. 'You might need this.'

She nodded taking the glass from him. Her hands were steadier than she expected. She knocked it back, flinching. Placing the glass down, she closed her eyes and she let the music from upstairs sooth her. Alex wrapped his arms around her, singing along to 'Just the Way You Look Tonight'. They had danced to this. Her heart broke again, picturing Gran and Gramps moving across this floor and their laughter.

'Thank you.' She pulled away.

He gave her a searching look.

'I need to find Mum and tell her,' she said.

He nodded. 'Do you want help?'

'I think I'd better do this myself.'

'I'll be here and checking on George.'

'Thank you.' She gave him a wobbly smile and set out into the garden. The day could not have been more beautiful and somehow that made it hurt all the more. But she wouldn't cry. Tears wouldn't help anything. Lottie needed to be in control to tell her mother. She just didn't know how she would take the news.

80

Diana

Diana sat on the platform of the watchtower, staring out onto the bay and letting the sound of the sea soothe her. Her mother killed her father. Her first response had been anger as she marched into the bedroom where she stopped, seeing her mother on the bed. Rage still flooded through her. She had stood there asking, 'How could you do that? How could you kill him? I loved him?'

Her mother had opened her eyes and sorrow filled them.

'How could you ask me to forgive you? You killed him.' Diana had stood there with her stomach in knots. 'How can you say you loved me? How could you?' Her mother had closed her eyes and that was it.

The fight had left Diana and she turned away, walking out of there. She should go back. The last words her mother heard from her shouldn't be angry ones. Her mother had done her duty. Her father was a traitor, he had betrayed them all.

She looked down as she heard Lottie climbing the steps. Her heart tightened seeing the solemn look on her daughter's face. Diana had left it too late to go and speak to her mother again. It was hard to breathe.

'She's gone, isn't she?'

Lottie nodded. 'Did you speak to her?'

'Yes.' Glancing down at her clenched hands she wished she hadn't. It would have been better if she hadn't known the truth.

'Did she speak to you?' Lottie came up to her and sat beside her.

'No.' She wished she had. She wished she had defended herself but all she had done was to look at Diana with sorrow and . . . love. Her mother had loved her. She swallowed before she asked, 'Did she speak again?'

Lottie nodded. 'One word: always.'

'Always?' Diana raised her eyebrows. She'd seen that word somewhere unusual recently but couldn't recall where. 'George?'

'He was with her and so was I . . . and Alex.'

Diana closed her eyes. She hadn't been there. She had managed to put even more distance between them by confronting her, by acting out. There was nothing she could do now. 'I'm pleased she wasn't alone, she was surrounded by love.'

Lottie grabbed her hand. 'I love you.'

'Thank you.' She turned to her. 'I love you.' She stood, releasing Lottie's hand. 'I need to go and see her even though it's too late to put things right.'

Lottie nodded. 'I'm going to stay here for a bit.'

Diana stroked her daughter's head. 'It's peaceful.' She left and strolled slowly back to the house. Things didn't feel real. Her mother had been alive when she left the house and now she was gone.

Stopping on the path as soon as the house came into view, she smiled. It was beautiful, and its position couldn't be better. There had been love here and she had to hold on to that. Inside, the newspapers were on the hallway table and the flowers that Lottie had put there looked magnificent in the afternoon light. All was as it should be, except her mother was dead. She walked up the stairs slowly, trying to remember her eight-year-old self who had realized she'd played a role in her father's death. That hadn't changed. Her mother may have killed him, but she was partially responsible. God how she wished her mother was alive now, so she could ask for her forgiveness.

'George?' Diana tapped on the bedroom door. He was standing by the window looking out at the bay.

'I can't believe she's gone.' He turned, shaking his head.

'I feel the same.' She took a few steps in, still not looking at her mother on the bed yet feeling her presence. 'What will you do?'

'Do you want me to leave?' he asked, leaning heavily on his cane.

She looked at the frail old man standing in front of her, offering to leave his home. 'Not unless you want to.'

He shook his head. 'I arrived at Boskenna for the first time fifty-six years ago. I saw your mother and fell in love with her and the house at the same time.'

She smiled, picturing her mother then. She would imagine his wasn't the only heart she had stolen.

'It took me thirteen years to convince her to even consider me and once she said yes, I didn't give her a chance to change her mind.'

She walked closer to him and held out a hand. 'Sorry I was such a cow.'

He laughed. 'Well, I understood and so did your mother.'

She squinted into the distance, seeing the beauty in front of her. 'Not sure I deserved it.'

'You did.' He took her hand and gave it a squeeze.

'But you want to stay here?'

He looked around the room then his gaze stopped on her mother. 'I do. She loved this place.'

Diana nodded. 'I think I did once, too.'

'You did.'

Today was another beautiful day in a summer filled with beautiful ones yet it was different. Out the window Lottie was marching up the lawn with Alex not far behind. 'Lottie loves it here and she loved my mother.'

'True on both counts.' He smiled gently.

'I don't feel like I knew her at all.'

He closed his eyes for a moment then said, 'Not many of us did.'

'Would you mind if I spent a few minutes alone with her and maybe went through her things? I've been through everything in the hallway closets.'

'Of course. Are you looking for something in particular?' He walked to the door.

'Yes – my mother, if I'm honest.'

He nodded. 'Of course.'

She watched him leave then turned to the bed. Her mother looked peaceful. She could be sleeping except for the stillness. Someone had taken off the oxygen tube and combed her hair. Diana went to the bed and picked up her mother's hand, wishing she was still here.

'I'm sorry, Mum.' There was so much more she could say, but that was the most important and she'd left it too late. A tear rolled down her cheek and Diana brushed it away. She could no longer do anything to fix this relationship, but she could do something about hers with Lottie. That would be how she would show her mother, wherever she was, that she had learned something. Carefully placing her mother's hand down, she stood then kissed her cheek. 'I promise you I won't waste any more years with Lottie.'

Turning from her, Diana looked at the big wardrobe. Would she find Narnia in there or would she discover a bunch of cashmere sweaters wrapped in dried lavender? Pulling the door open, she was enveloped in her mother's scent. In order of length were five dresses which would cover any occasion she had been to in recent years. So different from the rich silks and bright colours of her past wardrobe. There were four skirts, and four pairs of trousers plus five jackets and six white blouses of different fabrics. The other side of the wardrobe was as neat with folded t-shirts, jumpers, shorts and jeans.

Opening the drawers, everything was in place. It was nothing more than a larger version of Diana's capsule wardrobe for travelling. The only colour to be found was in the collection of Hermes scarves. She felt around in the knicker drawer and came across all the letters she had written from boarding school. They were in date order. The older she became, the fewer the letters. That told a story in itself.

She sank onto the bed looking at the handwriting on the envelopes. It would take more strength than she had to open them now. She put them aside and looked at the handbags on the bottom of the wardrobe under the hanging clothes. They were simple and elegant. Inside each she found no more than a folded hanky.

Nothing. There was no story to tell or to find here. Diana began putting the bags back when a memory returned. She bent down and ran her hand along the bottom of the wardrobe. A piece of wood shifted, and her hands touched leather. She pulled out a case that was instantly recognisable in royal blue leather with her mother's initials in gold on the top. It was thick with dust and she used one of the hankies to wipe it before she opened it. Lottie would love this, so she picked it up and went in search of her daughter.

81

Joan

5 August 1962, 1.15 p.m.

As I walk into the kitchen, I sense the change in atmosphere. The local policeman, Pat Treneer, is seated with a notepad open and Tom has his head in his hands. How long before London will be brought in? I glance at my wrist. It is one o'clock. No doubt someone is on their way by now. A phone call would have been made, if not by Tom then by George or both.

'Mrs Trewin.' Pat Treneer stands.

'Hello Sergeant.'

'I'm afraid I need to ask a few questions . . . ' He turned to the doorway. 'We'll need to take a look at your bedroom.'

'Of course.' I bow my head slightly. Everything was as it should be in there. 'I'm afraid it's a bit untidy.'

'Not to concern yourself about that.' He picks up his notepad. 'Could we go someplace more private?'

'Yes, of course.' I glance at Tom. His skin is pale and there is a haunted look in his eyes. Mrs Hoskine fusses about the kitchen. I haven't really seen anyone except Tom and George in passing. Tom reaches out and grabs my hand and he gives it a squeeze. I close my eyes for a moment then pull away.

'Follow me.' I walk instinctively to my father's study. Even though Allan had been using it as his since my mother died, it still carries my father's imprint on it. Many of the books lining one wall are his and not Allan's. I stop at the desk, realising that aside from the teddy bear in my daughter's arms and the clothes in the cupboard, Allan has not left an imprint on Boskenna. How could I have been married to him for eight years and find our home so untouched by him?

Sitting in the chair beside the desk, I indicate that Pat should take the one at the desk. He sits and opens his pad, tapping his pencil. His eyes dart around, and his discomfort amuses me. It shouldn't. It is completely the wrong emotion to have. 'How can I help?' I cross my legs at the ankles and fold my hands on my lap, as demure as I can be. I must put him at ease and make him feel in control.

'Sorry to have to go through this.' He clears his throat and twiddles the pencil, and I suppress the urge to slap it out of his hand.

Giving my head a quick shake, I say, 'It's your job and it's necessary.'

'Thank you for your understanding.' He twists the pencil in his hands again. 'Now, could you tell me about last night?'

'Well.' I take a deep breath. 'We had a dinner party for Allan's birthday.'

'Were all the guests staying at the house?'

I nod then stop. 'No, sorry. The Venns, an American couple who have rented Penweathers, were here last night for the party.' I swallow. I don't need them questioned. 'They left the party via their tender not too long after we finished dinner. I think it was certainly before midnight.'

'Can you be more precise?' He looks up at me and if he twists the pencil again, I won't be responsible for my actions.

Giving him a small smile, I say, 'Well, I was checking on Diana who I discovered awake and reading. So, by the time I'd settled her and returned to the party they had gone.'

'I see.'

'Other than the Venns, everyone was here. The first to retire was Anthea and her husband, Rupert, and everyone bar myself and Allan had gone to bed by two thirty.' Silence falls while he jots that information down and I wonder how he will phrase the next question.

'So you went to . . . you retired together?'

I shake my head. 'I left Allan downstairs about three o'clock. He wanted another cigar and another cognac.' I close my eyes, picturing it. It is the truth. 'I kissed him goodnight and watched him head out into the garden. I couldn't keep my eyes open.'

'I see. How did he seem to you?'

'A bit worse for wear but it had been his party.' I play with my hands. 'I wish I had stayed with him.'

'From what we've gathered, he must have gone to the watch-tower.'

I let a brief smile hover on my lips. 'We often went there after a long evening. Normally we would sit together have a drink and do a post-mortem on the party.' I frown. 'Sorry, that's a bad choice of words.

'Are you certain that you didn't go with him?'

'Yes.' My stomach clenches.

'It's just that there are a woman's footprints up there.'

'Oh. Well I was up there earlier in the day.'

'Why?'

'Most of my guests were out sailing. I went there to see if I could catch sight of them so that I would have a better feel for timing.'

He stares at me.

'I also go there to think and have a cigarette.'

'I see.'

But I am sure he doesn't.

He taps the pencil on the pad. 'When did you realize that your husband was missing?'

'When I woke up to Diana practising the piano this morning.'

'Were you concerned that he wasn't with you?'

'To be honest, not unduly. He's been known to fall asleep in a chair when he's had a few too many.' I look down at my hands. The diamonds in my wedding ring catches the sunlight. I spin it round.

'So what did you do?'

'I came downstairs and began to look for him, but he wasn't in the usual spots as Diana and I checked the house.'

'Did you think he might be with another guest?'

I raise an eyebrow. 'I'm not sure what you think of us but there was no bedroom hopping here last night.'

'How can you be so sure?'

'Large quantities of gin, wine, champagne, port and cognac put paid to even the most ardent of ventures.'

'Fair point. Everyone drank heavily last night?'

'Yes, no one except Diana and the Hoskines would have been sober.'

'The Venns?' he asks.

'They weren't either.' I don't want to think about them in

any way, but I know I will have questions of another sort to answer soon.

'They drove?'

'No, they took their tender.'

He taps his pencil on the paper again. 'What do you know about them?'

'Not much at all. Allan and Diana met them a day or two after we arrived on holiday.'

He runs his finger down his notes before looking at me. 'What made you check the beach this morning?'

'Well, I had sent Diana with Pete Hoskine to search the garden and I thought we might find Allan asleep on the beach.'

'Why?'

'Habit. Along with the watchtower he would head to the beach in the small hours of the morning to think.'

'Had he been doing that recently?'

I pause. 'Yes, actually quite a bit.'

'Would you say he hadn't been himself?'

I furrow my brows, knowing the truth. 'No, he was on good form and loving the holiday despite the awful weather we've had until yesterday.' I glance out the window towards the sea. 'You're not suggesting that he killed himself?'

'It has to be looked at.'

I place a hand at my throat.

'Sorry to distress you but it could be that he was drunk and went too close to the edge or he might have done it deliberately.'

'Dear God.' I pause, taking a breath. 'I hadn't considered that.'

I stood. 'Can you keep this possibility far away from Diana?'

He remains silent.

'She will have enough to deal with without thinking that her father chose to leave her.'

'I see your point.'

I run my hand over the edge of the desk. 'I will appreciate your discretion on this matter, for Diana's sake.'

'I'll do my best.'

'Thank you.' I smile.

'We will need to speak with her.' He rose to his feet.

I straighten a picture frame on top of the revolving bookcase. 'If you must.'

'I must, especially as Thomas Martin said he saw Mr Trewin coming out of Diana's room looking worried at about midnight.'

If Tom were with me right now, I would hit him. 'I see. Well, I gave her a half a sleeping tablet a little while ago so I'm not sure when she'll wake. The doctor will need to see her, and I will need to be with Diana when you speak with her.'

'Of course. There is no rush.'

'Thank you. Do you have any further questions?' I stand with one foot slightly in front of the other and clasp my hands as I was taught at finishing school. Poise, it had taught me poise and that was exactly what I need at the moment.

'None for the moment.'

'Very well.' I nod and leave him in the office. How am I going to survive this? And what of my poor child?

82

Lottie

5 August 2018, 1.45 p.m.

Lottie walked up the stairs to her room, her heart heavy. Despite the strong coffee at Mrs Hoskine's this morning, she was wiped out. She needed to close her eyes for a few moments and gather her thoughts.

At the top of the stairs her mother walked towards her carrying a blue leather box.

'What's that?' Lottie frowned.

'Your grandmother's jewels, I think.' She smiled. 'I thought they might inspire you for your upcoming exhibition.' She stopped in front of Lottie. 'Because of everything that has happened, I haven't had a chance to congratulate you on being chosen.'

The colour drained from Lottie's face. What should she say? She could just accept the congratulations and move on, postponing the inevitable problem, or come clean.

'Are you feeling OK?' Her mother tilted her head.

'Mum . . . ' Lottie began but stopped. 'Mum, I won't be exhibiting.'

'What?' Her mother leaned against the wall. 'You were selected.'

'True. I was but there is a problem.'

Her mother's eyes narrowed.

Lottie coached herself to just say what happened. It would all come out eventually. 'Look, I trusted Paul, he . . . '

'He what?'

'He walked off with all my finished pieces and all my materials and designs.'

'How did you let that happen?'

Lottie closed her eyes. The whole situation was far worse. 'Because we worked together, he knew the safe codes.' *And he was my husband*, she added silently.

'You told the police?'

She nodded. 'But because he knew the codes there was no theft, so to speak, or at least as far as my insurance goes.'

'But you have time to remake the work?'

'True but that would take a lot of money.'

'Re-mortgage your flat.'

'I'd extended my mortgage already to give him a loan.'

'You what?'

'I know. I was stupid and gullible yet again. But he'd been helpful to me, nurturing my talent.'

'He was jealous of your talent.'

Lottie flinched. 'So when he asked for my help, I gave it to him. But now he's gone, and my flat is sold, and my debts will be paid.'

Her mother shook her head. 'I never thought much of him and this proves I was right.' She huffed. 'You're too bloody trusting.' She paused then asked, 'Did you say you've lost your flat?'

Lottie nodded.

'Have you told your grandfather?'

Lottie looked through the nearest bedroom window to the sea. This was what she was dreading most. The deposit had been his gift to her. 'Not yet.'

'I see.' She pressed her lips together and Lottie watched the thought process and prepared herself. 'When were you going to tell me?' She leaned closer and Lottie sympathised with all the people she'd interviewed.

'You don't make it easy.' Lottie crossed her arms. 'And there's nothing that can be done now. There was no point mentioning it with everything going on.'

'It's your life. You should know better.' Her mother put the box on the table next to the flowers Lottie had brought in on Friday. Could today only be Sunday?

'One of the reasons I didn't rush to tell you was just this.' She took a deep breath. 'You always take me apart. It's not something I was proud of but it's a fact.'

'Since when has pride come into the equation? You've lied.'

Lottie swallowed. It always came back to this. 'I didn't lie, I just didn't tell you.'

'There are such a thing as lies by omission.' Her mother flattened her mouth into a straight line.

Lottie sighed. 'Trust you to know about different types of lies.'

'There are at least seven types, but you always favour lies by omission.'

'Look, Mum, that isn't the point here.'

'No, but telling the truth makes things better.'

Lottie shook her head 'Does it? I don't agree. Sometimes lying protects people.'

'Hardly ever and I don't believe it.'

'Don't tell me you haven't lied, or that you've neglected to mention you were a journalist.'

Her mother frowned.

'Look this isn't about lying. It isn't important.'

'I thought after ten years you'd learned your lesson. You promised you wouldn't lie to me.'

'I didn't.'

'You did.' She fixed Lottie with that look. 'The truth is always better. I may be angry but not as angry as when I'm lied to.'

'Fine. I'm broke. I have to inform the V&A tomorrow that I won't be one of their rising stars.' She dropped her hands to her sides and stretched her fingers flat. 'That's the whole truth and nothing but the truth . . . ' She looked away knowing this time she was actually lying. It wasn't the whole truth. She just couldn't add in the last bit. It was too awful and her mother's opinion of her would hit rock bottom.

Her mother sighed and shook her head. Angry words would have been better. 'What hurts more than the lie is that you didn't trust me enough to tell me.'

'Mum, it's not trust. I didn't want to appear even less than I already do in your eyes.'

Her mother opened her mouth, but no sound came out. Lottie had rarely seen her speechless.

'I'm sorry that I've given you that impression.' She picked up Lottie's hand. 'It's not what I intended.'

'Mum, you're so accomplished. Double first at Cambridge, a top war correspondent, awarded an MBE and you are a champion of oppressed women without voices of their own. There is nothing I could ever do that would reach that. My goal has just been not to let your opinion of me drop lower.' Lottie took a breath. 'I knew what happened with Paul would do that.'

'Oh, God, I never knew you felt that way.'

Lottie nodded.

'I'm angry at the moment because I could have and should have helped.'

'Mum, I made this mess and I need to fix it.' Lottie looked away. She felt so vulnerable, like a crab in transition. She needed that new shell in place fast.

Her mother ran her fingers over the initials on the box. 'I'm sorry.'

'Thank you. We all have our secrets . . . '

Her mother looked up.

'Well, you have never told me anything about my father.'

Her mother picked up the leather case. 'Let's look through these and see if we can salvage your career with them.'

'Mum?'

Her mother didn't respond but opened the box. She pushed aside a silk bow. Lottie swayed.

Her mother grabbed her. 'Are you OK? I know the jewels are impressive.' She lifted a diamond necklace that part of Lottie's mind registered was classic Cartier. 'But what is truly interesting is that many of these pieces are Russian, possibly Fabergé.' She dug down and pulled out a yellow sheet of paper. 'Countess Elena was a cousin and she left them to my mother.'

She turned to Lottie. 'I think you need to sit down.'

Lottie picked up the bow.

'Funny thing to have in your jewellery case.'

Lottie nodded.

'It must have fallen off one of her dresses.' Her mother picked up an enamelled locket. 'I remember her wearing this.' She pressed the clasp and opened it. 'Me as a baby and . . . ' She ran her finger over the other picture. 'My mother with my father and Tom Martin.'

Lottie held fast to the silk bow and looked at the locket. The photos were lovely and the locket itself exquisite, from the white enamel to the sapphires picking out the details on the diamond ribbon bow at the top. Glancing down into the case it was more like a treasure chest overflowing pearls, diamonds, rubies . . .

'Mum where did you find this?'

'In the false bottom in the big wardrobe.' She looked at Lottie. 'I think my mother put it away fifty-six years ago and then forgot it.'

Lottie nodded but she knew her grandmother had not forgotten it. She had buried it.

83

Diana

5 August 2018, 3.00 p.m.

Diana studied her daughter as if she'd never seen her before. Those grey eyes were serious and, right at this moment, full of sorrow. Diana had seen that look before on Lottie's father's face. A few hours ago, Lottie had asked her about her father, Arash. Diana hadn't allowed herself to even think his name for years but looking at Lottie this morning she couldn't deny her this anymore.

'Mum, I have a question.' Lottie hesitated as she spoke. Her eyes downcast one moment and fearful the next.

'Fire away.' Diana smiled, hoping she was wrong about what was coming next.

She took a deep breath. 'I want to ask you about my father.'

'What father?' Diana sat down on the sofa. She had dreaded the very idea of this conversation for so long.

'Exactly.' She huffed. 'One of the last things Paul said to me is that he had located my father.'

'That's how he got to you.'

'Probably. My father has always been my weak spot.' She rocked from one foot to the other.

'So, what did he say?'

'Afghanistan.'

'I'm sure you worked that out yourself.'

She nodded.

'And you have probably made some guesses about how you came to be.'

'Well you were held hostage.'

Diana nodded. She didn't want to talk about it, but Lottie had a right to know.

'Your father's name was Arash, he was my guard.'

'He took advan . . . ' Lottie's voice faded away.

'No, not at all. He was my guardian angel.' Diana's throat tightened. Even now after so many years, different emotions warred within her. Fear, hatred but mostly it was love. A longing and loss both so deep that to look back would make looking forward impossible.

'What do you mean?'

'I suppose in a way through our enforced proximity, eventually we fell in love, deeply in love, which in turn lead to marriage.'

'What? How?' Lottie stood then sat again. 'Married?'

'Not one that would be recognised outside of Afghanistan.'

'You loved him?'

She nodded. That didn't say enough. The word didn't capture the emotion, the need. 'We made plans for me to stay.'

Lottie's eyes widened, her shock evident.

'But things changed, and it wasn't safe. There was money offered for me to be killed.'

Lottie gasped.

'Arash risked everything to get me to safety.' Diana's hand went to her throat.

'Oh God . . . ' Lottie walked over and sat beside her. 'Did he know about me?'

She shook her head. 'I think he did, but I didn't.'

Lottie frowned.

'I lost track of time and food was in short supply.' Diana closed her eyes and she could still see the hills. The hills that acted as a natural prison and the hills they crossed risking everything. 'I didn't know until I was examined by a doctor. But Arash was more attuned to life.'

'Oh Mum.'

Her eyes were his and her kindness was his. 'What happened to him?'

'He was killed saving me.' His eyes looked at Diana now. With her heart wide open, Diana could see him.

'I'm so sorry.' Lottie picked up her hands.

'No, I'm the one who is sorry. You are so like him.'

'And you couldn't bear it.'

Diana nodded for there were no words that could express the pain in her heart. 'Forgive me.'

'I love you, Mum. I always have.'

'I know and that's been the hardest part.' Diana never should have pushed her away. She would have had him with her the whole time. It was the last thing he would have wanted. Diana pulled her daughter into her arms, allowing herself to love her.

84

Lottie

5 August 2018, 3.30 p.m

Gramps hobbled into the drawing room where Lottie sat making a list, and he smiled at her. She fought the urge to cry again. She had just pulled herself together but there were too many things to process while she wrote a list that included call vicar, call funeral director, call lawyer, call the private investigator and call the V&A. She reached for her phone but it wasn't in her pocket. She must have left it somewhere.

'My darling girl.' He held out his hand to her. She stood and went to his side.

'Oh Gramps.'

'What is it?' He gave her an encouraging smile.

'I need to tell you something.' She looked down.

He took her hand. 'Nothing can be that bad.' He gave it a squeeze. 'You are here with me.'

She snuffled. 'True but I'm afraid I've made a real mess of things.'

'It's not that bad.' He pulled her close to him.

'It's not good.' She took a deep breath, thinking of Paul and the mess she'd made of her life and her career. 'Because of some bad decisions and terrible judgement . . . I've lost the flat.'

His eyes narrowed. 'What happened?'

'Paul asked for a short-term loan to enlarge his workshop and buy the materials for a new contract.' She shook her head. 'I believed him and extended my mortgage by . . . £20,000.' She swallowed.

'And he blew it?'

'I'm not sure because it's worse than just that. We shared a workshop and he took all my designs, creations and raw materials from the safe.'

'I see.'

'It was everything I'd done in preparation for the young designers' exhibition and I can't claim on insurance because there has been no break-in.'

'And the culprit?'

'Gone. Vanished.' She choked on the last word. 'My career up in smoke and the flat sold to pay the debts.'

'And has it?'

'Yes.'

'Good.'

'You're not upset?' She frowned.

'You are well and as I said at the start, you are with me.' He placed a hand under her chin. 'No one died.'

She flinched. 'True.'

'It can be fixed.' He gave her a little smile.

'Yes.' But she wasn't sure how.

'I wished you'd asked for my help.' He led them to the sofa.

'I couldn't.'

He shook his head. 'Everything is easier when it's shared.'

'You and Gran.'

They sat side by side.

'I miss her.' His voice wobbled.

'You two had such great love.'

'We did.'

'Bonded through shared experience.' He looked down.

She wrapped her arm around him. 'I'm so grateful she had you and I have too.'

'Thank you, Lottie.' He wiped the tears from his cheeks with his hankie. Mrs Hoskine's words about Gran finding peace came to her. Her mother needed to find peace. She hoped she could.

Gramps' eyes closed. His exhaustion was deep, and Lottie felt it in her bones.

Alex walked into the snug, holding her phone as if it was poisonous. 'This has been ringing non-stop.' As she took it, the screen flashed with a text.

Have located your husband Paul. All is not lost, he's not in Thailand but Birmingham. Call me ASAP.

Lottie dared to glance at Alex. His expression was neutral, and he avoided her gaze.

'So, he's not your boyfriend but your husband.' Alex's voice was quiet, but Gramps heard him.

'Lottie?'

'I'm sorry, Gramps.'

He shook his head and sank into his chair. 'Why didn't you say?'

'Why didn't she say what?' Her mother came into the room.

Lottie's heart sank further but she pulled her shoulders back. 'I'm sorry that I didn't tell you all that I married Paul in Vegas in April.'

'What?' Her mother stopped walking in mid-step. 'You've been married for months and you didn't tell me?'

'We were drunk, and it seemed a good idea at the time.' Lottie looked at the floor. She'd known the next day that she'd made a huge mistake. Even now her stupidity made her stomach sour.

'Oh Lottie.' Her mother went to her just as Lottie's phone rang again.

'It's the private investigator. I need to take this.' With her head down, Lottie walked out the front. She should be happy. Paul had been found and if nothing else, it would make the divorce easier if not swifter.

85

Joan

5 August 1962, 4.00 p.m.

I sit watching Diana sleep with her arms still tight around Ben. Reaching out, I brush the hair from her face. My hands shake. They are the same hands that pushed her father to his death. My stomach turns. This game seemed so simple when it was going well. But now I have crossed a border. It isn't a game and I have taken a father from my child. There will be no more happy moments watching him sit with her while she practises. No more bedtime stories. I close my eyes and wish it had been me who had gone over the cliff.

'Mummy.' Diana looks at me. 'Mummy, please. Please don't cry.'

I can't stop the tears. Diana sits and throws her arms around me. I shake with the sobs that come from deep within.

'Here, take Ben.' She thrusts the old bear at me. 'He's held me like Daddy did.'

I cry out. My pain has no place to go as my daughter wraps her small arms around me and the bear. 'Shush, Mummy, shush.' She kisses my forehead. 'I love you,' she says as she tries to rock me like she was soothing a baby.

'Daddy loved you.'

I suck in air.

'He didn't love Mr Venn.'

My hand flies to my mouth. No.

'Daddy . . . '

I interrupt her. 'Darling, you must never mention Mr Venn again.'

'But Mummy—'

I take her hands in mine. 'Look at me. You must forget what you saw.' I swallow hard. 'It never happened.'

'But it did.'

Shaking my head violently, I try not to squeeze her hands too tightly. 'Please, Diana, do not ever speak of what you saw to anyone.'

She frowns.

'Promise me.'

I can see the questions running through her mind.

'What if someone asks me?'

'Then you must lie.' Her eyes are wide and there is an expression of pleading. They don't understand.

'But . . . '

'No buts. You must lie.'

'But you've told me not to.'

I take a deep breath in. She's eight, so young in so many ways and yet so clever beyond her years. 'The best thing to do is to forget it.'

'But how? How do you forget?'

Pulling her into my arms, I say, 'I don't know, darling, but somehow we must try.' The sun streams through the window and the sound of sea vies with the happy squeals of delight as families enjoy their holidays. We will never forget while we are here. We must leave Boskenna.

DESIRE LINES

86

Joan

'You've got to eat something.' Mrs Hoskine stands with her hands on her hips. She peers at me as if she is trying to see what is inside and that is the last thing that I want anyone to see. Inside is black and it is withering. I can't believe that I was so sloppy, and she caught me with the gown.

'I just can't face food.'

'Diana needs to see you eating.' Her glance pierces me with its intensity.

'I see.'

'Do you?'

I nod and pick up the piece of bread on the table. Outside rain pelts down. It is the bank holiday so of course there is rain. I had longed for it yesterday but today sun would help. Now we are trapped in the house in more ways than one. The chief inspector arrived yesterday, late afternoon.

I feel like I'm caught in a detective novel. But worse than that is that I know who the killer was, and so does George. He has kept his distance. There is so much at stake. What about the next drop? I now have no cover story, no reason to go back to

Moscow except to pack up our things. I've already had a phone call from the ambassador. The news of Allan's death has spread quickly. Mrs Hoskine and Tom are taking all the phone calls. But Tom, I am concerned about him. Haunted is the only word I can use and I haven't had time for him. Diana needs me. She is inconsolable and trying to be brave for me.

I wash the dry crumbs of the toast down with cold tea. I have to pull myself together for Diana. They are going to question her shortly. I put the cup on the table. 'Thank you, Mrs Hoskine.'

She nods, and the force of her look leaves me reprimanded. Her stare doesn't leave me and I begin to wonder if somehow she knows. But the logical part of my mind has been over the evening repeatedly. No one was awake in the house and there had been no lights on in the cottage. I'd been careful. I'd even cleaned my plimsoles when I'd returned. Nothing should give away my part. Nothing. But of course, I am guilty and I have never needed to look less guilty in my life. Last night in bed I rolled over and could still smell his cologne on the pillow. I hugged it to me and let the tears come. Only in the dark hours could I let go, but I didn't know what I was crying for. It worried me that I was not so much grieving for Allan, as the me that had existed just a few days ago.

Climbing the stairs to Diana's room, I find her sitting by the window with her finger tracing the raindrops as they race down the glass. Her cheeks are blotchy and wet from tears. My heart contracts as I go to her and place a hand on her shoulder. She turns and looks up. I could drown in the despair in her eyes.

'My girl.' I open my arms and she rests her head against my stomach as I hold her tight. She is now the only child I will ever have, which only days ago was just what I'd wanted. But I had wanted us to be a complete family, Allan, Diana and me.

'Mummy, do I have to talk to the policeman?'

I nod.

'But how can I?'

I see her holding back words and I know the effort it is taking. 'Just answer the questions they ask as best as you can.'

'But Mummy, Daddy said something when he tucked me in.'

I hug her tighter. 'That he loved you.'

She sniffed. 'He did say that but . . . '

'That's all you need to remember.'

'But Mummy he said he was dead already.'

I freeze. 'Forget that. I'm sure he meant something else.' I stroke her hair. 'It was just a tragic accident.'

'Are you sure?'

Meeting her glance, I say, 'Yes, and remember you promised me.'

She nods. 'But why?'

'Because it would confuse things.'

'I must lie.' Her eyes are wide and tear-filled.

'It's just not saying. It's just forgetting.' I watch her beautiful face. Her thoughts are so clear. 'It's just not important. Let it go.'

'But . . . '

I pull her tight against me. 'Just forget what you saw. It is unimportant.'

'If you say so, Mummy.' She picks up her dolls from the windowsill and nests them.

'I do. Now promise me.'

'I promise.' She puts the dolls down again then pushes them from her.

Kissing her forehead, I pray. She is such an honest child, but I know she can do this. I'm not asking too much of her. I can't be. She has to lie.

399

'Mummy, when you followed them, what did you see?'

I hold her away from me so that she can see my face. I school my expression, suppressing the memory. 'I found the two of them having a smoke and talking about the prospect for sailing the following day.'

'Oh.'

'So, it was nothing, darling. Just put it all from your mind.'

Diana presses her lips together for a moment. My heart aches. What am I doing to my child?

'I will.'

The doorbell rings. 'Now that will be the policeman. Are you ready, my love?'

She shakes her head, then looks down as she stands.

'Is there something else?'

She nods. Her small shoulders are hunched slightly forward. Gone is her immaculate ballet posture. I know there is something else but we can't postpone this any longer. I have to hope that if she hasn't told me, then she will not tell a stranger.

I hold out my hand and she grabs it. Together we leave her room and head down the stairs. It is the first time in ages she doesn't take them two at a time.

By the hallway table stand Mrs Hoskine, Tom and the chief inspector. All eyes are on us. Again, I am struck by the intensity of Mrs Hoskine's stare. Tom, however looks more diminished by the moment. His fair hair is in disarray and dark circles fill the hollows under his eyes. The world has dropped from under him. Allan was his best friend.

'Mrs Trewin.' The detective steps forward. 'Diana.' He pauses. 'Shall we go into the office?'

Nodding, I keep a firm hold of Diana's hand even after we

enter the small room. An extra chair has already been placed in there, making the room feel even smaller.

I let Diana choose where to sit. It is no surprise she selects her father's chair at the desk. Her little hands grip the wooden arms. Pushing away my guilt, I focus on Diana.

The detective takes a seat and I hover before sitting. If I could, I would run, run as far as I can from here. But glancing at my daughter's serious face, I know I will never be able to run away. My deeds will be with me always.

'Now, Diana. Can you tell me about Saturday?'

She nods but doesn't speak.

'Yes,' he said. She still doesn't say a word.

'He's waiting for you.' I smile.

'Oh.' She looks around and her hand reaches out for the pencil on the table. My heart stops. Her diary. What will she have written in that and where has she put it?

'Yes, I am. Tell me about what you remember about Saturday.'

'I woke up,' she says.

'Good. And?' He takes a breath then leans back into the chair.

'I had some porridge.'

I smother a smile.

'Then I practised the piano until Daddy . . . ' She stops.

'Until your father what?'

She swallows, and I just want to wrap her in my arms.

'He came to the drawing room and asked me to play more quietly.'

'I see. Then what else do you remember?'

'I had toast and asked Daddy about a goat in the newspaper.'

The detective frowns.

'There was an article in *The Times*,' I say. Typical of Diana to remember the goat story.

He clears his throat. 'Then?'

'We went sailing.' She frowns.

'Was everything fine?'

She wrinkles her nose. 'No.'

My stomach tightens.

'Can you tell me what wasn't right?'

Diana's knuckles go white. I hope the chief inspector doesn't notice. What had she seen on the boat?

'Something bothered you?'

I watch the emotions play across her face.

'OK, let's leave the boat trip. Can you tell us about the evening?'

'It was Daddy's birthday.' A smile hovers on her mouth.

'And?'

'We sang "Happy Birthday" and had cake.'

Where was the book she'd made for him? I hadn't seen it since she brought it to her room. My stomach sinks. There is a picture in there.

'You were happy?' he asks.

She nods.

'Then you went to bed?' He looks at me.

Again, she nods.

'Do you know what time that was?' he asks.

'Ten thirty, I think.' She looks towards the door and the clock chimes the half hour.

'Did you go to sleep?' He raises an eyebrow.

Diana looks to me and I smile encouragement.

'No, I was reading.'

'Couldn't you fall asleep?

'No, it was noisy.' She crosses her ankles, looking down.

'How so?'

'Music, laughter, singing.'

'I see.' He taps his fingers on the arm of his chair. 'How late did you stay awake?

She shrugs. 'Mummy came up.'

He turns to me. I had told him that I'd checked on Diana and had found her awake. 'And what did you do?'

Again, Diana glances at me and this time I reach out and take her hand giving it a gentle squeeze. 'She told me I could read another five pages then I had to put my book away.'

He pulls a cigarette case from his jacket and holds it out to me. I mouth no. I would kill for one but now is not the time. He lights one for himself and I push the ashtray towards him. 'And did you see your father again?'

She swallows, and his glance darts my way. I clasp my hands together, twisting them.

'He came up a bit later and kissed me,' she says.

'You were still awake?'

'Yes.' She drops her head.

'Reading?' he asks.

'Yes.' Her head pops back up and I give her a smile.

'So, you hadn't finished your five pages?'

She coughs. 'I read much more than that.' Turning to me she says, 'Sorry, Mummy.'

I stroke her cheek. 'It's fine, my darling.'

'Did you and your father chat?'

She bites her cheek. 'Not really.'

He sits up straighter. 'What did you do?'

'He gave me a hug.' She took a deep breath. 'He told me a story until I fell asleep.'

'A story?'

She squirms and a smile spreads across my face. She thinks she is too old for bedtime stories, but it was their special goodnight ritual.

'A story about a princess.' She sniffles. I hold tight to her hand. I send a stern look to the chief inspector.

'Anything else?'

She tilts her head to the side. 'No.'

'Thank you for being so helpful.' Each word is spoken slowly, and I frown.

'If you recall anything else, like what had bothered you when you were sailing, please let me know.

'May I go now?' She sits up straight.

'Yes.' He stands and Diana races from the room. I hear her footsteps up the stairs and then her door close.

He fixes me with an intense stare. 'I feel she is holding something back.'

'I don't.'

'But what about the boat comment?'

'That could simply be that her father had spoken harshly to her or someone else had while they were sailing.'

From his expression, I can tell he didn't believe me. 'Allan was very easy going but he was a stickler on a boat.'

'How so?'

'He had a boat full of people and many had never sailed before, so I imagine he was safety conscious rather than at ease as he is – was – when sailing normally with Diana.'

'Well, if she tells you any more, please let me know.'

'Certainly.' I leave him in the office. So much is pounding in my head. It wants to escape but it can't. If Tom had been the one to follow me and to have witnessed what I had done, then I would be able to talk to someone. But he hadn't, and it is George I have to rely on to sort this mess out. But I'm not sure how the Americans can put a lid on this without raising suspicions.

87

Lottie

6 August 2018, 1.00 p.m.

On her phone, Lottie finished typing the email to the coordinator at the V&A, explaining what had happened to her work and apologising for her necessary withdrawal. Her finger hovered over the send key and she looked up at the house. It appeared so serene while her insides were in turmoil. This exhibition had been her big chance. Did she want that any more? She didn't know. Her phone rang. It's the private investigator, Jamie. They had been playing phone tag. She pressed send and answers it.

'Jamie.'

'Lottie, finally, I have good news. We have located the jewels and precious metals.'

'What?'

'Yes, you heard me correctly. We've found him and the jewellery,' Jamie said.

Lottie swallowed, walking to the garden table, trying to let the words sink in. 'Truly?'

'Paul's in police custody.'

Her eyes opened wide. 'Thank you.' She pinched herself.

'A pleasure. The man has previous and, by the way, he's still married.'

'Yes, sadly, to me.' She pushed the gravel under the table with her toe. If only what happened in Vegas had stayed there.

'No, not to you. Or not just to you.'

'What?' The sun beat down on her and she began to wonder if she was hearing correctly.

'Not even to the woman you thought was his ex, but to a Karen Down who he went to school with. He never divorced her.'

'So . . . '

'You're not legally married, and we can get bigamy added to his charge sheet.'

She blinked and looked heavenward, thankful.

'You OK?' He cleared his throat. 'I'm sorry if you loved him . . . '

She laughed. 'Looking back, I'm not sure I ever did, but if I had, there was nothing left after he stole from me.'

'Phew. I do wonder if I blunder in sometimes.' He laughed.

'Thank you so much.'

'A pleasure and I'm happy to help a friend of Sally's anytime.'

Lottie smiled, thinking of her friend. She owed her a large glass of wine and then some. 'She'll be thrilled.'

'I know she is as she's here with me.'

Lottie heard her friend in the background say she'd call her later and that she was so sorry about Lottie's gran.

Letting out a deep breath, Lottie put her phone in her pocket, finally allowing herself to relax.

'You look happy.' Her mother walked towards her with a mug. 'Thought you could use this.'

Lottie took it. 'Thanks.'

'I know I've said it, but I need to say it again.'

'Mum . . . '

'No, I'm sorry I haven't been here for you.'

Lottie let go a deep breath and said, 'Thank you.' She took her mother's outstretched hand. 'I've had some good news.' She grinned.

'We could use some.' Her mother glanced up to Gran's room.

'Indeed, we could.' Lottie smiled.

Her mother nudged her. 'Well, don't keep me in suspense.'

'Is Gramps inside?' Lottie asked.

Her mother nodded.

'I might as well tell you both together.'

'That good?' Her mother raised an eyebrow.

'Definitely,' she said, as they walked into the drawing room to find Gramps.

'I love seeing you both smile,' he said as he tried to get up from the sofa and they both raced to his aid. 'Just hand me the darn cane, please.' Lottie gave it to him. 'I need to be able to do this on my own or you should put me in a home.'

'No!' Lottie said and her mother in unison.

Alex laughed as he walked through the door. 'Is that the first time you two have agreed on anything?'

Her mother looked sheepish. 'It might be.'

'Now, Lottie, this news,' said Gramps. 'I hope it's not like yesterday's.'

'Thankfully not.' She smiled. 'They have recovered all my jewellery and best of all, Paul is still married.'

'To you?' said Alex.

She looked up at him not sure how he would react. He'd been silent on the matter until now. 'No, to his first wife.'

A grin spread across her mother's face. 'So your marriage is void?'

Lottie nodded.

'Now that is good news.' Gramps walked to the drinks table. 'This calls for something more interesting than tea.'

'Yes, lunch,' said Alex. 'It's ready.'

'A sherry before, I think.' Gramps smiled and went to the decanter on the drinks trolley. He poured several glasses, offering one to Lottie then one to her mother.

'Why not?' Her mother took the glass, then linked her arm through Lottie's and they walked to the kitchen together.

88

Joan

6 August 1962, 5.00 p.m.

Diana is asleep in the snug clutching Allan's bear. All my guests have left, except Tom. He is in his room packing. Diana and I are leaving tomorrow. We will stay in London. It will be easier when everything isn't a reminder.

'Mrs Hoskine.' I whisper as she walks into the room. She nods and together we go out into the hall. The newspapers lay untouched on the table. No one can bear to read them. This weekend has provided enough tragedy for anyone.

'Your train tickets are here.' She hands them to me.

'Thank you.'

'It's not for me to say, but I will.' She pauses, and I brace myself. 'Leaving Boskenna isn't right and it especially isn't right for Diana.'

I purse my lips. I understand she needs to speak even if I disagree.

'She needs to feel safe and loved and to feel she is at home.'

'Thank you.'

'I've known you nearly all my life, Mrs Trewin.' She straightens her apron. 'And I have admired you, but I think you are wrong.' She gives me a knowing look. 'Two wrongs won't make a right.'

'Thank you.' I say again. Arguing won't help. 'I appreciate all you do for us, for me, and your role will be even more important going forward.'

She frowns and I continue, 'I will be letting the house out. Can you store everything personal and lock it up?'

'As you wish.' She turns on her heel and heads into the kitchen. I can rely on her but . . . I can't quite place my finger on it. I need to escape, to run from here and I can't explain that to anyone.

'Joan.' Tom puts his suitcase down and walks towards me. I wish he was coming to London with us and I wish I could talk to him, but I can't.

'Mr Hoskine is waiting to take me to the station.'

'Yes.' I straighten my shoulders.

A foot away from me he stops and says, 'I'll be back for the inquest.'

I swallow, dreading the thought of it. 'Thank you.'

'You will be fine.'

I nod. 'Tom?'

'Don't.' He takes my hand in both of his. Feeling silk on my palm, I swallow, and he pulls his hands away. I manage to stand unsupported, but it takes all the strength in me.

He picks up his bag and I walk with him out the front door with my hand tightly clasped. Our silence is punctuated only by the stormy sea below. The rain begins to sputter and I push my hair back from my face. Closing the car door, Tom rolls the window down and looks at me and says, 'Always.'

The car pulls away and I stand there long after it has disappeared, until the beat of the rain has increased and I am soaked through. The silk bow in my hand is bone dry.

89

Lottie

6 August 2018, 6.00 p.m.

The tide was disappearing and families were being replaced
by anglers. At present it was about forty per cent each. The
remaining numbers like herself were walking, thinking, being.
Although Lottie tried not to look to the headland, she couldn't
stop. Her grandfather was pushed from it and John had fallen
to his death exactly where the point jutted out furthest into the
bay. Several men were perched on the rocks casting their lines.
She thought of John's parents. They were right. It was time to
move forward and leave the shadow in the past. She couldn't
change it and it had shaped her. But she would forgive herself.
She had seen what happens when you don't. Poor Gran. Poor
Mum.

The sound of the sea and smell of the seaweed brought a sense
of well-being despite the past few days. Nothing had been as
it had appeared. Her mind struggled to process everything and
failed. Instead, she watched a child placing a rock on the tower
of a sandcastle. The father beside her beamed. She had missed
out on all of that but then she'd had Gramps. He'd built the
sandcastles, cleaned the scraped knees, and held her hand when

she was scared. And her father was Arash. It was a wonderful name and finally it was a part of her, that missing piece.

Her life at the moment was a bit like that sandcastle. It would last in that form until the tide returned. She would rebuild. Her life wouldn't include Gran, but she would hold all the love she had given her. Lottie understood her mother a bit more, too. Gran had said she was complete by herself. Had she known? Her mother had never sought love again. She had thrown herself into her work, giving that her everything. Lottie flinched. That hurt but at least now she understood why.

Picking up a smooth flat stone she felt its weight. Would it skip far? Or would it sink on the first bounce?

Alex walked up to her. 'Hi.'

'I don't want to talk to you.' She gave him a slight smile to take the edge off her words. They hadn't had a chance to speak with all things that had needed doing since Gran died.

'Look, I'm sorry.'

'You watched me trying to piece the whole thing together and you knew all along.'

He held up his hands. 'It wasn't my story to tell.'

She nodded and picked up a shell. 'No, but I'm cross Gramps could share it with you and . . . '

He reached for her hand. 'It wasn't entirely his story to tell.'

Lottie looked at his hand holding hers. It could be years ago, as if life hadn't happened. But it had.

Lacing his fingers through hers, he said, 'If it makes it easier, he wouldn't have told me either.'

She frowned.

'When I was helping George with your grandmother, she would say things like she did when I was with you.' He stepped closer. 'George felt he should explain, knowing I would never say anything.'

'Because of your background—'

'In naval intelligence, yes.'

'I see.' The sun was catching the ripples in the water, creating sparkling explosions. It was blinding. She thought of Gran's jewels, her work, her non-existent flat and she wondered what the hell was she going to do now.

'Penny for them.'

'Thinking about the disaster zone that is my personal life.'

'Ah, you were keeping that a secret.'

'Wouldn't you?' She shook her head. 'I'd made such a mess of things again.'

'But it's not so bad now.'

'True.' She laughed and began to stroll with his hand still in hers. 'I need to make a new start. Tomorrow I have to try to sort things out with the V&A, if I can, and once that's done, I need to find a job and a place to live.'

'What do you want to do?'

She looked around and saw his cousin closing the café. That bracelet. The mussel shell. The sea glass. 'Maybe I want to create jewellery inspired by the beach and by Cornwall.'

'Not grand designs?'

She laughed. 'Don't get me wrong. I enjoy that, but a bit like Gran's jewels, they don't get worn but sit in a box most of the time. It would be good to make more affordable pieces.' There had been one thing she'd glimpsed among Gran's jewels that had stirred her imagination. It was a brooch with a large central aquamarine encircled in ribbon-like threads of silver studded with small crystals. The colour of the stone had brought the sea glass cabochon in the entrance hall of Boskenna to mind. With sea glass, she could create pieces that could be worn every day and enjoyed.

'Then why don't you do it?'

'Easier said than done.'

'Well, there is more than enough space here at Boskenna for a workshop or four.'

She smiled.

'In fact, you could run jewellery-making workshops, you could even host weekend courses using the house to put people up.'

She turned to look up to the house. 'Gramps . . . '

'I don't think he'd object. He'd love the company.' He smiled.

'Maybe, but of course . . . '

'What?' He gave her a sideways glance.

'The house now belongs to Mum.'

'Oh.'

'She's keen on the V&A exhibition launching me again.'

'That's not a bad idea. Then you could begin your business again with that on your CV.'

'You make it all sound simple.'

'Nothing worthwhile is ever simple, but that doesn't mean it's impossible.'

She laughed and looked up at the cloudless sky. 'I'll think about it.'

'That's definitely a start. And you're not tied down to anyone.'

'No.' The relief was still overwhelming, but she felt lighter.

'So, a new beginning?'

'Possibly.' She took a step towards him and kissed him. He stilled, and regret ran over her like the sea over her feet at that very moment. But then she felt him smile against her lips and his arms wrap around her.

'I've been longing for this for years,' he whispered.

'Me too.' She smiled. 'I've dreamed of it.'

'A kiss to build a dream on . . . ' he said before he kissed her again.

90

Diana

6 August 1962, 6.30 p.m.

Dragging her feet, Diana went into the garden shed to find a small spade. She put the Russian dolls down on a shelf and looked through the various tools.

'There you are.' Mrs Hoskine stood at the door. 'Your mother is already in the car. We haven't been able to find you anywhere.' She shook her head and said, 'I never would have thought to find you in here.' She laughed and held open her arms. 'Come and give me a big hug, my lovely.'

Diana raced to her and breathed in the smell of fresh-baked scones. 'I'm going to miss you, little one.' She held her at a distance and Diana felt that Mrs Hoskine was trying to memorize every detail of her. Diana tried to do the same. Mrs Hoskine picked up her hand and they walked the gravel path beside the grass. Light rain fell. Boskenna was crying because they were leaving but Diana had to be brave. Mummy needed her to be because Mummy was sad.

She waited by the car under an umbrella and she wasn't smiling. More than almost anything, Diana wanted to see Mummy smile and laugh again. It was all Diana's fault.

'Be a good little thing.' Mrs Hoskine let her hand go and wiped her eyes with a hankie. 'I'm going to miss you but the good Lord willing, it won't be too long until you're back.'

Diana nodded and wrapped her arms around her. She didn't want to leave. But this was all because of her so she had to be good. Mummy handed Mrs Hoskine the umbrella then took Diana's hand, and they climbed into the back seat. Mr Hoskine drove and they went slowly through the gate. Diana rubbed a fist against her eyes, she would not cry. Mummy looked out of the window while Diana twisted around to watch until she couldn't see the gates anymore.

'Mummy!'

'Yes.' She looked at Diana.

'I left Ben on the bed, and my diary.'

Mummy turned her wrist over and looked at her watch. 'I'm afraid we haven't got time to go back and pick them up before our train. I'll have Mrs Hoskine send them.' She wrapped an arm around Diana and pulled her close, kissing the top of her head. 'This is all very hard, but we will be OK.' She smiled but her eyes didn't.

'Thank you, Mummy.' Diana twisted around again and through the back window she saw the last glimpse of St Austell Bay. She hoped she'd be home soon, and it wouldn't take too long for Mrs Hoskine to send Ben and the diary to her in London. Boskenna was hers and Mummy's home and she wanted with all her heart to be back there.

91

Diana

Diana sat at the desk and stared out of the window. Scattered in front of her were all the photographs of her early life. Boskenna had kept them safe. They were not faded or water damaged, but had been waiting. The question now was what to do with Boskenna? In her heart she didn't think that George would last long without her mother. His role was finished, he was no longer anchored to this earth.

Outside, Lottie and Alex were walking hand in hand, their heads close together and conspiratorial. Love, quite possibly. Memories of that feeling stirred. Arash. What would he have done?

Playing with her mother's enamelled locket around her neck, she stood and studied the books on the shelves, the gardening tomes and the photographs of Lottie. Although her heart ached for Arash and the missed years with her daughter, Diana had time, unlike her mother. Both she and Diana had travelled the world searching for something, but her mother had willingly come home to Boskenna. It had called to her. Was that what Diana's dreams had been doing?

Leaving the office, she walked through the house, wandering from room to room. She had loved it once. Could she now? George's snores drifted into the hallway. She smiled, looking at her watch. It was not like him to have missed cocktail hour. Turning, she strolled into the dining room. If she wanted to, she would have time to look at, if not read, every one of these books. What would they tell her about the people who had placed them here? She ran her fingers over the titles but didn't pull any off the shelves. Her glance was drawn to the far staircase. Somehow, she was certain this had been her favourite spot in the house as a child. She climbed to the halfway landing and looked up at the lantern light. The sky was blue and cloudless. Sitting on the step, she remembered she'd been happy here.

Lottie's voice carried through the house as she spoke to George and Alex. It was tinged with joy. This was a place of magic, Diana's father had told her years before. Closing her eyes, she saw her mother dancing in her father's arms laughing. Love encircled her. It was time to stop running. She stood, looked heavenward, and said a silent thank you before she walked to find the others.

In the drawing room, she lifted the piano lid and touched the keys. She hadn't played piano since she'd left, but now her fingers moved of their own accord, picking out 'Twinkle, Twinkle Little Star'. She would learn again, and she would play a new song. Closing the lid, she walked out of the French windows to join the others on the lawn. Alex was opening a bottle of champagne. The time had come to raise a toast to her mother and to Boskenna, her home.

Acknowledgements

I can't believe this is my seventh book. My first novel, *The Cornish House*, was published in 2012 and it fulfilled a lifelong dream. I am still pinching myself that people enjoy reading my stories. *The Path to the Sea* wouldn't have been written without my readers. I am so grateful for each and every person who has read and loved my books. Thank you.

There were many people who played a part in making this book happen but the first thanks go to my mother-in-law. In the 60s and 70s she kept a hostess diary chronicling her entertaining. It provided the first spark for the story and an insight into a very different world.

Porthpean House owned by the Petherick family is the inspiration for Boskenna. Martin Petherick has been gracious sharing his knowledge of the garden, the area and the history of the house. I could spend the rest of my days reading all the books on Cornwall contained in the library/dining room of the house.

As is always the way with me, the book takes many different paths until it finds the right road. David Blanning and Michael Wierenga, both retired policemen, set me straight on what would happen in 1962 and in 2008 if a death occurred from a cliff fall. All mistakes are my own. Chris Newman willingly subjected himself to my questions about the Navy . . . again all mistakes are my own.

The character of Ralf Venn was named by Nick Jacobs in honour of his dog, Ralf, after winning the auction at the Helford Village Regatta. The money raised went to support the RNLI and St John's Ambulance.

When I was having a dark night of the soul over this book and not sure where this story was going, Clare Maycock read and reread the story and helped me to keep my sanity intact! Thank you, thank you, thank you!!

Brigid Coady has brainstormed, plot-walked and drunk sherry in the service of this book. She deserves a medal for surviving my doubt. Julia Hayward has cast her exacting glance over the early portions and, as usual, set me straight on a few things. Wonderful fellow Cornish author Mandy James, put me in touch with her brother Martin White, a jewellery designer. He talked me through the training and degree course that Lottie would have done. Kit Falconer checked my Russian translation to make sure Google hadn't provided me with completely the wrong meaning. And for the curious, 'У меня не было выбора' means 'I had no choice' and 'Я не могла поступить иначе' means 'I couldn't do otherwise'.

I am so grateful for the support and sound advice of Luigi and Alison Bonomi.

Kate Mills has yet again pulled the best story out of me. It never ceases to amaze me. Huge thanks to Genevieve Pegg for her keen eye on the copyedits, to Victoria Moynes for her patience, and to the whole team at HQ for their hard work and enthusiasm.

For research, I subjected my whole extended family and friends to 1960s food and a black-tie evening at Porthpean House. They all went along with my crazy requests, while Clay Roberts played the piano until well after three in the morning and we all sang (badly), danced (badly), and generally had far too much fun. The family tolerated all my questions over dinner, breakfast and lunch of how a body would fall if pushed from a cliff as opposed to if it simply fell . . . and they didn't book me into the nearest asylum. Chris, Dom, Andrew and Sasha are all the best, the most tolerant, and the most fun family anyone could ask for . . . I love them all and am grateful everyday they are mine.

Fern
Britton
Picks

A NEW BOOK CLUB
Exclusively for
TESCO

EXCLUSIVE ADDITIONAL CONTENT
Includes an author Q&A and details
of how to get involved in *Fern's Picks*

Dear lovely readers,

This month, our Fern's Picks book club read is Liz Fenwick's sweeping story, *The Path to the Sea.*

Full of intrigue and mystery, the novel is set against the glorious Cornish coastline, and spans three generations of women from the Trewin family, each coming to terms with something in their past. Boskenna, their rambling family home on the cliffs, has played a different but crucial role in all their lives, and now Diana, Joan and Lottie are drawn back together there for a final time.

You'll feel the warmth of the summer sun and smell the sea as you read this utterly absorbing tale of family secrets, mystery and drama. Cornwall is a place close to my heart, as you know, and I look forward to hearing what you think about this powerful yet escapist story about mothers and daughters, love and letting go.

with love
Fern x

Q&A with Liz Fenwick

What was your inspiration for *The Path to the Sea*?

As with most story ideas, it was a case of finding interesting bits from snippets of conversation to myths and location and then settling on the right idea to pull them together. In the case of *The Path to the Sea*, it began with a notebook I inherited from my mother-in-law. It was stuffed with recipes cut from newspapers so I pushed it onto a shelf in my kitchen. Years later a writer friend, Brigid Coady, pulled it off the shelf by accident and began to read. The notebook detailed every dinner or drinks party that my mother-in-law ran during the Sixties and Seventies. It went through menus and guest lists in detail and even noted her outfit in some instances. It was a window to another world.

Talking about it, my husband mentioned remembering being in the kitchen when these parties were taking place and eagerly peering through the serving hatch waiting for leftovers of his favourites to come back. I suddenly thought … what if a child witnesses something they didn't understand which altered his or her life? There was the beginning of the story. The puzzle was finding the right setting. Browsing the internet on one of my breaks, I discovered that you could rent Porthpean House which was was used in the Richard Curtis film *About Time*. I knew in an instant that this was the perfect setting for the story.

How important is Cornwall to your writing?

I knew I wanted to set the historical thread in the Sixties because of my mother-in-law's notebook and the glamour of the era. So, I set about researching the historical events of the early Sixties until I settled on 1962 in the run up to the Cuban Missile Crisis. Once I had the date, I delved into newspapers to begin understanding what people were being told. Next step was to read books and watch films released at that time as well as studying the fashion and the music. Once the first draft was complete, I knew where more detailed research was required and I turned to history books on the Cold War and spies to fill in the details.

Describe a typical day's writing. Is there such a thing?

The writing day always begins with coffee and a five-or ten-minute writing prompt that has nothing to do with what I'm working on. This is a great way to flex the writing muscle. With the next cup of coffee, I will begin a writing 'sprint' of ten, fifteen or twenty minutes. I set a timer and just write – no distractions. Then I balance the writing with admin, housework and general life stuff plus ever-present social media. At the start of new a book, I will write slowly and I am happy if I manage 500 new words in a day. There is always research reading around the period/subject and garnering visuals that I normally put on Pinterest.

As I move through writing the story, the pace of the writing intensifies and by the end I will be sprinting all day and the word count can rise to 3,000 and sometimes more. I try to take what I call a 'plot walk' every day weather permitting. I don't set out on the walk to necessarily think plot, but there is something in the rhythm of the walk and open sky above that frees the subconscious and issues are resolved, or new ideas come to mind.

Can you tell us a little about your next novel?

I've always been fascinated by the River Tamar and how it divides not just counties but people. So a story set on both banks of the Tamar … forbidden love, forgotten crossings, a forlorn cottage, and new beginnings.

Questions for your book club

- How does Liz Fenwick explore the different relationships between mothers and daughters in the novel?

- How does the shadow of the Cold War reach the Trewin women?

- *'Boskenna was the house of her dreams…'* yet Diana hasn't stayed there for 54 years. How important are the places of our childhood to us in later life?

- How did you feel about Diana, Lottie and Joan? In what ways are they similar?

- Discuss the impact of the landscape of Cornwall on the story.

Daughters of Cornwall

Callyzion, Cornwall. December 1918.

I leant my head on the cold glass of the train window, drinking in the outside scenery. Bertie had described all this to me time and time again. He had insisted on reciting all the romantic names of the Cornish station stops.

'As soon as you are over the bridge, you come to Saltash. The Gateway to Cornwall.'

'Why is it called Saltash?' I had asked.

'No idea. Then after Saltash it's St Germans, Menheniot, Liskeard—'

I interrupted him. 'I'll never remember all those names. Just tell me where I need to get off?'

'I'm getting to that, Miss Impatience.' He inhaled comically and continued. 'Saltash, St Germans, Menheniot, Liskeard and then Bodmin. I shall be waiting for you at Bodmin.'

'Will you really?' We had been lying in the tiny bed of our Ealing home. 'I'm not sure I have had anyone wait for me anywhere before.'

'What sort of blighter would I be if I didn't pick up my beloved fiancée after she's travelled all that way to see me?'

'You'd be a very bad blighter indeed,' I smiled.

He held me closer, dropping a kiss on to my hair. 'I can't wait for you to meet my family. Father will adore you. Mother too, though she may not show it at first, she's always cautious of new people. But Amy and you will be great friends. She's always wanted a sister. My brother Ernest can be a pompous ass but he's not a bad egg.'

'It'll be wonderful to feel part of a family again.'

'You are the bravest person I have ever met.' He squeezed me tightly, his arms encircling me. 'My stoic little squirrel.'

I am sorry to say I had already told a few lies to Bertie about my upbringing. Needs must sometimes.

'My parents were wonderful,' I fibbed, 'and I miss them every day, but I feel they would be very happy for me now.' Shameless, I know.

'Do you think they'd approve of me?' he asked.

'Oh Bertie,' I smiled. 'They would adore you.'

In the peace of my carriage, I searched my little bag for my handkerchief, angrily wiping away hot tears as, with a jolt, the mighty train wheels, powered by coal and steam, started to slow down.

The train guard was walking the corridors as he did before arriving at each station.

'Bodmin Road. Next stop Bodmin Road.' I readied myself to disembark.

Standing on the platform, I watched as the train chuffed its way down the line and out of sight on its journey towards Penzance. The Cornish winter air blew gently on my skin, and I took in lungfuls of the scent of damp earth.

Bertie had told me that it was warm enough down here to grow palm trees.

'You are pulling my leg.' I had laughed.

'No, I'm telling the truth. We have one in our garden. I will show it to you.'

I picked up my bag and walked past the signal box painted smartly in black and white, towards the ticket office where a sign with the word TAXI pointed. Even now, the half-expected hope that Bertie would be waiting for me made me breathless with longing. I imagined him running towards me, his long legs carrying him effortlessly. His strong arms collecting me up easily, lifting me from the ground so that my face was above his. The look of love shining between us.

'Excuse me, Miss.' A man with a peaked hat was walking towards me. 'Would you be Miss Carter?'

'Yes.'

'I thought so. You looked a bit lost on your own.' He had a kind face, but not too many teeth. 'Welcome to Cornwall.'

Coming 2020
Pre-order now!

ONE PLACE. MANY STORIES

Bold, innovative and
empowering publishing.

FOLLOW US ON:

@HQStories